W9-BAM-106

Portrait of a
Conspiracy

Da Vinci's Disciples
BOOK ONE

DONNA RUSSO MORIN

DIVERSIONBOOKS

Diversion Books
A Division of Diversion Publishing Corp.
443 Park Avenue South, Suite 1008
New York, New York 10016
www.DiversionBooks.com

Copyright © 2016 by Donna Russo Morin
All rights reserved, including the right to reproduce this book or portions thereof
in any form whatsoever.

This is a work of fiction. Names, characters, places and incidents either are the
product of the author's imagination or are used fictitiously. Any resemblance to
actual persons, living or dead, events or locales is entirely coincidental.

For more information, email info@diversionbooks.com

First Diversion Books edition May 2016.
Print ISBN: 978-1-68230-060-2
eBook ISBN: 978-1-68230-059-6

To Jennifer Way,
My JWay:
Forever beautiful,
Forever young,
Forever in my heart.

RENAISSANCE FLORENCE

A Home of Viviana del Marrone
B Home of Fiammetta Maffei
C Home of Lapaccia Cavalcanti
D Home of Natasia Soderini
E Home of Mattea Zamperini
F Home of Isabetta Fioravanti
G Palazzo de' Medici
H Cathedral of Santa Maria del Fiore (Duomo)
I Baptistery

J Palazzo della Signoria
K Church of Santo Spirito
L Church of Santo Croce
M Church of San Lorenzo
N Enclave of Pazzi Family Palazzos
O Bargello
P Ponte alla Carraia
Q Ponte Santa Trinita
R Ponte Vecchio

S Ponte alle Grazie
T Porta San Piero Gattolino
U Porta alla Croce/Gallows
V Porta a San Gallo
W Santa Giuliano Convent
X Santa Apollonia
Y Santa Caterina de Siena
Z Santa Caterina della Abbandonate

Personaggi

*denotes historical character

Viviana del Marrone – a founding member of a secret group of women artists; the daughter of a long line of wealthy vintners; born 1444

Orfeo del Marrone – Viviana's husband; a merchant; born 1434

Contessa Fiammetta Ruspoli Maffei – a member of the secret group of women artists; daughter to one of the great noble houses of Florence; born 1442

*Lorenzo de' Medici – entitled *Il Magnifico* by the people of Florence; renowned Italian statesman and unofficial ruler of the Florentine government; merchant banker; a great patron of the arts; Platonist; poet; born 1449

*Giuliano de' Medici – younger brother of Lorenzo de' Medici; co-ruler of Florence though less politically active; patron of the arts; athlete; born 1453

Lapaccia Cavalcanti – member of the secret group of women artists; widow of Messer Andrea Cavalcanti; born 1438

*Messer Jacopo de' Pazzi – ruling patriarch of the Pazzi family; merchant banker; born 1421

*Francesco de' Pazzi – oldest nephew of Jacopo de' Pazzi; merchant banker; born 1444

*Guglielmo de' Pazzi – nephew of Jacopo de' Pazzi; younger brother to Francesco de' Pazzi; husband to Bianca de' Medici; one time Prior of Florence and member of the Eight; born 1437

Conte Patrizio Maffei – Fiammetta's husband; a high-ranking nobleman; born 1437

*Cardinal of San Giorgio, Raffaele Riario – nephew of Pope Sixtus IV; first adolescent elevated to College of Cardinals; patron of the arts; born 1461

*Bernardo Bandini Baroncelli – banker with the Pazzi organization; born 1421

*Archbishop of Pisa, Francesco Salviati – appointed Archbishop by Pope Sixtus IV; born 1443

Sansone Caivano – professional soldier from northern Venice, born 1450

*Cesare Petrucci – Gonfaloniere (governor) of Florence; veteran militiaman

Natasia Soderini – the youngest member of the secret group of women artists; a member of one of the most powerful and noble houses of Florence; born 1462

*Alessandro di Mariano di Vanni Filipepi, better known as Sandro Botticelli – Italian Renaissance painter of Florentine School; belonged to court of Lorenzo de' Medici; born 1445

Mattea Zamperini – last member to join the secret group of women artists; daughter of a deceased merchant; born 1461

Andreano Cavalcanti – son of Lapaccia; member of the *Consiglio dei Cento*, Council of One Hundred; born 1456

Isabetta Fioravanti – a member of the secret group of women artists; a mainland Venetian brought to Florence by her husband, a once successful butcher; born 1454

Father Raffaello, Tomaso Soderini – Natasia Soderini's brother; parish priest of Santo Spirito; born 1457

*Leonardo da Vinci – polymath; born 1452

God was watching.
And He shuddered in horror at what He saw.

Chapter One

"Gathering Clouds."

Time rules all; it does not discriminate nor exalt. They could not run from it, though they did try to hide.

The six women hung their voluminous smocks upon the wall pegs by the locked door. In a dance choreographed by frequency and none other, they formed a circle, each facing the back of the one before them. At once and together they turned, now perusing the woman on the other side with the same intense and critical eye. They turned again, facing each other in pairs now, partners in the dance, and examined more. With eyes trained and strained for the very purpose, they scoured each other's clothing—every inch of gown and overgown, in every slashed sleeve and every partlet covered bodice—searching for the smallest of damning evidence…a strand of a feather brush, a smudge of charcoal, a splotch of paint.

For these women, for this secret group, to be caught with even the slightest bit of incrimination upon their person…it could be the very worst thing in the world to happen.

It could be.

• • •

Viviana longed to tell him to go to hell, but she dared not; the words were there, hanging on the curves of her lips and the hate in her heart, but she had only ever imagined herself saying them.

"Is there nothing I can do to have you change your mind and

accompany me?" she asked instead.

She saw the lump of him—shriveled under the coverlet of their bed—in the reflection of the mottled looking glass in front of her; even in half sleep, the face peeking out of the linens was a scrunched and folded mask of discontent.

"It is a great honor to attend Mass at the Duomo, as the guest of such a well-positioned family, and on such a momentous occasion. We should be very grateful to Conte Maffei for the invitation," she cajoled still, hopeful yet, hating the thin tone of pleading in her voice as she tucked a stray chestnut curl back into the russet caul posed on the back of her head. "It was so kind of the contessa to ask, given our casual acquaintance."

Though not as casual as Orfeo knew, in their studio, as well as in society, the two women existed no more than on the outskirts of each other's lives, for Fiammetta's position was far above her own. Today was merely charity from a woman who liked to appear charitable. Viviana knew it but brushed the truth of it away, expecting no more than to be grateful for the opportunity.

A quick glance at her attire and a stab of insecurity jabbed her, at the minuteness of the diamond chips trimming the straight neckline of her evergreen gown, the slightly worn look of the thin lace partlet above it, the smallness of the brooch hanging from the plain headband encircling her plucked brow. Sumptuary laws or no, one's appearance was a reflection of one's stature and she feared hers was the truth of it, a portrait of a low ranking noblewoman who's family's wealth had been squandered by a lazy spouse. She was mollified, somewhat, as she donned the newly made *gamurra,* that the sleeveless overgown of gold and the same emerald green as her gown gave her at least the aura of fashionable flair.

With one blue eye upon her husband, Viviana del Marrone scurried one finger in her jewelry box, looking for the necklace. She found it quickly, for there was far less in the carved mahogany chest than there used to be. Viviana lifted her chin an inch higher as she dropped the long, Y-shaped necklace upon her bosom, a gift from her sons, young men who spoiled their mother with keen relish. It sat well upon her, beside the chain and its key pendant, that which never came off her neck.

Viviana turned and faced her husband though his head remained upon the pillow, his heavy-lidded eyes still closed. Her stabbing stare of envy was keen.

How dare you squander such freedom? Her mind chewed upon the familiar thought. *Were I blessed with the freedom of a man, the paint brush I dare to hold would never leave my hand.*

She shrugged slim shoulders, brushing away her frequent companion of dissatisfaction.

"Fiammetta assured me that not only will the Medicis be there, but many other fine dignitaries as well. It was quite the impressive crowd arriving with the Cardinal of San Giorgio and the Archbishop of Pisa, was it not? And we will stand at the very front alongside them, far more forward than we would ever…" she choked on her words with a cough, hearing them as his easily perturbed ego would. With a light step of trepidation, Viviana moved toward the bed. "Many will envy our very privileged position. It would be a most opportune occasion to pay our respects."

Orfeo spun round, slapped the feather ticking below him with both hands, and thrashed up.

Viviana stumbled back, her words having finally wrought a reaction, but not one she desired.

"What use have I of dignitaries, of the Medici…" Orfeo snarled, a repugnant sight, dark-skinned face a contortion of splenetic temper, the few strands left upon his head a tangled, stuck out mess, the revealed bare torso—saggy flesh and protruding belly—quavering with his anger. "Upon their whims they have cast me from their favor. No amount of supplication will change that. You know it!"

He stabbed the air with a stubby finger as if he stabbed her with his misplaced blame.

"How dare you toss it in my face?"

"I only thought you might try—"

"You thought," Orfeo snarled. "You think nothing, and do not try, for you might hurt yourself."

Orfeo flung himself back down on the bed and snapped the linens once more about the small bunch of his curled body.

"I am done. They will not let me back in the fold." It was a mewling of a pathetic animal, if not tainted by the venomous rage.

Viviana turned to her dressing table once more, ignoring the shake of her hand as she retrieved the small, embellished drawstring purse.

If you are done, she thought as she tied the delicate emerald silk pouch to the pale pink satin band high upon her waist, *it is only because you have given up, yet again.*

Without another word or glance back, Viviana left her stewing husband to wallow in his silent discontent.

Chapter Two

"Clouds gather only where a storm brews."

"Are you excited, Mona Viviana?" Fiammetta's husband Patrizio greeted her at his palazzo door with an almost girlish twitter, plump cheeks dimpling as he held his free arm out to her. His grandly bedecked wife already took her position on his other.

"I am thrilled, dear Patrizio," Viviana replied, taking the offered limb. "And I am grateful to be with you both, as always."

Around the short man, the women shared bemused smiles, indulgence tinged with shared secrets.

"Have you ever seen the city so beautiful?" Viviana asked, the splendor of the moment enveloping her—erasing her husband's virulence from her mind—as they made their way through streets teeming with smiling neighbors.

"It has been some time," Patrizio agreed as he strutted along.

Viviana sighed, gaze full of Florence embraced by spring, cleaned to perfection, adorned in its finest costume. Festoons of flowers hung on every doorjamb and balcony, their sweet aroma filling the air; family banners fluttered, snapping softly in the gentle breeze.

"*Magnifico* asked us to put on our best for his guests," Fiammetta said without a smile. "And what Lorenzo de' Medici bids, we *fiorentinos* do."

"Whatever the reason," Viviana held her head high as they walked the crowded, cobbled streets, "I am glad for it."

With a single gong, the church bells of the city began their clamoring, a splendid concerto, every bell in use to call this, the High Mass of Ascension Sunday, to order. Those so privileged or given special dispensation, rushed to the doors of the Duomo, while the rest of the city made their way to their own parishes in hopes of equal salvation or to the piazza to watch the privileged pass. Friends were in that crowd, special friends of all sorts; Viviana's critical gaze swept the faces for those dear to her, but to no avail.

"You have made us late again, Patrizio!" Fiammetta shouted at her husband. Though he walked right beside her, the tolling grew louder, the urgency of sound quickened her step, speed and breeze forced her free hand to hold fast to the jeweled veil atop her straw-like hair.

"I am moving as fast as I can." The very bald, very round man hurried to keep up with his scurrying wife, pulling Viviana with him, his knees popping outward, his belly jiggling.

With the turn of a corner, the grand and golden Duomo rose up before them, a blazing testament to the glory of Florence; Viviana felt the familiar hitch in her breath at the magnificent sight. As they hurried over the irregular cobbled rectangle of the Piazza del Duomo, her gaze scurried over its sights: from Giotto's *campanile*, the Column of Saint Zenobius, the Baptistry, to the dome itself— the round, golden vault—Filippo Brunelleschi's wonder.

"But what is this?" Patrizio slowed his pace, holding them back with a tick of his chin.

There, on the left side of the Duomo, they spied a small group of men hastening *away* from the side entrance, led by none other than the powerful Medici brothers.

"But...but..." Viviana stammered, a hand lifted to her cheek. "Mass could only have just begun, if at all."

"It is your fault," Fiammetta grumbled at her husband. "It is because we are so late."

Patrizio slanted a petulant look upon his wife. He rushed the women forward, bringing them ever closer to the towering front door of the cathedral, the scrolled pediment above, and the sculptures standing guard on each side.

"Slower," Fiammetta hissed as they drew nearer, and Viviana bit back a smile. She knew there was nothing in Heaven or the cathedral to impel her inquisitive friend to enter its confines until she saw for herself what had impelled the dignitaries out.

But they need wait no longer. From the narrow Via Larga degli Spada—the straight street of the sword forgers leading directly from the Medici palace to the Cathedral de Santa Maria del Fiore—they spied the return of the Medicis, their group enlarged to an imposing *brigata*, bright with cardinal red, archbishop purple, fine velvets, and shiny leather. As the trio of friends converged on the front entrance, the Medici contingent did so from the west side.

"Oooh," Fiammetta luxuriated on the picture. "And now they return with their guests."

Viviana gaped at the group of men, their power, their eminence apparent as each step brought them closer. Yet the more she stared at them, the more she knew them, not for who they were…everyone would recognize Cardinal Riario and Archbishop Salviati, even the small and smarmy Francesco de' Pazzi…but she *knew* them, as a group, but she could not recall from where. Something about them together struck a chord in her mind, a discordant note. She tilted her head, study and stare ever more intense, still she could not name it. Her pale eyes narrowed against a bright flash of light, a reflection…

…But no, it could not be. Her sight played tricks upon her mind. What an absurdity; what she saw was nothing but a glint from a strand of fine rosary beads. She believed it, only with a shiver of unease.

Fiammetta salivated on such a juicy tidbit of gossip. "A mistake has been made it would seem. It looks as if the Medici were to meet the guests at their palazzo, not the cathedral, but—"

"But I will truly be angry with you, my wife, if we do not enter before they do," Patrizio hissed between clenched teeth.

"What in the name of…" Viviana hissed in turn.

Within the Medici contingent, a man had suddenly stopped and embraced the man beside him, none other than Lorenzo's younger brother, Giuliano. Awkward surprise contorted the handsome young man's face until the other released him.

"Bernardo Bandini, what are you about?" Patrizio whispered aloud. Without thought, Viviana squeezed his arm; he had seen it too. Together they watched as Bandini released Giuliano, as he turned to whisper in the Archbishop's ear, who whispered in another's. The argument ended as the Archbishop left the man for the more accommodating company of two priests.

"What? What is that you say?" Fiammetta slowed her pace once more.

"Come. No more now," Patrizio replied, yanking her forward without answer.

He hurried them into the cathedral, his wife leaning backward to get a last glimpse of the strange contingent, Viviana leaning forward.

• • •

For the third time that morning, Lapaccia Cavalcanti climbed the stairs to the third floor of her spacious home, one she had searched for the better part of an hour; her aging knees screeched, inflicted lungs struggled for breath. She could find no sign of her son.

Andreano had promised to escort her to Mass and he had never gone back on his promises, not in all the years of her widowhood. The deceased Andrea Cavalcanti, one of the greatest knights in all of Italy, a title earned by blood, both inherited and shed, would be disappointed in his son were he to renege on his promise to his mother, any promise.

As Lapaccia looked in her son's room one more time, her shoulders drooped in surrender. His ornamental sword was gone from its resting place on the bedpost; his boots lay nowhere on the floor—Andreano's notion of "put away." There was nothing for it; he had left and early, for she was a dawn riser. She would return to her own rooms and have her maids remove her splendid gown, for she had never, and would not, venture out alone socially, regardless that Viviana and Fiammetta awaited her.

Lapaccia trudged to her chambers, forgetting why as soon as she entered. Crossing thick tapestry set atop gray stone floor, she stopped before the wall of windows and the balcony beyond. The vista took in the better part of the western quadrant, the old section of Florence long since taken over by brothels and their clientele. It was a world of lascivious dirt within a city of elegant beauty.

Lapaccia watched, enthralled.

Droves of men flowed from ramshackle inns sandwiched between brightly painted bordellos—stern-faced, adorned in dark leather and boots, yet their path could bring them nowhere other than the Duomo. Lapaccia had seen many things from these windows, but never had she seen such a contingent making for Mass.

She turned from the dichotomous sight, one thought alone nagging at her.

Where are you, Andreano?

• • •

Viviana stood near the front of the congregation beside the Conte and Contessa, for once as enthralled with Fiammetta's rank as Fiammetta always had been. She forgot any and all earlier concerns; her slippered feet—her best pair, though worn—tapped upon patterned marble, her thumbs twirled around in the clasp of her hands. It was the best attempt at quiet reverence she could manage within the multitude of distractions.

The Gothic vaults of the central nave towered above, guarded by the columns and round arches of ancient Rome, so high only birds could reach its apex, set aglow by the sweet light streaming in through the mammoth clerestory windows. It was a cave of wonders built by the hand of man, a hand guided by God.

Viviana aimed her eyes forward, on the priest standing in wait, small and encapsulated within the chancel and the cupola over it.

"Where is our Lapaccia?" Fiammetta leaned close to whisper, and Viviana could merely shrug in ignorance. They had planned to be together on this special occasion but the woman and her son were nowhere in sight.

Mass was often no more than an excuse to see and be seen, but never before had Viviana witnessed so many watching so many others. Yes, it was Ascension Day and with a cardinal coming to celebrate it at that. Still, the congregation appeared incongruently heavy with men…well-dressed, well-outfitted, standing side by side, and yet apart.

A metal hinge creaked; Viviana blinked as sunlight and the Medici brothers burst through the door. The chorus struck a rousing chord as if to sing their praises and not those of God. Both brothers accompanied the cardinal to his seat beneath the cupola. Viviana lowered her head as the priests began their parade of blessing, thuribles clacking, releasing the spicy scent of the incense that did little to mask the odor of so many bodies packed side by side.

The brothers separated, each taking the head of one side of the congregation, as far apart and as far forward as they could, Lorenzo to the left, Giuliano to just a few rows before Viviana. She wondered if perhaps they separated to discourage contrast of one so powerful and one so beautiful. With them and their group, the church filled— dignitaries, nobles, clergy, and dashing soldiers; Viviana tried not to stare at the luminaries but failed. A few she recognized as those she had seen approach with the Medici contingent, malcontent slick upon their faces, shrouded in a disquiet out of sorts with such a hallowed place.

Many congregants marveled at the sight of the Medici brothers and their guests. Viviana felt it too, their magnetism. But at the glimpse of one of the men among them, at the tall, thin man most simply called da Vinci, her breath became a shallow, elusive thing. Her emulation of the artist bordered on obsession, regardless of the salacious rumors that swirled around him like a storm.

Movement snatched her attention. Archbishop Salviati, the hem of his rich purple cappa magna slapping at his ankles, scampered down the far aisle on his short legs. Viviana turned rudely from the altar—eyes wide, brows high—following the clergyman hurrying past the ranks. Oh, over there now—an equally disruptive sight.

Messer Jacopo de' Pazzi, the presiding patriarch of the powerful family, yanked her gaze to the right as he too rushed from the cathedral, and out the opposite door.

Viviana looked round, forehead creased, wide blue eyes beseeching; had none of the other congregants seen what she had, did they not find it baffling? True, she was not so familiar with Mass among esteemed patrons, but none considered such displays of disrespect normal. Did they?

"Bene dictam, adscrí ptam, ra tam, rationábilem, acceptabilém fácere dignéris."

Viviana pinned her gaze forward, shaking her head softly to set aside and away all confusing thoughts, for the priest was making the sign of the cross, three times, over the great chalice. The Consecration had begun, the blessing of the body and blood of Christ.

In this moment, she often found the greatest connection to Jesus.

Today it was not to be.

The bell rang, the host was elevated, and...

"HERE, TRAITOR!"

The scream tore through the church, a shrieking, evil explosion. Viviana's breath faltered, her heart hammered. Directly in front of her, directly beside Giuliano de' Medici, a mad man came to life. He was not alone.

"Look out!" Viviana screeched and pointed at the daggers raised high. Just as the priest upon the altar raised the host, the shiny steel flashed in her gaze, the flaying weapon intent upon spreading pure madness. Downward they plunged.

Viviana's world turned blood-red.

Chapter Three

"What I have seen, I can no longer not have seen it."

The bells of Giotto's campanile clanged as the world crashed in anger.

Time changed. Seconds took hours. All color drained to shades of gray save the irreverent red of blood splattering the floor, the walls, the people closest to the carnage. Viviana did not know which way to look, so she looked everywhere.

The congregants in the row in front of her, the people between her and Giuliano, pushed and barged into her. The screams of scattering women mingled with the grunts of fighting men, but Viviana could not move—and could not turn away.

A flash of light glinted off the raised blade. She followed the blade downward, found the burning eyes of a lunatic set in the grotesquely twisted face of Bernardo Bandini. Viviana knew his cry had started the maelstrom.

Giuliano de' Medici turned slowly, too slowly…and the jagged-edged dagger plunged into his side unabated by any armor. In that moment, Viviana understood Bandini's bizarre embrace outside the church.

The blood erupted, the reddest blood Viviana had ever seen. It gushed upon a bleached existence, a mortal rip in the fabric of a world gone mad. The beautiful face, so desired, changed, etched grotesquely by chisels of shock and horror.

Instinctively, her hands reached out as she watched the body convulse under the assault. Her hands, her heart, flung out to Giuliano as they would to one of her sons; how much he reminded her of her own Marcello. Viviana had only one thought.

What madness is this?

The men sandwiched their victim; Bernardo Bandini stood in front of Giuliano, the bloody dagger, once plunged into his victim's chest, hung limply in his hands.

But the bedlamite came at him from behind.

"Francesco de' Pazzi," Viviana croaked the name of the second assassin, unbelieving, even as he joined Bandini.

Face snarled, mouth hanging open, spewing incomprehensible grunts and curses from between gnarled lips, Francesco struck again and again at the body of Giuliano de' Medici with a hatred not of this world, possessed by a madness Viviana had never been witness to, had never—could never—imagine existed in a human heart. The air filled with the coppery, acidic scent of blood; bile heaved into Viviana's mouth.

Giuliano held his arms up in front of his face, but she could see the defense was useless; the weak appendages offered little protection, slashed away with each blow. Giuliano staggered forward and to the right, toward the door leading to the Via de' Servi, dark waves of silky hair falling in his face, sticky with blood.

Viviana lunged in the same direction, her feet following the tottering Giuliano, her body colliding painfully as she bounced off the rushing, retreating horde moving in the opposite direction.

"Stop, oh please, dear God, make it stop," Viviana pleaded to the deity surrounding her, but her words were gobbled up by the uproar in the cavernous space. Would the great cupola of the Duomo finally come crashing down as so many had feared since its creation?

Giuliano fell and Francesco de' Pazzi slashed at him, shredding the body. So frenzied was he that de' Pazzi plunged the blade into his own thigh, but yanked it out and kept on, oblivious to any pain.

Closer to Giuliano now, Viviana heard the bleeding man whisper, "Where is Lorenzo?"

She followed his gaze. Her whole body began to shake.

• • •

Lorenzo did not hear his brother from where he stood on the southern side near the old sacristy, where madness found another niche.

Another cry, this one from his brother-in-law, Guglielmo de' Pazzi, filled Lorenzo's ears. "I know not of this!" he screamed. "I am innocent. I vow, Lorenzo, I vow. Forgive me!"

The young man scrambled about, unsure which direction to run, only trying hard to do so.

Lorenzo reached out, wrenching him back by the shoulder, "Of what folly do you speak?" but received no answer as more lunacy erupted.

The almost childlike cardinal, Raffaele Riario, shrieked. Lunging forward, he dropped to his knees on the altar, hands up in prayer, mumbling incoherently, rocking back and forth.

"What madness is this?" Lorenzo asked the world.

But he should have been watching the priests. He had seen them, just seconds earlier, two priests in simple soutanes, inching toward him.

From behind, a steely fist gripped Lorenzo's shoulder, spun him round. A dagger flashed, aimed for his heart.

With the swiftness of the soldier he had once been, with one graceful move, Lorenzo raised his mantle up, winding it about his left arm—a padded shield. With his right, he drew his short sword.

Lorenzo plied no more than a parry or two until he was surrounded, a human shield formed about his person by those who called him friend and master, Francesco Nori—employee, dear friend—leading the charge of defenders, moving them toward the altar. Leonardo da Vinci, unarmed, wrapped his arms about his friend, his sponsor, forming a human shield.

Within this circle, Lorenzo could think of but one.

"Giuliano!" He bellowed the name, of the spirit and bane of his youth, of the one he swore to protect with his life. "Giuliano! Giuliano!"

Lorenzo screamed as he searched about, jumping up to see

over the heads of the chaotic crowd bolting from the church in primal panic. But he saw nothing…nothing but the bobbing body of Francesco de' Pazzi as he swung his blade up and down on the far side of the church.

• • •

They heard it too; Viviana saw it in their split second hesitance, at the turn of their heads. Francesco de' Pazzi and Bernardo Bandini twitched at the strain of Lorenzo—still alive—calling for his brother. With one glance at the plundered body at their feet, they made their decision.

"*Il Magnifico! Beware!*" Viviana screamed as the murderers headed his way, stepping closer to Giuliano in their wake.

It was a full-scale war beneath the statues standing guard in the cathedral, but they could not come to life and bring peace to such insanity.

With guttural shouts, Pazzi and Bandini engaged Nori and the others, reaching out in rage for Lorenzo; arms thrashed, swords flashed, cries of hate and pain erupted.

Nori's black gaze turned for one instant from his attacker to the door just beyond the railing, to the north of the altar. Viviana saw it then too, the door to the new sacristy.

The crazed Pazzi lunged. Nori jumped between Lorenzo and de' Pazzi, taking the strike to the upper arm.

Wounded now, Nori raised his sword once more, beating the wounded Pazzi back with his swinging blade. At the same time, he pushed Lorenzo, forcing him to jump the low wooden rail into the octagonal altar.

The throng of assassins followed; the railing crashed beneath their weight. So determined, the Medici defenders held them back. From the left side, the other priest came at Lorenzo, a sword and small buckler in hands that once held the chalice and wafer, but was denied by a liveried servant in red and gold Medici colors.

"Lorenzo…"

Viviana barely understood the gurgled cough. Looking down she saw Giuliano lived still, barely. She knelt by his side and took his hand, but he gave her no acknowledgment. She followed his gaze, moaning much as he did; no impediments obstructed the view from the cold stone floor. Beside the brutalized man, she watched as Lorenzo's assailants made one last push.

A young Cavalcanti man, another Lorenzo by name, took a blade to the arm, crying out as his now useless limb dropped his sword.

Il Magnifico, Nori shielding him, reached the sacristy door, but he would not enter.

"Giuliano!" He cried once more, even as Nori, da Vinci, and the others pushed him.

Bandini lunged forward as the wounded Cavalcanti staggered back, and with a guttural grunt and a hate-filled thrust, plunged his sword into the stomach of Francesco Nori.

"Dio mio, no!" Viviana cried out, free hand reaching out helplessly as if to reach him through the churning crowd.

Nori looked down in silent disbelief as the bloodied sword retracted from his abdomen. Pure hatred curled his lip, powered his arm to lash out at Bandini, hurtling the man back as the tip of his sword slashed Bandini's cheek.

The other Medici protectors encircled Nori now, dragging him into the sacristy as they pushed Lorenzo in. In that instant, brother found brother.

"Giuliano!"

At the sound of his name, the sound of his brother's voice, the hand in Viviana's twitched and she saw the moment his eyes locked with Lorenzo's. She saw it all, all that ever lived between them— every moment, every word, all their love, the same love and indelible bond of brothers her own sons shared—spoken for the last time.

Giuliano's bloodless lips spread as if in a smile, watching his brother disappear from his sight, alive and safe, beyond the heavy bronze doors, and into the sacristy.

Viviana felt it then, Giuliano's last breath; the presence of life slipped from his body as his hand slipped from hers.

Still kneeling beside the now lifeless body, Viviana saw it—saw the battle end as any unharmed perpetrators carried out their wounded conspirators, rats jumping off a sinking ship.

In the wake, madness lived still, for it had taken residence in her soul.

She curled over, hands on the floor, face in her hands, and sobbed.

Chapter Four

"Disease is contagious, as is Madness."

"Viviana. Viviana! You must come away, now!"

Whether prodded by the urgency in his voice or the tugging of his insistent hand on her arm, Viviana came into awareness, away from the sight of Giuliano de' Medici's journey to death.

Looking upward, gaze ablur with tears, her mouth open yet silent, she found the stricken face of Patrizio inches away. He bobbled and staggered as he tugged on her arm

Fiammetta wailed, desperate and despairing. She slapped at her husband's grip, longing to be free of it, longing to flee. But Patrizio would not let go of either of them.

Viviana pushed to her feet, uncurling slowly as if the pain of her heart infested her body. For an instant, she put her hands to her ears to dull the cacophony—Fiammetta's yowling, the screams of so many still fleeing the cathedral, the shouts of men trying to gain control. Above all, Lorenzo's pleas escaping out the cracks of the closed sacristy door, crying his brother's name, begging for an answer in each anguished call. She could not bear another moment of it.

Squatting beside the body of Giuliano, blood running from him in a widening pool of glistening red, Viviana reached out a quivering hand and closed the dead man's eyes, feeling the warmth belying the end of his life. She draped a piece of tattered linen ripped from the edge of her chemise over his torso and head and rose up with a wavering breath, having done the best—the only—thing she could.

"Now, Viviana." Patrizio pulled again.

"Yes, now." She nodded and turned away, never to turn back again.

. . .

Blinded at first, the sun too bright after the bleached and dim interior, colors and light assaulted her. Viviana blinked, but to no avail; what she saw was the truth—the contained chaos inside the cathedral had spread to the piazza, spread and expanded, a beastly thing.

People streamed out of the Duomo, but they were not the same who had entered less than an hour ago; now they were pale ghosts of their former selves. Loosened animals ran amok at their feet, their squeaks and squawks adding to the din, tripping people in a pandemic rush.

Viviana searched the crowd for her sons—soldiers garrisoned for months—for Isabetta, for Mattea, for Lapaccia.

"Viviana!"

Patrizio had released his hold on her but would not release her from his security. He called her out of paralysis as his still wailing wife yanked him down the few narrow marble steps. Viviana staggered toward them.

Amongst the churning humanity, the three turned south, toward their home quarter.

At the corner of the stairs, Patrizio pulled the two women out of the fray, pulled them against the stone of the Duomo.

"It will be hard going." He took his wife's face in his hands, his words, his glare, cutting through her mania. "We must hold tight and fast, yes?"

Fiammetta, mouth finally closed, quietly nodded, as did Viviana, dropping her forehead in her hand; she could bear to see no more, yet more came.

At her feet, a young boy crouched in the small, shadowy corner where stairs met wall. Huddled into a tight ball, he looked no more than eight or nine years old, was barely visible except from her vantage point. He showed no fear; his black eyes bulged wide with eager curiosity.

"Do not look, child," she berated softly. It sickened her to see him seeing.

Her words brought Patrizio's attention to the child.

"Niccolo, to your home," Patrizio spoke unkindly, a man already overburdened.

"No, signore, I must see."

Patrizio swiped his hands together twice, switching one across the other, and raised them in the air in washed surrender. "At least stay out of the way." Taking each woman once more by the hand, he pulled them forward, head bent as if walking into a storm.

Viviana hesitated, fighting the tug of her escort. "Is he an urchin?"

Orphaned boys lived on the streets of Florence in droves, stealing their way through life. The conte shook his head, kept them running. "No, the Machiavellis live just over the Ponte Vecchio, in Santo Spirito. His father is a fine consigliore."

Viviana steeled a look back at the boy, at the shining, gruesome curiosity on his young face. A shiver of fear ran up her back. "We must—"

"We must get you home." The conte yelled above the screaming crowds. "You must return to your husband. He will be worried for your well-being."

Even as Patrizio compelled her, two men pushed him roughly, unconscionably, rushing away. As they whirled past, Viviana knew them for the devils who had brought evil upon her world, knew them as Bernardo Bandini and Francesco de' Pazzi.

Mouth agape, she watched Francesco hobbling as fast as he could, leaning on Bandini's arms, wounded thigh dropping scarlet circles of blood in their wake. Her blood surged, her heart pounded in her ears.

She grabbed her skirts, lifted them, and shot out after the fleeing murderers.

The yank on her arm snapped her head back like a whip.

"They will kill you without thought," Patrizio hissed, his lips so close his spittle splashed cold on her hot skin.

Heaving with anger, she stared at her friend, hearing the cries of his wife, the annoying bleat of a sheep in the field. Viviana knew Patrizio was right, but it did little to curb her craving for retribution. She had never known the feeling called blood lust…till now.

"Orfeo, Viviana. You must go to Orfeo."

Patrizio's words caught her up sharply; in the tumult of this inhuman moment, the truth almost slipped from her soul. She shook her head, denying it. "Yes, of course. To my husband I must go."

Chapter Five

"Saving and sacrifice; without the one the other cannot be done."

Lapaccia could not bear the waiting. A pernicious knowing burned in her throat, raw from the coughing, sweat beading on her creased brow. She whirled from the window, the decision made.

Placing a veil upon her pinned locks and donning a simple, light camlet upon her shoulders, Lapaccia rushed from home.

She escaped her own palazzo, sight unseen by any servant. The triumph of the moment fled with its reality. She had never walked a street without someone—family member, friend, or servant—by her side. She felt so small even as each step struck the stones harder.

Turning west, it touched her...the malice crackling in the air like lightning. Lapaccia berated herself for such a notion; it was only because of Andreano's absence, as was the nausea she felt.

Passing the corner of her home, she lowered her head, not wanting any member of the other palazzo on the block to see her, one belonging to the Pucci family. They possessed a genealogy as revered as her own; they would be scandalized to see her out and about alone.

Lapaccia turned the corner onto the Via Martelli with gratitude. The street here, as it headed crookedly south, was much narrowed and far less occupied. It would lead her past the back of the Duomo and into the heart of the city, to the Palazzo della Signoria. Surely someone at the government center may know where her Andreano was; perhaps he was on assignment as one of the newer council members. Or perhaps she would find some of his most favored companions; they would know something of him.

As she approached the cathedral, expecting to find the tranquil oasis that surrounds a church in the midst of Mass, she found bedlam.

This back passage was flooded as people ran in all directions. Lapaccia's already churning gut clenched at the sight of unrecognizable wraiths…white-faced, mouths agape.

Lapaccia became one of them; she ran.

• • •

The stream running through the Via Calzaiuoli moved in two directions: the curious headed south; the frightened rushed north in escape. Snippets of words found Lapaccia, but she longed to toss them away—words of assassins and the Medici, words of brutality and death. But every time her brocade slippers slapped upon the road, her son's name yelped in her mind.

Lapaccia froze at the lane's mouth, near the opening to the piazza, at the back of the Church of Saint Cecilia. Before her was a sight she had never imagined in her darkest of thoughts.

"This is what hell looks like," she muttered to herself, but the man rushing past heard.

"Take yourself away, signora. It is the end of the world."

His ominous declaration jolted her. "What do y—"

The man was gone, lost in the stream roiling away.

The Piazza della Signoria could not be seen; it was there, she knew, marked by the towering rough-hewn stone campanile of the palazzo. Yet filled with such a frenzied crowd, the grandest courtyard of Florence was unrecognizable.

There! Her pale gray eyes latched upon the figure. Russet, wavy locks falling to his shoulders, slim but muscular figure cut nicely in a doublet of navy—her son's favorite color. It must be him, running toward and into the government palace.

She picked up her skirts, lifted one foot, and—

The horse and rider bolted straight toward her. Though still in the middle of the square, its aim was like an arrow. A girl of no more than five stood frozen in front of Lapaccia, sobbing, her plain muslin gown tattered and torn.

"Run!" Lapaccia screamed at the child. "Run!" Lapaccia screamed again, this time to herself.

She ran without thought, without care. Like converging armies, she and the horse and rider trod a collision course, only the small body between them.

The churning crowd slowed the horse's stampede; adrenaline fired Lapaccia faster. The throng parted. Her arms opened. The clamor of beating hooves pounded upon stone. The child's cry hitched for air. Lapaccia's arm reached out. The rider saw nothing as Lapaccia captured the child in her embrace, whisked her off her feet, and threw them both to the left, out of the path of the charging animal and his mount, into the relative safety of the moiling mob.

She fell then, not in a stumble but in relief, and the child plopped herself upon Lapaccia's stomach as if it were a chair.

With an oomph of air, Lapaccia raised her head and almost laughed to see the little girl upon her. Sitting up, she wrapped her arms around the child, an embrace of gratitude. Pushing back the long, untethered strands of black hair falling about the pixie face, Lapaccia wiped the tears and dirt from the child's eyes, her own squinting in recognition.

"I know you, little one, don't I?" Lapaccia asked with a smile.

The child's black eyes popped out as she jumped up.

"S—sorry, madonna." The child squeaked. Without lifting her skirt as she should, the small girl attempted a curtsey and Lapaccia's heart ached with the dearness of the sad endeavor.

"Have no fear, little one, you have done nothing wrong." Standing, Lapaccia leaned down and took the child by the hand. "Your family owns a shop, yes? Here on the piazza?"

Lapaccia scanned the circumference of the square, hoping for a glimpse of recognition connecting this child to her home, but it was impossible in the turmoil.

"Where is your *madre?*" she finally asked.

Freed from fright by the presence of the noblewoman, the child turned and whirled, looking now at people where before there lurked only monsters. Pulling upon Lapaccia's skirts, the girl spun her toward the southern corner.

"*Mammina*," she peeped, a dimpled finger pointing to a woman pacing in the doorway of a Venetian glass shop, one Lapaccia had frequented on many occasions. From here, Lapaccia and her ward could see the woman's mouth opening and closing, but could not hear her cry.

Lapaccia squatted beside the child, "Go while I watch. Do not leave again."

The child nodded with fearful, enthusiastic obedience.

"Promise me," Lapaccia did not release the child's hand. "Promise me, *piccolo cara mia*, you will stay by your mother's side."

Did she speak to this child or her own, the missing son she still called her "dear little one," even though he now stood head and shoulders above her.

The little girl nodded again. Then away, away she ran.

Lapaccia disappeared then, swallowed by the gaping mouth of the Palazzo della Signoria, noticed by no one but a child and her grateful mother.

• • •

"The palazzo is under attack! Salviati fights the Gonfaloniere! Perugians fight our militia!" The shrieks rushed by her like gale winds as Viviana made her way through the palazzo and into the side streets. The squall brought the sounds of metal clanging hard against metal.

Viviana covered her ears, still running, but could not drown out the scream, the worst yet.

"*Popolo! Liberti!*"

She knew that voice, that of the great patriarch Jacopo de' Pazzi; she knew the cry of revolt, "People! Liberty!" How many times had such a cry brought upheaval, and how many lives had ended in response? But she heard no answer from the people, no agreement to take up arms against the Medici. What she heard instead gave her the strength to continue.

The countering yells began, sparsely at first, like the thin fluttering waves of the tide turning in. Soon they swelled to crashing breakers.

"Palle! Palle!" It was the rallying cry of the Medici, a reference to the balls upon the family's crest, a cry declaring, "I am for the Medici!"

Sobbing now, with joy and pride for her people, with the shock of the lifetime she had lived in a few hours, Viviana turned the last corner, tripping on her skirts. With a cry, she thrust out her arms as the ground rose up to meet her. But it never did...he caught her.

Viviana looked up into the green eyes, those that haunted her, those forever hovering on the outskirts of her thoughts since the moment she had seen them almost two years prior.

He held her for an instant, held her head against his chest, and with a frown sent her on her way.

"Go!" he commanded, the first words spoken between them since that night. "Go. I will watch your back. Always."

She knew so little of him, had seen him but a handful of times since the first, but, somehow, she trusted him, believed him.

Denying all she felt, Viviana turned and ran.

Chapter Six

'The tide turns slowly but inexorably,
And none in Heaven or on Earth can stop it.'

"Orfeo!" Viviana cried his name even before she pushed open the heavy paneled door, rattling the brass anchor of the Marrone family crest. He must have received word of the nightmare overtaking their city by now, must have realized his wife could be trapped in the heart of it. Worry is a catalyst powerful enough to warm the coldest of hearts, surely it was.

"Orfeo!"

Viviana twirled about in the small foyer, unsure if her husband was still abed or elsewhere in the modest home.

"Mona Viviana!"

The distraught squeak came from behind, and Viviana whirled about to find Jemma rushing toward her, a small bundle of energy and emotion.

Her lady's maid's dark, round eyes bulged at the sight of her blood-covered mistress; her mouth emptied at the appalling apparition.

"My husband, where is—"

"Are you hurt? Are you injured?" Jemma grabbed Viviana's bloodied hands, turning them about, grabbing Viviana by the shoulders, searching her mistress's body for a wound.

Viviana denied the question with a shake of her head. "No, I am not. I must—"

"What has happened to you? Out there?" Jemma thrust an accusing finger at the door. "We have only heard rumors…and… and the sounds."

Viviana had no time to explain, she needed to see her husband, to tell him, to be comforted by him. Grabbing Jemma by the shoulders, she gave the girl a gentle shake.

"Where…is…my…husband?"

Jemma stared at her mistress as if she had never seen her in her life. The girl pointed to the set of rooms off the right of the foyer. Viviana released the girl, grabbed her skirts, and ran.

Around the short gallery, one hand upon the rail, Viviana dashed to the master's chamber. There, she saw him through the open door standing before his wardrobe, buttoning his finest doublet, and she flung herself across the threshold.

"Orfeo, thank God." Viviana rushed to his side.

With a jutting elbow, he pushed her off.

She stumbled backward, astonished but not to be deterred.

"Orfeo, I must tell you what happened…what I have seen—"

"You need tell me nothing." Her husband spared her a dismissive look over his shoulder as he finished the arrangement of his attire, pulling down upon the frayed edge of his doublet as if doing so allowed his scrawny physique to grow muscles. "A messenger came from Friar di Carlo. I am on my way to the Palazzo della Signoria this very moment."

"You cannot…" Viviana's protest dried upon her tongue at a sudden realization.

He knew! As she thought, her husband did know what had happened, where it happened, knew she was there. Yet he uttered not one word of concern, even as she stood before him with a dead man's blood upon her person; it was as if he stabbed her…the sharpest ignominy.

"Why did you not send word?" The snide accusation slipped from between his teeth. "I expected you would hurry to tell me yourself, rather than letting me find out by an acquaintance."

"Why did I not…?" Viviana threw hands to her temples, to her ears; it was not condemnation she heard, it could not be. "You know where I was. If you know what happened, you know I was in the thick of it. I barely made it through the streets. I could have been killed. Have you given that any thought?"

She heard it, the deep, dark anger in her plunging voice, the unfamiliar inner self who had been born by such treatment as this. It burned her and she shook with ire. "I have seen things no human should ever see. The face of the devil was no more than inches from me. I held the dying body of Giuliano de' Medici in my arms."

"Good," Orfeo decreed flatly, smoothing the pathetic wires of straggly hair down upon his round pate, applying the pungent goose grease in an attempt to stick it there and hide the advancing baldness. "Perhaps *Il Magnifico* will award us for your actions."

"A—award us?" She grabbed his shoulder and spun him round. "The world has gone mad, Orfeo. The man's family has been attacked. The *government* is under attack. Are you truly foolish enough to care about award in this upheaval?"

With a whirling hand, he threw off her hold, and she stumbled backward. She saw him then; the man who had alienated himself from any political or financial ally, the man who had squandered her inheritance, and the man who blamed everyone save himself for his troubles.

"I am no fool," he hissed, snarling, trying to stand tall enough to loom over her; he was too small a man in every sense. "A man who can make himself useful in a crisis is a man valued. This could be my chance."

Viviana almost gagged; she longed to spit in the face of such self-absorption, of such disregard for others' devastation. In her husband's black eyes, she saw the same lunacy as in Francesco de' Pazzi's.

She said nothing—did nothing—to keep him there for a moment longer.

Her silence worked and Viviana knew, in Orfeo's delusional mind, he took it as a victory. She cared not a whit.

With one last glance in the cloudy looking glass, Orfeo quit the room without another word or gesture.

Viviana listened as he thumped down the stairs, threw open the door, and slammed it behind him. She ran from the virulent man's room to her sitting room through the adjoining door, one she had dreamed of barring more times than she could count.

Even here, among her lovely things, among her silly trifles and frothy covered pillows and colorful chairs and settees, she found no solace. Viviana paced the room—from her sofa to her table to the window and back, a triangular path taking her nowhere. Confusion and uncertainty plagued her; she could not reconcile all she had seen to the Florence she had always known.

"Marcello, Rudolfo." Without conscious thought, the names of her sons slipped from her tongue. They were all that mattered now...her children, her friends, and their secret work.

Viviana found herself by her settee once more and there she dropped hard to her knees.

"Please dear God, powers of Divinity, please watch over my sons." She dropped her head into her hands, her hands upon the pale sage silk. Both her boys—young men in the prime of life— were staunch supporters of the Medici, she knew they would put themselves in danger for the powerful family; it could both protect them and put them in harm's way.

"Protect my sisterhood, dear Lord, for they are worthy of your care; without them I am of little consequence." Viviana had no way of knowing where the other members of her secret group were in the miasma outside her door, she hoped only for their safety. They had saved her life, though they didn't know it; the women, their work, and the guild of secret artists they created had given her a renewed jest for life when she had begun to almost long for its end.

For hours, Viviana rocked upon her knees. It was then that his face materialized in her mind.

"Keep him safe. Oh please, keep him safe."

She cried then...not for her sons, or the society, or the man whose face lingered always in her mind. She cried for the Medici, for the Pazzi so filled with hate, for all *fiorentini* whose lives would never again be the same. She cried for herself, the illness to body and mind from the last few hours finally bringing her low. Still, she could not bring herself to forego the habits and duty of so many years.

"And watch over Orfeo, for he is far too stupid to do so himself."

Chapter Seven

"Truth can be so much harsher than lies."

The pounding on the door below jolted her awake, brought her up from the floor where she had crumbled.

"Madonna?" Jemma stood in the threshold, eyes bulging.

Viviana stood with a wince and a moan.

"I will see to it, Jemma." She relieved the girl as the thudding continued. "Stay here. Lock yourself in if you wish."

Jemma said nothing but stepped aside to allow her mistress exit.

Viviana rushed down the stairs, fearing not the reaper, but his crier.

The banging stopped only when she threw off the small wooden barricade and wrenched the door open. She blinked at the hallucination upon her stoop.

"Andreano?" Viviana squinted into the growing light of a coming dawn.

"Have you seen my mother, Mona Marrone? Tell me that you have?"

With his wavy hair of wood brown, a beautiful mane now dampened with dirt, falling in his face, the young man with the amber eyes resembled nothing of the dashing nobleman he was. He reached out a hand and grabbed her arm.

"Have you seen my mother?"

"I have not. We were supposed to meet in the cathedral—"

"She has not been seen since yesterday morn. She never

returned home."

"Oh, Andreano." She reached out a hand, taking his. A thought struck her. She clenched tighter; now she would wrench truth from him. "My sons, Andreano, do you know of my sons?"

"Yes, signora, they are well." Andreano nodded vigorously. "They were part of the force calming the city yesterday, but they are garrisoned today, unhurt and resting, I assure you."

Viviana threw her arms about the young man's broad shoulders, crushing him to her in soundless gratitude, her silent tears wetting the dark navy of his doublet.

"But all else is in riot."

Viviana put a hand to her chest. "*Il...Il Magnifico?*"

"Lives. He lives, madonna."

"Oh, thank the—"

"But he is crazed with vengeance. He is killing everyone involved, anyone he thinks is involved, the Pazzis, Salviatis...more."

Andreano told her a tale she would not soon forget, of bodies hurled from the windows of the Palazzo della Signoria, of the Archbishop and Francesco de' Pazzi. She could bear no more.

"Stop, please Andreano, stop." She held him with a squeeze of her hand. "Let us try to think of where your mother could be."

"I have no time." Andreano kissed the hand, turning away. "I must find her."

A step out the door, he spun back. "You will ask the...her other friends?"

Viviana nodded without pause. She always thought Lapaccia had told her son of their group; the older woman had always been far braver than she. She knew what he asked, knew the danger of it, but it mattered not at all. The women must meet, must help, as soon as possible.

"I swear it to you," Viviana promised. "As fast as we can."

With the assurance, a nod of his head, a blink of moist eyes, he was gone.

• • •

They ran through deserted back streets with hands clasped like links in a chain, Viviana hidden in her cloak, Jemma cowering in hers. They scurried through the twisting pathways to the south, to the mouth of the Ponte Vecchio, to the very edge of the quarter of Santa Maria Novella.

By the time they reached the statuette, both were out of breath, rushing to put the sign out fast in hopes the women of the art sorority, or the few servants with knowledge of it, would have time to see it and return to the safety of home.

Viviana leaned against the shelf of the corner niche, hands upon the waist-high stone lip. Filling her lungs with much needed air, she peered up to the devout face of Saint Caterina. Though it was not the Caterina that had launched the women on their clandestine undertaking, they had made this shrine theirs, one of hundreds scattered throughout the city, using it to inform members of meeting days and times. Such reliquaries punctuated many an intersection and were oft-tended with fresh flowers and candles.

With shaking hands, Viviana removed the dead flowers from the vase at the saint's feet, replacing them with eight fresh, brilliantly white lilies, pilfered on their way past a resplendent palazzo garden. Around the saint's feet she arranged eight small stones from the pile always kept at the base of the niche, all on the eastern side, where the morning light would shine upon them.

Stepping back, she studied her work as she would study one of her paintings, looking for flaws in the laying of the sign, one disguised to be, to the unaffiliated, nothing more than an oblation. Satisfied but not quite, she turned to Jemma, who gave her mistress another of her efficient nods. It was all Viviana needed. She grabbed the girl's hand, and again they ran.

Chapter Eight

"The saving of the one, outweighs the safety of all."

Viviana climbed out of the rented carriage without help of a footman, a treacherous act in her voluminous gown. Keeping her veiled head dipped downward, she dropped the coins into the driver's hands and watched as he rerouted the vehicle and clattered away.

Once out of sight, Viviana scampered along on the toes of her worn, beribboned slippers, around the far corner and up the hill along the Via de' Marsili. She slipped through two narrow and deserted streets; every door she passed had been closed tightly—shutters too. It was as if the city itself had died two days ago. If not in mourning, many hid in fear, frightened of the vengeful fist of *Il Magnifico* pounding anyone remotely culpable.

She clambered uphill in the lofty and wealthy Oltrarno quarter, and quickly made her way to the base of the great church. Services marking Terce were soon to begin, though with hardly a congregant to be found.

As she made her way to the middle door, the largest of the three, Viviana crossed into the strangely shaped shadow of Brunelleschi's architecture, the curved Byzantine silhouette. She spared a quick glance up to the single round window many feet above, and the small modest cross atop the barely pointed steeple. Its creamy plaster façade, accented in dark gray *pietra serena* stonework, spoke of simplicity and serenity.

Inside, however, its truth lay revealed. Almost forty side chapels bespoke its depth, each with its own altarpiece. The long, wide center aisle, lined with columns topped by scrolled capitals, led the eye, and the penitent, to the altar and the simple *baldacchino*, under which the priest offered Mass.

Viviana rarely ventured into this part of Santo Spirito, but on this day, more than in many, she felt the need to light a candle; she would light them all if she could. She had come to find her spirit in the classical faiths, rather than those of Catholicism, much like Lorenzo de' Medici. But there was a shadow of it on her soul.

Viviana stepped through the small back door in the corner of the north transept, then lightly through the petite square garden, past the lush green sprouts poking up and out of the dark earth. The postern swung loose in the tooth-like gate.

As always, she found the outside door of the baptistery open. Ignoring the first inner door just inside the darkly paneled interior—a locked room, the true guardroom for the church's sacred reliquaries—she turned left, grabbed a lit lantern from a sideboard with one hand, lifted her skirts with the other, and made her way along a dark corridor. It narrowed as she went, slippers shuffling on dusty stone, powdery sand lifting to dance in the pale rays of light. The lantern held aloft revealed the small simple door ahead, a portal to another world.

Here was the moment she relished like the anticipation of a lover's lips. She drew the chain out from between her breasts and grasped the key in her hand. Leaning down, she entered the elaborately scrolled piece of metal in its port and sighed with contentment when she heard the click of release.

Only seven keys to this room existed; each woman of the fellowship wore theirs about their neck, strung upon a finely wrought chain. They wore these keys day and night, sometimes hidden beneath their clothes and nightshifts, sometimes as a part of a jangle of jewels adorning resplendent gowns. They wore them as the knight wears his armor, as the warrior wields his sword, for it was both their protection and their weapon.

The seventh key belonged to the man who gave them their

home; the parish priest of Santo Spirito, Father Raffaello, brother to Natasia, one of the younger members. As much a devotee of art as the group itself, he was truly a man of God's graciousness, for he cared not a whit by whose hand art was created. Creation itself was by the hand of God, mortal beings were merely the conduit.

Social order deemed there were only two places women were to be, at home or at church. A church, then, was the perfect place for this secret art society to call home and no great cajolery had been required for them to gain access to Santo Spirito's secret chamber. For not only was Father Raffaello Natasia's brother, he was a doting one at that.

To be a male artist was to find a banquet of support and sponsorships—the sculptors were members of the Guild of Masons, while the painters belonged to a branch of the Guild of Doctors and Apothecaries. Such affiliation came after years of apprenticeship, some starting as small children as young as nine years old.

For women, there was nowhere to start, nowhere to go. Viviana hoped this assemblage, secret though it may be, would be the beginning of the end of such exclusion. It was a ridiculously lofty notion, but she had no other way to think. She was a woman passionate about her craft, and all the more tortured for it.

Viviana's presence was the first to break the sacred stillness of the room. For a moment she did nothing more than stare at the chamber and its contents in wonder.

The six roughly hewn workbenches of dark wood lined the room with precision, three to a side, facing each other and the open area in the middle. The easels stood tall and proud beside them, some boasting finished works, others in progress, and some with blank, stretched canvasses, their vacant paleness begging for attention. She picked up brush and palette from her own bench, one a bit cluttered, a bit splotched—signs of her zeal, not untidiness. Though not ready to work, she needed the feel of her tools in her hands.

Her loving gaze circled about the room. Each workbench told its owner's story: the hammer and chisel upon Isabetta's—

her dearest friend—told of her inner darkness; the exquisite, fine line sketches spoke of the loving Mattea's attention to detail; upon Lapaccia's bench were her tools, far more perfectly organized than any others; Fiammetta's held the most expensive of tools, of course; and Natasia's was nearly empty, the young girl had been too obsessed of late with the coming of her nuptials.

The latter three she knew not well, did not speak with them over much, and yet they were an intrinsic part of her world. What they were doing together was as vital as who she was as a solitary being, secret though their connection may be.

They need not share all, as long as they shared this. The thought flashed as she gripped the handle of her brush a pulse tighter, as she looked down and saw the myriad of colors on her palette…there they were, the women of the art league.

Along the base of the three stonewalls, wet canvasses stood in a row, propped away to dry. On the walls themselves, frescoes hid beneath other frescoes. Boxes and chests jutted out like boulders on a cliff side. So much storage was required in an artist's *studiolo*. The aromas of spices and tinctures used to create the paints enveloped all with pungency and bite.

The rising sun found its way in through the southern wall of windows, diffused by thin tracing paper tacked over the thick glass. It afforded the artists light for most of the day. How proud they had been when they first created this place, the hours spent in merry camaraderie, in deep study, and in experimental work with Caterina's books and journals and sketches before them.

Viviana came full circle, stopping again before her work, analyzing it with a harsh eye. She knew what it said of her, or what the lack of popular subjects revealed. There were no religious symbols, nor those of love, nothing except barren wastelands, landscapes bereft of people, abounding with roads and paths leading off and away. At least she created them with the new technique, with the lifelike dimensionality Giotto and Masaccio had brought to the craft, open windows on a fully rounded world, not the flat depictions of previous eras.

"What was once the most vital has become the very essence of the trivial." Fiammetta's booming voice broke Viviana's reverie as the stout contessa lumbered in.

"The world has changed for us all," Viviana lamented. "Are you rec—"

The question remained unasked and unanswered.

"Oh, you are here!" The trill announced Natasia's arrival…and her relief. "After yesterday, I did not dare to hope we would ever meet again. I thought it was the end of the world and we would never see each other, save for in the hereafter."

"It may still be." Fiammetta took the young woman in her hefty arms, the strands of their necklaces clinking together with delicate notes.

"Such a sight to behold, one I thought I may never see again." Isabetta had crept up on them in her stealthy way.

Viviana embraced her, arms quivering. "I was so very worried about you."

The tall woman scoffed. "I reside with the poor folk. This mayhem belongs to those hungry for power and glory." A hint of her northern accent remained, and all of her bluntness, as stark as her pale hair.

They were harsh words, not fully uninformed; none dared deny them. Viviana would say nothing of Lapaccia until the last member arrived, though she would make their number only five. Viviana had no expectations to see the sixth arrive, though her heart thudded with hope.

"Your husband, Isabetta, how is—"

"The same." The woman rushed past the topic as she always did when any tried to ask after her husband and his health. Her pale eyes met theirs without a blink.

The silence in the wake of her rebuttal grew and grew heavy; each woman took the opportunity to make for their workstation, though there were few thoughts of actual work. Isabetta brushed unseen stone chips from her crude wood table, the dust clinging to her pale tresses. Fiammetta fiddled with her brushes as she always did upon arrival—cleaning them meticulously, arranging them by size. Natasia stood before the finished works at the base of the wall by her table, pointing a finger at each one—an introduction heartily made on every arrival.

Light, quick footfalls pattered along the corridor, metal grated upon metal as key merged with keyhole and twisted.

With Mattea's arrival, they came together again. It was as if the very air about them had somehow changed; haphazard streaks forming a painting with the last and final stroke applied. It happened whenever they were together. They gathered themselves together in grateful silence, forming a circle of joined arms, hearts beating with the same rhythm of relief. For a moment, they wallowed in it. It gave the group—and the women in it—their power.

Viviana knew the moment had come; the stalling grew unbearable.

"I called us together to—"

"Stop." Isabetta held her. "Will you not wait for Lapaccia?"

Viviana's stomach flopped, her body quivered on a deep, indrawn breath.

"She...she won't be coming." Viviana leaned against a table, hands clasped tightly; a dispassionate telling was the prescription for this tale. "She won't be coming, for she is missing."

A collective gasp arose, one bursting with outrage and horror.

"Tell us, Viviana," Fiammetta ordered. "Tell us all...now."

Viviana squared her shoulders, and did.

"Dear Lapaccia." Natasia sank into a chair, covering her face with her hands as Isabetta held her shaking shoulders.

"Poor Andreano," Mattea whispered, tears of her own unshed, staring out into nothing.

"The Pazzi have broken us." The words escaped. Viviana bit her full bottom lip; she knew they were the wrong ones to say the moment they were out of her mouth.

The reaction, when it came, as quick as it came, was no surprise.

Thrusting her hands on her wide hips, Fiammetta turned on her, face puckered sourly.

"The Medici asked too much, took too much." The woman's ire splotched her bulbous cheeks, as always when she and Viviana talked of the two most powerful families of the land and their divergent loyalties. They tried, with every effort, to simply not discuss it. There were cracks in the bonds of every family. But avoidance may not be possible anymore. "If they had only—"

"If *they* had—" Viviana's face contorted in shock. She pointed a sharp finger. "You were in the cathedral, Fiammetta. You saw what the Pazzi did."

"They may have felt they had good reason to—"

"There is never a good reason for such carnage, for cold-blooded murder!" Viviana shouted. Fiammetta's face turned a vivid purple to match her brocade gown.

"Please, my friends, please," Mattea stepped between them. "We must not talk of this now. We must talk of Lapaccia."

Viviana turned, fuming. But Mattea was right; she had called them together to decide how they could help Lapaccia, for no woman of such a rank went missing for this long without a troublesome reason at the heart of it.

"Yes, Lapaccia," Fiammetta said. "She was not closely aligned with either family. The Cavalcanti need secure themselves to no one."

They all nodded; there were few more noble families in the entire region.

"I cannot believe she would venture out on her own," Isabetta said with flat disbelief.

"I have no doubt she was looking for Andreano," Viviana added.

"You do not think..." Natasia's tremulous cheep withered away.

"Think what?"

"You do not think they found out about us, about the group? And they took Lapaccia for her involvement in it. Perhaps they shall come for us all?"

"Listen to me, Natasia." Isabetta's tone was soft yet sharply made. "What we do here is deemed unlawful, but do you really suppose in this moment, with two great families—the greatest men of our city—setting out to destroy one another, that anyone, *anyone*,

49

would care about an association of women who liked to draw?"

Silence met her supposition, but only for a moment. Viviana cracked first. It was a small snicker loosening the floodgates. Soon even Natasia chuckled at the ridiculous notion she had suggested. Leave it to Isabetta to find the amusing reality amidst the maelstrom.

"But if not because of this group, then what?" Mattea asked the better question.

Not a one had a chance to answer.

Heavy and arrhythmic footfalls clod outside the door and the women turned in fright; Mattea had left the door unlocked. Isabetta reached out and grabbed her heavy metal, pointed chisel, brandishing it like a sword as she stepped in front of them, a human shield of righteousness if not of might.

Father Raffaello opened the door with a whoosh, swooping backward at the sight of the armed Isabetta. He threw his hands up, yet remained in the threshold.

"Madonna, *mi scuse*," his deep baritone squeaked. "I am so sorry. I did not mean to frighten you."

Isabetta lowered her artist's weapon. The priest entered the room, slapping his forehead.

"I should have thought, should have known, in these days, how easily we are all scared."

Natasia rushed to her brother's side. Of similar coloring and stature, big boned and tall, his made all the more corpulent by the voluminous robes, there could be no denying their kinship.

"What brings you, Tomaso?" Her brother had been a priest for many a year, but he had been her brother first, a wild young man saved when he had heard God's calling, as his priestly name implied.

"There is word of your friend, Lapaccia." He put a hand upon his sister's, one holding his arm so very tightly. "The city is rife with talk of her, Lapaccia and a painting."

"A painting?" Viviana's voice cracked as it rose. The group gathered closer to the cleric.

"Yes, a painting, one gone missing from the Palazzo della Signoria and...and they accuse her of its theft."

• • •

"And so we have left the insane to enter the absurd." Isabetta's sarcasm broke the appalled silence.

"A…a painting, from the palazzo…" Fiammetta repeated the words to make sense of them. "Do you know how many paintings there are in that palace?"

"It is one of the newer paintings, or so the scuttlebutt proclaims. The one hung just after Christmas, the mysterious group portrait no one ever claimed." The priest shut the door as he entered fully and took a step closer to the circle of women in the center of the room. "For some reason, its absence has become quite noticeable. It is now considered part of the investigation."

"A part of…" Viviana's voice trailed off; there were too many thoughts bumping against each other in her mind. "Let us take this a step at a time. A painting is missing, it is certain?"

Father Raffaello nodded. "Most definitely."

"Whatever could make them think it has something to do with the atrocity?" Isabetta asked.

"It seems, as the painting was of a gathering," the priest explained, "it is believed to be a portrait of the conspirators themselves."

"Good Lord!" Isabetta spat. "My apologies, Father."

Father Raffaello patted her slim hand with his chubby one.

"I am sorry, but I am not surprised. The ego of men, of powerful men, it is the work of your devil, yes?"

The priest nodded, slow and pensive.

"The adoration of their own brilliance impelled them to have such a painting rendered," Viviana added. "But it would have taken time."

"I remember this painting," Mattea raised a thin finger. "We went to sketch it, all of us, I think. Or perhaps just Viviana, Isabetta, and myself. It was quite the talk at the time. How could it be of the killers?"

"Quite easily, I think," Natasia declared. "I heard Giovanna degli Albizzi tell papa. Word is spreading that the plan was more than two years in the making, plenty of time for such a painting to be rendered, no?"

Fiammetta swatted the air. "It is all bruited nonsense."

"Is it?" Isabetta insisted. "And yet a conspiracy there was. An assassination there was. This is not rumor, but fact. It is in the realm of possibility, as surely as anything that has happened these past few days."

Viviana tutted, "A plan of such magnitude would take much time in the making. Acts of such a heinous nature are rarely done on spur of the moment thoughts."

"Ah ha!" Mattea crowed. With a large parchment in hand, she wormed her way into the center of the group, holding the paper up and out, displaying the work.

Two weeks after Christmas this painting had appeared, an anonymous donation to the growing collection at the Palazzo della Signoria, and now, four months later, its master was still unknown... four months and still its notoriety clung to it like the last layer of varnish. It was a mammoth work, a group portrait mimicking one of the great moments in Christianity. There had to be more than thirty men within the large and elaborate room depicted, not to mention servants and furniture. Yet the dimensionality, the new trend breathing true life into the art of painting, was employed with brilliance.

"I *do* remember that painting!" Fiammetta exclaimed.

"As do I," Viviana agreed. "I went more than once. I was quite enraptured with the technique of perspective rendering such a large group in a confined space. Typically, so many would be captured among nature, without confinement, easier to replicate the proper dimensions."

Mattea made the connection. "It is the Feast of Herod."

The Feast of Herod was currently one of the most favored topics; an ideal scene in which to capture many faces, a technique and trend of the age, where the rich sponsor paying the artist's commission demanded their faces, and those of family and friends, be made part of the portrait.

"We all have sketches of it then," Isabetta scrunched her eyes. "I am remembering it. It was not Filippo Lippi's, though it was in the style of his famous one. The mimicry brought the painting its notoriety, I think."

"It was not signed, was it?" Fiammetta asked, searching her mind as she cudgeled her memory. "I cannot seem to recall a signature."

"I think you're right, Fiammetta." Mattea bobbed her head. "I don't show any sign of it here, though I have more sketches at home."

Viviana paced, "Well, there is no question of the painting's existence. But what could possibly connect Lapaccia to its disappearance?"

"Those who speak of it say she and the painting went missing at the same time," Father Raffaello spoke up. "The last anyone saw of her was at the Palazzo della Signoria, *that* day. It is also the last day the painting was seen."

Mattea scoffed, "Preposterous. She would never."

"It doesn't matter, dear women." The priest brought them to silence. "It only matters that they *think* she took it."

To this, they said nothing.

With a kiss upon his sister's cheek and a respectful bow to all the women, Father Raffaello took himself away.

"We have many sketches, yes?" Viviana broke the silence in his wake.

Every woman nodded.

"Then there are two things we must do."

"Two?" Isabetta tilted her head.

"*Sì*, two. First, we must recreate the painting and return it as soon as possible."

"Are you mad?" Natasia barked.

"If it is returned, perhaps the government, perhaps *Il Magnifico*, will stop looking for Lapaccia."

"Ah, yes, but it is only half our battle." Isabetta said with dawning clarity.

"Not the easy half," Fiammetta sniped.

"No, it *is* the easy half, for we are all masters, are we not?" There was such righteous pride in Viviana's words, not a one would, or could, naysay her. "Though I admit, it would be far easier were our 'studio' to have a true *maestro*, one with a true talent for the modern techniques."

"We will find no such woman," Isabetta muttered.

"Not yet," Mattea said with her shy smile.

"That is a challenge for another day," Viviana brought them back to the task at hand. "For now, our most formidable task is finding Lapaccia ourselves."

Chapter Nine

*"A well-rooted tree fights against the wind;
its branches waver but never break."*

After sharing loving embraces and making their pledge to ferret out every sketch of the accursed painting, the women made their way from their sanctuary, staggered in small groups. Soon someone would call for another meeting—within a day or two, no more.

"Your sketches, Mattea," Viviana said to her young friend, "as soon as you can." Mattea was the best with charcoal; it was often her *cartone*, the basic miniature sketch or perfect downsized copy of a larger painting, the women used to grid and composite their works. Hers may well give them more insight than any other's would.

Mattea nodded and, arm and arm with Isabetta, made for home.

Fiammetta and Viviana brought Natasia through the Piazza Santo Spirito, along the short stretch of the Via San Agostino, and to her door. It was the way of them, to escort the unmarried Natasia home. And as often happened, Fiammetta chose to stay on, to socialize with the great Soderini family, while Viviana made grateful use of one of the family's carriages to return her home.

With their familiar, perfunctory politeness, Viviana took her leave of them, entering the enclosed carriage but keeping the curtains open, the unobstructed view giving her a chance to see the state of the city.

More and more people were venturing out, though all in groups of at least four or more, and only for market or church, as their baskets and veils evidenced. No decomposing bodies littered the streets of this most affluent quarter of the city on the far side of the river from both the Duomo and the Palazzo della Signoria. Viviana knew men were missing from these stately homes, men whose allegiance lay mortally with the Pazzi.

The carriage pulled up before the dark doors of the del Marrone household. Viviana fluttered her gaze between the façade and the street leading to the Piazza della Signoria. Neither told the true tale of what lay in store for her nor was the choice easily made. A dark part of her itched to see what lay in the city's largest courtyard, to see the bodies hanging from the windows for herself, yet it was no place for a woman alone to venture. But through those doors could await discomposure of a more dangerous sort.

Bolstering her courage, she opened the carriage door and stepped out. With a straightening of her shoulders, she turned toward her own front door, until she saw him.

He stood at the far corner, at the edge of the Palazzo Bartolini. Tall and lean, she immediately recognized the green eyes bright in the sun, beautiful beacons of light reaching out to her, though it was under a starry sky she remembered them best and remembered them often.

Could it be two years ago? It was at an evening fête at Lapaccia's palazzo, in celebration of her son's election to *consiglione del commune*, the upper house of the legislature. The images turned over in Viviana's mind like leaves rustling along a wind-swept lane. The ballroom seemed to have been lit by a thousand candles, rivaled only by the plethora of stars in the clear summer sky.

Viviana knew she had looked especially fetching in a brand new gown of forest green, though she had not heard a word of it from Orfeo as he led her into the room. She was merely another appendage, albeit one to show off, upon his velvet-clad arm. With the Cavalcantis as their guide, the del Marrones had been introduced to those in the room they did not know. Though there were not many, there was one who stood out.

"Gentlemen," Andreano drew the attention of a small group

of men standing in a circle as they approached, "please be so kind as to pay your respects to one of my mother's dearest friends and her husband. I present Messer Orfeo del Marrone and his wife, Mona Viviana."

As a group, they bowed, as did Orfeo; Viviana dipped her most graceful curtsey. Rising up, she looked into his eyes, the greenest eyes she had ever seen. For a moment, she forgot to breathe.

She heard little after that—voices rumbling, names passing, and only as Andreano turned to him, the tallest man with silken hair, the color of dark honey, falling about his ruddy-skinned face, did she hear his name: Sansone Caivano.

"Signore," Orfeo bowed to him as he had to each of the others as proper introductions were made. "Are you a member of the delegation as well, as Messer Abbatano here is?"

"No, signore," Viviana heard a warm bass commanding an orchestra. "I am a soldier. It has been my honor and privilege to serve with our host on occasion."

"Ah." It was Orfeo's only response, save to turn his back on the man, knowing he was no use to him, the same back he showed his wife.

Viviana looked up at Sansone, brow furrowed, cheeks burning, eyes filled with an apology she could not speak aloud.

The small smile came then, one so understated yet so disarmingly charming she felt the corners of her lips rise. With the grin came a small shrug of wide shoulders and an almost imperceptible roll of the eyes.

Just as she thought she could stand it no longer, the orchestra—perched upon a corner dais—took up their instruments and music filled the spaces where her turmoil might reveal itself.

"Signore del Marrone?"

She looked up as Sansone called her husband's name, then called again when Orfeo did not turn. When he did, it was with clear disdain.

"Might I have your permission to dance with your wife?"

Viviana thrust her bulging gaze downward.

"Yes, yes, of course," Orfeo hissed between closed teeth, his imitation of a cordial smile, turning back without a glance toward the woman in question.

First an *allemande* and then a *coranto*, they twirled and whirled together, in perfect step, as if they had danced together on many an occasion. For such a tall man, Sansone moved with remarkable elegance and Viviana found allowance for her own abilities to shine instead of reining them in as she must when dancing with her ungainly husband.

They danced and they danced. With each new song, Sansone returned her to her husband who dismissed them both with barely a glance, with a flick of a hand as he plied the powerful among the Florentine politicos. Sansone responded almost the same way each time.

"As you wish," he bowed to Orfeo, who had already turned away. Then Sansone turned once more to Viviana, his small, charming smile, a raised brow asking, her quick nod answering. And with that, his large hand led her back to the dance floor, led her firmly yet with devastating grace about the floor and through the complicated turns.

It was after a *lavolta*, after the intimate dance that brought the couple close together, that brought Viviana into his arms, lifted like a weightless flower into the air as he made a three-quarter turn, that she spoke without thought.

As Sansone made to lead her once more to her husband, she had turned them away.

"Oh, let us not bother him." Or had she said let us not bother *with* him; perhaps such words were only thoughts. "I need some air. Would you be so kind as to escort me to the balcony?"

She saw it, though it was but a flash…a glint of light in his remarkable eyes, a jump of the muscles upon his strong jawline.

"It would be my pleasure, Mona Marrone." He held his arm out to her and she laid her hand upon it gladly.

"We have been dancing all night," Viviana giggled. When had she done that last? "I think it would be quite acceptable to call me Viviana."

Did his step stutter as he looked down at her? She did not know; she knew only that when he said, "It will be my pleasure... Viviana," her chest tightened and her heart beat wildly in her throat.

His fine hair fell forward, as if it too leaned toward her. A soft ashen brown, the sun had swooped its brush upon random strands and glorified it with its golden depth. The effect was a dewy color that brushed so close to the meadow that was his eyes.

They stepped out the leaded glass doors as if they stepped into the firmament, so full was the moonless sky with the brilliance of stars. With the magnificence of Florence carpeting the earth below them, they spoke, slowly at first, then soon with ease. Viviana told him of her quiet childhood on the vineyard—left much to herself to read too much, to imagine too much.

They laughed together as he told her of his diminutive mother, still alive in the small town of his birth near Naples, who would stand on a chair to hit him on the back of the head. Viviana laughed so hard she forgot herself, forgot all else save the glory of the moment, and put a hand upon his arm as their laughter wafted out and up to the stars shining down upon them. His large hand covered hers and the shock of it, the lightning crackle of the touch, jolted them both.

Viviana turned as he did, spoke as he spoke...

"You are the most..." said he, her hand still in his.

"You are such..." she said.

And that's when his finger found the ring upon her hand.

All their words dried up in the parched desert of her reality.

Yet he took a step closer, stood inches from her. "Mona Viviana del Marrone, you are like no woman I have ever met," Sansone's voice was the low sung song of yearning; his head lowered yet closer...and stopped, "but you are another man's wife and I...I..."

Viviana squeezed his hand, demanding him to finish, feeling the same bitter angst that broke his strong voice.

Sansone straightened. She watched the battle within as he brought himself under control; in the act, he won her respect and broke her heart. "But I would not want my mother to have to stand on a chair and hit me yet again."

Viviana had sniffed a small laugh, had smiled a broken smile, and had let him lead her away from what could be, to what was.

She looked back up to the corner of the Palazzo Bartolini and saw the same disarmingly charming grin upon Sansone's ruddy countenance, as if he had journeyed back in time with her, as if, though they were a row of large homes apart, they were together once more upon the balcony beneath the stars.

He dipped his head, a barely perceptible nod and, as if seeing her arrive home were his cue, he stepped gracefully and swiftly away, disappearing around the corner with two strides of his long legs.

Viviana breathed once more, and entered her house, no longer afraid.

Chapter Ten

"Inner Truths must be well tended and well guarded."

She stood, alone, a stranger in her own house, in her own world. She turned about her sitting room as if it belonged to another.

Viviana dropped herself into her chair by the window. For a brief, warm moment, she burrowed into it, hiding. In the space of aloneness, in this treasured place, she allowed herself to be grateful for Orfeo's continued absence.

Her body prickled with numbness; her head swam. She had barely eaten in two days and the lack of food abetted her weakness. Viviana knew what was happening to her, knew she was the rock upon the shore, pounded by waves ferocious with a storm.

Beneath the quilt her *nonni* had made as a wedding present, the *cassone* stood in almost absolute anonymity. There were storage chests in every room of a Florentine house; it was where all things were kept, it was yet another symbol of a family's status. This one belonged to Viviana alone.

Purpose filled her; refuge was within her grasp, and perhaps Lapaccia's salvation as well. Viviana stood, rushed across the room, and unveiled the *forziere* from its protective garb. Wanting both comforts, she pulled the storage box across the room to sit beside the chair.

Viviana opened the trunk, releasing the two heavy clasps with a creak of metal, a groan of old wood disturbed. The heavy and earthy smell of the dark wood filled her senses, calming her nerves.

Her secrets lay within the exquisitely hammered metal interior, all save one, and she gazed upon them as one does jewels. Reaching in, Viviana brought out the small string of prayer beads. So like the Christian rosary, it was shorter in length and ended with a *triquetra*, a continuous line forming three pointed ovals, a symbol of the connection of mind, body, and soul.

She squeezed the amulet in the palm of her hand, much as she did whenever Orfeo mistreated her. Viviana trembled with fear should Orfeo ever find this chest and all that lay within it; how badly he would punish her then. There would be no prayers for such salvation.

With quivering hands, Viviana spied the most precious items. Placing the beads and amulet in her lap, she leaned over and picked up the first leather bound book. She brought the tome to her nose and breathed deeply of the smooth and worn buckskin, the musty yet appealing smell of leather more than fifty years old. It had all begun with this, this diary and the others accompanying it.

As always, Viviana opened the book delicately, with respect for its age, its origins, and its contents. With the pad of her index finger she ran her hand over the three words on the first page, caressed them as she would a beloved's face.

Caterina dei Vigri

Viviana held the book to her chest, eyes rising to the wall opposite and the painting upon it. In the flat, lifeless style of the era in which Caterina worked, the central figure of Ursula loomed large with her crown of gold. With both hands, the saint unfurled her cloak trimmed with ermine, revealing two groups of kneeling virgins, hands clasped together in prayer, heads anointed with their own crowns. Few knew the painting that once hung above the nun's bed, and which now hung above Viviana's settee, was the work of a woman named Caterina. Those few who did were the members of the special guild, her group pledged to continue Caterina's work.

Though she had only met the cousin but a time or two, Viviana's father had told her of his dead sister's daughter.

The dei Vigri family was of the great noble clans of Bologna.

Caterina's father Giovanni had served as ambassador to Niccolò, the Marchese of Ferrara. Giovanni's was a loving heart; his was an open mind when it came to his daughter's education. Taught to read and write, in her dialect as well as in Latin, taught to play an instrument and to sing, and tutored in the skill of paint and illumination, the shy and fragile child was nevertheless woefully unskilled at the ways of courtly life, despite growing up at the court of Ferrara. Her spirit showed no signs of becoming a worldly woman, and when her father died, the fourteen-year-old girl found herself adrift.

Though ingenuous, Caterina was not unwise, and she knew the only place suitable for her. She entered the convent of Poor Clares of Corpus Domini, a popular retreat for the well-born women of Ferrara. There she remained for the rest of her life, chosen as abbess when Poor Clares colonized in Bologna, and remained so until her death a few years ago.

It was in this cloistered environment—this protective atmosphere—that the shy girl prospered and thrived into a talented and benevolent woman. Here Caterina discovered that her true gift lay not only in her piety, but in her hands, hands able to wield a paint-soaked brush with the prowess of a master. Such mastery Caterina brought upon herself, through years and years of practice and experimentation. Such learning Caterina had documented, in the very journals Viviana possessed: the one in her hand, and the five more in the chest.

The day Caterina's diaries—her treatises and recipes for the composition of pigments—were delivered to Viviana, her only living relative, was the day Viviana's life changed forever.

She had been floundering, much as Caterina had. Her sons were grown and gone, out and about and living their own lives, and though they spared many an hour for their mother, they needed her less. Their absence had thrown Viviana into a void, one of aimlessness other women seemed to embrace with little compunction. Even now, amidst all the lunacy possessing her world, Viviana wondered if she would have embraced her newfound purpose with such rigor if her marriage to Orfeo were different. Blessings are so often disguised as curses.

Isabetta. The woman leapt into Viviana's mind. Not the cynical woman so at war with the hardships life had thrown at her, but the vibrant, vivacious character—once like Viviana, the wife of a wealthy merchant—who had crooned with enchantment when Viviana had shown her the diaries. From that moment on, things had moved quickly. Isabetta brought Mattea Zamperini, when Isabetta came upon Mattea drawing in a church. Mattea, who worked as a talented embroiderer, enticed Natasia Soderini to the fold after the noblewoman had shown Mattea some sketches for fabric embroidery she wished to commission. Natasia recruited Fiammetta while Lapaccia Cavalcanti came at the invitation of Fiammetta. They were among the richest and the poorest of the city; more than thirty years spanned the ages of the youngest to the oldest. It didn't matter. None of it.

Together they would learn and master their craft, work toward the same goal: to one day know the same joy Giotto and Masaccio, Celini and Botticelli knew, to embrace art as a discipline, not as a frivolous pastime. One day they would be free to sign their work and show it to the world.

Viviana jerked upward—her revelry broken—at the sounds of voices, male voices, in the empty warehouse of the ground floor.

"Jemma!" she cried, jumping up, protruding eyes searching the room for some form of weapon. She grabbed the heavy vase from the table by her chair, dumping the flowers and their water on the floor with no regard even as the footsteps sounded on the stairs below, as the voices grew closer.

Chapter Eleven

"Yearning finds us all, in all its forms."

Few people gave notice to the plainly-dressed woman hurrying down the Via delle Caldaie, crossing the Via Santa Maria to the Via Romana, leading not only through, but out of the Porta San Piero Gattolino.

For the first time when making this retreat, Isabetta scanned the road behind and before her, fearful any should see her hurried get-away. Such action could be seen as escape, escape as guilt; but it was only the truth of her own existence from which she ran.

Once beyond the battlemented gate, Isabetta quickly stepped off the road in favor of the narrow, well-trod path beckoning from the right. It was one she had taken on many occasions, telling no one she was going. She never did on such sojourns.

Her step became a scamper. Her need to find release from her worries, greater with the disappearance of her friend, urged her on. Scurrying now, her breath grew labored as softly rolling meadow turned to hill.

Unlike much of the surrounding landscape, where hundreds of villas jutted from their tucks in the cliffside, or where the vineyards and olive groves drew lines upon their faces, this hill was as it was born, wild with whatever nature decided should grow upon it. Outcroppings of rock shared space with bright tufts of newly sprouting grass speckled with the purples and yellows of fresh blooms.

Isabetta climbed the first hill and turned round. From here, she could see her city sprawled out like a tapestry of golden and russet threads laid upon the earth. Enclosed by gigantic walls portioned off between twelve mammoth gates, the city—once nothing more than an encampment of the great Julius Caesar in the years before the birth of Christ—*Florentina*, the Latin word for flourishing, had become a magnificent citadel, cleaved in two by the gently curving Arno River. The Black Death had taken many, yet her home still boasted one of the largest populations in the world, as much or more than the places she read about: Rome, Milan, and somewhere called Lon-don, such a strange sounding word. Like a bird wafting above, her gaze scanned the mosaic below her and she could not help but wonder what magic lay in the few miles between these walls.

Was it something in the water they drank or the air they breathed? Some otherworldly singularity creating so many extreme talents in one place? Dante, Petrarch, Donatello, Boccaccio, Giotto…all gone now, but not their influences—their legacies. Alberti, Brunelleschi, Botticelli. Painters, sculptors, writers, architects—the greatest the world had ever produced—all within these walls. How many more untold talents were there? She knew the work the sisterhood produced, knew more than some of it belonged on the walls beside those of Giotto, in sculptor gardens next to a Donatello, denied their glory by the feminine hands creating it. It blossomed within the confines of these city walls still, like a grape that had weathered a frost.

Isabetta crested the hill, entering the loving arms of the forest. She snuggled through the short and full bay laurels. She ducked beneath the prickly branches of the pines, twirling about them with one hand on their rough, thick trunks as if she danced a *canario* with them.

She climbed and climbed some more, until the tall, fuzzy firs hid her within their protective branches and the gurgling of the stream—her stream—beckoned her to the top of the tallest hill. It was a copse where the stream bubbled up from the earth and the trees formed a protective circle around it. It was nature's fountain. She esteemed it as a religious zealot would the most beautiful of altars. It was her favorite place in the world, where earth met sky, and sky met water. It was her place, belonging only to—

She saw him then.

How dare he? It was a ferocious scream in her head.

On the almost perfectly flat, jutting rock daring to hang a few inches above the stream's head, he sat. He sat upon *her* seat.

She suffered a personal violation; to have someone—anyone—in the one place she felt pure private ownership, the one place where she escaped all without fear of discovery or interruption, his presence was an assault upon her as surely as a fist to her gullet.

It was a man, she was still certain of it, but his hair belonged on a woman—long, light brown, shot with hints of red, silkily beautiful, falling to his mid-back in gentle waves. He was slim but powerful; she could see the broadness of his shoulders and the sinew of his arms, even under the gray knee-length tunic of substandard linen and the equally shoddy wool mantle he wore. He was tall, for he had to curl his legs beneath him, where she could let hers dangle without threat of touching the water.

Isabetta's forehead crinkled. What sort of man wore a tunic and an overgown? It was the typical dress of an older man, though she could tell, by the smoothness of the skin on his hands, that this was a youthful man. In truth, it was his hands capturing her gaze. Long, lissome, and slender fingers moved with a grace she found both strange and sensuous.

Upon his lap sat a small wooden cage, flat bottomed, oval topped, and made of the slimmest of willow wood. She had seen many such contrivances in the market place, where the wealthy bought birds for pets. Inside it, Isabetta saw three softly cooing doves.

With his nimble hands, the man opened the small rectangular gate and held the cage itself on the edge of his knees. With coaxing mutters the man charmed the birds from their prison. The doves launched themselves from the edge of the cage, lifting effortlessly into the air with a graceful flapping of their feathers.

"Do you see it?" the man spoke, voice thick. "Do you see the muscles in their wings, stretching up along their necks?"

He turned then, blue-gray eyes glowing.

"It is a wonder of creation," Isabetta said, not an iota of fear to be alone with a strange man in the woods.

"You are a lover of nature too, *sì*, signorina?"

Isabetta turned from the flight of the doves with a dip of her chin and a small smile. It had been some time since anyone addressed her as signorina; her vanity delighted in it.

"I...I...yes, I do," she replied, "I feel a part of it, a part of something...bigger...bigger than me, bigger than us all."

"You are, perhaps, a follower of the Sacred Goddess?" the man asked, such a personal question, such a dangerous question; Isabetta flinched back, only for a moment.

"Among other things, yes, I am."

"Ah," the man said, turning back round and setting aside the now empty cage for another object. "It is well for you."

Moving closer, she took a place upon a large rock beside him. And gasped.

Upon the man's lap lay a fine piece of vellum, thick and stretched smooth; in his hand was a piece of trimmed and pointed charcoal. He held it delicately, though he worked it furiously upon the vellum. Before her eyes, the doves returned. Quickly, but precisely, he created the birds in flight, the movement of the wings witnessed again.

"You are an artist," Isabetta announced in a breathy whisper.

The man snorted with amusement. "So they tell me, *signorina*. In truth, I am many things or only one, a simple human being." He finished the sketch of the bird's neck with the wisp of a few strokes and turned.

Isabetta saw now the fineness of his features—smooth, pale golden skin lay upon high-set, prominent cheekbones and a long, slim, arched nose. His dark brows and lashes made the paleness of his eyes all the more striking. For the first time in a very long while, Isabetta felt something, something she thought lost forever...desire.

"Do you appreciate art, signorina?"

"Fioravanti. I am Isabetta Fioravanti." She heard it, the untold truth; it was a very small dagger.

"Signorina Fioravanti," the man took her hand, and from his sitting position, bowed elegantly over it. "I am Leonardo, Leonardo di ser Piero da Vinci."

If she had been standing, she would have stumbled; if she had been speaking, she would have stuttered. The name of da Vinci echoed on the streets of Florence, in the artistic circles and on the tongues of spiteful gossips, for some time now, two years or more. And here he sat, in her favorite of places. It seemed destined.

"*Sì*, Signore da Vinci, I have a profound appreciation of art, including yours," Isabetta proclaimed with calm boldness.

He gave her the shy smile again, easily seen between the clipped mustache and the full flowing beard. "You know me?"

Isabetta settled her back against a rocky outcropping. It would take a ferocious event to pry her away from this man and this meeting. "The Angel."

The man snorted again, softly through his slim nostrils, still smiling; small and charming, it was a pleased expression.

With his father's blessing and assistance, Leonardo had left the small hamlet of Vinci for the city of Florence a little over a decade ago. Apprenticed to Andrea di Cione where he lived and worked, the young Leonardo learned quickly. Verrocchio, as di Cione was more commonly known, conducted one of the most highly esteemed studios in all of Florence, but soon found himself overshadowed by his own pupil. The *Baptism of Christ*, still hanging in the Church of San Salvi, had been a collaboration of master and apprentice, as most studio work was. It was unfortunate for Verrocchio that da Vinci's small angel in the corner, he who held the robe of Christ, far outshone the rest of the painting. It was rumored Verrocchio had not painted since.

With a twist of fate like a knife in the back, it was the same year as the tragedy, or travesty, of da Vinci's life, depending on who spoke of it. Leonardo became famous and infamous in the span of a few months. To be known for one's work and not judged must be pleasing indeed.

"Yes, the Angel." Leonardo worked upon his vellum. This time his fingers captured the landscape: the treed valley below, each bush, tree, and rock coming to life—a blur and tangle of curved lines, never straight—yet the depth was there. The valley below their feet, the movement of the water, the diminishing appearance of the stream as it ran from their sight.

"You have seen the painting?" he asked her without lifting his hand.

"Indeed I have. I have heard your name in the tavern where I sometimes work. Many artists spend their leisure there. Such talk impelled me to see it for myself." Once more Isabetta divulged a facet of her life known to not a single friend, for the truth of it shamed her. Why then did she feel no such compunction in telling this man her truth? Was it because she knew so much of his, the good and the bad? She didn't think so.

"Which inn, signorina?" Leonardo's lithe hand began to move again; a lush-tailed squirrel scampered on the stream bank across from them and across the page in seconds.

Isabetta lost all thought save the study of his technique, watching how often his eye strayed from the page to the subject, how he dropped his head from one side and then to the other, changing the perspective of his sight as he adjusted the perspective of his drawing.

"There are three sorts of people in our world, signorina, those who see, those who see when they are shown, and those who shall never see."

Isabetta found his gaze upon her.

"I believe you are one who sees."

To this stranger who she felt was a stranger no more, Isabetta replied, "*Sì*, Signore da Vinci, I am."

Her wide smile answered his slim, charming one.

"Please, call me Leonardo."

Isabetta felt her own eyes bulge just a tad before she could stop them. His request was highly improper; just being here, alone with him, was the height of impropriety. Any other woman would have left long ago.

"Then you must call me Isabetta."

Leonardo tucked his chin, pale eyes crinkling at the corners, and shrugged. "If I must, then I must."

They lapsed into companionable silence, one stretching on for how long she did not know or care. He worked, she watched, closing her eyes at times to find the stillness within, one only heightened by his presence. It was only when she saw the shifting of his shadowing did she realize the time had come for her to leave.

Isabetta rose reluctantly, brushing the leaves and twigs from the skirt of her gown. Leonardo's gaze followed with almost childlike innocence.

"I must go," she said grudgingly.

"Duty calls," Leonardo replied, as if he knew more.

"It does," she nodded, "as does the Inn of the Three Turtles."

A small furrow formed between the man's dark brows, "The one which stands on the Corso dei Tintori?"

"The very same."

"I have been there. Will you be quite safe making your way?"

Isabetta knew what he did not say; the tavern was in a rather disreputable part of the city, close to the river and the shanties housing the very poor. Little did he know she lived just north of there, on the very edge where the lines of poverty and prosperity blurred, thrown there by the calamity of her husband's health.

"Thank you, Leonardo, for your concern." The taste of his name was sweet upon her tongue. "Many know me on those streets. I will be quite safe."

"If you are sure," he replied, though he seemed not entirely convinced. "*Buonasera*, Isabetta."

Among the trees and the animals, Isabetta became the lady she had once been as he spoke her name. She gave a fine curtsey, fanning her skirt with grace. "*Buonasera*, Leonardo."

Isabetta could linger no longer. She turned and began her way back along the trail.

"Isabetta?"

His call stopped her short and she turned back with far too

much willingness.

Leonardo smiled over his pointed shoulder. "Perhaps we will see each other here again."

There was hope in his words, wasn't there?

"That would be lovely, Leonardo," she said quickly, before she could stop herself, hurrying swiftly on her way.

• • •

She stood at the threshold of their bedchamber. Vittorio slept soundly beneath a thin linen. The small room felt still and warm with the last of the day's sunlight streaming through the one small, unglazed window.

He had a bad day, Isabetta thought with a pang of guilt. He had not the strength to light the lanterns or the tapers. His breathing came raggedly and his chest rose and fell in fits and starts.

The memory of him bloomed in her mind; the tall, ruggedly handsome young man who had come into her father's glass factory in Venice a little more than seven years ago, the man she had loved from the moment he aimed his wide smile her way. It took only months for their love to bloom and grow, for her to leave her family and her homeland behind for the sake of the man who became her husband.

Did the troubles start when they knew there would be no children for them or were there no children because he became ill?

Isabetta shook her head at the question, one asked far too many times. The answer would make no difference.

She made for the small kitchen and the embers still glowing in the bottom of the cooking grate. Coaxing it up to a fire, she put the kettle of broth on the spit to warm and lit a taper. From this small flame, she lit others, and a lantern as well.

Vittorio, awake and aware, struggled to sit up.

Dropping the lantern quickly on the chest by the door, Isabetta rushed to help him.

"You must at least let me try," he said, his once smooth voice now rough and raw, his throat damaged by years of coughing. He let her pull him to a sitting position, allowed her to arrange the bolsters behind his back so he did not slip back down. "How will I get strong if I do not try?"

How she admired his hopeful outlook, one she did not share. How she loathed a world that turned love into an anchor.

She kissed his forehead, relieved to find it cool. "Let me get your broth."

Isabetta sat on the edge of the bed and helped him eat the thin soup. It was all the food remaining since before *that* day, since she had been able to get some ingredients to make more.

They spoke of what went on in the city. Isabetta told him what she had learned of the state of affairs. Vittorio didn't ask where she had been or to whom she had spoken. He never did, not anymore. Isabetta was no longer sure if he knew when she was there and when she wasn't as the days of his illness stretched beyond two years. She knew only how he delighted in her company, as much as in those first, blissful days, and she gave him as much as she could and as much as she could bear.

Isabetta lifted the spoon again. This time he shook his head, and with a gentle touch pushed her hand away.

"Look how well you did." Isabetta put on her smile, one she had learned just for him, and showed him the bowl, almost empty, before placing it on the bedside table. "I have not seen you eat this much in many a day."

He smiled, dry lips cracking with the effort. "It is your fine cooking and lovely company, *cara mia*."

Always my chivalrous gentleman, Isabetta thought with yet another twinge of onus. She had grown used to them, as she had to her husband's condition. Isabetta saw how much their time together and the effort to eat had tired him. She talked softly, talked of nothingness, allowing her voice to grow quieter with each word. Within minutes he was once more asleep.

Standing, she gently removed the bolsters, easily slipped his wasting form down upon the ticking, and tucked him into his linen yet again. She stood over him until the tears threatened and then she turned, only to be aimed for her next duty, for such was her life, a series of duties dotted now and again with the brightness of paint.

Isabetta could be thankful for one thing: Vittorio slept before she left for the tavern. How he hated that their circumstances forced her to such lowly work. She had no choice if they were to pay for the taxes on their small shop. Without the shop, they would lose all. They would become a part of those wretched lives existing in shanties along the river.

As she removed one gown and put on another—the simple muslin she wore to the tavern—her eyes held upon her own body clothed in no more than chemise and kirtle. Firm still with her youth, curves abounded, aching to be touched. Isabetta allowed her own hands to slip down the sides of her hips, eyes closed, imagining. It was not the hands of the sickly man in the other room, nor of the young, vital man he had once been. It was the long and lithe hands of Leonardo she saw on her body.

• • •

"You are late," the gruff squawk reached her from the back corner of the tavern. The inn was almost half-full, more than she expected in light of events. Those among this clientele were not the sort to fear much; they were mostly feared.

"My husb—" she began.

"Yes, yes, your sick husband," Drago yelled as he approached her. He tottered like a child learning to walk. He shoved the cloth and bucket of dirty water in her hands. "We have heard your story too many times. Get to work."

"Yes, Drago."

She worked feverishly, the energy coming easily on the wave of all the happenings of the day replaying in her mind. Her fear for Lapaccia spurred her on, to make her way back home, to look for any sketches of the missing painting she might have made. Visions of Leonardo, the beauty of the man set among her favorite of places—his eyes, his hands, the trees, the sky. Isabetta needed to expend the forces building up within her.

She thought she was alone as she began to mop the filthy floor; no doubt it had not been done for the last few days, the last time she herself had done it. When the gentle hand came to rest on her shoulder, she jumped in fear.

"Oh, my pardon, Isabetta, I am sorry to have frightened you."

"No, no 'tis fine, Delfina," Isabetta said.

"Do not let his grousing bother you." Delfina ticked her head over her shoulder toward the back room of the tavern. Orphaned young, taken in by the underworld, Isabetta's unique acquaintance had been lost to the darkness of life as a poverty stricken stray. Like other prostitutes, Isabetta's friend sat as an artist's model, making a pittance in comparison to what she made on her back. Isabetta had asked her to sit for her, clothes on for once. Delfina returned the kindness, appeasing Drago whenever he threatened to fire Isabetta. "His prick is as limp as the noodles he cooks."

"Hah!" Isabetta barked a laugh. "You are terrible, Delfina."

She drew closer to Isabetta as she whispered, "I am sorry to hear of your friend, *la donna* Cavalcanti."

"What do you mean, Delfina?"

The woman put a hand to her heart. "Now I am truly sorry, Isabetta. I thought you would have heard. I know you had mentioned a fine acquaintance with the lady so I thought...I mean surely by now you...oh dear."

Delfina dumped herself into a chair.

"Worry not, Delfina. I do know. I was just...so very surprised to hear someone speak of it. I would not think many knew."

"Men are going missing by the dozens, most finding their way to the end of a rope." The woman's gaze flitted about. "It's true some women have been exiled, but it is mostly Pazzi women so far. Not a woman has gone missing, no one but the lady herself."

Isabetta took in all this with a stoic face, even as her mind screamed with growing fear. She had mentioned Lapaccia by accident one day when in Delfina's company, that they knew each other through Lapaccia's work at the orphanage, charity work Isabetta herself conducted before she herself had become a charity. She would never reveal even a thought of the group itself, not to a soul.

"How did you come to know of it?" she asked Delfina.

Delfina leaned across the table, brought her voice down to a whisper. "There is a friend of mine, a man who thinks himself important in the government. He likes to boast about his grandness, as if it would excite me." Delfina gave a shrug. "He may be old and corpulent, but he is quick and generous. If he wants to talk politics during, I let him. He talked about Mona Cavalcanti's disappearance at length just last eve."

"At length?"

"Well, yes, I think so." Delfina scrunched her face with thought. "About her missing and how they were looking for her. The Medici. And something about a painting, I think."

"Any word on where they think she may be?"

Delfina shook her head, sloppily piled hairs dancing with the motion. "Nothing I recall."

Isabetta brought steepled fingers to her lips. "Thank you, Delfina, I appr—"

"Do you search for her?" Delfina cut her off. And suddenly, strangely, the girl's cheeks blossomed and her eyes twinkled again. "Because if you do, I may know a way you could learn more."

Chapter Twelve

"Heaven and Hell, both may bring the pain."

"I must go out again, mama." Mattea dropped the veil over her braided auburn hair. Her skin itched; she could not find a place to put herself at ease. Fear niggled at her; not only for Lapaccia, but for them all, what they dared to do. And yet the thought of reproducing such a creation…her body tingled with the expectation of it. She had to walk.

"But you have only just returned."

"*Dio mio.*"

"Language, Mattea, if you please."

"I left my rosary at church." Mattea looked away from the sharp black eyes piercing her. "I could not forgive myself if they were lost."

She put a hand to the door once more.

"You will not find a husband walking the streets alone and in such desolate days," Concetta Zamperini chided her only child.

Mattea sniffed, "The chances of me finding a husband are not good on any day." They were harsh words, if quietly said, and she turned back to her mother, regretting them more at the forlorn sight.

The woman's lower lip trembled. "He did as much for us as he could with the time God gave him." Concetta reached out a veiny hand to place upon her daughter's unblemished one. "I know you have felt his absence deeply. What young girl wouldn't?"

Mattea began to shake her head, but it would be meaningless;

indeed, what young girl wouldn't miss her father, growing up without the most important of all men to tell her she was beautiful.

"He provided," her mother continued. "He sold the business without the government knowing and we will always have the money we need to pay the taxes. We will never lose our home, he made sure."

Releasing her hold on the door, she held her mother's hand instead. "He did, mama. He did better than many other men would have done."

Her words brought a smile to her mother's pale face. "You shall see. You have your dowry fund. It will bring you a fine man."

"I must go, mama." The words had turned her, and Mattea longed once more for escape. "I will return quickly, I promise. I will be here to make your supper."

She slipped out then, before her mother could say more.

Meandering back toward the Church of Santo Spirito, should she be seen by any of her mother's friends, Mattea dragged her plain, worn slippers over the pavement stones.

She felt at ease in the desolate streets of the wealthy quarter. Free, for once, from supercilious eyes raking her with their judgment, the denigration of a single young woman walking the streets. Her poverty clung to her, as did her threadbare gown; no one would ever think her part of the Pazzi plot. No one would *see* her—few ever did. Heartsick at the scourge upon her homeland she may be, she ambled in the quiet and the freedom.

She turned onto the Borgo San Jacopo to follow the river out of the far less opulent Santa Croce district where she and her mother lived, and she almost laughed at her mother's brand of chastisement.

There was money in her government dowry fund. Put there by her late father since her birth, it was money she would lose if she did not marry in the next few years. There was enough to buy her a simple man, but it was not a simple man haunting her dreams, bringing her the only other satisfaction in her world. It was a satisfaction of such magnificence, it made her shudder at the very thought of him. A man of such high standing, it would be an outrage for them to consider a life together, yet she could think of a life with no other.

The frustration ate at her.

She saw him in her mind—a Greek god come to life: the body of Hercules, the face of Adonis, topped by a thick head of raven hair falling in waves to his shoulders. They wafted behind him when he walked, like a banner of privilege, and set his whole being on fire when the sun touched him. He set her on fire just thinking of his touch.

Frustration.

Mattea heaved a sigh full of it as she wandered onto the Via Bardi, the road taking its place along the Arno. She would forsake the river's crossing at the Ponte Vecchio. Though she was sure most of the fine shops along the gently arching bridge would still be closed, she had no wish to even see the fine wares in their windows.

Someday, I will have more of—

The man grabbed her from behind, snatching her and her thoughts away.

"Gesumarie!" Mattea released a cry. But then she saw the face— his face—and all dread and distress disappeared.

It was him, as if conjured by her very thoughts, of things wanted but just out of reach.

Mattea laughed as she quickened her step, all too eager to keep up, to follow his long cape, a banner unfurling behind him. He turned them right, down one of the narrowest of streets, no more than an alleyway, but she followed him without question, the excitement in her chest pounding against her ribs, thrumming in her ears.

Costa San Giorgio tapered as they followed its winding path, the buildings on either side so close together not a ray of descending sun crept in.

"Where do you take me?"

He only smiled over his shoulder, light brown eyes sparkling with mischief, a sensual laugh emerging from deep in his chest. A wave of desire made her weaker. Mattea knew what she did with him was a sin, yet she had not made the rules they must live by, had not built the societal walls separating them. If he and what they did together were the fires of hell, she would gladly burn.

He pulled her once more to the right, along the back of the abandoned San Girolamo Convent. Built more than two hundred years ago, once a convent for Franciscan nuns, it was in the middle of renovations, work suspended, at least for the time being, since the riotous events of Sunday.

Her man pulled her into the garden at the back, rushing her through the flowers and vegetables, wild and untended, rustling and rasping against their legs as they rushed through to the very back corner of the building and the encompassing solitude of the location.

He pulled her in front of him, plunged her against the wall, and thrust his body against hers, his lips upon her mouth.

Mattea moaned with breathless rapture, the feel of his lips, his hard body. He kissed her with relish—the rushing thrill of lust, yes, of course it was, she knew. He kissed her as if they were drowning and only shared passion could save them. But she knew it was worship as well, adoration snatching his breath with magnificent thievery.

He moved his lips down her throat as she laid her head to rest against the wall behind her, holding fast to him, lest she fall to the ground limply. Mattea opened her eyes, for she would watch him, see him as much as she could. He was the epitome of the new man, a man of the rebirth taking place in their city, zealous and expert in all facets of his life, be it art or sport or politics. Or love.

His lips moved to hers again, but this time she denied them.

"I was so worried for you," she whispered, though she knew none were near to hear, only the crickets chirping around them as evening fell. Their love lived in these dark corners, in the secret places of the city, sometimes in the forest outside the city walls. It was only in her dreams that they walked, hand in hand, through the Piazza della Signoria, or into the Duomo, with the greatest of Florence's families smiling benevolently at them. "I knew you would be, must be, in the thick of this."

The young man nodded, pulling his face no more than inches

from hers, eyes caressing her lovely features, fingers brushing them with a feathery touch. "I must be. But I had to see you. Had to hold you."

"Are you well?"

He leaned in, his lips teasing her ear, making her tremble. "As well as can be."

Pulling back abruptly, he held her by the shoulders. "You and your mama, do you have all you need? Is there anything I can get you?"

And there it was—the concern transforming lust to love. Mattea held to it tightly.

"We are fine. Signore Bostiana brought us some milk and cheese just this morning. We will be fine. I will go to the market soon."

"You will ask one of your friends to accompany you, yes?" he said sternly, as he would to a child, or a wife. "No matter where you go, you will do nothing foolish. I know what her disappearance must mean to you, how kindly she looks upon you, but you must do nothing to put yourself in harm's way."

"We...I...must do what I can," she argued. "Surely, you know I must."

He shook his head, but said, "Of course, I would expect nothing less of you." He kissed the top of her head, pulling back again, quickly. "But you must do it ever so carefully. You could be hurt, imprisoned. I cannot lose you t—"

Mattea took his mouth, took his fear, until she felt the tense, tight muscles of his body relax once more.

"Promise me," he demanded. "Promise me you will be careful."

Mattea smiled then; her compliance, her gratitude, and her lust lived in the small expression.

"I promise," she vowed, and pulled him to her, unable to bear his lips not upon her.

He groaned at her brazenness, his kisses growing hard, forceful. He grabbed her by the back of her hair, opening her mouth to him with unfettered abandon. As he lifted her skirts, his hands slid so slowly up her thighs, a tantalizing tease, knowing what it would do to her. Mattea ached to grab them, to put his hands where they would do the most good. She clutched at them and he laughed in her mouth as his tongue played with hers.

Grabbing each of her thighs with a powerful hand, he bent ever so slightly, only to straighten, lift her off the ground, and pin her against the wall. Holding her there with the force of his body, he drew his cape around them to create a secret haven for their bodies should anyone wander into this forsaken garden. Within the confines of his concealing garb, their bodies pressed close, their need urgent.

Mattea could think no more; she could but feel and do.

• • •

He brought her along the outer edge of the city, for he would not allow her to walk home in the gloaming, no matter the danger of being seen together. Only at the edge of the row of small houses did he part, with a last fluttering kiss upon her swollen mouth. From there he could watch in the shadows, watch as she traveled the last few steps to her door.

Mattea held the tears, as she always did, until she had turned fully from him, holding her shoulders straight, walking swiftly so he would not need to dally overlong.

She cried not at his parting, for she knew she would see him again, as soon as he could. She cried not for his presence in her life, for she would be bereft at its loss. Mattea cried silent tears of confusion, not knowing how life could be so magnificent and so brutal at the same time.

Chapter Thirteen

"There are always roses among the thorns."

"Truly, mama, if you take much longer, I will…"

"Rudolfo!"

Viviana threw open the door, her mouth split wide at the sight of both sons. Halfway up the curved staircase, so handsome, so young and strong, each with his own swagger yet with brotherhood undenied in the curve of the eye, in the width of the smile—her smile.

"Marcello!"

The very essence of life changed in that moment.

She was a young girl again, running after the round cheeked little boys, so full of life, hair of curls, mouths boasting only a few teeth. As they climbed to greet her, Viviana flung herself into their arms. She pulled them close, as if she were drowning and they were all that kept her afloat.

"*Madre mia*," Marcello, the eldest, croaked a complaint. "You are strangling me."

With bright laughter, Viviana released them, only to pull them back into the full embrace of her arms.

Viviana stood on tiptoes to embrace her eldest, a man nearing twenty years who stood a half foot above her. She quivered to have him in her arms, to feel the strength of him, to know he was truly well and unharmed.

"I am fine, mama," Marcello whispered as if he read her mind.

He seemed able to do so the whole of his life. He pushed her gently from him and scrutinized her closely. "And you, you are well?"

She ruffled his cap of black curls, a habit from his childhood. "I am well, all considered."

With open arms, she turned to her youngest, less than a year younger than the older brother he idolized. She held Rudolfo tightly. This affectionate boy, this loving man, had always been effusive and demonstrative; age had not disavowed him of his truth.

He put his forehead to hers, his eyes, soft brown—golden green if the sun or the heart touched them just so—tender on her face. "I am fine as well, mama." His full lips cracked into a smile as they so often did. Rudolfo loved to laugh, still silly for all his years. "A bit hungry though."

Viviana pulled back, laughing. "Then we will have a big, wonderful *pranzo* to fill you up."

She patted his stomach. Broader than his slim but stately brother, Rudolfo's muscles needed fuel, constantly it seemed.

"Are there the makings for such a repast?" Rudolfo asked skeptically.

"I will make it as fine with what we have," Viviana replied.

"You are going to cook, mama?" Marcello's deep voice squeaked, as much from trepidation as from surprise.

Viviana laughed. She never pretended to be a master in the kitchen. "Beatrice has not been here in two days, not since…but Jemma will help me."

"And you should not be out either," Rudolfo remonstrated. "You have been to Mass today, haven't you? You wear your dress for it."

"You have no business being out, seeing what goes on," Marcello chided her.

Viviana shook her head. "It is far too late, my son. I have seen far too much. I was there. I was in the cathedral."

"What!" Marcello barked.

"No, it cannot be." Rudolfo shook his head.

"I will share all, I promise. But not only have I been to Mass, I have been with the Contessa de Maffei, and I am a bit weary. Allow me some rest and we will eat, drink, and talk, yes?"

Rudolfo leaned down and kissed her cheek tenderly. "Of course, mama. You rest. I need to ask Jemma to clean some of my shirts. I fear they are offending my fellows."

Viviana laughed again. She had no doubt they had come to assure themselves of her well-being. If they could eat and get their clothes laundered as well, such was simply a matter of course, and she adored it.

"Ask Nunzio for help with your clothes. Your father has not been home for a few days, and he has had little to do."

Marcello's mouth tightened into a thin line. The jaw of Rudolfo's long face hardened. The year before these brothers went together to the notary and petitioned successfully for legal emancipation from their father. The laws of Florence provided sons to acquire parental manumission through two means only: the legal path these young men had taken, or marriage. Neither cared to wait for a wife to be free of a father for whom they had no respect, nor cared to enter into business with him. Viviana had never told her sons how their father had made her pay for their actions; they need never know, though she was certain they had a notion of it. They had seen the monster for themselves for the whole of their lives. Now they served their time with the militia, relishing the lively social life Florence provided for such young, dashing, free men. Their talk of opening a business together had yet to be resolved.

"I will speak to Jemma of our meal." Marcello kissed her this time, turning her round and setting her toward her room with a gentle nudge. "You take your rest."

Viviana blew them a kiss over her shoulder, sending silent words of gratitude to all the gods for their well-being. But as soon as she entered her small salon, as soon as she shut the door gently behind her, all Viviana could think about were the sketches, the painting, and Lapaccia. Her friend knew little of the harsh ways of life and had little experience dealing with it.

With little worry of discovery, Viviana knelt before her *forziere*, tossing aside the cover hastily replaced at the first sound of her sons' footfalls and throwing off the heavy clasps once more. With slow respect, she put favored tools and Caterina's journals aside, finding the stack of her sketches, those of landscapes and formidable edifices, and the many masterpieces enriching the city. Those she could sketch without fear.

Like a beggar given a purse of gold, Viviana held the pack of papers close to her chest and rushed to the light of the window. Rustling took on a rhythm with her discordant grunts as she failed to discover the correct drawings, as she picked up one after the other only to put it aside.

"*Dio mio!*" It was a cursed whisper. There it was, in her hand, a sketch of the Feast of Herod. Squinting her eyes to see her small notations in the bottom right corner, made as she always did when sketching, noting the date and title of the piece, the artist if she knew it. Written in her tight, curly scrawl...*25 February, in the year 1478, Palazzo della Signoria, anonymous,* her own hand provided the incontrovertible evidence.

She studied the parchment below it and the next and the next. Viviana could not believe her good fortune; there were four sketches in all. One of the painting in its entirety; the other three breaking it down into parts. There was so very much to see.

As Viviana continued her rapacious perusal, so much became clear, so very much became ominous and frightening. Many of the men she had sketched in form only, leaving their faces devoid of features, as if their missing eyes, noses, and lips were in some way a portent of what was to come. Her gazed followed every line she had made, on every square of parchment, at once critical of her creation and perceptive to what the composition and the content might mean.

On the third, her sweeping scrutiny stopped. On this particular drawing, she had concentrated on the right background, the far back right corner of the room. There, unmistakably, were two laurel plants—two withering, browning, laurel plants.

Viviana dropped her hands and the parchments in her lap, perplexed at her own lack of sight, questioning the very veracity of her daring to call herself an artist, for was not seeing truth the only way to paint it?

With such thought, she wondered how no one else could have seen it for what it was? The Latin origin of the word laurel was *Laurus,* the symbol for noble or famous. In the Tuscan dialect, it is a word from which a man's name is derived—that name? Lorenzo. To paint a dying laurel is to paint a dying Lorenzo. Viviana hunched over the parchments, unable to turn away.

Before she realized it, her shoulders ached with the strain of hunching over them, and the sun had changed its stand in the sky.

Viviana had not lied; she was indeed so very tired.

• • •

"You held him in your arms? As he was dying, you held him?" The pain in Marcello's voice was undeniable. He thought of Giuliano, a man of a same age and like temperament, with great respect.

"Praise be for Conte Maffei," Rudolfo said. "You would have run after him, wouldn't you? Run after Francesco de' Pazzi?"

Viviana shook her head no, even as she spoke the truth. "If you had seen what I had…the brutality…the insanity…the blood…" her jaw ached with the grinding of her teeth. Grabbing the goblet, she drank long of the light and fruity Trebbiano wine.

"What would you have done?" Rudolfo leaned forward.

Viviana stabbed him with her gaze. "I would have beaten him with all the hate in my mind and in my heart."

Her boys sat back, food and drink forgotten. More than anyone, they knew of her anger and hatred. To have it delivered upon a man, any man, would have been a sight to behold. She saw in their faces what she herself feared—her hate would one day eat her alive.

"I could not bear the thought of him escaping." Viviana shrugged her shoulders, as if it was enough. For them it was.

Viviana knew with certainty, more certainty than she knew anything else, how much her sons loved her, how much they would forgive. For a moment, she thought to tell them of her work, of her association with the group, even of her cousin Caterina. She felt certain they would approve, or if not approve, at least accept.

Her sons told her their part in bringing the city to some semblance of order, of the arrests they had been party to, of the executions they had witnessed.

"And what of him? When was *he* last here?" Marcello refused to speak his father's name; his care for the man's whereabouts were for his mother alone.

"He was here when I returned from the cathedral." Viviana stared a few steps backward in time. "I was covered in blood, Giuliano's only. But he did not even ask if any was mine."

"*Stronzo*," Rudolfo spat the crude denouncement.

"I have been thinking, mama," Marcello continued on, "I think I should give up my commission and return home. With so much violence all around, others may be caught up in the mania of it."

"No, I will not have it, not from either of you." She took one of their hands in each of hers. "He is far too concerned with using this catastrophe to his own advantage to worry about me."

Her sons stared at her with their intrusive eyes, those who knew her better than any other living souls.

"Very well," Rudolfo conceded for them both, "but you cannot know, or object, if our friends pass by, perhaps a few times a day."

Viviana knew of one who already did just that. "No, I would not know, nor would I mind."

"And we will visit more often, I think, in these precarious days," Marcello ruminated. "I do not think the taverns will be very lively at any point. No reason for some of us to visit them *whenever* we are off duty."

He winked at his mother as his brother gave his shoulder a swat. Viviana smiled at the sibling teasing that had always been so affectionately jived. It changed the air yet again.

Their talk turned to lighter things, recent outings and adventures in the days before the tragedy, Marcello's favorite new composers, Rudolfo's latest injury upon the training ground as he tended to be more than a little prone to injury, though often in the most amusing way. As they ate their food and delighted in the few sweets Jemma was able to make with the last bit of sugar, as the wine flowed into their glasses and down their throats and their laughter grew louder and quicker and filled the house with its beauty, Viviana said naught of her secrets.

Yes, perhaps they would understand, but she could never put them at risk, could never risk losing them. She would denounce the work and her love of it, she would give up the very air she breathed, before she would give up their love.

Chapter Fourteen

"There are flowers among the weeds; innocent among the guilty."

To free the mind of one worry, one must introduce another.

It was an illogical supposition, but it was the only one Mattea could think of to relieve her mind of thoughts of him and his touch upon her body.

She had cooked for her mama upon her return, as promised. Concetta now dozed over embroidery haphazardly done with fingers grown knobby with age. Mattea felt certain she could bring out her sketches without fear of discovery.

One foot into her room and Mattea sank to her knees, moving so quickly she slid a bit, straight toward the *guardaroba* that held her meager selection of gowns. Most were plain and showed signs of wear. Those boasting some style—style long out of fashion—were too small for her; they fit the body she owned at the time of her father's passing. But with his passing she had learned the truth— such trifles as gowns were meaningless in this life.

From her perch on the floor, she opened the wardrobe door, shoulders popping up to her ears at the screech of the old hinges.

Mattea held her breath, listening for any evidence that the sound had roused her mother. Allowing herself to breathe again, Mattea stuck her head into the wardrobe, posterior rising in the air as her head bent downward, down to the false bottom she had built when she first became part of the group of women artists. Here, in this small cubby, she kept the sketches she brought home to work on during the nights she could not sleep—those too many nights.

"What in the name of heaven are you doing?"

Mattea jumped, hitting her head against the door. She grunted, rubbing the offending spot as she twisted about, laying eyes upon her mother—wide-awake and far too curious—standing in her doorway.

"Must you sneak up on me like that?"

Concetta frowned, raising one thinning gray brow. "I do not sneak," she announced as if insulted. "I walked gracefully, as I always do. It is not my fault you were unable to hear me with your head stuck in there. Bringing me to ask again *what are you doing?*"

Mattea rubbed her head some more though the flinch of pain had subsided. She needed a moment to think, to explain such an awkward position.

"I am...um...I'm going through my gowns." Mattea swung round and stood. "I'm going through my gowns to see which I may add some embroidery to. Seems silly not to put my skills to my own advantage, not just those who pay me to do so," she said. "Perhaps..." she knew where she was going, she knew exactly which words to say to distract her mother, "perhaps if my gowns were more appealing, I may attract the eye of a suitor."

"Oh, oh Mattea!" Concetta threw her arms about her daughter's body, crushing her head to Mattea's chest. "At long last you think to find a husband. My prayers have finally been answered."

Mattea rolled her eyes; she had opened this kettle of fish, but it would be she that would fry for it.

"I am just planning, mama, no more. Let us not think too much of this." Guiding her mother gently toward the door, Mattea continued, "You return to your work, and I will return to mine. We will talk more of this another day, yes?"

Still teary-eyed, but smiling, Concetta gave her daughter yet another hug, scurrying away sprightly on tiptoes. Mattea returned to the wardrobe.

Quickly this time, she lifted the flat wood of the false bottom, pulled the stack of parchment and vellum—both the large pieces and the scraps—from its depths, and thrust them to her chest. With an eye to the door and the empty hall beyond, she scuttled into the small space between her bed and the wall in a crouch, rested the horde upon her knees, and her back upon the bed. Forgetting all else save the memory of the painting, she began her investigation.

It didn't take long to become impatient with herself, with her voracious sketching and the overwhelming amount of drawings she waded through.

But then finally she found them, those of the painting. Mattea dropped to the floor, sitting, legs akimbo, and mouth hanging open, not a single thought in her mind for gowns or men.

There were so many of them. As she analyzed them, over and over, the unremarkable suddenly became obvious. So many details glaring with truth, unseen for all their brilliance.

The first jumped out at her, as if the dimensionality of the painting truly existed. The garland of roses woven into the candelabrum above the gathering of men, its symbolism one of the most oft used in paintings. What was discussed beneath the roses, *sub rosa*—under the rose—was held in sacred confidence. It immediately identified the men below it—some whose faces she recognized, some who no longer lived—as belonging to each other, bound by secrets.

"Did you know—" Once more her mother had crept up upon her, once more she had been caught unaware by the small woman's stealth.

"Oh...*Dio mio*...mama!" Mattea shoved the odd pile of papers under her bed, turning round in one swift movement, and flopping her torso onto the ticking, her head in her hands.

"I only thought to tell you—"

"Can you not tell me in the morning?" Mattea raised her head. In doing so, she saw the hopeful look upon her mother's face, a hope misplaced, but it brought color to the elderly woman's cheeks, a brightness Mattea had not seen there in many a day.

"Tell me now, dear *mamina*," she said softly.

"I thought you might like to know that I've heard the vintner's son is looking for a wife."

As if she told the secret of the universe, Concetta smiled smugly at her daughter, hands folding across her chest.

Mattea blinked. "The *vintner's* son? Do you mean the cross-eyed one, or the one so fat they had to widen the door to allow him to enter his own room?"

Mattea looked to the heavens. Perhaps the last was an exaggeration, but the young man was hideously corpulent. The thought of being his wife, of doing with him what she did with…

Mattea shivered, it could not be borne.

"I will not have the vintner's son, *either* of them," Mattea tried her best to keep the cutting edge of exasperation from her voice. "There is the right man for me out there, mama, I know there is. We just have to be…"

In her mind, Mattea heard the words, those denying the possibility of him and a life together, but she pushed them away.

"…hopeful. We just have to be hopeful, *sì?*"

Concetta's bright smile fell away. "*Sì*, yes, of course. Hopeful."

Her mother needed no further prodding. With a kiss upon her daughter's cheek, she shuffled away, to her room, and the bed awaiting her there.

Mattea watched the small figure retreat, waiting for the sound of her mother's door to click as it shut, and scurried back to her niche by her bed, retrieving the abandoned sheaves.

She peered closer still, studying the finer details of the full rendering. It was a scene within a scene. There, in the small, round, stained glass window centered in the wall behind the large table that dominated the picture. It showed the tiniest depiction of the god and her triumphal vehicle, but it was her, there could be no doubt of it. The vehicle was a decorated barge being slowly pulled through low waves by graceful harnessed swans. It was the vehicle of April.

Aphrilis is derived from the Greek "Aphrodite," Mattea closed her eyes as she remembered her schooling, *one could surmise that the month was named for the Greek goddess of love, whom the Romans called Venus.*

"And one could," Mattea said to herself with decisiveness, "surmise that this tiny picture made implicit the timing of the attack."

She shook her head, pulling out blank parchment and a sharpened piece of charcoal, for she had no time to prepare the paper for her silverpoint.

"Oh, the folly of men," she muttered.

These details needed enlarging, not only to present her evidence to the group, but to allow them to reproduce them more exactly. She touched the tip of the charcoal, she felt the rush just before the moment of creation. Mattea's hand began to move.

It flowed fast here at the beginning, the technique they had all adopted after reading and rereading Caterina's journals. *Move quickly at first. Render lightly the basic shape and proportions.*

This Mattea did and with ease. Soon she drew life from such lines, altering the thickness and thinness of her strokes. In this manner, she made them work for her, emphasizing the rhythm of the objects, the metaphorical and symbolic power of each shape. A master at the technique of foreshortening—that which allowed for the addition of dimension—Mattea became lost to the ecstasy of making art. It was unlike any feeling she had ever known, even that which she felt when in his arms.

Remember the power of negative space. Let it ride along the outside of the form.

Place the object skillfully in its environment, it will breathe life into the work.

Caterina's words were the prayers inside her head as she worked quickly, ever more quickly. Sketching was fast work—to do it slowly would be to lose the movement of the object, the life of it.

She would give life to these sketches, the women would give life to the painting, and to the men within it, they would bring their end.

Chapter Fifteen

"Knowing and seeing are not always believing."

The brittle quiet held the city in a firm, stifling grip, and a bitter wind pushed hard at Viviana. She trod the same route she had taken a few days ago, the same route she had taken for years, yet it was through a strange land that she now trudged. The sun itself, still clinging to the horizon, hid behind a blur of clouds, as if in fear of what it might see. The beauty and brightness of Ascension Sunday had been swept away with a dark and dirty broom. Her boys had returned to their barracks, her husband had not yet returned to his home, only under such absence of male dominion did she have the freedom for what some may call her foolish excursion.

Viviana dared go to the *Mercato*, as she did every day, as every Florentine did most days, this day with Jemma shuffling by her side. The market was the nexus of everyday life. At dawn, the gates of the city opened, the space filling with people, donkeys, horses, and carts, scrambling to be the first to reach the arcade.

In turn, the people of the city clamored to reach the marketplace first, to put the best these farmers and merchants had to offer in their baskets.

But not today.

At a time when the Via Calimara should be crowded with people, nothing save dust and litter rolled in the street, and no more than a few stragglers showed themselves. Those who did wander about— strange men with ill-fitting and ragged clothes casting squinted eyes up and down beleaguered streets—made Viviana glad to have worn her plainest gown and partlet with no adorning *gamurra* and not a single piece of jewelry, save the hidden chain and the key. Viviana looked around and found the world closed; the shutters of each house and shop remained latched, save for a few.

And the quiet, it was ceaseless. She had often heard many complain of the inner city noise, preferring the quiet of the surrounding hillsides outside the walls. Viviana found this noise the music of her life and she reveled in its vibrancy. Today, she shivered at its lack.

"We should not be out," Jemma hissed, shuffling closer to her mistress.

Viviana frowned at her with tender pity. It should rightly be Beatrice, the cook and housekeeper, accompanying her, but the portly woman had not shown up. Circumstances forced Viviana to bring Jemma along in the woman's stead. Circumstances included that the purse of del Marrone had grown too shallow for any save Jemma and Orfeo's valet to live in the house.

"No one should be out," Jemma grumbled. "We must have a care for what comes next."

Entwining her arm in Jemma's, Viviana nudged her playfully with a full, round hip. How wise this young girl was, this foundling Viviana had taken from the orphanage to be her maid, a common occurrence among the nobility and the merchants. She had seen the wisdom in the child's eyes then; she had never once since been disappointed.

"The worst is over. I am sure, little one," Viviana forced her voice into a bird-like chirp. "Besides we have no eggs and no milk. How will we make the biscuits you love so much?"

Jemma pulled her mistress's arm tighter in hers and walked along without further complaint. Viviana knew she had done right by not telling the girl her whole truth, that she needed supplies to make the pigments. The girl's cynicism would have turned quickly to outrage.

They passed the *Arte della Seta*; it too remained shuttered and closed. It was an odd day indeed when the guildhall of the silk merchants failed to open its doors. As they turned from the large building and onto the Por S. Maria, they found many more people in the streets...

...but they were all dead.

Viviana put hands to her mouth, gut heaving. Jemma shut her eyes into tight creases of flesh.

The human refuse bulged from the paving stones like boulders upon a rocky path, growing in number where the street flowed into the Piazza della Signoria.

"Come, Jemma. Come away." Viviana spun the girl away. Rushing behind Saint Cecilia's, she propelled them onto the Via Calimara. Moving as fast as possible, she silently berated herself for her own nonsense. How dare she think the danger was at an end? How dare she bring this girl out into a city still under siege, an onslaught wearing a myriad of faces? Viviana knew herself to be—had always been—too inquisitive for her own good. The girl's staunch loyalty deserved better than to be dragged out into this living nightmare.

They quickly passed the *Arte della Lana,* and the hall of the wool guild was also closed and barren. Viviana tugged on Jemma's hand as the girl tried to look about, not daring to imagine what other sights might await them.

Viviana almost shed a tear of relief at the sight of people, living folk, meandering in a small huddle about the market place.

"See, the *Mercato* is open." Viviana shook Jemma's hand still in hers and gave her the best smile she could muster.

The young girl's dark brows rose skeptically.

There were, at most, four or five stalls out of thirty with their flaps open and set upon the poles. No more than twenty people hovered about these stalls, clearly uneasy to be out, clearly dissatisfied with the wares available.

"We shall get what we can and call it a victory, yes?"

Rushing into the small fray, Viviana found milk but no eggs, so she purchased bread. One vendor was open for business. His root vegetables—the carrots and parsnips *fiorentinos* preferred—showed signs of discoloration and were soft to the touch, clearly not recently plucked. Beside them, the tuna seller offered fresh wares, as did the man who sold the salt, their unique dialects blending into a vocal stew. Without her usual relish in price haggling, Viviana purchased what she could with the coins she had brought, and did so with gratitude for these people and the courage that brought them to the tumultuous city.

Neither the herbalist nor the flower seller were on hand. Viviana's hopes of purchasing any of the necessary ingredients to make the paint remained unrequited. She shrugged her shoulders at Jemma and turned them away, her eye catching on a befuddling sight.

There he was again, Leonardo da Vinci himself. Though they lived in the same small city, Viviana had seen him but three times, twice in the last few days. She felt first a sense of relief, unspeakable delight that he had survived the attack, seemingly unharmed. But within seconds she felt naught but sympathy.

Da Vinci was a tall man and his long legs ate up the ground with his stride. But even still, Viviana could tell he walked at an exerted pace. If he could run without appearing unseemly she believed he would. But from what did he run?

At that moment, he turned his sharply boned face, no more than a flinched glance over his thin shoulders. Viviana followed his gaze and found them.

A hungry pack of *giovani*—the gangs of young men that roamed the city—were fast on his heels, juvenile men for whom da Vinci's innocence was not believed, evil rapscallions who viewed the quiet man as easy prey for their games of degradation.

Viviana wanted to shout at them to stop, to leave the brilliant artist alone. She wanted to run and catch up to da Vinci, to walk beside him in support. She did—could do—neither. She could but watch as da Vinci quickly made his way out of the market square and turn a corner, hoping he would slip from the gang and their hurtful games.

She turned back to Jemma, her cloak of sadness a bit thicker.

"Come, I feel the need to return ho—"

"Viviana!" It was a prayer intoned; it was a bursting of joyful relief.

Viviana swung about and nearly dropped the basket and all her purchases to the ground.

"What the devil are you doing out alone, Mattea? Are you mad?" she chided even as she embraced her friend.

Mattea's small, rounded lips formed a moue. "My mother insisted I come out. She demanded to know the state of things this day."

It was a forceful, well-rehearsed statement, Viviana thought.

"Have you ever seen it like this?" Mattea prattled on quickly, in keeping with her usual stoicism. "If my father had lived to see this he would surely have died with grief for his beloved city."

Keeping the young woman's hands in hers, Viviana stroked tenderly the tiny needle-puncture marks dotting the girl's fingers.

"It is the doings of the devil, it must be, no? Such evil as this?" The younger woman cleaved to Viviana for answers, as she had so often in the past. Viviana had little to give Mattea. Little she would want to hear.

Viviana shook her head. "It is the evil of men that brought this, nothing else and no less."

"But why?" Mattea begged the question, voice thick with her naiveté.

"Where does one begin?" Viviana gave a shrug, gaze scanning the landscape of a changed Florence, as if she could see the domino of events leading them to this moment. "Orfeo tells me bits and pieces, but that is it all it takes, no? Bits and pieces to break us?"

"Are you—" Mattea began, concern etching a thin line between her brows.

"The Pazzis never accepted the power of the Medicis," Viviana said before Mattea finished asking her question, one Viviana might have no care to answer. "It was a power gained as the Medici family crawled up the steps to glory as opposed to winning it on the battlefield, as did the Pazzis. They have pushed and pulled at each other for years, all under the cloak of a Lord Prior, or a Gonfaloniere, or some such government position. Then the Medicis trifled with the elections, but the Pazzis outwitted them. The Medicis refused a loan to the Pope and the Pope went to the Pazzis."

Mattea's long thin fingers clamped upon Viviana's arms. "You don't think the Holy Father…"

Bitter cynicism glinted in Viviana's cold blue eyes. "In truth I am afraid to think, but some things cannot be denied. The Pope turned to the Pazzis for the loan and transferred all the Vatican business to their hands. He put himself in the heart of the feud with his own actions. The Medicis retaliated, how could they not? Back and forth it went. One insult heaped upon another. One maneuver for power countered, until…this."

Viviana leaned down slowly, placing her basket upon the cobbles, as if it carried the weight of her words.

"Men and their games of power will end this world someday."

Mattea frowned; it was a look she might have given someone she didn't know, for rarely did Viviana speak of such darkness of life, of such doom.

"Surely—"

The marching of feet rumbled like the pounding of drums; the clattering armor like the clashing of thunder. The quiet pall hanging over the city ripped at the seams.

The women swiveled their heads here and there.

"Help us, dear Lord," the whisper escaped Viviana's lips.

The red uniformed force of the Podestà, the highest criminal lawmen of the land, had surged into the square, turning right with regimental precision onto the Via Calzaiuoli.

The streets overflowed now with Florentine militia, men of power, frightening in their white and red uniforms, the colors bright in the harsh glare of a rising sun. With a purpose and strategy Viviana could only guess at, the men approached a house, seemingly at random but surely not, and without knock or preamble, broke the door open and rushed in. From within, the screams came, and here and there a clang of steel where a few were courageous enough to resist. By an arm, by a leg, even by their hair, the soldiers pulled the men from their homes, dragging them through the streets, the direction all the same, to the Palazzo della Signoria.

"Are they taking everyone?" Jemma's haunted whisper came from behind.

"No, look." Viviana jutted her chin down the road. "They do not enter every home. It is only this one, then another further down. They know something. There is some reason behind which men are taken and which are not."

"But is it a good reason?" Jemma asked softly.

Like the others at market, the triumvirate of women followed timidly behind, unable not to as the enforcers burst into a modest if elegant palazzo just two doors down the street.

Clinging to each other, the women scrunched their shoulders up at the crashing of wood, at the screaming of women, and the debased begging and pleading of a man.

Other doors on the street burst open. Some cracked only enough for frightened eyes to cast about, seduced out by the sounds, gated in by fear.

As they wrenched the man of the house from his home, the street filled with people, relieved, for a brief moment, to find that the soldiers of red had not come for them.

With a clench upon her heart, Viviana realized she knew this man. He was a *consigliar*, a lawyer who created justice for those wholly underserving of it by the twisting of facts and words. The irony of his fate was not lost on her, though she worried for the twinge of satisfaction she found in it.

Apart and aside from the fleeting satisfaction, a thought seared her mind.

The horrors. They begin again.

Eyes forward, impervious to the man's screams or struggles, the *condottieri rosso* dragged him on the cobbles, his body bouncing with each uneven stone, blood spurting from his mouth, a tooth left behind.

Close behind the perverted procession, his wife followed,

heedless of her appearance—her nightshift and robe barely obliterated her curves; her hair, loose and disheveled, was the halo about her features, etched with fear. Her high-pitched pleas went unheard by the captors, but not by those of the city, and within moments a parade of onlookers formed behind her, stifled by the horror of what they witnessed, morbid in their craven need to see.

The man's unrelenting wails carried them to the Piazza della Signoria, Viviana and her two companions as well, hands and arms entwined.

As soon as her feet touched the stones of the courtyard, Viviana dropped her chin, demanding that her gaze look only as first one then the other slippered foot peeked out from the folds of her wind-buffeted skirts; there had never been a more conscious, stabbing gaze.

And yet it failed.

Viviana looked up.

She had not the choice.

They hung just as Andreano had told her—the two bodies locked together hung from the same third-floor window. Archbishop Salviati's teeth still remained sunk in the naked Francesco de' Pazzi's shoulder, the state he had been executed in, a death throe bite from one co-conspirator upon another, conjoined as they would be throughout eternity in Hell.

Only the more desperate cries of the condemned lawyer had the weight to pull her sight from the dead men, and the others similarly demised from other windows of the palace.

The soldiers dragged him through the growing crowd of the piazza and into the palazzo, the giant, carven doors slamming shut behind them with a booming crash, as if sucking the very air from the square.

The women and those around them stood, bewildered and frightened, unable to do anything for it.

Just as they made to turn, the black doors whooshed open once more, the throng flinching back. Gasps arose at the sight of the man on the threshold.

Robed and turbaned in black, the severity of attire heightened his pallor as well as the bindings splotched with small dollops of blood upon his neck. Nevertheless, *Il Magnifico* stood like a mighty statue in the door of the palazzo.

It took a thin moment for the astonishment to pass, for the chant to begin.

"Palle! Palle!"

The crescendo rose, Viviana's voice within it. She knew he had survived—Andreano had told her so—but seeing him so, as one who had seen the attack, was a relief to her mind and spirit. She raised her face to the sky and those who watched over them, closing her eyes and nodding with a genuflection of gratitude for his life. The crowd grew, some falling to their knees in relief at the sight of Lorenzo de' Medici, alive, well, and once more in charge of their city.

It was not a smile *Il Magnifico* greeted his people with, but a hard and stern countenance, a raised hand in both greeting and authority. From behind him, men brought out a sturdy box, and a soldier's hand helped the Medici to climb upon it.

Upon this loft, all eyes in the piazza caught a glimpse of their revered, if unofficial, leader.

"My wounded heart is healed by your devotion." Lorenzo's gratitude echoed across the piazza, as it would in the days to come. "Good people of Florence, I am here to assure you that justice for the assault upon our most honored persons, upon our city, will be imposed."

The simple pronouncement made, Lorenzo gave a look up and over his shoulder.

Every gaze in the square followed. There, in the middle window of the second floor of the palazzo, the *consigliore* stood, his weepy face a garish mask of the man he had once been. At the sight, his wife screamed and dropped to the piazza stones.

Lorenzo spared her not a glance. With a tick of his head, hands unseen pushed the man from the window. He swung for only a moment, for his neck snapped with the force of the throw, the breaking of the bones the crack of a whip, and his lifeless body came to a quick halt.

"I swear to you," Lorenzo bellowed, the condemnation of a god high above. "I swear to you, all who have done this will suffer the same."

His promise given, he stepped off his perch and into the palace where the swift closing of the door ensured his safety along with the five *condottieri* who took a post before it.

Viviana and Mattea held each other, ballasts in the storm, forcing their eyes away from the hanging man. "Eternal Spirit, Earth-maker," Viviana's voice quivered as she intoned the prayer, one no Christian or Catholic would speak except in solitude. "In times of temptation and test, strengthen us. From trials too great to endure, spare us. From the grip of all that is evil, free us."

"Amen," Mattea replied.

Raising their heads, the three women saw their fear writ harshly on the others' faces. Until Mattea's burst open—mouth, eyes— rupturing with surprise. Viviana followed her gaze and she too felt a moment's respite. Rushing toward them strode Andreano Cavalcanti.

He pushed and pressed his way through the crowd, reaching out and grabbing Mattea's hand.

"Any word on your mother?" she asked.

Her question seemed to answer his; he shook his head as his chin dropped. "I had hoped you had."

"We have heard nothing," Mattea said, placing a soft and sympathetic hand on his arm.

"Return to your homes, dear ladies." His amber gaze seared their faces. "Times only grow worse, I fear."

"We are doing what we can," Viviana said.

"No," he snapped, taking a breath before speaking more kindly this time. "This madness is too big. It is too dangerous. I must attend council, then I will look some more."

With a parting nod, a passing glance upon each face, he ran off for the palazzo, to disappear as the guards parted and the doors swallowed him up.

It took no more than a moment. Viviana knew what must

be done.

Placing a hand upon her shoulder, she said to Mattea, "We must gather the league again and set to work, quickly. We cannot wait another day."

The young woman seemed not to hear. Her eyes squinted with worry as they remained upon the door Andreano had vanished through.

"Mattea?" Viviana gave her a gentle, insistent shake.

"*Sì*, Viviana." Mattea came round. "Yes, the group must know the latest. They must know the arrests grow and continue. We must set to our task." Her gaze flitted back to the palazzo. "Poor Andreano."

"I will ready the shrine this moment. We can meet tonight af—"

"Madonna," it was no more than a whisper, from Jemma, "the curfew."

"Yes, the curfew," Viviana murmured, deep in thought.

The criers had announced its change all through the previous night, from Compline to Vespers, three hours earlier, to the time of the setting sun. On many a social occasion, Viviana had been out and about with her husband past the evening deadline and the streets had teemed, bursting with life as if to mock the very notion. She knew on this night and the many to follow, the curfew would be enforced.

"I will set it on my way home," Mattea offered. "For two days hence. All the women should have found what we need by then."

Chapter Sixteen

"Once craven comeuppance has begun, it is often hard to stop."

As soon as they reached the kitchen on the upper floor of the medieval tower house, Jemma dumped the basket of meager goods on the table and flopped herself into a chair. Viviana followed, caring little that she sat at the servant's table, too grateful to be in her own home and for them both to be safe.

The sun had still not appeared from behind the billows clinging to the city though the hour neared noon. The morning chill, brought into the house through the open loggia above, had not been chased from its corners. Instead, it reached out to them with the same eagerness that disaster gobbled up their city.

Rousing herself, Jemma struck at the flint, many a time, until at last a spark flew and a kindle ignited within the large hooded grate in the center of the interior wall. With Beatrice's absence, the cooking fire had yet to be lit. Though it was late in the spring to light one for warmth, both women needed it.

Viviana filled the kettle with mulled wine and hung it from the spit above; it was not long before they sat in heavy silence, sipping the warm liquid.

"I should see if Orfeo has returned," Viviana said with little enthusiasm.

Jemma's chair scraped as she pushed away from the table, surveying the contents of the items still in the basket before her. "I will make something of this."

Viviana's small smile blessed her for the efforts, this child she loved as her own. With a parting hand upon Jemma's arm, Viviana made for the lower level.

She wandered the rooms of the first floor, the family's living quarters. How disappointed Orfeo's grandparents would be if they saw the home they had built in such a state of neglect. In the Great Room, the wall above the fireplace showed the stain of too many years without new stucco. More than half of the fine paintings were gone; pale squares and rectangles of emptiness spoke of their former presence, ghosts left behind to haunt the family of declining fortune.

At least the marble has its sheen, Viviana thought as she stepped across it. Beatrice may not have come today, but she was a dedicated worker.

Viviana poked her head in the *Sala dei Pappagalli*, the family dining room. The frescoes of the parrots upon the walls, once so colorful, were almost as invisible as any sight of Orfeo.

She hurried on to the master chamber, to her sitting room, though he never stepped foot in her private place of refuge for he had no interest in what interested her. His study was as undisturbed as it had been yesterday.

With a silly flutter of hope, Viviana stuck her head in the room her sons had once shared. The beds remained for those nights they came to stay, though they came less and less frequently. Even their child's *cazzoni*, filled with silly toys and small bronze soldier statues, she kept just as they were. She had not the heart to remove them, except perhaps, someday in the future, to make room for those of a grandchild.

Though she heard not a peep from the floor below, she knew she would not feel her search fully executed if she didn't check the ground floor and the rooms serving as Orfeo's business offices. As Viviana expected, these rooms were empty, as was the cavernous loggia below. The three mammoth doors set in arches—allowing for the entrance of horse-pulled carts—were shut tightly.

She scampered through the storage cavern and out into the

courtyard. Even on this cloudy day, the table and chairs tucked into the small square fecund with flowering bushes and trees beckoned like an oasis, one she would deny. She had never more needed a lie down, and perhaps a cool cloth for her forehead.

• • •

"Signora del Marrone! Signora!"

Viviana jolted up from the settee. She heard the trampling of feet as they ran down the stairs, from the kitchen and servant floor the call and stampede came in search of her. Her rest had been no more than a quick respite.

Beatrice stood on the threshold, the much smaller Jemma almost hidden behind her back.

"Beatrice," Viviana stood and took her by the hand, sat her in one of the small chairs, the woman's ample posterior wiggling to fit in. "It is good to see you. I was worried so."

"And I for you, madonna. Bernardo would not allow me out. I had to wait until he himself ventured about." Gruff of manners as he may be, the woman's husband of more than thirty years cared for her well, a reminder to Viviana that such men did exist.

"You really didn't need to come. We would have managed, wouldn't we, Jemma?"

The young girl nodded, barely.

"I had not planned to come, though I longed to know you were well. But then…then…oh, *Dio mio.*" With the lord's name upon her lips, the large woman flung herself back in the chair and slapped a hand upon each round cheek.

"Get her some wine, Jemma, would you?"

The girl took off like an arrow shot, light footsteps returning as fast as they had retreated.

After a few sips, Beatrice seemed to have regained some, if not all, of her composure.

"What I have seen this day."

"What, what have you seen?"

From just beyond Viviana's shoulder, Jemma inched into the room and perched herself on the edge of the settee.

"Take your time, Beatrice," Viviana said as she sat in her high-backed wing chair beside the housekeeper. "Tell us what has happened, but do not tax yourself."

"They've found him. Jacopo de' Pazzi. They have captured and killed him!"

Viviana longed to put her hands to her ears, to hear of no more horrors. She knew with certainty, horror still ran amok.

"Tell us, all. But quickly, please."

"He was hiding in the hills, just to the north and east. The peasants themselves, those of Castagno di San Godenzo, found him, tied him up, threw him over a horse's back, and brought him in." Her black eyes bulged. "They almost didn't let them in the gates. Messer de' Pazzi's own screams disclosed his identity. Men of the Eight took him then, straight to the Palazzo. He offered them gold, it was whispered about among the crowd, a great deal of gold, to let him go. Not a one would hear a word of it. Ack, no." She shook her head with abhorrence. "In the crowd, I stood outside waiting to see him swing from a window. Me!"

She said it with such amazement. "And did he..." Jemma prodded, "...did he swing?"

"Oh yes, but not at first, not right away, for he had much, too much, to say. I heard someone mutter he blamed Francesco, his own dead nephew. That he, Jacopo was innocent. It did him no good, no good at all."

She stopped to quench her flapping tongue with a sip of wine, oblivious to the impatience of her audience.

"He would swing, oh indeed he would. Not until he screamed at the crowd."

"He screamed at them?" Viviana balked. The audacity of the man! He had worn a cloak of arrogance all his life, one he would wear straight through eternity, straight to Hell.

"What did he say?" This from Jemma.

In the way of the people of Florence, Beatrice thrust her hands up and apart in a gesture of both disbelief and enormity.

"He stood upon the window casing wearing his purple gown and silk hose and that ridiculous white belt of his and he...he cursed *Il Magnifico!*"

"*Santo cielo!* He did not!" Viviana scoffed.

"He did," Beatrice insisted with a hiss, leaning forward in her chair, bosom rising and falling fast. "He called him a traitor and commended his soul to the devil." She threw her hands up once more. "Well, you can just imagine the outrage from those in the piazza who heard, which was everyone, of course. Everyone started screaming back at him. Some young men even tried to stone him.

"You could see the worry on the soldiers of the palazzo. They feared the crowd would riot again. They hung him then before he said any more. But the crowd..." she dropped her head, rolls forming beneath her chin, and shook it as if in shame, "...the crowd wanted more. They wanted his blood on their hands. They stood just below him, yelling for the guards to cut him down, though he was still alive and thrashing."

"Did they?" Viviana whispered fearfully.

"No. They waited for death to take him and then they hauled him back in."

"They what?" This was a story filled with shock upon shock.

"It is true." Beatrice leaned in close to share her tale intimately, as gossipers do. "No one knows for sure, but many of us waited for some of the soldiers to come out. Marcella knows Simonetta whose son Arturo is one of the men of the Eight and she, Simonetta, told Marcella, who told me, they were going to bury him, and at his own family chapel, no less."

Viviana knew her words as truth. Beatrice was never one to exaggerate for all the drama used to tell the tale. Nor did the final resting place come as a surprise. Messer Jacopo was one of Florence's greatest sons, or he had been. How badly Viviana wanted to believe the rumors of his confession, of the blame resting firmly on the slanted shoulders of the slimy Francesco.

As a young girl, she had looked up to Messer Jacopo like a

hero, for such was how the people of Florence spoke of him. How desperately she needed a male hero in her life, as much then as now. It was so very easy to put the badge upon his already decorated chest.

Now she wondered, was there never to be a man in her life she could truly call a champion? For this *cavaliere,* this knight who stood upon the top of government buildings and defiled the name of others as the devil, this was no hero. Her already damaged heart suffered yet another crack.

Chapter Seventeen

"Every life holds its own horrors."

"Did you not hear me call?"

Viviana flinched in her chair. Half the sketches upon her lap slipped down onto the floor.

She dropped to her knees as if thrown, gathering them up before her husband could see them, could see the subject matter upon them, for surely Orfeo knew by now of Lapaccia's disappearance, the rumors of the painting, and her alleged thievery.

"Forgive me, husband, I did not hear you with the door closed."

Orfeo stood in the threshold of the now open portal, eyes raking the parchments and Viviana with the same contemptuous glance.

"You waste your time with your silly drawings again. Did we not speak of this? Can you not find something more intellectually fitting to do?"

"Yes, Orfeo, we have discussed it, but—"

"Do not bother me with your excuses. If you need stimulations, I suggest you contemplate the Bible and all it has to teach you, including obeisance to your husband. Is there supper for me?"

"I am quite sure Beatrice can—"

"Make sure," he snipped, and spun on his heel, stomping into his own chamber.

Viviana hid the sketches once more in the bottom of the chest. Orfeo had been gone so long and she studied them so often, she had not been bothering to hide them. Rising, she wished fervently he made for a change of clothes. He reeked in those he had worn for days. As she rushed upstairs to the kitchen, she prayed Beatrice had indeed begun an evening repast, for a hungry Orfeo was a terrible creature, one that made his normal conduct appear near to saintly.

Thankfully, she did find *cena* prepared and pleasant, and almost ready.

Within minutes, a freshly attired Orfeo sat across from her. On the table between them was a finely prepared *tomaselle*, the liver sausage, one of Orfeo's favorite dishes, as well as freshly baked bread, fresh peaches, and thin slices of *parmigiano*, its potent aroma adding a zest to the meal and its biting taste flavor to the still warm bread.

"How goes it at the Signoria, Orfeo? Is all still in chaos?" Viviana nibbled.

"*Il Magnifico* has written to Milan, asking for military support." As he shoveled food into his mouth with stubby fingers, Orfeo was all too eager to tell of the events of the last two days, as if he had a hand in them.

"Will there be war?" she asked.

He nodded his head, mouth too full for a moment to speak, his greasy grin giving his opinion on the matter.

"All but one Pazzi brother and cousin have been taken," Orfeo began his lecture with a salacious pronouncement. "We were not able to get our hands on Antonio, Bishop of Sarno, and Mileto, one of Jacopo's nephews, but he has been condemned in absentia, confined for life to his diocese. All Pazzi men have been charged with conspiracy, murder, and attempt to murder."

"All?" Viviana raised her brows at this. There were so many Pazzi men, of many branches; she found it difficult to accept they were all part of this heinous act.

Orfeo nodded. "They do not speak. Silence is tantamount to treason. It is enough."

Viviana could not object to such a thought. If she were accused of such a crime, she would scream her innocence until she had neither voice nor breath left within her.

Orfeo stood, suddenly finished, without thanks or preamble.

"I am for bed. I have been without the comfort of it for far too many days."

Viviana dipped her chin in silent prayer for his leave-taking, but too soon.

"You are with me." It was not a request, but a demand.

It was well she had not eaten much, for surely were her stomach full, she would be retching it up at the thought of what was to come. Her husband's sexual practice—never could it be called love-making—was selfish and quick, but to have his hands upon her filled her with disgust. She had long since learned to hide it and pretend satisfaction, for her sake, not his. It was never an act of coupling, but of control.

Viviana rose slowly, following behind at a sluggish pace, and entered the bedchamber as if she entered the Palazzo della Signoria as one of the Pazzi. She stood by the bed, neither moving nor disrobing.

"What of the others?" Viviana prompted, as he removed his doublet. Perhaps she could keep him talking until fatigue overtook him.

"There have been at least another ten hangings, perhaps more. Men who were known associates of the Pazzi. The younger Pazzi have been exiled to Volterra."

"Which ones?" Viviana kept her mind whirling with questions to ask.

Orfeo waved his hand in a dismissive, all-encompassing gesture. "Galeotto, Lionardo, Raffaele. More still. I forget their names."

Viviana held her tongue at the mention of such young boys, their ages ranging from fifteen to seven, lives forever ruined by the action of a few of their brethren.

"And what of Renato? You have not mentioned him?"

Orfeo laughed, a darkly contemptuous laugh she knew well. "Ah, yes, Renato, the oldest nephew. We had a fine time with him."

Viviana's hands clenched by her side.

"He tried running, the fool," Orfeo chuckled, "but only as far as his villa in Mugello. He claimed he had been there since before the attack and therefore could have had no part in it, but none believed him."

He pulled his shirt over his head. Orfeo stood before her in a bumptious pose, sagging breasts and flaccid flesh jutted, arms akimbo as if he were one of Donatello's most regal statues.

"But his own cleverness was his undoing. He was too clever, too esteemed, we could not let such a Pazzi survive, such a lineage continue." Orfeo's sneer was of a man well-pleased with himself and his doings. "Not only did we hang him, we hung him in a peasant's costume."

Viviana cocked her head. "In what?"

"In the clothes of a dead beggar; a skimpy gown, dirt gray and made of coarse wool. That and nothing else, save his boots and spurs."

"I...it must have been quite the sight. I am quite sure the Signoria sent a strong message with such an act."

"Indeed." Orfeo stepped closer, pulling at the pins holding her long nut-brown hair atop her head. It dropped upon her shoulders and down her back, and he shook it out with his fingers. But then he held, dropping his hand to his side. "Yes, you would think it was a statement to silence all others, but it has not. There is a faction of the people—Pazzi followers—though they would not attest to it if questioned, who are spreading a tale that Renato was opposed to the conspiracy, that he spoke against it to his family members."

Viviana had met the man; he was indeed an amiable and non-confrontational sort. "Perhaps such a tale is true. Certainly not all Pazzis can be cut of the same cloth."

"You dare defend them?"

The back of his open hand against her face expulsed all air from her lungs. Viviana fell back upon the bed. In a breath, he hurled his body upon hers, pinning her to the ticking. She felt it, the anger coursing through him, vibrating through his scrawny body, anger lit by seeing her with the sketches, further enflamed by her questioning words.

With one hand he threw up her skirts, with the other he unlaced his breeches.

With one thrust, he enforced his will upon her without invitation. Orfeo ripped into her, sneering down at her, victorious.

Viviana gasped, biting her lip. She turned her head from the gargoyle above her. One silent tear ran down her temple as he pounded her, but she would not cry out, she would not beg for relief even as she wondered if this would be the one time, of so many like it, she did not survive. With brutal sex, he did what he could not do in life—best her.

• • •

She moved not an inch. Was it minutes or hours? She knew not. But she barely dared to breathe as she waited for him to fall asleep. He made it plain when he did, for the noises began almost instantaneously. Orfeo snored with a cornucopia of sounds, as if every instrument of an orchestra blared out of tune and at once. In the sanctuary of his slumber, Viviana slithered out of bed, fearful of waking him even now, fearful of a reprisal.

Viviana, the wraith, walked the house on the pads of her bare feet, looking in each empty room, at the furniture she had purchased as a young hopeful bride, at the accumulated objects meant to mark the joyful passages of her life. But the more she walked, the more rooms she peeked in, the emptier she saw the house.

Entering her salon, she could not bear to light a candle, to look at yet more meaningless things. The ewer beside the corner perched basin was full, as always, with tepid rose water. She found it in the gray light of a half moon, its elusive illumination casting all it touched with a strange half-existence. Eagerly she dropped the stained silk and lace chemise. Vigorously, angrily, she scrubbed her skin with the tinctured cloth, until every inch was red, until every scent of him had been banished. Abandoning the chemise in its crumple upon the floor, she took up another from the wardrobe as well as a fresh wrapping gown.

Pulling the worn, soft fabric tighter round her body, she sat gently on her fine settee, but even its softness could not protect her from the pain of contact on the battered, most delicate parts of her body. Curling up in a ball on the small couch, she stared unblinking at the blank wall before her, until her mind became equally as blank, until she finally, mercifully, slept.

Chapter Eighteen

"An all too willing accomplice comes when most needed."

Isabetta stood at the tip of the square, where one lane diverged to two. In one direction lay the craving of her heart, in the other her duty. Isabetta took the lane to the right, leading to the market square, the butcher's row, and her husband's shop.

"Signora, ah signora, Heaven itself has led you here."

He pounced on her shadow, not but a foot yet across the threshold. Marzio Beccaio may be a master cleaver, a charmer with customers, but he was a wretched businessman. That was her husband's purview, or at least it had been.

"The customers, signora, they are growing angrier and angrier. They pound on the door for us to open." Marzio wiped his short, wide hands on a blood-spattered apron, ringing them with the harsh canvas. "They want meat and our vendor has not arrived for three days."

"I understand, Marzio," Isabetta cooed as she would to small animals and children. She walked through the empty shop, heading for the curtain and the small cubby behind it.

Marzio followed quickly on her heels, reminding her of a man whose growth stopped halfway, except for his feet, for they were far larger than his short, slim frame required.

"The beef and veal ran out days ago. All we have is pork and I save that for the few who have been with us since the beginning. I had no choice but to close."

The lament pushed her into the back room, to the rickety walnut table serving as a desk and the small stool before it. Even as she brought more order to the already well-arranged papers, she allowed Marzio to continue his whimpering. It was the only way he would stop.

"When will your husband return, signora? Vittorio may know another source of goods."

Isabetta looked up, a sharp retort on the tip of her tongue, one she bit back and swallowed. The man's small eyes, dots of black in a paling face, were as mopish as the deep frown upon his almost lipless mouth. She reached out and patted him on his still quaking hands. He could not know that she had kept this business functioning for the last two years; she would not hold his ignorance against him.

"Fear not, Marzio. Vittorio is still not well enough to return, b—"

"Oh, *Dio mio!*" Marzio wailed.

"But," Isabetta continued, raising her voice, holding up a folded piece of parchment, "he gave me distinct instruction on what to order and from whom for now. He also gave me instructions on how to work the ledger a bit more." Isabetta cast her gaze downward, hoping the lie would be forgiven when it came time for her final judgment. She knew more of ledger keeping than Vittorio ever hoped to. "So have no fear. Please tell our customers more meat will be here within a day, two at the very most, and we shall reopen then."

Marzio threw up his callused hands, crossed himself with one, kissing the tips of his fingers in the final flare of the gesture. "Praise be, signora, praise be."

"Now return to your work, Marzio, and I will to mine."

"Yes, yes, of course. *Grazie,* signora, *grazie tante.*"

The thud of the cleaver meeting the heavy block of bloodied wood resumed, and she turned to the small fire chasing the morning chill from the little office and dropped the blank piece of creased paper into it. There was more meat coming, not the wealth of product the shop typically offered, but enough. She had seen to the order herself that morning. Such truth Marzio need not know.

• • •

Isabetta hurried down the Via dei Benci, across the bridge and through the Porta San Miniato, the southeastern gate, closest to the shop. She needed a quick escape above all else.

She scampered into the woods, flaxen hair fluttering, eyes glimpsing over her shoulder. Every step brightened with yearning as she followed the path snaking up the hill, up and away from the city imprisoning her, each pointed cypress a dark foliaged finger pointing to the cloudless sky as if in exclamation of its loveliness.

Cresting a small rise, Isabetta held. Bending forward, she squinted her eyes to see the figure on the path in the near distance. It could not be; it simply could not be. But there was no mistaking the reddish golden floss, no matter that it was protected today by a brimmed *beretto* of dark gray wool, one matching his short artist's tunic.

Isabetta's heart fluttered in her chest. Her feet followed Leonardo da Vinci for many minutes, through thicket and bramble, as the path became less distinct, and the hill ascended higher.

As she reached the peak and the trail's end, all manner of effort was well rewarded.

Isabetta stood at the very edge of a treeless dell, one revealing a tumbled down ruin the size of wealthy man's palazzo, scattered remnants dropped haphazardly as a fall tree drops its leaves. Here, a cluster of stones marked a partial circular design, the remainder of a hamlet's protective wall. Over there a broken column, still somehow majestic with its bleached marble and its uneven, tattered top. Everywhere blocks of stones lay cast about, some partly buried in the ground and embraced by thick vines, others mottled by moss and time.

And there, perched high atop a square stone leaning in a zigzag pattern against two others, sat Leonardo himself, his elegant beauty never more at home than among such magnificence. In all the years Isabetta had climbed these hills, finding refuge among them, she had never come upon this place of rubble beauty. She stepped closer.

"Sig...Isabetta," he called.

Isabetta clutched the book she carried, how glad for it she was, how grateful for the excuse of quiet reading she would use.

"You found me," Leonardo chirped merrily.

Perhaps there would be no fooling this man after all.

"So it would seem," Isabetta replied, and made her way carefully around the debris of what once was, until she reached the artist and his lofty perch. She held a hand above her eyes to shield them from the glare of the midday sun.

"I do not think I shall try to come up," she laughed.

"Then I shall come down."

Leonardo clasped his leather portfolio tightly and scurried down the large boulders. "How does the day find you, mistress?" He smiled with his small, lovely curved mouth, blue eyes piercing in the bright light of midday.

"Well, thank you," Isabetta replied, though she longed to say *better now.* "And you, Leonardo?"

"Very well, indeed."

And he seemed so, seemed bursting with light and brightness and life.

They found a place where they both could sit comfortably among the rocks and stones. Here the sun found its way through the trees; the warmth of it reached her, chasing away the morning cold.

Leonardo opened his leather folio. His request when it came, softly, lyrically, was like the presentation of a gift.

"May I draw you, Isabetta?"

It was as if he asked to make love to her, so intimate was the request, so stirred was she by the thought. But it was not the request of an inexperienced lover, but of a master. To be drawn by an artist such as da Vinci was the height of compliment. She kept the discomposure his request kindled tight within, laughing silently as she thought of what Viviana would do. Her friend would have yelped her assent until she chased the birds from their nests.

"If you wish," she acquiesced with what she hoped was amiable nonchalance. "I did come to read." Isabetta waved the book about as if doing so would make it true.

Leonardo grinned. "Yes, I see. It is Dante, *sì*? Which?"

"It is *La Vita Nouva*," Isabetta's voice dropped almost to a whisper. She knew it then, for herself, the obvious intent of her choice, felt her cheeks warm with a blush.

"A fine piece. It is, perhaps, his best," Leonardo mused as he leaned over to reach into the heavy leather satchel at the base of the rock, extracting a block of malleable poplar wood. This he placed on his lap and prepared a quill, removing any remnants of plume that might prick his fingers. "Or at least, his best in the Volgare style."

"Exactly," Isabetta quipped, pleased.

Leonardo placed the thinnest sort of paper upon the poplar. Isabetta understood; he would produce two sketches then, one on the paper, the other indented on the wood below.

"Though I would not have thought the topic of courtly love to your liking," he said it casually, but now Isabetta did indeed feel caught up.

"Well, it…I…as you say, it is the best example of literature in the Florentine dialect rather than the Latin." Isabetta could have kicked herself for her stammer. "It is a great thing he has done here. Making great literature available for all, not just those privileged with a thorough education, is a wondrous thing. It…well, it could change the world. I believe it has already."

"As do I." Leonardo nodded, slowly, gently, his pale gaze looking at something far off in the distance. "Have you ever noticed time?"

"Noticed…time?" Isabetta cocked her head.

"Yes, the passage of time." The artist shifted on his rock so he faced her, leaning forward with elbows on knees. "Time comes and goes in fits and starts. Slow times are marked by mundane passages where little changes, little dust rises from the streets of progress. Oh, but when time comes at you, it becomes a rushing battalion armed with catapults of change, fair boulders of it. Time stays long enough for anyone who will use it."

"It is a blessing to be a witness to it," she turned, "to be a part of it."

Leonardo smiled back, understanding unspoken, unnecessary. Isabetta's heart beat with the same fits and starts of time.

"And education," she reverted the conversation; she had to. "The education of the masses will only bring the movement of time, the progression of civility, ticking faster."

Once more, she inwardly chastised herself for her rush of words; she knew of his early rustic life in the small village of Vinci— one revealed now and again in his accent—and his lack of formal education as a bastard son.

"In truth, I hope it will help rid me of my own telling dialect," she said as quickly.

Six years in Florence as Vittorio's wife, as a Florentine citizen, had done little to deny the other sixteen in Venice.

"It is very faint," Leonardo said kindly. "From the north, yes? Venice perhaps?"

Isabetta's eyes gleamed. "You've been there?"

Leonardo shook his head. "I have not, but yet feel sure I will someday." His tools now assembled, the last in place, a small vial of iron gall ink set upon the stone just to his left, he made ready. He looked intently at her, but not her, she knew from her own work, but as the object he would draw. "Open the book upon your lap. Yes, *bene*. Now turn your head to the left. Ah, not too much, just a bit."

"You plan a three quarter rendering." More telling words escaping before she could shut the gate of her lips. She flicked a quick slip of a glance at him.

Now he did look upon her, at the woman before him, his brows puckered, the furrow beginning to etch itself permanently into his young skin between them. "*Sì*, three quarters."

It was all he said, but she could see, within his eyes, it was not all he thought. Had he guessed, had words exchanged at both their meetings given her away? Isabetta thought it had, but with the same conclusion came another. This was a man who would not object. He would, in fact, be delighted at her truth. An artist who loved art for its own sake.

The tip of the quill flowed about on the page with ease, powered by the mastery of his hand. At times, he conducted an orchestra of design with long sweeping gestures, at others he leaned over closely, making the smallest of marks. It was with such fluidity he moved, gentle yet commanding, soft yet sure. And always, the flicking of his heavy-lashed lids, the stab of blue eyes upon her again and again.

Isabetta did her best to lock her gaze upon the distance, head held as instructed, but it was a hopeless struggle. She needed to see his hand move, to see the motion creating the murmuring as his skin brushed along the finely textured paper.

Even when she held herself in her pose, eyes turned from him, his gaze touched her, as if lithe fingers sloped down her check, flowing along the curve of her neck, brushing against the roundness of her breasts. Her skin prickled with goose-flesh at each slow, sensual swoosh of his hand. Isabetta swallowed, unable to look at him, willing the warm flush from her face.

There would be no satisfaction in this and yet she could not deny it. Isabetta could only rein it in—as she had done for so long now. The small flicker of hope that perhaps in a world filled with wondrous things, unchangeable things could be changed. Such a hope she could not deny.

She risked a glance at the artist and his work, thunderstruck. She saw herself clearly upon his page and a myriad of notes in a strange scrawling hand bordering the picture, tucked into each corner.

"How will you proceed from there?"

"I will use boiled linseed oil and perhaps some crushed stones to burn the lines in," he answered without looking up, for now he worked on shadows and diminishing lines, now he brought the depth of life to his rendering. "I prefer animal fur though others tend toward bird feathers, but such things are hard to come by these days. From there I will make a rubbing upon canvas which will serve as the basis for the painting."

"Painting?" Isabetta squeaked like a child.

"Do you object, madonna?" His gaze pierced her, alert to her reaction.

She shook her head, gently, a half-smile upon her lips. "No, I do not mind at all. I am honored."

"Just a few more minutes," he turned back to his work and Isabetta turned back to watching him.

Even as the sun moved across the sky and the church bells in the valley city below them struck *None*, the hour of mid-afternoon prayer, she felt no compulsion to leave this place, or this man. Isabetta the woman was gone; Isabetta the artist remained, lost in the study of his technique.

Her mouth fell as the thought struck her. It was an epiphany and she longed to behave as Viviana might, with loud exuberance.

"Are you free Tuesday next?" The soft-spoken words burst from her without regret.

Leonardo looked up with surprise, but tinged with a flash of sadness dulling his eyes to somber gray.

"Signorina, I—"

But she would not hear what he thought he had to say, what she thought he might say. She raised a hand to silence him.

"There is a group, a group of artists in need of your help." Even as she spoke, the idea became fully formed in her mind. "But I must know, Leonardo...are you adept at keeping secrets?"

Chapter Nineteen

"Bindings and bonds; cracks and fissures,
All must be carefully made and guarded against."

At the front of the secret studio, the women moved two of the smaller tables together, a difficult task in their long skirts and the layers beneath. They laughed at their own awkwardness as the hard oak squawked resistance, legs dragging across uneven stone.

Viviana and Mattea, Fiammetta and Natasia spread their sketches of the painting across the tables. The anonymously painted but infamously known *Feast of Herod* lay across the now wide and accommodating surface.

Four different versions of the same painting, the same subject, were displayed before them. Some emphasized capturing the dimension of cloth—its folds and drapes and hanging—for this painting had done much to further the treatment of the subject. For others it was the men themselves—the realism of faces, especially of shape and color. In others, the room took precedence—the décor and the placement of men and furniture, giving it depth.

"Have you made inquiries, Fiammetta? Have you had any word?" Viviana asked.

"I have, but her friends speak of nothing but fear."

"I have knocked upon her door twice," Natasia chimed in, "but received no answer at all."

"I haven't had the chance to ask at the market." Mattea walked a circle about the table, studying the sketches from all angles. "I don't know if Isabetta has."

"It is quite rude of her to call the meeting yet be the last to arrive," this from Fiammetta.

Viviana's shoulders slumped, "Perhaps it is her husband keeping her from—"

But a grating tolled as metal met metal, as the key inserted unlocked the door, and Isabetta entered. Upon her heel, but hovering at the threshold, stood a companion—a male companion, his visage hidden by Isabetta's shadow.

Mattea gasped. Natasia and Viviana eked startled yelps, though they, at least, had the good sense to throw themselves upon the scattered sketches, to attempt to hide them.

No man, save Father Raffaello, had ever visited their sanctuary. No persons, other than themselves and a handful of servants sworn to secrecy, knew about this place, this group, and what they did there. Even as Viviana rushed to capture parchment and flip it over, her mind screamed at Isabetta, at vows broken.

"What do you mean by…?" Viviana's demand stuck in her throat, her gaze upon the tall man became a pop-eyed glare. Disbelief, astonishment, burned bright splotches on Viviana's cheeks. Though Isabetta's actions were an affront to their friendship as well as to the group, this man's presence took all precedence.

"How dare you?" Fiammetta barked.

"Fiammetta, wait," Viviana held a hand out. "Do you not realize who—"

Isabetta steadied herself. "Please, my sisters, calm yourselves. Let me make the introductions."

The man with the long reddish blond hair stepped hesitantly into the chamber. Dressed in a long tunic, a *cioppa*, and a brimmed *beretto* upon his head, his attire made him unplaceable. Few noblemen wore the long sleeveless outer robes unless it was over a bejeweled tunic, not one as simple as this man wore. Those who wore such simple tunics were typically men of some religious order, but they would never be seen in a *cioppa* or a *beretto*. His very outward appearance confused them, Viviana could see it in their befuddled expressions.

He smiled at them shyly. The impact of his penetrating gaze made all the more powerful with the light color of the iris seeming to reflect both wisdom and experience. The man swept his gaze about the room, to the worktables, the easels and canvases, the paint mixing station with its riot of splashed color, and his shoulders lowered, his smile traveled up to his eyes, and the hand holding a leather portfolio before him like a shield eased its grip.

Isabetta preened, "My friends, I would like to introduce you to Leonardo da Vinci."

"Certainly not? Truly?" Natasia quacked.

Isabetta brought her hands together with a clap in either relief or delight. "Truly."

Of all the men to walk into this sanctuary, of all the people dared to be told their truth, Viviana could not think of another more startling, yet more appropriate.

Leonardo made his way to Natasia and took her hand, bowing over it and asking her name, as he did to all, ending with Fiammetta. Viviana knew her upbringing, her inbred manners, prevented the grandiose *nobildonna* from snubbing the man completely, but she acquiesced with little joviality. Instead, she turned her ire upon Isabetta.

"Why have you brought him here?" Fiammetta asked as if the man did not stand but two feet from her.

Isabetta squared her shoulders at the demanding woman, unflinching. "He is here to help us with the painting."

"What painting?"

"*The* painting?"

The outcry rose again. Viviana reached back to knead tense neck muscles.

"Worry not," Isabetta told them. "I have told him all. He is acquainted with Lapaccia. He is all too eager to help."

"Is he eager to keep his mouth closed?" this from Fiammetta.

"Beauty and its creation know nothing of men or women and who or which its creator is, it just allows itself to be created. The greatest deception men suffer is from their own opinions."

Leonardo's long face grew almost deathly still. "I will guard your secret like no other, to this I swear."

"What are you working on, *maestro?*" Mattea asked with a small bounce on her toes.

But Leonardo held up a long-fingered hand. "I have not earned that title, signorina, though I thank you greatly for the compliment of its use. Someday perhaps."

The women would not divest him of his modesty; it sat too well on shoulders too thin.

"I am presently setting up my own studio," Leonardo told them, receiving, graciously, the oohs and aahs such a proclamation deserved. "*Il Magnifico* himself is assisting me, though I would imagine progress will stall, for a time at least."

Lorenzo de' Medici had taken him in as the artist's troubles resolved themselves, though not indisputably. Only a chosen few, the greatest of talents, were brought under *Il Magnifico's* wing, a finely feathered one.

"But we are not here for you to hear my tale. I am here to serve you, to help you in your creation," Leonardo graciously turned the conversation away. "But first I must learn a bit about you, about you as artists, about your *studiolo*. Who is the *maestro* here?"

"We are all learning, signore," Viviana answered. "There can be no *maestro*."

"I have been painting the longest, no doubt." Fiammetta crowed.

Beside her, Viviana saw Isabetta roll eyes at Mattea, who smiled to hide a smirk.

"It was Viviana's cousin, Caterina, who truly brought us together," Isabetta offered. "She was a nun, if you would believe it. But she kept careful notes and journals of her progress as a painter. They were the beginning of our study. We've based our alliance and our work upon them."

Leonardo spun on Viviana; she flinched back against a man moving on her so quickly.

"Your cousin was Caterina of Bologna?" he whispered urgently, almost breathless.

Viviana blinked, at his vehemence, at hearing her relative called thusly. "You know of her?"

"My dear," Leonardo took Viviana's hands in his, "All true artists know of her. Giotto, Masaccio, even my master, Verrocchio, spoke of her. She was the first some…" he shook his head, "…she was the only woman any have yet speak of as artist. I am…grateful, deeply grateful, to meet her heir."

It was then it happened; Viviana fell under his spell. With this man's words, his reverence, unlike ever before, Viviana realized the importance of the work they did here, not just for themselves, but for the women who would come after them, women who should be allowed to wield a brush, to brandish hammer and chisel. If progress could not be made for their own sakes, she would dedicate her life to creating it for others.

She dipped her head with true gratitude. "The pleasure, sig—"

"Leonardo."

Viviana smiled. "The pleasure, Leonardo, is all mine."

The air changed then, in that pinpoint of time; he became one of them. The reedy man put hands to hips. "Now, you must all show me your work. I can only tell you where to go if I know where we begin."

As it was closest, they led Leonardo to Mattea's easel, and the partially painted canvas upon it. He could not know she was the least experienced among them, or the most hesitant, regardless of her proficiency. Once their apprentice, she didn't realize how talented they thought her.

Leonardo stood before the half-finished painting propped against the triangular wood stand. The *cartone* had been drawn upon it, the fully articulated composition in the thinnest of lines, and the artist had just begun to fill in the nearly empty meadow landscape with its color. Mattea chewed upon her bottom lip as Leonardo's gaze touched every inch of the painting's surface—as he squinted, as he pulled back, all in the sake of differing viewpoints.

"You have washed your colors with an abundance of *gesso, sì?*" he asked her. "Egg white, I think."

Mattea's thin pointed brows jumped up her high forehead. "I have, yes. Should I…is it wrong?"

He turned, head tilting as he pulled on one ear. "Do *you* think it is wrong?"

Mattea studied her own painting, as did the others. Viviana thought the girl had perfectly captured the depth of the scene; it appeared as if the field continued as far as the eye could see, as if one could run through it with abandon, never reaching the end, never to be found. Her pale colors of citrine and jonquil merged and overlapped in a dreamy wash, as if looking through squinted eyes or a waterfall.

"No," Mattea's soft answer broke the silent scrutiny, the ever slight straightening of her shoulders broke her self-doubt. "No, it is as I wish it to be."

Leonardo lips spread beneath the bristles of his facial hair and Viviana saw the girl's pleasure in the dip of her round chin and the flush on her pink skin.

"All our knowledge has its origins in our perceptions." The truth of his words gave them pause.

"Why do you paint?" Leonardo asked her, a question out of nowhere, but the *only* question.

Mattea looked at him shyly, through the tops of her eyes.

"It is not something I *want* to do or would *like* to do, though it is both. It is…more." She closed her cherubic mouth, opened it, and closed it again. And then, "It is something I *have* to do, an itch I must scratch or go mad."

Viviana turned to catch a glimpse of her own work. But her gaze got stuck, caught on Isabetta's face. While the others perused Mattea's work, Isabetta perused Leonardo, brightly, as the thief craves his prize.

Viviana almost groaned aloud; as thrilled as she was to have *the* Leonardo da Vinci as an honorary member of their group, clouds scudded across the joy of his tutelage. Isabetta's desire could bring them trouble, could only bring her friend heartache.

As the man traversed the room, Viviana kept to his side, kept insinuating herself between Isabetta and the handsome artist, but she soon lost herself to his thoughts and opinions, as he had something distinctive and unique to say about each of their styles and accomplishments.

Leonardo exclaimed brightly over the fine rooms Fiammetta preferred to capture. He blushed at the deeply romantic tones of Natasia's work, at the flesh so perfectly rendered, the brush of hands upon faces, lips upon lips. Leonardo offered his congratulations at the news of her betrothal and Viviana smiled at the girl's passionate whimsy.

"Are you truly convinced this is wise?" Fiammetta hissed in Viviana's ear.

Viviana held her tongue, but only for a moment. The right and wrong came quick and clear.

"Yes, Fiammetta, I do," she whispered back, fearing to offend the man least he overhear. "I can well appreciate the risk we take by bringing him into our confidence, but we have great need of him, of his knowledge and expertise, for Lapaccia's sake as well as our own."

Fiammetta pursed her lips, nostrils flaring. "But he is a sodomite."

It was a nasty condemnation spoken with a nasty, hard edge. It was a damnation by its very vociferation. Viviana had never felt such impatience with her friend.

"It was never proved and you know it." Viviana snipped, a verbal push back.

Fiammetta threw her hands up, no longer attempting to keep their private conversation private, though she leaned in and hissed at the woman standing beside her.

"Not one, but two accusations." She held up two fingers in front of Viviana's eyes as if she spoke to an uncomprehending child. It served only to hinder her case.

"Accusations," Viviana laughed the word quietly. "Accusations such as these are made every other day."

Fiammetta could not refute this truth. The *tamburo* at the Palazzo della Signoria sometimes overflowed with denunciations. In this letterbox, one citizen could make a claim of wrongdoing against another. Created as a form of justice, such contentions had become contorted, a vehicle for vengeance, for rivalries to further elicit harm on one another.

Two such allegations had been made against Leonardo, that he and two other men, a goldsmith and a male prostitute—such as were often used as artist's models—had been party to wretched affairs and to pleasuring, each to the other, who requested such wickedness of him.

"And you know well, for it was you who told me," Viviana continued her defense as if she were da Vinci's *consigliore*, "these claims came at the same time as he began to gain notoriety with his brush, to outshine his master. Such envy incites the most false of denunciations."

"He knew the men, it was proved," Fiammetta countered.

"It was the only thing proved." Viviana entwined a stiff arm round the woman's arm, stiff as a branch in winter though it was, and walked her a few steps away. She hissed softly, "It is a discussion long since over. The charges were dismissed for no signature was writ upon them."

"But…" Fiammetta began, scrambling to counter, without a hold. Accusations could be made secretly, but not anonymously.

"Would *Il Magnifico* take a sodomite into his home? Into his life?"

Fiammetta's lips thinned into a slim line of fury, her angry gaze lingering upon Viviana's face. She mumbled as she withdrew—one word quite clear, spoken on fetid breath, "Medici."

Viviana would ask of it, but she had not the moment.

Leonardo and the others came to Viviana's table, finding no work in progress, for she had just finished her last. It stood propped against the wall drying. Leonardo regarded it silently for a time—too long to Viviana's mind. She saw it through the eyes of another for the first time.

The palazzo stood atop a rocky hill, alone, without neighbors. Its stone dark, its portals devoid of any light shining from within, the sky above gray and bleak with a coming storm.

"Your clouds," Leonardo said.

Viviana waited, breath baited.

He turned from the painting to drop his probing glare upon her. "They frighten me with their premonition."

"I—" she began, but to say more could only reveal more. This gallant man saved her.

"Your use of shadow and light without color is masterful," he patted her hand with the softest of touch.

All thoughts of her artistic mystery fell by the wayside; Leonardo da Vinci had used the word masterful in speaking of her work. She would live off the notion for a lifetime.

As he stood before Isabetta's endeavors, his handsome face darkened. His smooth skin crumpled. "This is not what I would have expected. Is it in response to the strife of the city?"

"No," Isabetta replied flatly. "This last was finished...before. It is part of a series."

Leonardo followed her pointing finger to the paintings leaning upon the walls; they were a series of nightmares, shades of gray and darkness, set to paint. Viviana almost nudged Isabetta, hoping she would tell the artist of her husband and the tribulations of the last few years. But she did not. Leonardo looked at Isabetta differently than when they had entered the chamber.

"So now." He opened his arms. "To the crux of the matter. To the *Feast of Herod*."

They led him to the two tables made into one and the sketches upon them.

"Ah yes, Isabetta," Leonardo nodded as he taped a tapered finger on his lips. "You spoke true. I do remember this work. It was quite the talk among the guilds, most particularly as no one took credit for it."

"Even in the taverns?" Mattea queried, finding it as strange as the others. "It seems too fine a work for no man to desire the accolades of its creation."

The women twittered, trying their best to not. But Leonardo joined them.

"Too true, mistress," he chuckled. "There is nothing so large as a man's assurance of his own prowess."

"But to take credit would be to take incrimination," Isabetta whispered harshly with dawning realization. They held a moment in the horrid truth of it. An artist was part of the despicable conspiracy.

"What if we..." he muttered, and with sure hands, moved the sketches about, using particular ones to elucidate different parts of the whole. Soon they saw his intent. Hands and parchment flew, put in place, discarded and replaced.

The rustling slowed, their dance about the table stilled, then ...stopped.

There it was. The painting lived upon the table, a haphazard rendering, true, but a wholly conceived one, one they could reproduce.

"Are you absolutely sure this is what you intend to do?" Leonardo asked.

He saw what they all did, the signs proclaiming the intentions of the men in the group portrait, the portent of what was to come. Many faces were unmasked. Together, the group knew almost all of them, almost. Nor were all dead, some not even captured.

"It is." Viviana spoke softly.

"It is well," he said, and they heard that he did indeed think it so. "Then the first thing you must do is decide whether just one of you will paint it or all?"

Mattea spoke, her voice quivering. "All. For if any one of us is asked, 'did you paint this painting?' we could all answer, in a truth of sorts, 'no, *I* did not.'"

Leonardo barked a laugh, took Mattea by her rounded chin, giving it an affectionate tweak. She blushed with pleasure.

The group knew the brilliance of it the moment they heard it. They would succeed or fail, together. It had always been their way.

"Then you must all decide on a technique all can replicate." Leonardo rubbed his hands together, rushed to a worktable and grabbed a piece of charcoal. Gently moving aside some drying paintings, he made the largest wall of the chamber his teaching canvas.

He made the simplest sketch, explaining the mathematical basis of dimensionality and depth, of the shortening of lines, of lines drawn closer together to give the illusion of distance, of diminishing perspective. Viviana watched every move, how he held the charcoal, how his arm moved. With every revelation, her breath quickened. How quickly and with such ease he designed. Apprenticed late, at fourteen, Leonardo had spent only six years under a master's tutelage and yet he spoke with utmost authority, moved without hesitation, created with the same ease with which he breathed.

Her wonder became a craving, as a starving man looks upon a rich man's table scraps. Leonardo moved by pure instinct. Viviana had such moments, remembered them with the clarity of a blazing fire, but they were not the norm. Too often she found herself struggling with her craft. But she knew too only more work could bring those blazing moments more frequently, a vow hard to keep when one was forced to work sporadically and secretly, hard to do when one was a woman forced to pretend her talent was nothing more than a hobby.

"You must learn to see through the same eye," Leonardo turned from the jumble of drawings upon the wall, pointing around the chamber to their individual works. "Look, see how each of you *sees* differently. What one notices the other doesn't—forms, shapes, shadows, light, lack of light, color, lack of color. Each viewpoint is, in a way, a reflection of the life of each woman."

Viviana suddenly worried if her work showed too much, exposed all she tried so hard to keep hidden.

Leonardo offered a knowing look as he continued. "A bird cannot fly if it carries too much weight. As you begin your work, you must study the others, and you must make your decision and learn cohesively from there. You should look at certain walls stained with dampness, or at stones of uneven color. If you have to invent some backgrounds you will be able to see in these the likeness of divine landscapes, adorned with mountains, ruins, rocks, woods, great plains, hills, and valleys in great variety. You will see expressions of faces and clothes and an infinity of things which you will be able to reduce to their complete and proper forms. In such walls the same thing happens as in the sound of bells, in whose stroke you may find every note imaginable."

The women began to murmur, the artist's enthusiasm infectious.

"May I ask a question?" Mattea held her hand up like a schoolchild, head buried between scrunched shoulders.

Leonardo bequeathed her with a most tender of smiles; Viviana found love for him, not the artist, but the man, in that smile.

"You may ask me anything, *cara*," he told the shy girl.

"What you have done here, could you explain it again, please?"

"Of course, of course," Leonardo replied gladly. This time putting the charcoal in her hand, instructing her to do it as he informed. "The true, scientific principles of painting...well, they are grasped by the mind alone, without recourse to any manual effort." The rest of the women crowded round, the questions coming fast and quick.

Viviana whirled round to find Isabetta beckoning her aside. Viviana went gladly, something of her own to say.

"You took a grave chance," she chided Isabetta with equal parts censure and admiration.

Isabetta shook her head, waved her hand before her friend's face in dismissal. "I know, but you are thrilled I did so."

Viviana waggled her head; she could not deny the truth of it.

Isabetta smiled conspiratorially, a child who won the toy. "There is another chance to take, one we must take together. I cannot do it alone and you are the only other among us who may."

Chapter Twenty

"Depravity ignited is impossible to extinguish."

It had been a good day. They all felt it, the coming together of their talents, merging them as one. It didn't matter if today was the second of May, there would be no *Calendimaggio*, no May Day Feast, for the entire republic was still in a state of civic mourning, its citizenry still suffocated in grief as well as fear. The news of the soldier's confession, Montesecco by name, had spread far and wide. The Eight still broke down doors, pulling men from their homes. The men of the black cloaks still chaperoned them on their path of doom. The bodies of the condemned still littered the streets.

Yet in their cohesion, these women had found not only solace but the strength and the spirit to move their brushes faster and with skill and finesse for the sake of their missing comrade. As long as the *Neri* brought people to their death, these women would give every possible moment to finding and protecting their Lapaccia.

Together they stretched and mounted the canvas on the oak frame Leonardo had made for them, the very size of it daunting, but not enough. Together they sized the canvas with rabbit skin glue; the concoction provided a smoother surface and protection upon the canvas fibers from the degrading force of the linoleic acid of the linseed oil, the basis for all paint mixtures.

He watched them scatter like fall leaves on a tender breeze, with grace and loveliness, each with their own peculiarity. He watched them until he could see them no more.

Leonardo made his way slowly down the Via del Gelsumino, crossing into the heart of the city via the Ponte Trinita. His feet knew his destination long before he did. So preoccupied with thinking, he allowed free reign to guide his body.

The artist's mind whirled with thoughts of what had transpired... no, what he had *experienced*, for meeting these women, agreeing to help them as he had was a wondrous and frightening experience.

Leonardo shook his head at himself, scruffling long fingers absently through his thick beard. Did he dare to associate himself with such an undertaking, one whose consequences could be damning in so many ways? An unmarried man with all these women, forging a painting that belonged to the government, a government that still looked a bit unkindly in his direction, assisting them in finding a woman who may be an enemy of his friend, and friends like the Medici—especially Lorenzo, especially in this moment— could be a fatal undertaking.

And yet, how could he *not* help them? His admiration for what they dared to do, not only in their efforts to find and save their colleague, but also in the very existence of their group and the work they carried out in secret, eclipsed anything he had ever felt toward the feminine gender, save that for the mother who died young. How could he not, having seen the joy, the passion, the obsession for their craft, one of his own beloved demons, writ on each and every face, even those with puckered expressions at his presence among them?

We can learn from every journey. Leonardo raised his head, his mind in harmony with his body and its target. *Am I not a disciple of experience?*

He stood almost at the mid-point of the bridge, the Arno churning with gentle gurgles below him, its mossy scent wafting up to him. A wave of grief struck him, unexpected, unprepared for.

Leonardo turned, grasping the stone edge of the bridge wall, to drop his head into the cleft between shoulders and arms. He had held it off—held it away—as much as he could, but even he could not control his heart completely.

The grief he felt for Giuliano's passing was a felling blow, it struck him deep in his gut and he bent further over the rough rocks of the barrier. He moaned low and guttural with the kick of it. The loss of love, unrequited though it may be, was the worst loss a man could suffer.

A memory flashed, his head popped up, eyes wide to the sun, and he laughed.

Giuliano knew, Leonardo was as sure of it as he was anything else in science and nature which could be proven as truth. Giuliano knew Leonardo loved him, loved him in a way no man should love another. And yet Giuliano loved him still, loved Leonardo with an unbreakable bond of friendship. It was all Giuliano could do for him, it was the best Giuliano did for him. For in that friendship was complete lack of judgment. Such love was true.

Leonardo began to walk again, steps more purposeful than ever.

If what I do with these women, with the forging of the painting, brings any of my dear Giuliano's assassins to meet their deserved end, then all the better for it.

It was the last time he would question the rightness of his actions.

• • •

He turned onto the Via Calzaiuoli and traversed the few blocks to the delicately effaced Palazzo Cavalcanti. Nestled between the churches of San Pier Coelorum and San Cristofano, it was splendid with the understated opulence only Leon Battista Alberti could design. Leonardo gave a silent nod to his colleague, an absent gesture of respect. The palazzo boasted the best in newer concepts of architecture. The grid-like façade of pale gray stone gave contrast to the rounded arched windows in the top two of the three floors, each arch using the innovative vertical keystones at center position.

Leonardo straightened himself, flicking stray brush strands from his tunic as he approached the door off-center on the street-front wall, then knocked upon it. There was a small place in his mind which niggled at him, needed him to ascertain for himself the lady's absence. Not that he questioned the women's veracity, merely to appease his own curiosity. He knocked once more with the same effect.

Could the servants be gone as well? He stepped back, raising a hand to shield his eyes, though the encroaching clouds maligned the sun. He scanned the windows for any sign of life.

"If no servants are in attendance as well, perhaps the lady has simply left the city," he muttered to himself as he would when devising a new technique or conducting a new experiment. He shook his head in answer to his own question. "No, she would not do so without telling her son."

Though he knew not Andreano Cavalcanti, he knew from the women how close mother and son were. He lifted his hand to knock one last time. The door cracked open, no more than a few inches. An elderly man's face appeared ghostly in the shadowy space.

"Good day, signore, I am Leonardo da Vinci," he announced quickly, for he knew his name was widely known, for many a reason. But Lapaccia's *maggiore domo* gave no sign of welcome and would not, it appeared, open the door further.

"I am here to discuss a commission with your mistress. Is she receiving?" He spoke with natural confidence, having said the same words at other doors on more than one occasion, and with no indication of contrary knowledge.

"No, signore, she is not in residence at present," the man replied with little courtesy, though not devoid of respect altogether.

Leonardo heard what he left unsaid.

"Not in residence?" He stepped closer to the door and the man hidden in its shadows. "Does this mean she has vac—"

The door shut in his face, the words left on his tongue. The lack of any answer was his answer.

Leonardo retreated the way he had come, heading south on the Via Calzaiuoli, past the stillness of the Duomo and the blood-stained steps before it. He thought to make for the Palazzo della Signoria—to know the condition of the body that was the city of Florence, he need only look at its heart. One step upon its cobbles told him all.

On any other Sunday afternoon, when the breeze caressed with the smooth warmth of spring, the piazza would be filled with Florentines of all varieties. It was a day of rest and socializing, of seeing friends and families without the bustle of a workday imposing its will upon them. Jugglers would entertain, perhaps even a marionette performance or two. Musicians would gather in the corners, serenading the spirited, hobnobbing horde.

But not today.

Today there was emptiness. Empty, save for the pigeons in full dominion of the piazza, roosting in every corner and on every ledge. There were no gatherings, no entertainers. One or two living souls crossed the piazza, eyes cast downward, footsteps swift with arms tight to their bodies, clearly in hurry to be gone. There was but one item in great abundance—bodies.

Lorenzo had seen the shore once, had seen a deserted stretch of smooth beige sand dotted with shells and stones. Such was a vista he gazed upon now. But here the scattered remains dotted the stones stained red with blood, the pieces of what had once been people, evil though they may have been, were the lumps that broke the plane of flat cobbles. A few men worked at their removal, rough looking men with ill-fitting, ragged clothes, some with rags tied about their mouths and noses. In silence, they picked up the bodies—the pieces—and tossed them unceremoniously in the back of a wagon, a pile mounting as they went, a pile destined for the river.

The artist swallowed hard, throat bobbing. He had dissected the human form in its deceased state, but he had done so with respect for the soul that once occupied it. This was depravity. He could look upon it no longer.

Leonardo had no wish, or fortitude, to cross the piazza. Instead he turned his boots to the west, onto San Romolo. It was the long way to the Corso dei Tintori and the Inn of the Three Turtles, but the detour was worth the courtesy to his sensibilities.

Breathing soundlessly through his nose, Leonardo allowed his mind to clear of the pictures he had no care to paint, of the images he longed to erase from his mind. There were so many now, rendered indelibly, one upon the other in his mind, ever since that Sunday he lost Giuliano. The quiet in his mind seemed to permeate the very air around him, and for the first time he found a modicum of gratitude for the hush that lay upon his city.

But it was not to last.

Fretful snippets found him, traveling up the wide lane of the Via dei Benci, a well-traveled thoroughfare turning him southward. As he neared the Piazza Santa Croce, heavy male voices raised in anger and outrage reached out to him, rumbles of a brewing storm drawing closer.

"*O Dio,*" he muttered harshly, "what now?"

The crowd milled before the shallow stone steps of the Santa Croce Basilica. It was an angry throng, a reviled horde consisting mostly of farmers, many with a brandished pitchfork, others with shovels. Among them stood a smattering of merchants and noblemen, their silks and brocades a discordance of bright blooms in a field of brown grass. Their voices raised in protest.

"He has no business here."

"It is a sacrilege."

Leonardo shuffled slowly along the back of the mob, behind the fountain and the playing field, to the corner of the Palazzo Cocchi, where he could watch and listen in relative safety. He had neither need nor desire to be recognized, most especially by a group of angry men.

"His own words cursed him," one of the farmers yelled, tall and broad, his booming voice carrying far and above the sonorous rabble. "His last words commended his soul to the devil."

They speak of Jacopo. His thought was no question, but a surety.

Everyone had heard the rumors of Jacopo de' Pazzi's confession, knew the fiend's reputation for blasphemy, and took his final utterance—one aligning himself with the force of greatest evil—as truth. Many had spoken against his burial in consecrated ground, in the Pazzi Chapel of Santa Croce. Not a soul believed he had received extreme unction—the blessing freeing a soul from sin, allowing for a holy interment—though some claimed he had.

"Did no one see this coming?" Leonardo muttered at the lack of thought. The revenge the Medici sought had infested the entire city. Were the men who ruled too shortsighted not to foresee the repugnance this body in this sacred place would cause?

"Our crops are dying. God punishes us all for the blasphemy." This from another farmer, his words inciting the very air to reek of vexation. The resulting cries concurred—his was not the only crop suffering, though not a one mentioned the days of rain that had just passed, an overabundance of precipitation easily blame-worthy for yellow, withering plants.

"He must be given to his devil," the first man yelled, stomping forward, his bulk parting the crowd, his looming mien driving the friars of Santa Croce and Ser Roncalli, one of the presiding Lord Priors, back upon the landing in front of the church entrance. Five heavily armed men of the Eight stood their ground before the cenobites and the politician, yet they were vastly outnumbered.

The man came to a stop at the bottom of the seven steps. "He must be put where he can no longer offend the Lord."

Another stepped up beside him, not nearly as imposing but as fiercely determined. "Give him to us or we will get him ourselves."

The friars flinched at the threat, huddling together, whispering with Ser Roncalli, who finally spoke for the group.

"The good friars will bring him out. They have no wish for their church to be desecrated. Surely we can agree upon this."

Leonardo thought the elderly man remarkably courageous; no more than wisps of gray remained upon his head, errant strands fluttering in the wind like feathers, his jowls shaking as he spoke, yet his voice held the authority that was his to wield.

"If we cannot agree, I will be forced to call in more of the Eight as well as the militia."

It was a daring gamble, for this maddened crowd could surely impose their will long before reinforcements could arrive.

The farmers huddled together as the friars had. A few appeared unsatisfied, most did not. The body, once retrieved, would be theirs to do with as they wished. Peaceful men at heart, it was all they desired.

The man at the head of the group addressed the protectors of Santa Croce.

"It is agreed. But only if it happens here and now."

The friars needed not another word. En masse, they turned and rushed quickly down the stairs and to the right of the church, entering the more modest secular structure attached to it. In this building resided the Pazzi chapel and its generations of the venerable family interred there.

In minutes, a band of six friars reappeared, three on each side of the casket.

Six men, including the large farmer who spoke for the throng, stepped to the coffin and wrenched it from the friars' hold, pushing the devout men, and began to carry it away from the sacred ground where it had no right to be.

It was a malevolent victory procession turning north onto the Via di Bonfanti.

Leonardo debated with himself. Did he follow? Did he indulge in the debased human need for revenge? Or did he keep himself devoid of such emotion, above such corruption of the soul?

He pulled his *beretto* lower upon his forehead, lowered his already heavy-lidded eyes, and began to follow.

In this nearly anonymous attendance, Leonardo turned as the parade did, west onto the Borgo alla Croce, becoming a piece of the tail of the beast winding its way through the city. For the first time in days, doors burst open, faces came to the windows, and other daring souls cried out, "Who do you carry?"

"Jacopo de' Pazzi!" came roaring answers. "We rid our city of his pestilence."

It was a rallying cry. Others quickly crossed their thresholds and joined the throng. The dyers—home from work on a Sunday—and their families, those who populated the area, streamed from their modest homes, congesting the road, swelling the ranks of the grisly parade to a flood. They threatened none and yet, even as they approached the Porta alla Croce, the militia guarding it, and the gallows beside it, they did so as an uncontestable force.

None came.

The men carrying the casket and the majority of the followers passed through the gate, toward the empty gallows with its rope swinging gently in the breeze, its creaking a banshee's call for a neck to embrace. Leonardo felt he could not have stopped himself did he wish to. He had no such wish.

But the sight was worth the effort.

As he made his way around the back of the gathering throng, as he found a crack in the crowd through which he could see to its front lines, he saw that the leaders of the crowd had dug a shallow grave in the field just beyond the gibbet. The tall man rose higher on stretched toes as the casket cover of the once great knight ripped from its hinges, and his stiff, but not yet decaying body, tumbled from the coffer.

What had been a righteous mission became a celebration of grisly success. As they covered the body with dirt and rocks, men spit at it, some dropped their breeches to defecate upon it. The crowd cheered and jeered raucously, rapturously.

Above it the cry rose, dark and righteous.

"Any who had a part in the great Giuliano's death," the man's voice boomed, God's wrath through the air, "you will suffer as this devil has!"

In the man's mania, Leonardo heard his own, and the sound was cacophonous to his ears. With a small modicum of guilt, he knew his need for revenge had been somewhat mollified, he knew too the biting bitter taste was not for him. He spat it away, set his shoulders in an act of finality, and turned from the ghastly and gruesome sight. His aim was now firmly set toward the women and their light.

Chapter Twenty-One

"Cheers match jeers,
As do tears and fears."

If Leonardo had been a young child instead of a young man, he would have clapped his hands with delight at the sight of the apothecary shop on the Ponte Vecchio. Its flap was up and secured on poles, its door a wide open and inviting maw. Just nearing it, one could smell the tang of herbs, the perfume of berried potions, and the sharpness of linseed oil. It was all there, especially artists' supplies.

Leonardo doffed his brimmed *beretta*, squinting into the dark and crowded interior. He sighed at the onslaught of aromas—so familiar, so beloved.

"Leonardo! You are here. How wonderful!"

"And happy I am to be here!" Leonardo returned the joyful greeting, spotting Dario Barbieri behind the counter. The chubby man's face split by a wide grin, yellow teeth exposed all the way to the back of his mouth, arms thrown wide.

The two men embraced as if they had not seen each other in an age. They held each other but an arm's length apart and, for the moment, simply rejoiced in the survival of the other.

"All is well with you?" Dario asked, just a hint of concern tainting the polite question.

"I am quite well, Dario, have no fear."

"But you are still living in the palazzo, *sì*? How is it with *Il Magnifico*?" This last the man asked with not a bit of subterfuge, his

147

sadness for Lorenzo de' Medici laid bare.

Leonardo shook his head. He still inhabited the small rooms Lorenzo had made available at the time of his troubles, but he had seen the man only twice since the death of Giuliano, once to convey his tear-filled condolences, the other at the funeral services. They had said no more than a few words to each other.

"I do not believe he has begun to heal," Leonardo said the truth quietly. "Hate possesses him utterly."

Dario pursed his lips, scratching the back of his nearly bald pate. "As well it should."

Leonardo merely tilted his head.

"You do not agree?" Dario recoiled.

"I think hate can be the ruin of us as much as our enemies."

"You are too wise for your age, Leonardo. You need to have more frivolity in your life."

Leonardo whipped out a short parchment filled with a long list from within the pouch of his tunic. "My work, my studies, these are my joys. Now prepare yourself, Dario, I have need of much."

For the next hour, the two men scoured every nook and cranny of the well-stocked apothecary. By the time their gathering was over, Leonardo could barely see Dario behind the pile heaped upon the counter.

The proprietor stood on tiptoes to stare at his friend. "So much, Leonardo, are you sure?"

The learned man, more than a painter or sculptor or philosopher or scientist, nodded with great spirit. "I am sure, my friend, quite sure."

Dario boxed up the goods, calling a young boy to bring a handcart to the front of the shop. "You have enough here to paint the whole of the city. What is it you work on?"

Leonardo offered the small grin so particularly his, shy yet full of knowing. But he gave no answer. In lieu of words, he placed in the merchant's hand two gold florins, each with the face of *Il Magnifico* engraved upon them.

The sight of Dario's bulging eyes did much to hearten

Leonardo, and did everything to stifle any more questions from the curious seller.

"I wish you the best of days," Leonardo called over his wide, bony shoulders as he dipped out of the shop.

"And you, dear Leonardo. Many thanks!" Dario called back.

Even as Leonardo began his walk off the bridge pulling the small cart, he could hear the call of *"mille grazie"* reaching him from within the apothecary's shop and he treasured the small grin it gave him as a gift.

Gifts.

That is what these women were to him, those anxiously awaiting his presence.

• • •

It took them so very long to settle down, to stop crowing with pleasure, to stop touching everything with coos of delight. It did not evade Viviana's notice, in the color rising on Leonardo's cheeks or his sparkling eyes, Leonardo's pure gratification in the giving she glimpsed each time she glanced at him. She shared his gratitude, not only for his gifts, but for the gift of his very presence.

Once they had calmed, once the women had distributed the goods proportionally and genially, they set to work.

Leonardo brought them before the large, prepared canvas, and they studied its surface.

"Do we agree it is dried thoroughly enough?" he asked and all concurred as they touched and smelled the overlay.

"Ah, *sì*, good." He stepped away, returning swiftly with a ball of string. "What I am going to show you now, though in truth I cannot believe I do so," this last he muttered like an old woman protesting the vagaries of life to no one but life itself. "Well, I do not recommend you ever use it again. I care not if Botticelli considers it a great tool. I deem it a fine cheat."

At this the women eyed each other, more than a little intrigued by the gossipy nature of the allusion. They watched with curiosity as

Leonardo used the string to form squares on the back of the canvas, creating, at the end, a perfect twelve square grid. Each segment was perhaps a little more than a foot in size, four across and three down. But when Leonardo turned the canvas back around, the grid disappeared.

"But how—" Mattea began, stilled as Leonardo held up a long hand.

From another table, he captured two lit candles, one in each hand, and stepped behind the canvas.

"Would you look at that?" Isabetta exclaimed.

By gridding the canvas with string and by placing the candle behind it, the shadows of the strings perfectly portioned the painting surface. One could now apposite which items belonged in which grids, giving a greater guide to positioning as well as proportion.

Leonardo stepped out from behind the canvas, saw the success of his work, and saw the surprise and elation on the faces of his women. He pointed a harsh finger at them all.

"I apply the method only as you are reproducing, not creating. You will promise me you will never use it in your own work or I will help you no more."

"We promise," a few said aloud with wonder, while others simply nodded, speechless.

"Very well," Leonardo accepted with a decisive if dubious nod. "Then it is time to make all those sketches," he pointed to the women's gather of parchment—the haphazard conglomerate of ill-matched drawings—set upon the table, "into one. Mattea, will you begin?"

Viviana felt the young woman beside her hesitate. Yes, she was the best at sketching among them, but she had yet to accept it, to believe and own it. Viviana placed a gentle hand on the small of her friend's back and pushed her forward.

Mattea picked up her favored piece of sharpened charcoal, setting herself before the primed canvas. With a last look at the women, her other family, she set the tip to the artist linen. It had begun.

• • •

Each took a turn, imitating Mattea's style at the guidance of Leonardo, but implanting and infusing what they thought were the most vital elements of the painting. But not a one ever worked alone; with the women beside them, at their back, whoever wielded the charcoal was tutored in technique, placement, and items.

With Isabetta at the helm, she added the small snake to the picture. It could barely be seen, hidden as it was, disguised as one of the tie-backs for the curtains on one of the three windows behind the table of men.

Viviana leaned forward and squinted at it. "I did not see it at all. Are you sure?"

Isabetta nodded. "Quite," she affirmed without hesitating in her work.

"The snake is the symbol for the Sforzas," Fiammetta said from Isabetta's other side.

Isabetta's hand hesitated then, like a single stutter, but continued on. She felt no need to mention it was the Sforzas causing so much of her troubles with the store, with their "regulations" on the selling of meat raised on their lands.

"May I?" Viviana held out a hand to Isabetta, one begging silently for the charcoal. With a few swift strokes, she embedded the smallest of daggers onto the picture, sitting untouched, almost hidden on one of the back corners of the table.

Standing back to scowl at her contribution, she handed the implement back to Isabetta.

"There was no knife in the painting, was there?"

Isabetta shook her head, as did Fiammetta on the other side of her.

Viviana cocked her head. "It is there, though. In all my sketches, I have placed it there."

"It is your trope," the male voice came from behind.

"My t—trope?" Viviana stumbled on the unfamiliar word.

Leonardo stood beside her. "You saw the evil in this picture, somehow you saw it. A trope is a metaphorical expression of what we want to say but cannot truly say, what we see but cannot name. For you, it is that dagger."

"Do we leave it in?" Isabetta queried with a whisper.

"It is so small, I do not think anyone but the artist would notice it. I think it has a rightful place. It is the signature of this group upon this work," Leonardo answered. Isabetta returned to her work, the small implement remaining.

As with any gathering, the work was not undertaken in silence. Between remarks on the work came the idle chatter of a group of friends. It began with Fiammetta's simple remark of regret.

"I missed *Calendimaggio* yesterday, very much. Would it not have been good for the city to have a little gaiety?"

Viviana harrumphed, "Perhaps. But it surely would have been the height of impropriety to the deceased Giuliano and his grieving family."

"Of course," Fiammetta snipped, turning her back on she who dared to correct her.

"There was a…a festival of a sort," Leonardo said, no more than a shamed mumble.

"A festival?" Mattea cocked her head to the side.

Da Vinci shrugged. "Perhaps it is the wrong word, but it was an event for certain. But first I must tell you, I spoke to Lapaccia's houseman."

"You did?" Viviana squawked, bright eyes darkening. "Why?"

"What did he say?" Fiammetta demanded.

Leonardo turned azure eyes toward Viviana, their outside corners drooping. "Please, madonna, do not think I mistrust or fail to believe you. I simply…well, I needed to know the situation at her home. To *feel* it. *Capiesce?*"

"I do understand, signore." She assured him.

"He said, 'she is not in residence.'"

"That's it?" Isabetta grumbled.

"That's it," Leonardo confirmed, "but then, as I thought to make for a tavern…" Leonardo shook his head, dark clouds crossing his face, "then things truly became interesting."

With this intriguing introduction, the artist launched into the tale of the previous day's adventures.

"It was the most astonishing of things I have ever seen." Dropping his long form into a chair, Leonardo took a deep draught of watered wine, not caring whether the chalice was his or not.

Isabetta took her place again as artist. She began to draw the figures themselves. Natasia, standing at her wing, began to giggle, and the loveliness of it drew them all to the work.

Without guile or timidity, though Leonardo joined the group, or perhaps because he did, Isabetta allowed her strokes to pay particular attention to the formation of the men and their most manly parts. As she turned her attention to one man, Fiammetta began to laugh.

"You do him far more justice than he deserves," she chortled. "He has nothing near that kind of…wealth."

The cackling was joyous.

Viviana struck an incredulous pose, her eyes gleaming. "And just how would you know how deeply his pockets fall?"

The question only ignited more laughter.

Fiammetta shrugged a shoulder with feigned though superior nonchalance, proclaiming the truth with the drama it deserved. "I saw it with my own eyes. In my own home!"

With brows so high on her forehead, they almost reached her plucked hairline, Isabetta scoffed, "You and this man?"

Everyone in the room knew who he was, who he used to be, for he was one of the first executed. Piero Felici was a diplomat of some sort, from the court of Urbino. He was very young, very thin, and very unimposing. The thought of him and Fiammetta, together, brought the most fanciful of images to mind.

"Do not be silly, Isabetta. You really must get hold of your priapic thoughts," Fiammetta quickly disavowed them of the ridiculous notion. "I actually walked in on him, and some woman, during a ball in my home." She shook her head and tutted, "It was so rude."

This time the women kept their giggles contained, for

Fiammetta's sake.

"Besides," she leaned in and squinted, "if I were to forsake my vows to Patrizio, it would be with someone with much more to offer."

That did it, the gales returned. Isabetta began to draw again. As she gave life to another, a taller man this time, with a long, almost delicate face none recognized, she gave him the same bounty of certain parts as she had before, expecting a similar response.

"Surely not!" Viviana squawked. With only her husband as a gauge, she found such abundance difficult to accept. If it was true, if a man could be built thusly, she was doubly deprived in life.

Isabetta just smiled, but this time Leonardo answered.

Leaning in, peering over Isabetta's shoulders, he pulled back with a slim smirk.

"Oh no, that one you most certainly can leave as it is."

The women's jaws dropped as if in concert. Viviana put a hand on his arm, a gesture full of her pleasure that he felt safe to speak so plainly with them. Only Isabetta failed to join in; she turned quickly away and began to sketch another man.

On this figure, she took her time, paying particular attention to all the details of his rendering. He wore a short tunic, cinched at the waist with gilded belt, and tight, multi-colored hose. His legs she sculpted with the deep lines of well-formed muscles, the torso she angled with a slim waist broadening in the chest and shoulders.

"Do you know this man?" It was Mattea who asked, Mattea who sounded skeptical.

Isabetta shook her head. "No, nor will anyone, I think. Wait for a moment."

She continued to sketch him with fine details, but this man's face she drew in profile. Though he stood at the back corner of the table, his body in a frontal pose, his face was turned to the side. His hair, lovely wavy locks, fell in front of his face like drawn curtains. One could see only a nicely straight nose and a strong chin, little more.

"I thought him very fine, very beautiful," Isabetta sighed wistfully, "Such beauty is often hard to pull away from."

Viviana frowned, knowing the yearning Isabetta felt, one seeming to stretch out like a never-ending road, one she recognized as her own.

Mattea studied the drawings but stayed at the table at the back of the room.

"Are you all right?" Isabetta called.

"We need to be very careful here."

Mattea spun round, small nose wrinkling, lips pursed pensively.

"What do you mean?" Leonardo asked of her, though they all felt the change in the air, the change in her.

"The Medici, the government, even the common men of the street, they seek this painting to identify those who were part of this crime, yes? And we do so to save Lapaccia?" She walked toward them, pointing to the sketch as if in accusation. "But what of the other men in it?"

Every glance turned to the large canvas. The faces of those drawn in were of those already denounced and dead. Those with blank features had not been drawn, and were therefore unidentified.

"We take on a serious burden here. We cannot put anyone into this painting, this irreparable and damning evidence, who hasn't already been arrested or executed. We could be committing them to death, whether deservedly so or not."

It was another layer of their deception to which none had given any thought. Like the others, Viviana was stunned they had not. How could they not?

Quiet suffused the room; the gurgling of the water in the small garden fountain just outside the windows grew and took precedence.

"You may be right," Isabetta said, breaking the brittle stillness, though gently. "But I know this man. I know his embodiment as well as I know my own. Nor can we really tell who he is, though oft times I thought he looked familiar."

"Then you see—"

"What I see is a gathering of men so enamored of their own power, beguiled by what they perceived as their own intelligence and cunning that they chose to have this painting created. They *chose* to do it." Isabetta shook her head, mouth curling grotesquely. "If he is a part of this conspiracy, it is his trouble to have."

"Please, Isabetta, wait," Mattea tried once more. "We have to…" But her words failed her, while those of others—voices in conversation not far from their closed door—broke in.

"Who is it?" Viviana hissed, brow furrowing, eyes bulging.

"What can I do for you, Ser Ufficiale?" It was Natasia's brother, Father Raffaello, speaking, very loudly, and to some sort of government representative.

"Lord save us all," Natasia whispered in prayer. "What have we done?"

"Shush," Viviana silenced her.

Isabetta went to the door, mouth set in a hard, firm line not to be denied, even when she opened the door and tiptoed out into the corridor, closing the door behind her.

Viviana thought she would vomit, such was the clenching grasp fear had upon her. From their sweaty brows and their wringing hands, she knew the others felt the same. There was no air, nor did it matter, for not a one seemed capable of breathing.

When the door cracked open once more, they did not know what to expect. Isabetta dashed any hopes with a single finger tapping hard and repeatedly against her pursed lips as she locked the door behind her.

Silently, with exaggerated mouthing, she told the others the worst of the news. "They are coming." Her lips formed the words while her hands swirled around to all parts of the room, pointing into cupboards and under tables. The message was clear. They were coming to search.

Self-preservation banished all fear, turned it into action. Viviana ran to the table, gathering the sketches together, wincing as the parchments scratched against each other with a sound so small, any other time it wouldn't be heard. Leonardo snatched the canvas from the easel, shoving it into Mattea's hands.

The voices outside the door grew louder; footsteps clattered arrhythmically.

"It's one of these keys, I am sure of it," Father Raffaello laughed at himself.

Both hands now free, Leonardo took Mattea's arm in one, Natasia's in the other, fairly dragged them across the room, shoving both of them—Mattea clutching the painting—into the single large cupboard.

Fiammetta dropped her girth behind Isabetta's plinth and threw a paint-smattered, long forgotten piece of canvas over her, one they had used to practice creating fresco dimensions.

Only Leonardo, Isabetta, and Viviana remained exposed, vulnerable.

The grating of key after key sounded in the lock.

"Give it to me," a disgruntled male voice insisted from the other side of the door, and the jangle announced his possession of the keys.

In the space of time, Leonardo threw remnants of cloths—most used for cleaning—over one table, turning it quickly into a tent of sorts.

"Aha!" came the cry from without.

Leonardo grabbed the women, pulled them around the back of the table, and shoved them under, crowding them in as he curled his long body into a ball beside them, head and shoulders so curled, his long face hanging squelched between raised knees. Safely hidden from the front, yet if the inquisitors walked the circumference of the room, they would soon be uncovered.

The door opened with a whoosh, followed by a stamping of feet.

"As you see, signore, it is as I said, an art *studiolo*." There was but the slightest quaver in the priest's voice; only those who knew him would hear it.

"Are you allowed such an amusement, father?" this from the same voice belonging to he who had taken the keys.

"Well, there have been many famous men of the cloth who accomplished a great deal artistically, such as Fra Filippo Lippi," Natasia's brother laughed nervously, perfectly fitting for this conversation. "Of course he was not of my order. Perhaps, just perhaps mind you, this work of mine would be, shall we say, frowned upon. Why do you think the door was locked?"

Viviana could have cheered for the brilliance of his words, at the lengths he would go to protect them. Even as she shared small smiles with the two crouched beside her, she knew Father Raffaello would condemn himself to many days of penance for his lies.

"Surely in these times, a painting priest is of little concern?" he continued.

She heard it then. Viviana heard the sniffle and her eyes bulged. She knew it came from Natasia. Had the men heard it too?

"It is sorry I am not to have more to show you. I have no current work in progress at the moment," Father Raffaello performed wonderfully; Viviana almost believed he *was* sorry.

"Very well then," the man grumbled with disappointment. "See to your true duties, priest. The city has great need of them."

"I will. Oh, I certainly will. This way, gentlemen."

Even as they heard the door shut, even as they heard the key turn again in the lock, they didn't move. No one moved. They waited.

It seemed like an hour, but was not more than a handful of minutes before the key returned to its home and the door opened.

"It is safe. Are you here? It is safe, I swear it." The dear priest sounded close to tears.

They came out then, each from their own hiding place. Father Raffaello rushed to his sniffling sister, cradling her in the basket of his arms. The remainder of the group came together in the middle of the chamber, each asking others, all at once in a jumble of words, if everyone was all right.

"My knees are no doubt bruised from kneeling so long," Fiammetta groused, but it was not to be the worst thing she would say. "We must let this go."

"What? No!" Viviana's voice was not the only one raised in protest.

"If you were missing, if you were hunted by the authorities, would you want us to stop?" Mattea asked her with more than a tincture of her previous anger.

"It is not me," was Fiammetta's answer, a poor one even in Viviana's ears.

They all began to talk at once—Fiammetta for the end, Natasia wondering if she spoke true, Mattea and Isabetta antagonistic against them. Leonardo stepped away silently.

Viviana could stand it no more.

"Silence!" she commanded. "All of you. Be still. It is not just about this painting." Viviana's blue eyes were aflame with righteous indignation. "It is not even just about Lapaccia. It could be any one of us, at any given time. The world has gone mad and we are more blessed than all the women out there. And I for one refuse to see it riven. To have meaningful purpose should be the challenge of everyone, man or woman. There is no price, no life more worthy than another. There is no price on loyalty."

Chapter Twenty-Two

"Curiosity indulged, is often satisfied on a jagged edge of regret."

As Viviana gathered the aberrant array of belongings into the large satchel, her hands quivered. To take tangible action in the search for Lapaccia filled Viviana with a sense of power, of action. The risk of it, the blatant idiocy, fired her adrenaline. Jemma entered the room, shaking out a cloak.

"Are you sure you want this?" Jemma held it out from her body, barely holding it with thumb and forefinger, nose crinkled on her face turned as far from the garment as possible.

"Yes, I am quite sure," she replied, folding it into the satchel. "We are ready."

As the two women made for the door, Viviana repeated a litany of instructions, a prayer recited many times over the last few days.

"You will stay at Signoria Fioravanti's home until we return. You will not ask, not now, not ever, where we go. Only, *only*, if we do not return by morning will you find my husband and alert him to our lack of reappearance. Understood?"

Jemma gave her a frown and a narrow-eyed stare, disapproval and concern conjoined.

Viviana stopped at her front door, and took the young woman's arm. "Understood?"

Jemma nodded, whispered, "Understood," and opened the door.

• • •

"I thought perhaps you may not be able to get away from Orfeo." Isabetta whooshed her door open, heaving with relief, greeting her guests with quick curtseys, and shutting the door.

"He left once more for the Signoria this morning," Viviana replied, "I do not expect him for at least a day or two. It has become his way."

Isabetta frowned. "It is a long time to leave his wife in these days."

"Yes, well, he considers his attendance there a necessity." This time Viviana's bitterness blared like a trumpet. She heard it herself and rushed to disguise it. "Your home looks lovely, Isabetta, but so dark. I did not expect you to be so fearful, to live with your shutters closed."

"It is not fear." Isabetta led the women through the small sitting room and its meager furnishings and into her bedchamber. She tipped her head across the hall and lowered her voice. "It is Vittorio. The light seems to induce the head pains."

Viviana put a hand upon her chest. "He is in such a bad way?"

"He is very ill, Viviana. I think he may be near the end."

They sat then, two friends, side by side upon Isabetta's bed. From there she told Viviana of the ever-growing seriousness of Vittorio's condition, of his sleeping in the servants' quarters for they no longer could afford any, the difficulties at the shop and the troublesome condition of their finances. Isabetta left the only ignominy—that of her work at the tavern—unspoken.

"I am so very sorry, my dear. Why did you not tell me, any of us?"

"When I am with you, with the sisterhood," Isabetta began, "it is a different world, a world free of worry and strife." The jut of her sharp chin returned; her shoulders squared once more. "I would not have my place of sanctuary tainted."

Viviana almost laughed, ready to share like emotions, but the chance flitted away.

"Come, we must dress," Isabetta said. "Time is tight."

With Jemma's help, the women donned the garish gowns

Viviana had procured from one of the convents, a haven where fallen women unable to live the life of prostitution any longer found refuge and a place to live out the remainder of their years. With Jemma's help, Viviana kept her bruises, those just beginning to fade, from Isabetta's gaze. Someday she would confess her torturous truth, as Isabetta had just been so courageous to do, but today was not that day.

Brash of color, one of burnt pumpkin, the other of dingy olive, both were made of far less fabric than either woman was familiar with wearing, both heavy with the odors of the bodies that had worn them and the sickly perfumes such women had used to mask it.

Though the orange gown would suit Isabetta's platinum hair and the olive gown would the auburn of Viviana, they purposefully made the switch. The sleeves, though ballooned, were unslashed, a style many years abandoned. The olive gown boasted a high, sashed waistline, while the other fell straight from a gather below the bust. Both displayed most of the women's décolletage.

"I cannot wear this in public," Viviana hissed. Jemma bleated agreement like an old goat. So low was the square neckline of the kirtle, so transparent was the V-neck of the partlet, that little covered her full breasts, the material barely disguising her nipples.

Isabetta glanced up from the ministrations of her own costume, and bit her lips tightly together, eyes flashing with bursting hilarity.

Viviana glowered at Isabetta. "Do not laugh at me. Do not dare."

But there was nothing for it. As Viviana attempted to shove her voluptuous bosom below the kirtle's neckline, squishing them down, Isabetta fell into a chair, laughter overwhelming her.

Viviana snarled, but it was half scowl, half sneer, for she could see how she appeared in Isabetta's cloudy looking glass. Her copper hair, ridiculously coifed and embellished high upon her head, clashing so atrociously with the orange hue. She attempted to push her breasts into a space ill-equipped to accommodate them.

Isabetta reached into her gown, pulling first one breast, then the other, as high as she could, revealing as much of them as she could. She began to prance about the bed, chest stuck up and out.

"Look, it is I, the top-heavy Viviana."

All three women gave into it then, the ridiculousness.

The laughter made it difficult to paint their faces—the crushed pearl dust (the same many used to clean their teeth), the saffron applied to lips and cheeks in sharp, bright contrast—only made them laugh more, for they no longer recognized each other or, in truth, themselves.

"It is just as well," Viviana muttered, mind returning to their mission. "It is not me." They left Isabetta's house, leaving Jemma to watch over the sleeping Vittorio.

They hurried past the cathedral, the bas reliefs of Ghiberti visible on the bronze paneled doors of the Baptistery even in the fading light. As they turned onto the Via Sasseta, following it up into the more seedy part of the city, the air grew thick, the buildings ramshackle, and the people unsavory. Even in these dark days, raucous noises—voices of lowly dialect, bawdy laughter, blustering music—reached out into the streets on waves of strong aromas. For here were rows of brothels sandwiched between rowdy inns like the Hotel at the Crown and the Inn of the Bell. This was Florence's most lecherous district, and neither woman had ever set foot within its purview, had never desired nor dared to. Before now.

Viviana dared to peek out and over her shoulder from her hood, and she saw him. He stood leaning against the corner of San Miniato tra le Torri, the church between the towers. Even in this dim light, she could see his bemused skepticism—the finely curved brows perched high on his forehead, and though his arms were crossed firmly across his wide chest, one corner of his mouth curved upward.

Viviana offered a shrug.

Her green-eyed man placed one hand on his chest, while pointing a finger to the ground where he stood. He would be right there if she needed him. She sighed with the pleasure and pain of it.

"There," Isabetta ticked her head at the corner building, a three-story home of muddied brick and crooked shutters, each thrown open, light wafting out in square yellow beams. "Around back."

As soon as the women turned the corner onto the Via Alfani, they saw her. Standing by the rickety back door of peeling red paint, Delfina leaned against a wall, ignoring and unperturbed by a drunken group of young men. Seeing Isabetta, her face lit up.

Delfina hurried them on with a flapping, beckoning hand. As they grew close, Viviana lost all embarrassment from her attire, for Delfina's was far worse. The young woman's kirtle was lower than Viviana's, pink nipples clearly visible through the transparent partlet.

"He is here. He arrived early," Delfina told them in hushed tones.

Isabetta shared only first names, introducing Delfina as a distant cousin of her husband's.

Viviana could barely contain her distress as the courtesan led them through the brothel. Though the art she studied so often depicted humans without clothes, rarely had she glimpsed them in open coupling in such a public, debased manner.

Viviana was neither a fool nor naïve. She knew that what passed between she and her husband was perfunctory at best, save when he took her in anger. She knew, from vague mentions by Fiammetta and Isabetta, and from the way she felt when she glimpsed Sansone's face, be it months apart, that there was more, much more that could happen when a man and a woman shared carnal knowledge of each other in a sensual manner. But she knew too that what she witnessed now, the lewd acts taking place with little privacy, was not as it should be either.

Delfina took their cloaks, hanging them on wall pegs by the door, and brought them to a narrow staircase, whispering over her shoulder.

"In the room I take you to, there is a space, no more than the width of a wardrobe, but it has its own door and cannot be seen by those in the adjoining room. The holes in the wall are well disguised, but they are there. Through them, one can hear and see all. There are some, not many mind, but some who like to watch. There are still others who like to be watched. This is the room we use for such people."

"People?" Viviana squeaked. "Women?"

Isabetta shushed her; Delfina shrugged.

Viviana swallowed hard at the breadth of life of which she knew so little.

Delfina brought them to a door, *the* door, opened it, and warned them, "Do not lean upon the wall. Put only your eyes or ears against it, for it is not sturdy."

They nodded as Delfina shut them in

The darkness was not the worst of it. Pin-pricks found their way through, beams of light catching dust motes in their slim streams, enough to locate the holes. But the smells. The malodorous scents forced them to cover their noses with a slap, preferring their own scent to the odors of all manner of bodily fluids trapped in the fetid, unstirred air.

They heard the door in the adjoining room open, heard Delfina's voice, and they rushed to find a place to look and listen, hurried to become still.

"I am so sorry, signore, I did not mean to make you wait. You know I long for your arrival." The girl's voice turned to a cajoling purr. "Why have you stayed away so long?"

"You know my duties, my dear. I fear I am more in demand than ever."

Viviana rolled her eyes; how like Orfeo the man sounded with his pompous grandiosity. She felt quite sure he was as inconsequential as her husband.

Like Isabetta beside her, Viviana squinted through the small hole for a quick glance, pulling back to share a look. Together they shook their heads; neither recognized him.

Narrow-eyed and mostly bald, save for a few scraggly hairs rimming the back and side of his head, Viviana wondered if Delfina would be able to find his manhood beneath the girth of flesh hanging grossly over his belt. But she need not worry, a good prostitute was a good actress.

Delfina led her client into the room and sat him upon the bed. Opening his legs, she took a stand between them, her unconcealed breasts inches from his face. With slow, languid movements, she began to undress him.

"Oh yes, signore, I know how very important you are. Tell me of your work." She leaned down and with a small pink tongue, licked his neck from base to ear. The man leaned toward the caress with eyes aflutter. "It makes me desire you all the more."

She leaned ever forward, her breasts fully displayed as she unlaced his tunic, caressing his chest between each pull of a string. Tell her he did, but so much of it was of an irrelevant nature— no doubt all he was truly privy to—that Isabetta and Viviana grew impatient. Delfina drew near the end of the laces.

Delfina knew her job. She kissed him, licking his lips, darting her tongue in and out of his mouth, in and out of his ear, along his fully bared chest.

"Tell me more," she panted. "It would excite me so to know whom you have captured, whom you hunt."

She shimmied onto the bed behind him then, and pulled off his *farsetto*, revealing a sweaty linen shirt beneath, its wide neck flapping open to reveal a hairy chest and breasts plump enough to rival Viviana's own. Delfina began the slow untethering of the laces on the back of the man's breeches.

The man was all too happy to comply. He dropped names like trees did their fall leaves.

Viviana bit her lip at the mention of such men as Roberto da Sanseverino, Lorenzo Giustini, and others, but his prattling brought little satisfaction other than surprise. Delfina knew her true work that night.

She turned the man round on the bed, her now open legs wrapping themselves around his girth, and she pulled her kirtle even lower, releasing a plump breast from any remaining binding, reaching down and placing the man's hand upon it.

"I remember," she growled, using her hand to make his squeeze and probe her flesh. The man took on the haze of one drugged and possessed. "I remember you told me they seek a woman. Is it true? Do they seek her still?"

"It is," the man said, removing neither hand nor gaze from Delfina's body. "Signora Cavalcanti is the one they seek."

Delfina gave a squeal of pleasure, one well-rehearsed. "Certainly not. She is a great noblewoman. I have seen her in the marketplace so many times. She is as sweet as my own *nonni*. Why would they want her?"

The man began to stroke Delfina of his own accord, his thumb moving in wide circles closer and closer to the pink nipple, teasing it out to full plumpness. "They believe she stole a painting, though everyone is quite vague about it. I think some are just after her to remove any power the son may gain as the offspring of such a nobleman."

The man removed his hand from the engorged nipple, stroking the flesh of Delfina's stomach, but he did not desert her breast entirely. Instead, he lapped at it, languished it with a moist tongue and full lips.

Viviana began to quell at what they did, for more reasons than she cared to acknowledge.

As Delfina's head fell back, surrendering, it would seem, to the delight of the sensations, she kept true to her task. "But what prompted the Priors to accuse her in the first place?"

Viviana heard, but didn't. She watched the rapture soften the woman's face, saw her look toward the wall, their wall. With a hard swallow, she realized Delfina was a woman who enjoyed being watched; she enjoyed her task this night. Viviana raised a hand to her own face in question: had it ever shone with such rapture?

The man's answer however, when it came, trumped all thoughts.

"Because Signora Cavalcanti was seen that very morning." His muffled words came as his mouth switched from one nipple to the other, his free hand pushing the linens up Delfina's legs and round her pale buttocks, giving it a stroke, then one to his own swollen self, taking Delfina's hand and placing it upon him. Keeping his over hers, together they stroked him to further hardness. Yet still he bragged as their breathing grew ragged, as their hands moved up and down, faster, harder. "They won't rest until they find her, for more than a few say they saw her running from the Palazzo della Signora, and they say she carried something, something large and rectangular."

Viviana flinched back from the partition as if struck.

"Seen?" She mouthed to Isabetta. She too had retreated from the wall. "*Seen* with it?"

It was almost too outlandish to be believed. All this time they worked with faith, believing the accusation was false. But if Lapaccia was *seen* with it...

Both women put their eyes back to their peepholes, but there would be no more information gained this night. The man set hard to his task now—a mouth to a breast, one hand lost beneath the folds of Delfina's flimsy skirts. The only sounds were those of humans at their most animalistic.

Viviana stepped away and toward the door, taking Isabetta by the hand and pulling her along, whispering, "We must go."

Here Viviana blanched—at Isabetta's unyielding stance, at the amusement on her friend's parted lips, and the desire in her eyes. Yet who was Viviana to disparage her? Was it not the same, deep within, which ignited Viviana's longing to run?

With another tug, Isabetta gave way, and the two women slithered from the hidden closet on tiptoes and into the corridor. Viviana moved left, unsure of the way out.

"No, this way," Isabetta hissed, taking a step to the right.

Yet with a sudden yank, she spun them back round, tugging Viviana once more to the left, grabbing her by the shoulder, and turning her abruptly. Viviana's words of protest were lost, pilfered by deep, lecherous laughter from further down the narrow, dim corridor.

But it was not so far or so dark for the man's features to be concealed, for Viviana not to recognize her own husband.

His laughter—she could not remember the last time she had heard it. It was the strange thought screaming in her head as she stood immobilized. In this mummified disbelief, Viviana watched as Orfeo entered a room on the opposite side of the corridor, one hand working frantically on the front laces of his breeches. His other hand he kept firmly in place on the prostitute's bare ass.

Chapter Twenty-Three

"There is a great disgrace as to be defiled by indignity."

Viviana expected no callers. The knock upon her small front door took her by surprise. She opened it to find Leonardo da Vinci and Isabetta, another surprise. But here they stood, a blooming flush on Isabetta's face, and Leonardo, himself, with the shy, endearing grin he wore so well.

"I realize how rude it is of us to come unannounced," Isabetta chirruped, hands aflutter. "But I've run into Leonardo and we've decided upon a wonderful outing. We hope you'll join us, as no one else seems available."

Viviana heard what Isabetta did not say—that though Isabetta wished it, the married woman could not walk about alone with the unmarried Leonardo.

"Besides," Isabetta's voice grew tender, "I did think you might benefit the most to be out and about."

Once more, the true words were left unspoken. Isabetta knew there was no love to be lost from what Viviana had seen of Orfeo last night, but there were more places in the heart that could be broken.

"What sort of an outing?" Viviana asked, and if cynicism crept into her tone, it was for this and this alone.

"*Scusi*, signora," Leonardo's dulcet voice soothed Viviana's ruffled brow. "I had a thought that perhaps it would aid the group to visit and study paintings, those of a similar composition and treatment." *As that which you forge,* he refrained from adding.

Viviana needed little convincing. She had not slept the night before, too disrupted by anger and disgust. Viviana could have borne a mistress; there were few wives these days who did not, in this age of experimentation and change. But it was within one's own community, a mix of a decent variety. Even a well-kept courtesan she could have accepted. Was it not enough to suffer his ill-treatment, his disrespect of word and deed, his anger and his humiliation? Must she be further humiliated by his association with a tawdry prostitute? It made his crimes against her all the more castigating, all the more denigrating.

She ran to her chamber, grabbed a veil and her own sleeveless overgown, and returned, stepping out into the late afternoon with a distinct sigh of relief. The rain of the morning had wasted away to a drizzle, but it did little to impede the contentment of a promenade. It filled the air with an earthy, acidic scent, as if it had been washed and sterilized.

Though they had been at the studio often, it seemed only to have replaced one confinement with another, so stifling had life in the guarded city become. As they stepped onto the Via Porto Rosso, it appeared they were not the only ones feeling the ill effects of a restrained existence, not the only *popolo* to long to take back at least a modicum of their city.

The streets, once empty at all hours, showed signs of life, small shoots of spring bursting through the barren dirt of winter, though nothing of the full richness typically found on the streets. Viviana was pleasantly surprised, nonetheless, to see so many strolling along, once more taking up the tradition of the *passeggiata*. The walk taken before the evening meal had been a ritual of the city since before Viviana could remember. It was a time for socializing, for catching up on the lives of neighbors, and often it was a time for flirtations and meeting potential mates, as it had been for decades.

"Where do you take us, signore?" Viviana took the arm the tall artist offered her as he led the women southward, along the Lungarno Corsini and across the Ponte alla Carrara.

"Well, as I thought of such places, I realized there was one in this city that boasted not only some of the greatest works to be found here, but also a great many of them."

"Do not tease us, Leonardo," Isabetta laughed merrily.

Viviana frowned.

"We, our group, often make such instructional outings under the guise of visitations," Viviana spoke quickly, before her friend behaved untoward publicly. "But I am surprised to find you do so as well, being already so masterful at your craft, Leonardo."

"The acquisition of knowledge is always useful to the intellect," he intoned. "The worthless can be rejected, the good retained. Nothing can be either hated or loved until one has had some knowledge of it."

"But surely," Isabetta interceded, "you know what you love by now."

"Ah, but what I love is ever changing, as is the craft of painting," Leonardo replied. "Sad is the pupil who does not surpass his master."

He turned them left, into a vast and quiet piazza, and Viviana threw her free hand up in delighted recognition.

"Of course, the Brancacci Chapel," she chirped.

A gleam in his pale blue eyes, Leonardo exhaled, "*Sì*, the Brancacci Chapel."

The small family chapel in Santa Maria del Carmine not only displayed more than ten amazing works, they were works by the forerunners of the new style—Masaccio, Masolino, and Lippi. The works themselves were considered the incunabula of it, so great was it in use.

"Though they are frescoes," Leonardo had dropped his voice to a respectful whisper, as all Italians would within a church, "there are two whose composition is worthy of study."

Leonardo stopped before the altarpiece and raised both arms. To the left, Viviana beheld Masaccio's *Rendering of the Tribute Money*, and to the right, *The Healing of the Cripple and the Raising of Tabitha* from Masolino da Panicale.

"Though frescoes, they both contain many figures in a

defined space."

Leonardo began, and Viviana recognized the voice of a tutor—their unrecognized *maestro*—as soon as she heard it. All thoughts, even those plaguing her since last night, fled as her mind opened to all this genius had to teach them.

"With the Masolino you can see his figures are deeply Gothic, but the technique with which he rendered them gives an astounding sense of perspective to their place within the work." He pointed. "See, see the two central figures? They stand before a building that is far behind them. And how do we know it is far behind? By the ratio of their size to that of the building, its windows, its doors."

Isabetta had brought out a small book, the first half of which was filled with notes and sketches. As Leonardo spoke, she added more.

Turning, da Vinci brought his hands together as if in prayer. "And here, the Masaccio, dear Masaccio. The realism with which he painted his characters, those both divine and not...the utterly, definitively expressed emotion, especially anger and confusion." He stepped closer to the painting, pointing at particular figures.

This painting related the story as told by the Apostle Matthew and rendered it with all its dramatic implications. In the center stood Christ surrounded by his disciples. A tax collector is moving towards him, about to demand the temple tax. In depicted movement, Jesus gives the order to Peter to catch a fish, saying he will find a coin in its mouth.

"Look how well we see Peter's hesitance and confusion, the tax collector's anger," Leonardo continued. "Can you see that the thoughts of Masaccio were—*must have been*—impacted by the truth of his own world. Thus we have perspective, we have movement, we have emotion, we have—"

His quickened lecture, his own unbridled emotions, came to a halt, and Leonardo turned from the masterpiece to the women.

"—we have truth," Leonardo da Vinci announced.

In the silence echoing after his words, the three artists—forever students—studied each brush stroke, each choice of color, of hue and shadow.

An hour, no more, had passed when Isabetta softly closed her book. The women took their place on each of Leonardo's arms and they made their way from the church and back through the city.

Crossing back over the bridge, it seemed to Viviana that Leonardo led them in the direction of the city center, a place she had no wish to go again, perhaps not for a long while to come.

"Where to next?" she asked.

Leonardo patted the arm entwined in his, as if he heard her reticence.

"Worry not, madonna. I lead us to the west, to a friend's home."

"Someone's home?" Isabetta's voice squeaked an octave higher.

"A palazzo, in fact," Leonardo teased.

"Ah, someone important," Isabetta smiled, and they continued on, a merry party on *passeggiati*.

From the path of other strollers, it was clear that this trio were not the only ones steering clear of the city center, fearing what may lay in the Piazza della Signoria. And yet, they should have known— horror was everywhere these days.

• • •

"Make way! Make way!" the gruffly barked command came from up ahead, just round the corner.

The triumvirate walked on, hearing but not listening, a niggling in the back of their minds to which they should have paid heed.

Turning at the Via del Giardino, the gang of boys and young men, the *giovani*, turned onto the Canto di Nello.

Three of them walked in a "V," leading the parade, sluicing through folks who dared to venture out. These *giovani*, gangs of city boys, ran roughshod over every street of the city, the lofty and the low, young sons of wealthy families with too much coin in their pockets and not enough work required to gain it. Their insouciance allowed them indulgence in the mayhem they found so amusing. In these days, where blood flowed like rain down street gutters and body parts were discarded with the same irreverent frequency as bones for a dog, the *giovani* had taken the calamity as permission to flaunt their disrespect with a far heavier hand.

"Move aside, I say," the lead boy yelled. Clad in expensive leather and silk, there was no more than jawline fuzz smudging his smooth skin, unlined by the passing of years, unspotted by sun that any work in the fields might bring. Black eyes sparkling, his hips swayed with sensual swagger as he pushed all aside—man, woman, child, or elder—a brushing hand to the left, a pushing one to the right.

"*O, Dio mio,*" Viviana breathed.

Isabetta planted her feet in the road, planted her hands on her hips. She was never less fearful than when threatened by those she deemed unjust.

"Ah, Mona Fioravanti, how very grand it is to see you," the young man bowed, but the exaggerated gesture was a mockery of respect, one serving only to rile Isabetta more.

"Isabetta, come away," Viviana hissed, knowing insolence when she saw it, for she saw it on her own spouse's face all too frequently.

"*Sì,* madonna," Leonardo joined in Viviana's pleas, "they will not listen."

"Is that you, Scevola Genovese?" Isabetta squinted, peering through the spotty facial hair and the dirt upon his cheeks. Dirt covered patches of his fine clothes as well, so out of character for these coxcombs. "What is the meaning of this nonsense? What game do you play?"

"It is no game, mistress." Scevola approached, his arrogance more affected. "We are purveyors of justice, true justice, upon the devil known as Jacopo de' Pazzi."

Isabetta stamped her foot at the nonsensical answer, which was no answer at all. "Whatever do you mean? He was buried in unconsecrated ground, was he not?"

She stood him down, toe to toe.

"It is not enough, not by half," he spat, pushing back his pitch-colored locks. "The wretch has brought the demons among us. Many have heard the noises, eerie sounds of haunting, sightings of satanic beings. His body has brought them, turned the ground into a place of demons."

Isabetta grabbed her head with both hands as it shook, as if it would shake clear off her shoulders. "You cannot belie—"

"Clear the streets for the arrival of a great and distinguished knight!" Ignoring her, the cocksure young man threw his arms wide. The remainder of his entourage turned the corner.

A large gaggle of *giovani* followed the lead three, bringing with them their honored guest, Jacopo de' Pazzi—or rather, what was left of him.

The body of the once prestigious *condottiere* had been buried with his noose still about his neck. The frayed rope had become his eternal chain of office. Two boys dragged the decomposing body of the Pazzi patriarch along the road. It bounced against the cobbles with moist thwacks.

Isabetta stood frozen in her tracks, no longer out of preeminence, but from pure horrified astonishment. Scevola approached, his feigned polite manner replaced with vicious intimidation.

"Remove yourself, madonna, or we will stone you," he spit as he spoke, so vehement his intent, so vile his demeanor. "We will stone you as we have others who dared stand in our way."

Viviana pulled her. "Come, Isabetta, come," she whispered, drawing her friend off to the side of the road. Isabetta hesitated until she saw Leonardo, his arms open and waiting to take her in. Silent though they were, tucked safely out of the path of the degrading parade, they could not look away.

"Make way for the great knight!" Scevola took up his call even as he gave them a blustery bow, a gesture as insulting as a thumb flicked from his teeth.

The crowd of louts spread themselves out, taking up almost the whole width of the lane.

"Do not tarry," one pack of the *giovani* called back to the cadaver. "There are many citizens waiting for you in the piazza."

Viviana stepped back and back again, Leonardo and Isabetta with her. As the *giovani* passed by, they saw more than one recognizable face, more than one son of good bloodlines. But none so shocking as the appearance of Lapaccia's son, Andreano.

"Andreano!" Viviana cried out with the terrifying truth of it. "Andreano!" This time it was sharp with rebuke, a demand for his attention.

The young man followed the sound of his name until he found his mother's friends. The bulge of his soft brown eyes exposed his surprise, and his shame. Running his hands through his dark hair, darker for the dirt crusting in it, he stepped closer.

"Get yourselves from here, my ladies, this is no place for you," he hissed.

Viviana could have slapped him, as she would have one of her own sons, had he the courage to come closer.

"It is you," she pointed a finger of damnation at him, jaw thrust forward. "You must get out of this. You cannot be a party to this despicable bacchanalia. Get out!"

Andreano only shook his head, albeit with little enthusiasm, calling back as he moved on. "I cannot."

Leonardo pulled on Isabetta's arm. Limp with revulsion, she barely gave resistance.

"We should leave, madonna," the artist whispered to her.

"Where do we go, Viviana?" Isabetta snapped, her anger overtaking her disgust. "I can see no more."

Viviana shut her own eyes for a moment, in the longing to surrender.

"I know, I know," she pacified. "But I feel we must follow, to be sure of Andreano's well-being. For the sake of Lapaccia, we must."

Were she the missing woman, were one of her sons amidst this detestable swarm, Viviana prayed her friends would do the same.

They followed along, doing their best to forget the decimated body slogged through the crowd before them, until a detached, forgotten finger forced them to step quickly aside. Viviana knew the distress this caused her companions, Isabetta with thoughts of her dying husband, Leonardo fearful of recognition and incurring the wrath of the *giovani*, as he had on too many an occasion.

As they followed the Borgo alla Croce, they saw members of the Eight as well as those of the Podestà. The women saw the law enforcers and the soldiers doing nothing about the *giovani* and their gruesome guest of honor. "It is an outrage," Isabetta found her voice. "How can they allow it to continue? Why do they not stop them?"

Viviana shook her head, for she had no answer, no sensible answer. She knew only what her heart told her, not only of the man's just rewards, but the destiny of all who defied human decency.

The gang brought the body to the edge of the Piazza della Signoria, but here the military force did their due diligence, barring them from entering the square with a barricade of well-built, well-armed men.

Without argument, the *giovani* turned away, unwilling to suffer physically for their fun.

"You see, Isabetta, they did——"

"Viviana! Isabetta! Signore da Vinci!"

Turning, the trio discovered Natasia and Mattea rushing toward them, the two young women clinging to each other as they ran.

"What happens here? What is amiss?" they fired the questions at them.

The group continued to follow the parade, as Viviana and Isabetta told of the conflagration in which they found themselves.

As they turned onto the Borgo degli Albizzi, it suddenly became clear to Viviana where they were going next, and she groaned with the thought of it.

"What, Viviana, what is it?" Mattea stood on tiptoe to see if she could see up ahead.

"I know where we are headed."

"Where?"

But Viviana need not answer, for it was a short distance to the next turn, to the Canto de Pazzi and the family's conclave of palaces.

Now the *giovani* brought what was left of the once great *cavaliere* to his very door. They took him by the head then—the largest of the young men using Jacopo's skull to knock upon the Pazzi door, while others yelled up at the windows.

"Who's in there? Who's inside?"

No one came to the door. The shutters remained fully closed and latched over the leaded panes of glass the Pazzi palazzo boasted. Whatever Pazzi remained inside, remained hidden there.

"Is no one here to receive the master and his entourage?" Scevola yelled to the crowd. "Enough of this. I am sickened by his stench." He aimed his group south, and south they went.

It pleased Viviana, if any pleasure could be found in such moments, to find Andreano always at the back of the pack, always with those of the *giovani* who did naught more than watch and swagger about. He intimidated with his presence, true, but he touched neither the body nor any of the people who tried to stop the carnage the gang wrought.

As the number of citizens swelled, as the body broke into more pieces, its entourage brought him brazenly passed the Bargello, the Palace of the Podestà, and the court of criminal justice. With no shame or guilt, they dragged him passed church after church—the Apollinaire, the Neri, and even San Firenze. All the way to the river, they brought him, and the Corso dei Tintori.

Here the poorest citizens of the great republic lived, if it could be called living, for the homes of these people who dyed the cloth in massive quantity for those rich enough to afford it, were no more than rickety timbered shacks, makeshift cabins tilted askew by the slightest wind, flooding in the rains. These poorest of the poor who lived in this squalor came rushing out at the ruckus, cheering to see one of the high and mighty taking such a fall.

As the cavalcade of the cadaver reached the water's edge, its purveyors dragged what remained of the body upstream and onto the Ponte Rubaconte. Crowds surged both sides of the river, pressed up against the barriers, some daring to join the *giovani* on the lengthy bridge itself, the longest and northernmost in the city.

Women of acquaintance came to stand with Viviana and her group, women whose tongues loved the waggle of rumor, rumors claiming the Eight were in collusion with the *giovani*, that it was *Il*

Magnifico's own coin, pressed into the palm of the leaders of the gangs, which brought about this desecration.

As loathsome as this charade was, Viviana cared little for Jacopo de' Pazzi and what the gangs did to him, save for the violence it kept alive in her city. She feared for the soul of Lorenzo de' Medici, for she knew the darkness of it, lived with the same. Consuming hatred turned souls black.

"The Eight are still pulling people from their homes. They are still hanging them from the windows of the palazzo without benefit of a hearing," Natasia whined as the group watched the gang rifle onto the bridge, peering here and there for the perfect spot.

Viviana scrunched her shoulders. "We cannot fault them for doing their duty."

"But what if some of them are innocent? They are then killing innocent people."

Viviana pierced the young, troubled girl with a cynical glare, knowing how well some could hide their evil ways. "How do we know they are innocent?"

"How do we know Lapaccia is innocent?" Natasia simpered. In her words, Viviana heard Fiammetta's influence.

"Natasia!" It was Mattea who chastised the woman. "You must not speak so."

The young girl hung her head, refusing to meet their eyes. "This is wrong," she muttered. "Yes, what the Pazzi did was an outrage, but this is no better."

Not the one refuted her. Viviana felt the niggling of doubt in the pit of her stomach. In Natasia's words, Viviana heard a vein of truth. If such all-encompassing power—power the Medici wielded—were allowed unchecked reign, where would it land next, where would it take the Medici control next? She understood the absolute lust for revenge. But there had to be limits. Who limits the man who creates the limits?

Viviana dropped her head into her hands, fingers pushing against her forehead. She felt a hand on her shoulder and turned to find Leonardo da Vinci leaning over her, eyes ablaze with concern.

"Are you all right?"

"Be gone Pazzi!" the cry rang out, saving Viviana from finding an answer.

All eyes turned to the *giovani* and the lifeless captive.

"Farewell Pazzi!" they yelled, lifting the body and tossing it into the Arno.

The body fell in utter silence, hovering, tattered rags of his once fine doublet flapping in the air. It hit the water with a decisive splash and a full splay of water.

"*Evviva! Evviva!*"

The rousing cheers erupted; the desecration turned into a festival.

Viviana could take no more; she had seen the very worst of human existence within the span of ten days. She must retreat.

"Come, Isabetta," she pulled on the angry woman's arm, finding no resistance.

Chapter Twenty-Four

"Knowing is not accepting."

"I will not be very long, mama," Mattea called as she opened the door. "I will find us some fresh tuna for our supper."

Mattea closed the door on the answering call. She would not return soon. It was not to the fish market she went.

She had received the note late yesterday, just as she returned from witnessing the drowning of Jacopo de' Pazzi's dead body. It could not have come at a more auspicious moment; nothing else could have lifted her spirits as did the words from her beloved.

The directives were clear and she could barely contain herself until this moment came.

Mattea hurried eastward and north, beyond the Palazzo della Signoria, beyond the Duomo and Giotto's campanile standing sentinel over the quiet city. The Eight still made their arrests, the hungry scurried to the market and back, and the *giovani* pranced here and there. But all seemed as though done in secret, as if no one wanted—cared or dared—to see the goings-on in their homeland.

All the better.

Mattea rushed up the Via del Maglio, drawing closer to the Porta a San Gallo, the main northern gate. Here there were fewer houses, fewer churches, and barely a soul in sight.

As the convent of San Domenico del Maglio came into site, Mattea trounced off the right edge of the road and into the vast space of undeveloped land. The gentle forest of wildflowers, cypress, and sturdy oak shared their home congenially. It was a place of magical secrecy, and Mattea delighted in romping through it, communing with nature in the privacy it afforded, though still within the confined safety of the city walls. This was not the first time she had met him here.

She entered the grove, their grove, only to find it empty. Mattea raised her gaze to the sky, to the clouds finally beginning to part and break away, to the glow of the sun through the gaps as well as a blue of pure azure, one so deep she longed to paint with it.

Mattea tipped her head to the side. It was not footsteps she heard, as she hoped, but music. It sounded like a *frottola*, though only the slimmest of the repetitive rhythms did she hear and feel, as if in the air around her, as if the lute player sat in the tops of the trees high above her.

She closed her eyes and began to sway. She imagined him in her arms, his warmth, his strength, as he guided her into the steps. Mattea inhaled, smelling his dark, cinnamon-like scent.

Her eyes popped open. It was no imagined scene. He was there, in her arms, holding her, leading her in a gently sensual movement of dance as the trees stood watch round them. Mattea almost cried with the ecstasy of it. Instead, she lay her head upon his shoulder. Closing her eyes once more, feeling his body rub against hers as they swayed together—never had she experienced such intimacy in the whole of her life, one far deeper than actual coupling brought, one she wished would last forever.

But, of course, it could not.

She gave no resistance as he kissed her, as his mouth captured and caressed hers, delicately at first, commandingly soon.

"How desperately I have missed you," he whispered, his mouth burning a trail up her neck to her ear. The words broke Mattea's fugue, and she pulled back, keeping his lips from hers though her eyes rested on them still.

"You are more involved in this than you are telling me, aren't you?"

"Does it matter?" he finally asked, licking his full lips as if he would taste her yet again.

"I have always known," she began softly, not wanting to make accusations, wanting only to know the truth of him, lest her fears take her to worse places than reality, wanting to be prepared if it was as frightening as she thought it could be. "I have always known you do not respect and adore the Medici as most *fiorentinos* do, as I do."

Only here in nature's hidden chamber would she dare speak such words, but dare she must.

Mattea stepped toward him once more, reached out with hands he took eagerly.

"Have they done something to you or your family perhaps, to make you feel this way?" It was a feeling she had always had, but only a feeling.

He answered her in kind.

"You know me well, but you see more than there may be. Do not let the maniacal days we live in infest you." It was no answer, just a vague response. Her glare told him it was not enough and he shrugged his wide shoulders. "Perhaps I simply have problems with authority, as my father, God rest him, was so wont to tell me. Perhaps I simply have problems with any one family wielding so much power."

"There is much fear among...my friends," she slipped over the words, even here not daring to speak of the group aloud. "We have learned more, more about the day one such friend disappeared, but it does not help us find her."

He nodded his head. "It is one of the reasons I asked to see you."

He kissed her then, with the depth of his emotion and desire.

"That is the most important reason," he smiled rakishly as he pulled away. "But there is something I wanted to tell you. I think there may be an opportunity for you to learn more."

Mattea perked up, shook off her desire.

"In a few days' time," he continued, "there is to be a gathering, a small social occasion of sorts, if you can imagine one in these days. It will take place at a young, rich man's *sala*, a visiting *condottiere*. He is said to know much of the city's secrets. Perhaps he may reveal something to a young beautiful woman."

"I cannot go alone," Mattea objected, scandalized. "Nor would I be admitted."

"Bring one of your friends. There must be one among you who would fit in, one who searches as you do," he said, or did he ask?

Mattea nodded. Yes, Natasia served all the criteria, but the timid woman would never dare. Yet there was one among them who looked at every dare as a challenge. Perhaps they could make their way through the miasma that was a social occasion among the privileged. Had Isabetta not been one herself, before disaster befell her?

She nodded, accepting his challenge.

He took her in his arms, an embrace of protection, speaking softly as his lips brushed the top of her head, as he rubbed his cheek against the soft auburn floss.

"Our city is becoming more and more a place of danger," the aberrant darkness in his voice demanded attention. "Even the innocent nobles are becoming fearful and dangerous. It may seem as if the Medici and their followers are gaining back ground but there is a fear of another sort infesting them. Do you know how to use a dagger?" The question came from him but out of nowhere.

"What? Hah!" Mattea staggered, snickered at the absurdity of it, but there was not one iota of amusement in his face.

From the back of the belt he wore upon his waist, between the body and the skirt of his *farsetto*, he pulled a dagger, one of gleaming steel, jeweled sheath, and hilt.

He held it out. "This is for you."

Before she could find words—any word—he knelt before her and removed the laces from his *camicia*. With the dagger in one hand and the laces in the other, he lifted her skirts with his wrists. Mattea felt her breath hitch, but remained motionless. He twirled the laces thrice about the middle of her calf, lips curving sensually as his touch brought out goose bumps upon her smooth flesh. Laces placed and tied, he slipped the dagger sheath snuggly against her leg.

"There you should always keep it. I wager you may have a thicker piece of leather or heavy cloth from which you could make a better garter for it, yes?"

Mattea nodded, pulling her skirt up and stepping her leg out like a man about to offer a bow. Instead, she stared at the dagger attached to her leg. Her dagger. She was an armed woman. How astounded those who knew her would be to learn of it.

She made to reach down, to take it in her hands, but he held her motion with a laugh.

"Not yet, *cara*. First I must teach you to use it."

"But how—" she began, giggling as she watched him rustle in the undergrowth, bringing up a long, thin stick and breaking it in half, a side for her, one for him, both the size of a dagger.

"Stay on your toes. Keep your knees slightly bent, never locked." He told her as he entered the posture, a ready stance for fighting.

Mattea mimicked him, and though he could not see her knees bent, she showed him the fluidity of her body with a slight up and down bounce. She raised her weapon hand, holding the "dagger" as if she would poke him with it, as one would poke a fire in the grate.

"You would think this way was the best way, I know, but watch."

He took her hand and moved the stick within it, so the "blade" extended from the back of her hand, not the front, out from her palm with blade pointing toward her, not from between thumb and forefinger pointing at him.

"Holding it thus will allow you two slashes in the motion of one."

He showed her then, showed her offensive moves—attacking moves—but mostly defensive ones, ones to make if attacked.

The sun rose high, their bodies became warm and slick with sweat, but still he kept her at it, until her blood thudded in her ears, her muscles ached, and she felt a power unlike any other she had ever experienced. It intoxicated her.

He came at her yet again, hands and arms raised, reaching, a fiend intent on grabbing her. Ducking beneath his arms, she twirled as if she whirled away, yet coming full round, in a dance, and popped back up. Taking him unaware, she slashed upward and to the left with her right hand—her "dagger" scraping along his chest between each arm—then back down again she sent the "knife," breaking the tiny twig at the base of his neck.

Were it steel in her hand, he would be dead.

He dropped his "weapon;" she scooped it up.

Her teacher, her lover, stood immobile, his face agape at the brilliant move she flourished.

He grabbed his neck, gurgling as if blood puddled in his throat, eyes rolling in their sockets as he staggered about like a drunken man.

Mattea laughed with delight, squealed with triumph as his dramatic death scene brought him to his knees, then to his back, splayed on leaves and flowers, unmoving as his throe passed.

But she was not done with him.

As the conquering hero, never had she felt so like one, Mattea lifted her skirts, stepped one leg over his body, and lowered herself onto him. His lustful groan sounded her reward.

Mattea took him then, but it was not with the weapon he gave her, but the one she was born with.

• • •

He remembered the night he sketched it. It came upon him, unbidden, unforeseen, after spending a day with the women who were now a permanent fixture in his life.

Like a man possessed he set to work. Drawing out a blank canvas, one already stretched and awaiting his touch, he plied it with absorbent ground, the chalk surfacing agent applied to a canvas, or panel, without oil, making the canvas more able to absorb the paint's own oil.

Without Botticelli's cheat, it took him but an hour or so to proportionally enlarge the *cartone* to a full sketch upon the blank sheath. Quickly he put Fiammetta standing at the canvas in the center. Using *costruzione legittima*, a system of perspective founded on a geometrically constructed picture plane, the height of the foremost figure—in this case, the abundance that was the contessa—became the module on which all proportions of the whole were predicated. His horizon, the middle of the space at the eye level of this figure—in this case the canvas within the canvas, a miniature of the actual accursed painting itself—became his vanishing point.

With colors as distinctive as the women themselves, he brought them to life with his brush, with the emotion for them he felt but could not express in any other manner. With his quick, almost stabbing-like technique, he rendered his new family. With scumbling, he gave them softness by painting thin layers of light color over dark; he brought them to life.

Leonardo played with his colors and the variants of them he devised with shadow and brightness, the latter most assuredly on the female artists' faces, for they had brought light back upon his own.

He worked until his arm ached, until no more than a few candles lit the room.

Stepping back, becoming now an objective observer of what he had created, as best as he could be, always the worst to look upon his own work. Eyes uncritical of form, focused on content.

Leonardo almost laughed.

He had intended to honor this group, yet what he had produced was nothing if not another of his puzzles. Which was the painting of the conspiracy, that which the women painted the one which had gone missing from the palazzo—or was it what he had rendered? The women painting the painting. He relished in the ironic convolution of it.

Chapter Twenty-Five

"A line once drawn, can never be erased."

Viviana's blood burned hot at the sight of him. Speechless, static, face a sculpture, hands fisted by her side—she was a steaming cauldron barely contained.

"Are your *duties* well-tended?" Viviana asked as Orfeo trounced through their home, past her sitting room. Her sarcasm was lost on him. How could he know what she knew? She could never reproach him for it. How could she explain her knowledge?

"Of course not," Orfeo scoffed, returning from the bedchamber where he had divested himself of belt and doublet. Though thin, his flabby middle section hung grossly over the edge of his hose. All Viviana could think about was the grisliest of pig sausage in its thin casing.

"But we have finally convinced *Il Magnifico* to take some rest." Orfeo puffed. "It is the perfect recess in which to change clothes and sleep in one's own bed."

"As opposed to someone else's," Viviana snapped without thought.

"What?"

He sat then, upon her settee. "I have quite the tale to tell, of a dead man, no less," his voice, like his small chest, swelled. "You would not believe what the *giovani* have done."

Viviana dropped her book in her lap. "You mean how they dug up the body of Jacopo de' Pazzi, dragged him through the streets, and threw him in the river?"

Orfeo's small mouth dropped open, gape narrowing to a sneer at the denied opportunity to laud his superior knowledge.

"H—how…how?" It was all he could manage.

"I saw it happen," Viviana reported far too jovially, but she could not seem to help it.

His shoulders dropped, his arms twisted against his meager chest. "You were out in it, in such a debacle?"

Viviana cared not a whit for his displeasure, in truth, she quite enjoyed it. "Isabetta and I were out for *passeggiata*. We ended up in the very path of the *giovani*. We followed. We saw it all."

Orfeo didn't ask of her safety or that of her friend. He stood and left the room without another word. Viviana rose, following, fairly skipping behind him as he entered the dining room.

Seeing her there, Orfeo's jaw twitched. He stepped to the banquet and poured himself a large goblet of strong *brunello*, the dark brew staining his teeth a tint browner with a single gulp.

"Foolish women," he mumbled, wiping his mouth with the back of his hand. Any other man would demand his wife not leave the house.

Orfeo took his place at table, waiting without request for his food.

Alerted to his return, Beatrice quickly filled the table with an impressive midday *pranzo*, a chicken pie, cooked to perfection with golden crust, and an *erbolata*, the cheese and herb tart, one of the master's favorite foods.

"You will not know of the letter," he spoke again, after a long stretch of silence as they ate, together yet apart. Viviana knew he had used the time to search for a token of his superiority.

"Of what letter do you speak?" Viviana asked with little curiosity, voice flat, continuing to eat. He did not deserve her undivided attention.

With dramatic aplomb Orfeo told her of the letter Lorenzo de' Medici had received from the Duke of Urbino, and how annoyed Lorenzo had been by it.

Orfeo held in his diatribe, forcing her to give his words their due.

With a clang, Viviana dropped her knife and her two-pronged fork, and glared at him. "And why was he agitated?"

The supercilious man leaned back in his chair. "It was disguised as a missive of condolence, but its tone, the content, the very closing offered little in the way of sympathy. He offered help to the Medici, to Florence, but with little enthusiasm." Orfeo shook his head with condemnation. "When we took it apart, the message, line by line, denuded it of its rhetoric and its formalities, the message was clear, and it was not one of warmth or support."

"What *was* the true message?"

"Montefeltro made it perfectly clear—Lorenzo should consider himself lucky not to be dead as well. And if he wanted to continue to stay alive, he had better keep his mouth shut and do nothing 'to disturb God' and his followers."

"Disturb God. There was something else meant there."

Orfeo's nostrils flared. "Yes. 'God' in this instance is meant in the worldly form," Orfeo took a slow drink. "God in this letter is none other than the most holy vicar, Pope Sixtus, and his followers, including Federico Montefeltro himself."

"Does he imagine the duke and the Pope to be part of the conspiracy?" Viviana blanched. She had spoken of it as a theory, but to hear evidence of it, there was no salvation to be found in a world defiled by such degradation. A sense of abandonment engulfed her.

Orfeo laughed, "A soldier's confession, Montesecco. It had already told the truth of it. And then there is the poem."

"Poem?"

"Oh yes, and quite the verse it is too, though no one has come forth to claim it. *Others of great condition, but it is better not to speak their names, although each of them was born of humble origins, so that anyone can guess who they are.*"

He sat back, pleased with himself, plopping his booted feet upon the corner of the table with a thump and a thump.

Viviana reached her limit; she could no longer allow this impotent cock to crow when the sun had been up for hours.

"Does this tell us something? In truth? Nothing. It could be anyone." She dismissed his contention as she dismissed him, with a flick of her hand, turning her attention back to her food.

Orfeo dropped his feet to the floor, his arms upon the table with a thud.

"You are so wise, aren't you?" There he was, the snide and cruel man, the truth of him. "I will tell you something you do not know, could not know."

He leaned over the table, a stubby finger pointed in her face.

"Your friend Lapaccia Cavalcanti is still very much on the arrest list. I have it on good authority—"

"Who?" Viviana squeezed the arms of her chair until her knuckles turned bloodless white.

"—they believe they are getting closer to learning her whereabouts."

"Who told you this?"

"Baccio Ugolini, Lorenzo's eyes and ears in Rome. I heard him tell Sigismondo della Stufa myself. I…" The contemptuous man's words withered on his flapping tongue. His reddened cheeks revealed his epiphany. He knew what he had confessed—he had not come by the information directly, but by eavesdropping, the act of a meaningless person. He slapped his hands upon the table with a thwack. "I need not tell you anymore."

"But you must, it is Lapaccia, one of my dearest friends." Viviana hated the thin edge of desperation in her voice.

"You will not become involved with her anymore, wherever she may be. You will not see her again. She has proven to be of the wrong sort."

Viviana's head jerked back as if slapped, a snarl undisguised on her lips.

It was the moment; the metamorphosis was complete. It was as if a great wind had thrashed its way through their home, snuffing out every candle, dousing their world into utter darkness.

"The 'wrong sort?' You now call the Cavalcanti the 'wrong sort?'"

Slowly, deliberately, Viviana took a long draught of the sweet

Trebbiano she so enjoyed. If there was a quiver in her hand, she ignored it. "Why I remember it was not so long ago you would have wiped the ass of a Cavalcanti if it would have done you some good."

Orfeo sat forward so fast, his chair almost slipped out from under him, his face turned purple. "You...you..." he choked on his anger.

Viviana watched Orfeo through new eyes. He was so different now. With a breath, Viviana cleared her mind, batted her eyes prettily, and smiled.

Orfeo jumped to his feet, chair tipping backwards and slamming against the floor, rushing to her with a hand raised across his body, the back of it aimed for her face.

But she was quicker.

"Touch me and I will plunge this into that soft gullet of yours."

She pointed her knife at his stomach, where it waited for the slightest effort to gouge him.

Orfeo was a fool and a dullard, but he was committed to self-preservation at all costs.

He lowered his hand and took two slow steps back.

With the smile still upon her face, knife still in her hand, Viviana rose and, with a curtsey, backed out of the room.

"You cannot be always on guard," he hissed at her like a snake just as she reached the door. "Nor can your sons."

She spun round, knife raised. "Harm my sons and I will kill you where you stand." She laughed malevolently. "Or sleep. I do know where you sleep, Orfeo, *all* of the time."

As she closed and locked both doors of her salon, she realized she had become much like *Il Magnifico*. She would cleanse her life of all its venomous toxicity, one way or another.

Chapter Twenty-Six

"At times, the worst to be done, is the best to be done."

The early morning sun shined warm on Viviana's shoulders as it bathed the world in tones of magenta and gold. She took herself across the Ponte Vecchio, toward Santo Spirito, the women and the work awaiting her. She didn't know if she could work at all, if the spirit of creativity could find its way through her darkness. A demon lived inside her these days; she could see it clearly, but she had found nothing to appease it.

"Such a sight I never thought to behold, Viviana is the last to arrive." The snide comment was her greeting from Fiammetta, as Viviana entered the busy and bustling studio. All were in attendance, including Leonardo, for a full, good day of work would find the painting finished.

"Did we stop for some shopping, perhaps? I noticed many of the shops on the bridge have reopened, some with fine new wares," Natasia teased her, though far more gently. Viviana ignored her, focusing instead on the painting. It could not be denied, the sight of it cheered her, thrilled her.

Reminiscent of Rimini's rendering a century ago, it glorified the evolution of painting progressing to full dimensionality. In lieu of rendering the men in the forefront as miniature to delineate depth, their positions were made clear by more subtle changes in size, as well as in color, both brightness and shadow. There was no blue, but a tender periwinkle. There were no flat colors as there were in the

Rimini, but every gradient of color created with a thick ink wash of roasted cobalt ore. It was just such mastery of shading, such jewels of color, which Leonardo had brought them and taught them to use.

Viviana went to his side, took his hand, and dipped him a curtsey. "We could never have done this without you."

Though they were nearly the same age, the man, looking so young in this moment, blushed beneath her gratitude. "Where the spirit does not work with the hand, there is no art. I merely helped you connect them, no more."

"Orfeo has told me some news, news of Lapaccia." Viviana's declaration held them fast. She relayed the part of her conversation with Orfeo concerning their missing friend.

"I had heard the diplomat arrived," Isabetta chimed in. "Baccio Ugolini is a very well-connected signori."

"It is not good news the man speaks of our Lapaccia," Mattea sighed heavily.

"No, it is not," Isabetta agreed. "But I do know he will be a guest at a fête, one but two nights hence, at the d'Estes." She turned to Fiammetta. "Surely you must have been invited as well."

Fiammetta became the definitive portrait of a mouse caught in a trap.

"The invitation did come, but we were not planning to attend. It is unseemly, no, in these days of mourning?"

Viviana fumed, longed to thrash the pompous woman, to tell Fiammetta what she herself had done for the sake of the cause. Instead, she insisted, "You must attend, Fiammetta. I feel sure there may be information gained. Diplomats are never so garrulous than at a fête, imbued by good food and good wine."

Fiammetta narrowed her eyes at Viviana. It was ever so faint a gesture, but it was one seen by all. "Very well. But we should not get our hopes up."

With a sudden epiphany, Viviana told what she and Isabetta had learned at the brothel, that Lapaccia had been seen leaving the Palazzo della Signoria with something the size of the painting, but without saying so, she intimated the information came from Orfeo as well.

"I still do not understand why," Fiammetta bleated, still a note of irritation at being forced to attend the fête in her tone. "She is not *in* the painting. Look, no women are."

"It must have something to do with one of these men," Isabetta moved closer and peered at the faces of those they did not recognize, as if staring at them long enough would bring their identity to light. "Perhaps she was romantically involved with one of them. And then there are three blank faces, those no one has sketched. Maybe one of them is her lover. We must finish them today."

The group nodded as one. This was the task assigned them this day, the task remaining. But none took up Isabetta's postulation, that one of the men was Lapaccia's lover. It didn't matter that he was deceased, Lapaccia's fidelity to her husband would stay true until they met yet again on the other side.

"Or," Fiammetta grumbled now, "she could still have been part of the conspiracy, though she does not appear here. Perhaps it was her function to remove the painting if the efforts to put the Pazzis in control were to fail."

The women around her replied with silent disregard at the ridiculous notion, save for Viviana, who awarded her with a look of ill-tempered impatience.

"What?" Fiammetta shrugged her wide shoulders in defense. "It could be. If these days have taught us anything, it is that behind every life, there are secrets."

The words were an arrow to Viviana's heart, a sign for one who truly believed in signs. This was the moment. She felt as if she couldn't breathe, as if she never would, then,

"One of the men without a face," it was a garbled whisper. Viviana cleared her throat with a tight swallow, tossed back her shoulders. "I know whose features to use for one of the missing faces."

"You do?"

"Who?"

The women pelted her with their curiosity, more than one and at once.

Viviana breathed deeply, closing her eyes for an instant as she exhaled through her nose.

Opening her lids, looking upon each and every one, she spat her announcement.

"Orfeo. Put Orfeo in the painting."

Silence.

• • •

They worked the entirety of the day, taking turns at the canvas. Isabetta and Viviana rendered Orfeo with such keen likeness that Viviana felt the same revulsion as when standing before him.

"They will kill him," Isabetta said in a hushed voice.

"He has been killing me, slowly, for years. He abuses me. He abuses me in every way a man can abuse a woman. It has been going on almost the whole of my marriage. And what was I to do? Take it to the Lord Priors? Ask for justice? There is no justice for women such as I, abused by her husband. It is allowed. For pity's sake, it is encouraged as a show of strength."

She gripped her brush, holding the fisted, armed hand up before Isabetta's face. It trembled with her passion and her fury. "Here. Here is our power, our tool of justice."

Isabetta, this intelligent woman of few words, spoke those most crucial. "They will come for you too."

Viviana continued to paint the visage of her husband.

"There will be a scar on your immortal soul," Fiammetta intoned from across the room, a stiff statue, a guard of her God.

"A scar on my soul?" Viviana snapped harshly. With both hands, she pulled down one corner of her partlet and gown, revealing a shoulder stained purple. "What of this scar? What of the many others like it? Will that scar be any different than these? I think not."

She turned from the stoic woman to continue her work. "I will, I must live with both scars. God will decide which defines my eternal soul."

Mattea, releasing held breath, turned back to her work, finishing one by herself. Though it was of the man with the beautiful physique Isabetta had rendered, the face Mattea gave him was so nondescript it could have been any man or every man. Fiammetta rendered the last and she made him as a foreigner from the south, with the dark and harsh features of the Sicilians, for they were rumored to be involved as well.

The late afternoon sun began its slow descent. The pure light streamed fully in the windows, the brightness of it revealing every stroke of the brush filling the canvas in its entirety.

The women embraced each other. It had become a victory unlike any they had ever known, ever thought to experience. It had become something far greater than simply a challenging artistic endeavor; it challenged their very beings, their beliefs, and their characters. In it, there was both great joy and debilitating sadness.

"Genius knows no gender," Leonardo said softly as his gaze flitted between the painting and the women who had created it. "I am proud to call you all, each and every one, a colleague."

"We could not have done it without your help, *maestro*." Isabetta turned her warmth upon him, the women agreeing, curtseying as they too murmured their gratitude.

"Oh, I think you could, madonna," he chided with his shy smile and a slight nodding. "It occurs to me the feminine sensibility, a woman's ability to *feel* more and far greater, far deeper than most men, would make them far more proficient for translating the human condition onto the canvas. And yet you are prohibited by the very fact." He shook his head, long hair undulating. "It seems inconceivable."

"Perhaps it will change someday," Mattea replied.

He smiled. "Perhaps it is you, this group, who may bring forth such change."

The women brightened at such a notion, a thought, a hope they locked away in their hearts and minds for safekeeping.

"So," Fiammetta stood before the painting, in her favorite

posture of arms akimbo, "how do we get it back into the Palazzo della Signoria?"

Leave it to Fiammetta to think of the practical, vital step not a one had yet to consider.

"I will take it."

This time the group turned resounding incomprehension toward Leonardo.

He shrugged one shoulder as if he spoke of what to have for a meal. "I walk in and out of the Palazzo without a single glance. The same is true for the Medici household itself." He folded his arms upon his chest. "Plus, I am a painter, of sorts, to be seen carrying a painting will be as natural as a mother carrying a child."

"It puts you at great risk, Leonardo," Viviana said.

The artist shrugged away her concern. "There is little they could do to me that has not already been done." There it was—the years of trial, the humiliation, the scars of it. "Consider it my gift in parting."

"Parting?" Isabetta squeaked. "Why should we be parting?"

Leonardo pointed to the painting. "It is finished, as is my work here. There is no reason for me to return."

"No, no you must—" Isabetta began, walking toward him, a hand outstretched.

"We still need you, Leonardo," Viviana stepped between them. There was no guile in her statement, no undue or misplaced flattery. "If we are to become the vehicle of change you proclaim we may be, then we must be the best, for only then will they pay attention."

Leonardo looked down at the woman before him. Viviana felt a kinship with him as she never had with a man of her own age.

"You are our brother. You are our *maestro*. There can be—should be—no other."

Leonardo held up both hands, shaking his head as he stepped back. "Oh…no…madonna…I could not—"

"Oh, but you must." Isabetta jumped up to stand beside Viviana. "You already are. Have you not told us of your dream to have your own studio, to be a *maestro*?"

Murmurs of agreement and assent crowded round him as did the other women.

"But...but I am not," Leonardo stammered, "that is to say..."

"You are not a woman, Leonardo, we do understand that part." Isabetta did not even try to hide her amusement.

"Then how could I be your *maestro*? Are you not committed to the forwarding of the female artist?"

"Because you are an artistic genius," Fiammetta said it flatly, acceptance of fact rather than compliment. "We must learn to further our mission and we cannot learn from each other. We can only learn from one who holds more knowledge than we, we can only learn from a master."

"*Learn from a master*," Viviana repeated the words, not Fiammetta's but Caterina's, exact words she had read in her cousin's journals. She stepped forward, taking Leonardo's hand, further astonishing the astounded artist. "I know this—" she waved her free hand about to encompass the room and the women in it, "—I know 'tis not exactly what you wished for, but perhaps it will do for now?"

Leonardo's eyes grew as deep as the ocean as he stared at her, and for a moment all thought he would refuse, until the small crack beside them gave his fey smile away.

"If it is what you wish—"

"It is! It is!" More than one of them cried, a delightful chorus.

"Then it will be so."

Chapter Twenty-Seven

"Victims, victors, vermin; captured one and all, immortally in paint."

The Piazza della Signoria had remained a vacant wasteland, abandoned by those who adored it, feared by those who abhorred it, as desolate as the ruins on the surrounding hillside.

But not anymore.

The artistic endeavor begun on the north wall, or the wall of the *Dogana*, brought them back out, enticed them, at first, with the hammering and the clamoring of a scaffold under construction. Then, the man who climbed it, none other than Sandro Botticelli, at last cajoled those few still reluctant out of their homes.

Now the city hummed with talk of it, on every street corner, in every tavern and home, from the low to the lofty. The *popolo* came out in droves to see what the artist was up to and the piazza became, once more, not a place of destruction, but one of creativity and socializing. The subject of his work seemed not to matter, though it reminded them all of what had transpired. The brutal consequences still echoed with screams of torment, and the bloodthirsty arrests held the breath of the city.

It had long been a tradition in the world-renowned city of *Firenze* to depict traitors and bankrupts on building façades. Most often such frescoes were rendered on the walls of the Bargello or the Stinche, the fortress of the chief police magistrate or the prison.

But not this time.

At Lorenzo de' Medici's insistence—he who had commissioned

Botticelli to conduct the work, a commission of forty large florins—the depiction was to be rendered on the wall of the government palace, facing the large courtyard in the city. Day after day, all would see it, a constant reminder to those who dare pit themselves against the great house of Medici.

In the heat of the day, the dusty smell of the warming paving stones rose up to meet the pungent odor of the fresh, wet limestone applied to the wall in readiness. Sandro Botticelli climbed the scaffold. Isabetta watched him, with Mattea by her side. He wore a scarlet cape trimmed with a thin row of fur.

"More to the left," he called out to the apprentices splaying the wet lime plaster on the wall in specified sections, Sandro following along with his tools.

"He need not add inscriptions," Isabetta said, bumping shoulders with Mattea.

Mattea sniffed, "No one will ever wonder who these fiends are."

Botticelli had been at work for only a few days, yet the identity of the first two men, merely rendered in life-sized outline at this point, could be none other than Francesco de' Pazzi and Archbishop Salviati. Simple sketches depicted with such mastery, the realism of the men captured in the moment of their gruesome death throes as they hung from windows of this very building were so startling, passersby shivered with frigid memories. Nowhere else would the new method of realism—of shadow, light, and dimensionality combined—be best put to use. Already the artwork served its purpose.

In what should have been the somnolent days of spring, when folks idled away their days in their gardens or in the rejoicing of the most popular days for *passeggiata,* the piazza had become the focal point of society. People came in droves to watch for hours, standing against the *Mercanzia,* the city's courthouse, while others brought chairs and tables, food and drink, and made a day of the theater of art playing out before them.

It was easy for Isabetta and Mattea to be lost in the crowd, easy for them to hold small squares of parchment or heavier vellum in the palms of their hands as they copied the sketches of the *maestro*. They made notes describing every tool Botticelli used, every technique he plied. And it was easy to scan the crowd for any glimpse of Lapaccia or anyone they may ask who may know something of her. As they sketched, as they mimicked the *maestro's* technique, they could not overcome their own concerns, those for Lapaccia, and now Viviana.

"Had Viviana ever told you about…" Mattea struggled, for she could not speak of Orfeo's treatment of her friend lightly. "Did she ever tell you the truth of their marriage?"

Isabetta shook her head without looking up from her notes. "No, never. I could tell theirs was not a love match. Not all of us are lucky enough to fall in love with those our family binds us to. I knew he was inattentive and slothful, that he had lost most of his inheritance, and hers. But never, in my wildest imagination, would I have thought…"

"I do not know how she bore the infliction of it for so long." There was a note of fear in Mattea's voice; she heard it herself. Her lover seemed the kindest, gentlest of men, but had not Viviana once thought the same of Orfeo? "I am not sure I could have endured such horror in silence."

Isabetta shrugged sadly. "Perhaps it was her pride, or perhaps it was her shame, which kept her from revealing the truth."

"Shame?" Mattea balked with a frown. "What had she to be ashamed of? He is the despicable one."

"True, true," Isabetta agreed. "But many women who endure, such as our Viviana has, feel they are somehow deserving of it, somehow they brought it upon themselves."

"Utter nonsense," Mattea snipped, a disgusted moue upon her young face.

Isabetta leaned closer, to speak her next words in a whisper, "I wonder if she has thought of life as a widow, the widow of a traitor."

"She should retain legal rights to their holdings, no? Her sons are emancipated. Perhaps all will go to them. They will take great care of her, I am sure."

"You speak as if she would be a normal widow. What will happen after—" Isabetta waggled her head. "She could face banishment as so many others have. She could lose all."

The thin piece of pointed lead and small squares of parchment began to shake in Mattea's hands. Until Isabetta reached out and took them into her own.

"Think not of it, not yet," she insisted with a squeeze. "Whatever happens, we will be there to help her."

"Yes, yes, of course. All will be well, for we shall make it so."

The declaration made, to Isabetta and to herself, Mattea lost herself gladly to the study of Botticelli and his movements. She watched with an eye to technique and method, until something else took root in her heart, something perhaps not as worthy or as kind, something more akin to hunger. To practice her art—her mastery— so publicly, could there be anything greater? A question jumped into her mind—how much would she sacrifice to practice her art as men do?

As Botticelli moved back and forth upon the scaffold, his arm grandly sweeping in bold gestures of color, she knew there had never been a stage more largely set nor a canvas so grand. She frowned at the small scrap in her hand and almost laughed at the pathetic sight.

Mattea snuffled away her melancholy; it was a product of more than just this moment, but the culmination of all the trying ones over the last weeks. Gaze shifting back up, her eyes glazed over. Now she saw herself upon the scaffold wearing a smock, neatly tied up and lace-trimmed, one of the other women by her side. It was the illusion—a magnificent vision—setting her back to her task, to watch and to learn, for the sake of learning itself, for it was all she and the fellowship could ever have. But perhaps Signore da Vinci was right; perhaps their work would pave the way for other women, females longing to create as they did, in public, not just as some disregarded, genteel hobby.

"Clearly Francesco will be as naked here as he was in his death," she muttered to Isabetta. "It appears as if Signore Botticelli will create the Archbishop's bite upon him as well, though they will face forward, not as they hung facing each other."

"I agree," her companion replied. "I don't know if the cruel postures are necessary to project the warning they are intended to convey. But what is the point of such an undertaking if not to do so with the grandest impact?"

"It is strange to think of it. Here we have the Pazzi and their ilk vilified while in other parts of the city, the Medici, both living and dead, are being glorified."

It was the sculptures Mattea spoke of, images of a victorious *Il Magnifico* commissioned by Lorenzo's family and friends.

"It is a shame we cannot witness that work as well," Isabetta replied.

"Verrocchio's." They said together and laughed, though not without a hint of bitterness.

Sculpting took place in the privacy of an artist's workshop, a place women were not allowed. If they could, they would watch the great Verrocchio collaborating with the modeler Orsino Benintendi to sculpt three life-sized figures of Lorenzo, intended for display in the three most attended churches in the city.

"One work would remind us always of who is dead, the other to assure us," Isabetta waved her hand to include the vast crowd in the piazza, "to assure all of us, that Lorenzo is very much alive, and so very much among us."

• • •

Leonardo could not have asked for a grander distraction than the one his friend Sandro provided. He stopped amidst the crowd for the briefest of moments to watch, shrugging off the twinge of envy. What artist would not wish for such a commission as this fresco? He almost laughed at Sandro's grandiosity, watching the short man sketch as if he conducted a lavish orchestra, creating with the same insolence he carried in his every day manner. Many held the distinctiveness against Botticelli, but not Leonardo. In truth, it amused him.

He hitched the painting, barely dry and covered by a thin linen, higher beneath his arm. Edging along the outskirts of the crowd clogging the piazza's north and west side, Leonardo made for the main entrance.

"Signore da Vinci," a member of the Eight, those who still stood guard at all the entrances to any building wherein a Medici may be, greeted the artist with a serious mien. "I must ask your business here today."

"As well you should," Leonardo said spiritedly. In an awkward twist of hands and torso, he lifted the painting up a few inches. "I must return this painting to the palazzo and the Gonfaloniere."

"Return?" The ruddy-skinned soldier's face grew darker still. "What do mean return?"

"Well, it came from the palazzo to begin with. I was..." Leonardo let his words fade. "Perhaps it would be best if you brought me to Gonfaloniere Petrucci's office and allowed me to explain it all to him."

But the soldier on the opposite side of the wide double door stepped quickly over to the painting, lifting the linen. Disciplined soldier though he maybe, he could not keep the surprise off his young—and handsome, thought Leonardo—face. Small though they were, it was the jumping jaw muscles, the spasm beneath the clean-shaven, strong bones, which laid bare his shock.

"Right this way, signore." Without another word, the soldier pushed open the right side door. With a clanking of armor, he led Leonardo up the grand staircase at the back of the foyer.

At the office door of the Gonfaloniere, the soldier held a hand up. "If you please, wait but a moment."

"Of course," Leonardo replied, biting his lips as the door closed in his face. He imagined the conversation taking place on the other side. He needn't imagine for long.

With a whoosh, the door dashed open. Gonfaloniere Petrucci himself stood in the threshold, long face bursting with high color and bright eyes.

"Signore da Vinci, what a wonderful surprise. How nice it is to see you. I hear you have something for me?" The man could not be more effusive, could not contain his ebullience, so like a child about to receive a treat.

"I do," Leonardo replied.

The soldier stepped aside, permitting the artist entry into the large and opulently outfitted office.

"Please, please, come in," Cesare Petrucci beckoned him further into the vast space, indicating, with a long hand, a chair before his desk.

"Thank you, Gonfaloniere, but I cannot tarry," Leonardo said. "It has recently come to my attention you may be looking for this painting."

Vague pronouncement made, Leonardo placed the canvas upon the chair, and with a flourish worthy of his friend Botticelli, threw off the linen.

Leonardo did not sit, but at the sight of the painting, the Gonfaloniere did.

He studied it intently, a silent tongue, a whirling mind. "How did you come by this?" It was a demand, whispered but not disguised.

"It was Giuliano himself," Leonardo began, stumbling over the story he had created, one he knew would be believed, but one not easy to fabricate. His grief he still held tight and close. "He asked me but a few days before…"

For a moment, Leonardo thought he should have sat. Calling up memories of the man he so greatly admired, a man he loved, was proving harder than imagined. He took a deep breath, rushing to finish.

"He told me it had been damaged in a leak, from the rains, and asked me to fix it."

Cesare's round eyes bore into him; Leonardo saw the tincture of skepticism in the gaze.

"Did you not know this painting has been searched for, for days? Did you not hear of what it represents?"

"I learned of it only last evening." Leonardo shook his head, wide-eyed. "I do my utmost not to listen to gossip. Surely you can understand."

Cesare Petrucci cleared his throat, or did he choke on his own words, it mattered not. He would ask nothing more. Instead, he offered gratitude.

"It would have been easy for you to put aside this task," the Gonfaloniere said, "in light of these devastating events."

"No," Leonardo snapped quickly. "No it would not. I could not. I made my promise to Giuliano. I would keep it."

"Of course, of course," Petrucci stood up, taking Leonardo's hand. "On behalf of the Medici and the Republic, I thank you for returning this to us. It will prove so very helpful, I assure you."

Leonardo bowed his head. Turning quickly upon his heels, he made from the office with as much unseemly swiftness as possible, before the Gonfaloniere could see the slight smile of satisfaction brimming on his lips.

The deed was done.

Chapter Twenty-Eight

"The time of reckoning comes for us all."

The world lay tucked into the gray blanket of dawn.

That's when they came for him.

Viviana heard the crash from her sitting room. Here she slept ever since threatening Orfeo with her knife. They had circled each other since then, lions waiting for the other to pounce, not a shred of marriage—of trust—left between them.

But none of that mattered anymore.

Viviana knew the time had come.

"Signore Orfeo del Marrone?" It was a deep, dark voice rising up from within the confines of the courtyard as if rising up from hell, echoing eerily off the cold stonewalls.

Viviana sat up and listened to the sounds of her husband rousing from his bed, the rustle of the silk sheets she had long been denied, the thumping of his bare feet on the floor as he marched to the door and answered the call.

"I am Orfeo del Marrone. Who is there? What do you want?"

"You." Came the simple, denouncing answer.

Viviana jumped up, grabbing a wrap as she rushed from the room, coming to stand behind Orfeo as the intruder climbed the stairs to the living quarters. His black leather-clad form barely fit in the narrow confines of the stairwell.

"Me?" Orfeo recoiled, neither contrite nor respectful, even in the face of this mammoth law enforcer, one whose presence could mean but one thing, and one thing alone.

"You are under arrest for colluding with conspirators." The man reached the top and stood over Orfeo, looking down at him like a small child. "You, sir, are a traitor of the state."

Orfeo blundered back a step. Viviana shifted to the side. She would not catch him.

"I…a traitor?" Orfeo's ruddy complexion drained of color, his eyes sunk into the dark, saggy skin surrounding them. "You are mistaken."

"We make no mistakes, signore." The soldier took Orfeo roughly by the upper arm, pulling the smaller man along as a child would a rag doll. "You are coming with us."

By now, both Jemma and Nunzio were awake, huddled together in the Great Room just beyond the door, viewing the events.

"No!" Orfeo shouted, reaching back, but for what Viviana could not tell, certainly it could not be for her. Perhaps a sword or a wrap. It mattered not.

They took him then, dragging him roughly, as he tumbled down the stairs, dressed only in the thin linen of his nightshirt—his skinny, hairy ankles and bare feet sticking out the bottom.

"Madonna…" Jemma began.

"Let us go," Viviana said as if she launched a trip to the market. She closed her wrap, ran back to her sitting room, and grabbed the simple *gamurra* she had shed the night before. Throwing it on as she ran, she followed her now wailing husband and his captors down the stairs.

Out in the street, a gathering of soldiers awaited their leader and his prisoner, ready in case the arrested man put up violent resistance. Viviana almost laughed at the absurd possibility.

"You have the wrong man, I tell you," Orfeo whined now, "I am innocent." He planted his feet upon the cobbles, but as another of the Eight grabbed his free and flaying arm, the two men lifted him straight off the ground, trounced with Orfeo in their grasp all the way up the Via Porto Rosso, straight into the Piazza della Signoria.

The remainder of the soldiers followed behind. Viviana and her two companions walked in their wake. She felt the eyes upon her. Viviana felt the heated stares of those who came out of their beds to watch their disagreeable neighbor swept away, into the clutches of the government, as well as those who did not dare step out, the few watching from between barely opened curtains and shutters.

Viviana gave them nothing of herself to see. No emotion whatsoever, though her upper lip glistened and her legs shook unseen beneath the folds of her gown. She held Jemma's hands, felt the supportive warmth of Nunzio's hand on her back. She walked on.

• • •

"Jemma," Viviana spoke with a voice as flat as the road before them. "Run to Isabetta's home. Tell her what is afoot."

The young girl did as instructed, running as if her own life depended on it.

By the time the procession reached the piazza, the sun began to crest the horizon of the hills surrounding the city, began to find its way into the vast space of the government plaza between the forest of buildings as crepuscular rays of light, God's pointed fingers of justice. And with the light came more people. Some yelling, some whispering, most now dressed for the day's beginning, none surprised to find yet another man under arrest and on his way to a sentencing. Judicial prudence was still suspended in these days of eradicating conspirators. The ceremony of the imposed sentence, however, had taken on ritualistic theatrics.

As he neared the Palazzo della Signoria, the worst of Orfeo's indignation and fight left him, his body fell limp in the soldiers' grasp, his toes bloody from scratching along the cobbles. As they ascended the stairs before the main entrance, the smaller door within the black and brown grid archway opened. In its threshold stood none other than *Il Magnifico* himself, accompanied by Gonfaloniere Petrucci. This latter man stepped forward as the soldiers threw Orfeo down to his knees upon the stone steps.

"P…please, Gonf—" Orfeo's begging caught in his throat,

strangled by the fracas of wheels upon cobbles, of the snapping of a horse's rein.

In the sudden stillness of the crowded piazza, the cart of the dead pulled up to the corner of the palace. Men of the *Neri*, clad in hooded robes of all black, stationed themselves at all sides of the wagon. Viviana shuddered at the sight of the accompanied wagon, though not at the thought of her husband in it.

Someone jostled Viviana from behind. She spun, finding Jemma returned, dressed now in one of Isabetta's simple gowns, Isabetta beside her. The women embraced her, one with an arm about her waist, one with an arm about her shoulder.

Orfeo cried in earnest now. "I beg you, Gonfaloniere. Listen to me. You know me."

Gonfaloniere Petrucci sniffed irritably with a shake of his head. "Oh yes, del Marrone, I do know you. I do know the fiendish betrayal you are capable of."

Viviana could not help the rise of her brows on her forehead. Given a moment's thought, she did not find the governor's proclamation surprising. Any man who would treat his wife and children as Orfeo had was capable of many other despicable acts. His was a morally and ethically corrupt soul. He was a man who would put his desires and his agendas before any others, to the detriment of any, even if it meant betrayal.

The Gonfaloniere spared a look behind him and two squires brought the painting forward.

"Do you deny this is your likeness?" The official pointed to the man seated to the right of Francesco de' Pazzi, one laughing along with the dead assassin, cups raised, clinking together.

Orfeo squinted, leaning forward. His face was bloodless, eyes and mouth empty maws. There was no denying the resemblance.

"I…it is…but it cannot…" Orfeo floundered.

Anyone with a modicum of intelligence could easily contend that someone had put him in the painting on purpose, to indict him falsely. It was quick defense and a likely one, for it was the truth as well as the truth of the prevailing winds that blew harshly through the city. No one was above suspicion. Neighbor gladly tossed neighbor upon the fire of investigation rather than be scorched by it themselves.

But as Viviana knew so well, Orfeo had much less than a smidgen of intelligence.

The crowd in the piazza, those close enough, all began to talk of the painting.

"I had heard of its existence." Viviana heard a man behind her say. "Word was it had gone missing or was stolen."

"Not at all," another replied. "Apparently da Vinci had it, was doing some restoration work on it. I've seen it once more upon the wall. It's quite the masterpiece."

"Is it?" the second grunted.

Though their faces remained passive, immobile, Isabetta squeezed Viviana's hand ever tighter and Viviana knew exactly what she felt: pride, unfettered pleasure to hear their work regarded with such admiration. The dichotomy of her emotions, of this moment, made the day ever more surreal.

Gonfaloniere Petrucci had run out of patience.

"Orfeo del Marrone," he yelled, loudly enough for all in the square to hear, "I denounce you as a traitor and I sentence you to torture and immediate death by hanging."

Orfeo screamed, as did many in the courtyard, disgust and pleasure melding.

Lorenzo de' Medici stepped out of the shadows, stopping a foot in front of Orfeo, skin mottled, splotched with bloody anger. He leaned over Orfeo and spat, a great glob of disgusting green phlegm. "Die," he growled. "Die as my brother did."

Viviana swayed, her head swimming. If not for her companions, she may have fallen. Did she regret what she had done? She shook her head. Perhaps she was only hungry.

Even as Orfeo kicked and thrashed, members of the Eight bound his hands behind his back, lifted him up, and dumped him harshly into the back of the cart.

The Eight followed close behind, but it was the fellows of the

Compagnia e' Neri—the Company of the Black Ones—who would escort Orfeo on his final journey upon the earth.

The men, shrouded in black, had become an all too familiar sight. In other cities they were called *La Compagnia di Santa Maria della Croce*—the Black Company in the Confraternity of St. Mary of the Cross—referred to more simply as the Black or Christ's Cavalry. It was their mission to keep the offender as calm as possible, to offer comfort as the Eight did their work, work meant not only to punish the criminal, but to frighten the voyeuristic population.

The cart swung round. Viviana followed behind the Eight. She heard every guttural curse and condemnation made upon Orfeo's head, from acquaintances and strangers alike, a bloodthirsty crowd lining both sides of the thoroughfare.

Through the haze of her thoughts, Viviana remembered a similar scene. How well she recalled the day the *consigliore* had been taken. Like his wife, Viviana followed behind, but Viviana did not cry out, did not plead for her husband's life. She couldn't.

As the procession turned northward onto the Via Calzaiuoli, the *Neri* chanted:

Mercy, O highest God and everlasting,

A man of the Black leaned over the rail of the cart, instructing Orfeo to repeat the prayer. But Orfeo shook his head in denial. The *Neri* continued without his participation, their droning mixing with the rhythmic thudding of the wooden cartwheels on the hard paving stones.

Here I am, dear Lord, at the final step
That every man must take
In this thieving, base and sighing world
I deserve the hellish and eternal fires.

"No," Orfeo screamed. "No, I do not."

He turned, bloodshot eyes searching frantically in the hostile crowd. They lit upon her face and, for an instant, showed a glimmer of hope.

"Viviana! Viviana you need to—"

And though the cart yanked him about, swaying as the road curved, it was not the motion arresting his words, but the look on his wife's face—one of stark, frigid indifference. His scrunched expression fraught with pleading fell away. In her narrowed, hardened eyes, in her curled lip, in her tightly set jaw, she said everything she needed to say, she gave him his ultimate verdict.

The wagon slowed as it entered the Piazza San Giovanni, the courtyard between the Baptistery and the great domed cathedral.

"Let me through! Let me pass!" The young woman's voice had a sharp edge that cut through the crowd. Viviana was not surprised when Mattea popped out.

"You do not have to be here," Mattea whispered in Viviana's ear.

Viviana pulled back, a hand to the young girl's soft cheek. "Yes, I do."

I repent my criminal ways,
And with this sobbing face and torment,
I think about your mortal woes on the Cross.

As the *Neri* finished the next portion of the prayer, three members of the Eight climbed onto the back of the cart. Two held Orfeo by the shoulders, firmly in their gauntleted hands, while the other stood before him, brandishing a dagger, its sharp edge glinting in the sun.

"Look away," Isabetta insisted of Viviana.

She did not.

Viviana watched as they hacked Orfeo's nose from his face, as the blood spurted, dripping down his ecru nightshirt, spewing across the floorboards. Gasps of horror, degenerate cheers fell away. Orfeo fell forward in a faint.

The first step in the punishment complete, the cart continued on, turning south on the Via Calimara, past the *Mercato*, full of morning shoppers, many of whom dropped their packed baskets and joined in the deathly procession. The journey continued, as did the *Neri*.

O Lord, snatch me from this weeping.

So large had the crowd become, so profuse did their cursing rise, the prayers barely rose above the racket. Not once did those marching behind her make to pass. Their sympathetic, almost respectful, attitude toward her was antithetical to the epitaphs shouted at Orfeo. Already she had become the grieving widow; but was it a role they would always allow her to claim?

The assemblage turned east, following the cart, onto the Via del Corso, the road passing straight by the Pazzi enclave. But it did not pass it by; it stopped before it.

Once more, men of the Eight climbed upon the wagon. Two held Orfeo, while the other lifted his nightshirt and, without preamble, castrated him.

While those in the near crowd moaned and wailed, Viviana spun from the gruesome sight. For a brief moment, she knew fear, not for Orfeo, but for her own empty heart.

Frenetic gaze flitting about, snippets of the unreal becoming real, she caught sight of Fiammetta.

Her oldest friend stood near the corner, in the archway of her courtyard, her dark eyes latched upon Viviana. A flicker of acknowledgment brightened her gaze, but she did nothing. She made not one sign of recognition; she did not step out to join the group.

Viviana gagged on bitterness. As the procession once more began to move, Viviana offered her friend no more than what she had received—an empty glare. Another irrevocable change came calling.

The death march continued past the Gate of the Cross, to the gallows and the chapel and cemetery, all under the purview of the Black.

The adjoining barracks of soldiers emptied out and Viviana's greatest fear came to light. Her sons stepped out with their fellow militia. She saw the dawning of dumbfounded comprehension cross their beautiful faces, though they held their soldiers' staid pose.

"Rudolfo! Marcello!" She screamed their names. "Do nothing,

I beg you."

More than anything, she feared they would try to undo what she had done, feared they would put their own lives in jeopardy to save their father.

They moved not an inch, save to turn their faces to the crowd, find hers among it, and offer her their love through the almost imperceptible softening of their gaze. On their faces, she saw what she felt in her heart. The time for righteous justice had come at last.

The decimated Orfeo was barely conscious. As the Company of the Black led the condemned man up the stairs of the gallows, as they carried him to the rope of destiny, they completed their litany:

> *My soul, come to the ends of the earth*
> *Cries out for your Divine help, so*
> *That you may put it among the blessed.*

Orfeo's head already hung limply in the noose set about his neck. With these last words spoken, one man pushed the lever. The floor dropped out from under Orfeo, his body dropped into the hole. His neck snapped with a crack at the end of the rope.

• • •

The crowd cheered and, as quickly as it had formed, it dispersed. The sight of an executed man no longer held the novelty it had a few weeks ago. They streamed away, swollen with bored contentment.

Viviana's friends and companions held her as they too walked away. She looked up to her sons, mouthing her love for them silently. They returned the sentiments with the barely appreciable dip of their chins their duty allowed.

She turned back away. Though it was still morning, she was exhausted and, knowing she held still the hearts of her sons, Viviana longed for nothing more than her bed. Only one thought did she have the strength to hold onto, *the beast forever stalking me is dead. I live free.*

Chapter Twenty-Nine

"Freedom once born is life's true gift."

She stood deathly still in the soundless courtyard.

Immediately upon their return to the house on the Via Porto Rosso, Viviana sent Jemma and Nunzio to their rest, though they tried to stay. She shushed them away instead, longing for solitude.

Yet now surrounded by it, she knew not what to do. But only for a moment.

Viviana rushed up the stairs, into her sitting room, and pulled out her chest of art supplies and sketches. She dragged it not only out of its hiding place but into the master bedchamber, where she was now master.

She stood in the room, but found no peace within these walls. Not yet. Her breath heaved. Her nostrils flared. Even now, the memory so fresh with the torture and death of her tormentor, the fear returned just entering the room.

Viviana stared at the bed. As in most households of similar stature, it was the grandest piece of furniture in the house. The two mattresses, the four bolsters, the richly carved wood frame, the canopy that had enclosed around her, imprisoning her. Running to the bed, she ripped at the canopy and curtain with clawed hands.

The linens were her next victims. Big and heavy though they were, she yanked them from the mattress, carried them in a bunch to the window, opened it, and tossed them out. Viviana laughed as the street urchins pounced on the expensive fabrics.

"Take them," she yelled down. "They are yours. I have no more need of them."

Next came his clothes. From out of the *guardaroba* she took them and carried them into the Great Room. Back and forth she went until a pile as tall as she grew in the middle of the room.

"Nunzio!" she cried out to the man who was not there. "Take these to whatever orphanage or monastery would have need of them most."

Rushing back into her sitting room, she threw herself upon the floor and, breaking fingernails, she pulled up two slats of floorboards. From beneath, she pulled out the collapsed easel. Viviana stumbled but did not fall as she strode into the bedchamber, unfurled the easel, and with a hard, resilient crash, planted it firmly before the south facing window of the room, that which let in the most light.

Laughing like a child on a Christmas morn, Viviana pulled out her brushes and paints, her palette, quills, and silverpoints. With particular placement, she set them about the room, a room now not only where she slept, but her own private *studiolo*, one she held dear with the reverence of a chapel.

She should paint this moment; Viviana knew she *had* to paint this moment.

Pulling the full-length looking glass beside her, she found her subject.

Chapter Thirty

"We do not always cherish freedom till it is denied."

The crash sounded just the same. Did she dream it?

Viviana jolted up in bed, just as she had almost a week ago. It was the same gray light of a dawn yet realized greeting her. She tipped her head, listening.

Since the return of the painting, the nights had once more become preternaturally silent, broken only by sudden, hideous cries as another home was assaulted, as another man was dragged from his home, dead or alive. People shivered beneath their covers, praying only that their door was not the next door to crash open.

Her sons had not yet returned, though their notes following their father's demise promised they would do so soon. Without a family burial, there was no reason for them to hurry. How glad of it Viviana was.

Another smash, a crack this time, of the wooden barricade put across the yet unfixed door to her home. Viviana rose slowly from her bed. She did not fear intrusion from miscreants.

She knew her time had come.

Viviana dressed quickly in a simple muslin gown, one with a few tiny spatters of paint upon it—all the more appropriate—and awaited them at the top of the stairs, door thrown wide.

When the man of the Eight, the same who had taken her husband, reached the top, she said not a word. Viviana held out her hands for him to bind.

• • •

Without her cries of anguish and protest, few in the neighborhood came out to see, only the one or two who had heard the crashing of the del Marrone door.

"Return to your beds," Viviana called to them, almost serenely. "All will be well."

It was what she had said to Jemma and Nunzio, prohibiting them from attending her, insisting they need not worry, assuring them her fate would be different. How glad she was for the early morning hour; at another time in the day he might have been there, her ever-present guard, he who brought light into her dreams. She could not have borne what his reaction would have been, what he might have done, and what might have happened to him for it.

She knew there was not a shred of evidence against her and there she found the ability to endure what she must. Not a woman had been executed, only banished. Without evidence, they would do no more to her.

They made for the Palazzo della Signoria. What she saw as they approached solidified Viviana's resolute notions of what lay ahead.

The large door stood closed. Neither the Gonfaloniere nor *Il Magnifico* stood waiting to condemn her. Instead, she and her guards reached it as quietly and calmly as if they strolled together on a night of courtship—the soldiers manning the doors opened them with equal composure.

Viviana could not help herself. She knew she was under arrest, knew too she would be questioned—possibly tortured—but she lost her thoughts to the beauty of her government's palace and the breathtaking art hanging upon its walls. She strained backwards to look into the Grand Hall and other rooms, but she was denied. Her guard tugged her along with a shake of his head. Viviana knew she perplexed him, but she cared not.

They spiraled ever higher. She slowed her pace once more, gazing at the Sala dei Gigli, for there, in the Room of the Lilies, was Donatello's bronze statue of Judith and Holofernes. They passed this room and made for the narrow and dusty stairwell just beyond it, one so slim, her guardsman pushed her ahead, for they could not fit side by side. There was only one place these stairs could take her, to the *Alberghettino*, the small prison cell within the bulging portion of the tower, a prison cell given its ironic name, the little hotel, when Cosimo the Elder, Lorenzo's grandfather, was incarcerated within its walls preceding his short exile.

By the rope binding her hands, her guard tossed her in, cut them loose, and stalked away, closing the door behind him.

Viviana stood within the vast space, empty save for a cot, a table, and a single chair.

Rubbing her raw wrists, she sat upon the cot.

"If it was good enough for the great Cosimo, 'tis certainly fine enough for me."

With this righteous declaration, Viviana lay back. Within seconds, she fell back to sleep.

• • •

"Rouse yourself, madonna, there is someone here to see you."

Viviana jerked awake. The men standing on the threshold were no more than silhouettes. She rubbed her eyes, chasing sleep away. There was the man she had expected to see all along, but he was not alone.

On each side of the tall, thin Gonfaloniere were two members of the Eight, both well-seasoned, faces as hard as she presumed their hearts to be.

So be it, Viviana thought for a second time and braced herself. She knew now what she could withstand, more than she would ever have imagined.

"Signora del Marrone," the Gonfaloniere entered and held out a hand, taking one of hers, surprising her as he bowed over it. She did her best to curtsey though her legs trembled and her hand in his shook. "I have some questions for you."

With a tick of his head, they brought the governor a chair and the two took a seat across the small table from each other.

"I hope I have answers which will please," Viviana croaked a response.

"Get the signora some water, if you please," the Gonfaloniere asked and another soldier, posted outside the door, rushed off to his task, returning just as quickly.

Viviana drank almost all of it in one gulp, grateful for the tincture of wine cleansing it and giving her strength at the same time.

"Better?" Cesare Petrucci asked.

"*Sì*, better."

"Tell me, how long was your husband involved with the Pazzis?"

Gonfaloniere Petrucci did his job well, dropping the incriminating question on the table between them before she had barely answered his polite one, hoping to jostle her to the truth, no doubt.

"I had no idea he was involved with the Pazzis, signore."

"Come, madonna, surely a wife knows her husband's secrets," Petrucci pressed.

"I tell you true, I have no knowledge of my husband's involvement with the Pazzi." Viviana lifted her shoulders and held them there. "I thought he disliked them."

The Gonfaloniere smiled, but it was a smirk saying he would not be cajoled by her charm. He barraged her then, with question after question, but they were in fact the same few questions, each time worded slightly differently in an effort to catch her up, to trap her into pronouncing her own guilt. But he never asked her the proper question, never forced her to answer it.

"And what of your friend, madonna, what of Lapaccia Cavalcanti?"

Her head snapped up, thinking, in her fatigue, he was telling her they had found Lapaccia.

"Lapaccia?" Now it was she who demanded information from him. "Is she here? Is she well?"

Petrucci's mouth formed a tight line as he sniffed out a breath and slunk back in his chair, clearly disappointed. "She is not. I had hoped you could tell me where she is."

Viviana's shoulders slumped. "I cannot for I know not."

The Gonfaloniere sat up quickly, making his move in her lethargy. "Why do you, my lady, sympathize with the Pazzis?"

She didn't know if it was the toil of the interrogation, the insensibility her life had taken on since the tragedy, or the insult to her loyalties. But this question Viviana could not—would not—tolerate. She had seen what they had done, every second of it.

Viviana jumped up, knocking her chair to the floor, grabbed the sides of the small table, and thrust her face within inches of the Gonfaloniere's, "How dare you? I am a Medicean. Always."

The guard inside the door took a step, brought his hand back, and brought the back of it crashing against Viviana's jaw, a blow so hard it dropped her to the dusty floor like a stone.

"My husband hits me harder than you." Derision bristled from her, struck and humiliated though she may be.

The Gonfaloniere stopped before her. She saw upon his face something she had not seen in the hours he had been questioning her. Belief.

He reached a hand out and she took it.

Cesare Petrucci lifted her gently and placed her equally so on the cot.

"Bring Signora del Mar—"

"Viviana, please," she asked of him, not bearing to be called by that name.

One side of Cesare's mouth twitched. "Please bring Mona Viviana something to eat," the Gonfaloniere ordered. To her, he said, "I take my leave of you, madonna."

"Gonfaloniere?" she caught him up, for the first time her voice soft and pleading. "If you are to execute me, do not let my sons watch. They have served the Republic and the Medici well. Please, do not let them see."

Cesare Petrucci exhaled. "I take my leave of you."

With a curt bow, the governor did, leaving Viviana to wonder what would become of her.

• • •

She paced the room for the length of the day, light creeping into her cell through the cracks in the roughly hewn door. Viviana walked and walked and walked some more, certain if she had walked a straight line, she would have reached Rome. She had played her part well, given the Gonfaloniere nothing to persecute her for, though she knew that meant nothing in these days.

"I am not yet ready to die." As she said the words to the cold stone walls around her, Viviana thought of the children of her children she had yet to hold in her arms, the creations she had yet to paint, love she had yet to know.

Only then, when no light save that of the single candle illuminated the room, when fear brought her low, did she lay her body on the cot, did she dare close her eyes squeezing out the tears, uncertain if they would open on another dawn.

They did not.

A gentle hand upon her shoulder waggled Viviana awake. It was the pitch of the night. He knelt by her rough bed. In the glow of the candle behind him, his hair glowed more wheaten than coppery gold, and she could barely see the features of his face, but she knew him.

"Leonardo?" It was a perplexed whisper; Viviana wondered if she dreamed his presence.

"Mona Viviana, 'tis I, indeed."

There it was; the smooth, rich timbre of the voice she had listened to for hours as he tutored her from an adequate painter to a fine one.

She sat up slowly, enervation still a heavy cloak upon her shoulders. "It *is* you, Leonardo. Whatever are you doing here?"

"I have come to take you home, madonna." Declaration made, he stood up and to the side. In doing so, he uncovered yet another figure in the threshold of the small cell, the silhouette of the Gonfaloniere. "*Il Magnifico* himself has honored you with clemency. He pledges you friendship in exchange for your loyalty."

Still in the stupor of somnolence, Viviana could barely

understand the incomprehensible, let alone believe it. She did so, though not without a stinging pinch of guilt, for she would save Lapaccia if she could, whatever her friend had done and to whom.

"We have no more need of your presence, Mona Viviana," Cesare Petrucci told her. With his next words, his tone dropped precipitously. "However, I must warn you, madonna, if we find you cavort with criminals, not even the favored da Vinci will be able to help you."

"If," the governor continued, "you should have the ear of someone the government cares to speak with, and you inveigle this person to come speak with us, of their own accord, then perhaps both your lives could be forever spared."

Viviana nodded. There was little more to hear, nothing more to say.

Leonardo held her crooked arm by the elbow and the hand as he escorted her from the room. Cesare Petrucci stepped aside to allow them leave, but Viviana stopped.

Placing a hand upon the Gonfaloniere's arm, she rose up on tiptoe and kissed his cheek, as lightly as the gentlest passing breeze. "*Mille grazie,* signore."

• • •

Leonardo led her in the strangest path from the Palazzo della Signoria to her home on the Via Porto Rosso. He headed south first, then west on the Borgo S.S. Apostoli.

Viviana's step hesitated, lips parting on the surprise of it. She continued on but not without a smile and a shake of her head. "I no longer know the world we live in, my friend."

"Nor I," Leonardo chuckled.

"But…but I would try to paint it. I hope I may."

"You have the talent for it."

"It is all I have," she confessed. "My sons, my art, and our group…they are all I have."

"What you did, madonna…" Leonardo's voice trailed off with

a distinct chime of admiration, "…you have much more in you than even you know."

Viviana thought hard upon his words; she knew she had begun to believe. From an open window of one of the many houses and palazzos they passed, the murmurs of slow, sensual lovemaking fluttered down, voices low and tender, furniture creaking, answered by delighted giggles filled with pleasure.

"I hope I may always call you friend," she teased, "even when you have become one of the most famous artists of all the lands."

Leonardo sniffed skeptically.

"Do not scoff," Viviana chided him. "You are a master, and I think you know it. All the world will be falling at your feet soon enough."

"Do not wish it upon me, my lady," he replied with a note of dark intensity.

"There will be many who will admire you, men and women," Viviana continued, but she did so as if to brace him for what she saw ahead, as he braced her, turning north on the Via Tornabuoni, but two blocks from her home. "Many, like Isabetta."

"She loves me for my beauty, naught more," Leonardo said bitterly. "Nor is she the first."

"We all love beauty."

"She does not accept who I really am."

Viviana shook her head. "Isabetta loves and accepts you for exactly who you are. What she cannot accept is that she cannot have you."

They turned the corner onto the Via Porto Rosso and Viviana tripped, her strength abandoning her even as she would rush ahead at the sight of her door and her home.

"Almost now, almost," Leonardo said, an arm firmly at her waist as she hurried forward.

The door opened, even as they were steps away.

"*O Dio, grazie, Dio mio,*" Viviana cried her thanks to God as the two young men rushed out the door, as she lunged out of Leonardo's arms and into those of her sons.

She covered their bristly faces with kisses as they held her tightly, leading led her to the door.

But she stopped at the threshold, turned, and rushed back to her savior.

Viviana threw her arms about Leonardo. And though the top of her head reached his chin, she squeezed him with all the might she had left, cheek pressed against his chest as his arms came around her back. She pulled back, rose on tiptoes, and kissed him on his full soft lips, delighted by the stunned smile she left upon them.

• • •

"Sleep deeply and worry free, *madre mia*," Marcello told her. "We'll be here when you awake."

"We will be here for a few days. We will take care of you," Rudolfo assured her.

Viviana heard them through the buzz of exhaustion, as she watched them tiptoe from her room through the slits in her eyes.

As the door closed behind them, she thanked whatever greatness had blessed her with such sons. She wondered and worried, as her mind grew more and more muddled with the onset of sleep, would she tell them the truth...should she?

These were not her last thoughts. Her last thoughts of the night she saved for Lapaccia. Gonfaloniere Petrucci had made the situation clear and simple: if the government found Lapaccia, Lapaccia may be killed; if Viviana found Lapaccia and did nothing, they could both be killed. The answer to it all lay with Lapaccia, her knowledge and the reason for her actions. The question followed Viviana into the deepest of sleep...

How could she save them both?

Chapter Thirty-One

"To some, make a forever farewell and good riddance too."

The unseasonable chill was a pall upon the late spring day; it wrapped itself about the city in the guise of a mist rising up and spreading over them from the Arno, smudging the bright city as if rubbed with charcoal.

Isabetta and Mattea had taken to spending more and more time together; the sharing of trauma will either bind souls or thrust them apart forever. Mattea rarely took to the streets without Isabetta by her side these days, and then she would only do so if she were to meet him, an occurrence far more rare now than ever before.

"I spent yesterday morn at the studio," Mattea told her companion as they walked toward the *Mercato*.

Isabetta pulled back, a bird with feathers ruffled. "You did? Why did you not come and get me?"

Mattea shrugged; she could not tell the truth of it, that she had been looking for some sign, some word, of him, but what she said was not far from it. "I just needed some time to sit by myself. It has become so much more, since—"

"Since we created our masterpiece," Isabetta finished the sentence without any of the guile holding Mattea's tongue.

"Yes, it's true," Mattea giggled, "I believe it of myself more. Does that make sense?"

"It makes perfect sense," Isabetta replied. "When you are told your whole life you cannot do something, you will, of course, believe it, whether it's true or not."

Isabetta stopped their stroll along the Lungarno. "But when you do something, with your mind, your own hands, that contradicts this belief, shatters it, then it becomes a truth none can gainsay."

Mattea smiled, nodding as she inhaled deeply of the pungent, fresh scent of the river, the air of the new world she had come to inhabit. "I so look forward to our next meeting. It is but two days hence. Viviana should be recovered by then."

"I believe she will." They continued east, heading for the Ponte Vecchio, where they would turn northward, into the city.

"Sometimes I wonder if anyone—what is that?" Mattea stopped mid-sentence. "What is that ruckus?"

Isabetta heard it too then, her eyes rolling heavenward. Who knew what to expect in these days replete with aberrations?

It was a crowd, yet another, but this time a cheering one, though that did not guarantee anything resembling gaiety. The crowds had become as bloodthirsty as their government.

The two young women allowed the commotion to direct their sight and suddenly they took note of the throng gathering at the river's edge, far down the end of the straight lane, near the last bridge to cross the Arno.

"Were they there before?" Isabetta asked.

Mattea shrugged her shoulders and shook her head. Her mind had been so full of their words, so thick with the paint she had plied on her latest work, she had seen nothing around them.

"Come," Isabetta roused her, pulling her along.

Caught up in the tangle of converging citizenry, the slim women somehow finagled their way closer to the river's edge, where the voices and the people charged. Squeezing between some large men, hands blackened from layers of dye, the friends saw the cause of congestion.

At the very shore of the river, where water met bank, a gaggle of young *giovani*, long sticks in hand, fished, but it was nothing edible they caught.

"Is it...?" Isabetta began.

"Oh dear, no, it cannot be," Mattea mumbled.

But as the fiendish boys pulled the body out of the water, there was no denying its identity, even though its flesh was more than half decomposed and missing. Once more the presence of Jacopo de' Pazzi made itself known in the city of Florence.

"Wherever did *he* come from?" Isabetta spat.

"They found him snagged there," one of the men beside her answered, pointing to a branch, more like half a tree, which had fallen into the river. "They've been trying to pull him out for some time now."

Mattea's pale blue eyes grew wide. "Why?"

The man popped his shoulders up then down. "Why not?"

Though both girls wanted nothing more than to run in the opposite direction, neither found their feet accommodating. They watched as the *giovani* untangled the remains from the river, pieces of flesh rippling off it with an odd grace in the weightlessness of the water.

The gang dislodged the body and yanked it onshore, standing round it, talking animatedly, gesticulating wildly.

Though Mattea and Isabetta could not hear their words, neither doubted that whatever these rapscallions decided, it would not be pleasant.

As the gang rushed away, their grisly prize rolled into a snatched sheet dragged behind them, the thick crowd followed.

"I cannot..." Mattea muttered.

"Nor can I."

There they stood, ballasts against an ill wind, trying hard not to listen to the sounds of humans behaving inhumanly. Yet all too soon they returned.

This time, when the *giovani* dumped the body once more in the Arno, the boys followed it, from each side of the river. With the long sticks they had used to haul the body out, they now used to keep the body in, pushing it offshore should it draw near the bank, as the man's lifeless tentacles reached out to the river grass as if to grasp it and pull itself out. Their game brought them, and the crowd, to where the river widened, to its vomiting mouth with its strong current.

Cries of "farewell" and "never return" launched the body into the strong pull of the water that would carry it toward Pisa and out to the sea.

"Though I may, someday, paint this, today I would see no more," Mattea said, pulling Isabetta away.

Chapter Thirty-Two

"A new world can only be built on common ground."

Marcello shook his head of dark curls. "You dreamed it, surely. It is far too fanciful a tale to be true."

Viviana chastised with a shake of a finger. "You question your mother's veracity?"

"It is just…I…you…" her son blundered.

"I know, my dear," she chuckled. "I would not believe it did it not happen to me."

She threw back a chalice, taking a deep, long chug, spying the faces of her boys over the rim of the goblet—the surprised grins, the brows raised in admiration. No doubt they thought only they had the knack for tossing back spirits. "The Medici are surprisingly amiable to me now. I believe there is great forgiveness and friendship to be had there. It will help us all I think." Viviana saw no reason to cite the conditions of such an alliance.

"But how? How did you survive?" Rodolfo probed, not disbelieving, only in disbelief. "They are killing everyone, even for reasons less tangible than this noodle."

Swirling the thick and darkly red Valpolicella in her hand, Viviana answered without looking up. "With the help of Leonardo da Vinci."

"Da Vinci?" Rudolfo's voice squeaked. "The…artist?"

Viviana heard the stumble for what it was. Rudolfo's tongue tripped on the resounding rumors swirling about her new friend, but he would never speak them. She had taught them better, taught them the true meaning of acceptance and love, against whatever example their father had shown them.

"*Sì*, the artist." Viviana smiled into the green-tinted brown eyes of her sons. She had told them so much already, was the rest truly worth keeping a secret?

• • •

"Our mother, a *dilettare*." Marcello dropped back in his chair, head as full as his belly. "I knew of your appreciation for art, but never your talent."

Viviana smiled into her cup, how it had loosened her tongue and given her strength, the daring to tell her sons of her secret life as an artist and of the group itself, to bring them to her room and show them her work, her completed self-portrait begun on the night she became a free woman. She would need far greater fortitude for the rest, to tell the entire story, which she must. But for now, she steeped herself in the magic of this moment.

"Whatever prompted you to do such a thing?" Rudolfo leaned forward, pouring himself more wine.

"It all began when I received my deceased cousin's belongings," Viviana told them, told them of Caterina's journals, treatises, and drawings, and what had happened when she shared them with the other women. "But it was more," she grew thoughtful, the witness she was to her own life dredging the deepest parts of it. "My husband is…was…a bastard. You boys grew up. I needed something. A greater purpose. Caterina showed me mine."

Viviana heard an edge of despair in her voice. She laughed it away. "At least until one of you hurry up and bless me with a grandchild."

Marcello smirked, "From what I hear, Rudolfo is working on it all the time."

"Hold your tongue, brother," the younger man chided, but the mauve stain working up his cheeks snatched away any true objections attempted. He gave up the ghost. With a dashing flick of his brows and a devilish half smile, her youngest told Viviana all she needed to know of his sexual exploits. It was all too much for the tipsy trio. Their laughter rang out well and loud.

Viviana sat back in her chair, in relief as much as relaxation. The building was the same, with the same room, the same furniture, yet it was a new place, a place it had never been. With Orfeo's death, it had become a home, a haven. Closing her eyes for an instant, the music of her sons' voices—the words indistinct as they continued to stuff cheese and tortes into their mouths, a lifetime of such breathtaking moments burst in her mind, moments that would be lived here in this, her home, with her sons, and their wives and their children. Such a future was worth the risk and the pain, and even the punishment that may yet await her in eternity.

"Will you be able to keep the house?" Marcello asked.

"I believe I will sell your father's business, with your permission. Or rather, *you* will, *sì?* I have no interest in fabrics, except to wear them. Between such proceeds and the income we still receive from my family's vineyards—the sale of the wine and the rents—there should be more than enough to cover the taxes and the upkeep."

"The warehouse and offices would make a fine spice shop," Rudolfo commented to Marcello.

"We'll see," his brother replied.

Viviana sighed with thick contentment. Though smaller by one, her family had never felt more complete. And yet, it would not be free of its ghosts until the whole story was told. She could only pray it would survive.

"There is one more thing I must tell you." Even as she spoke, her voice lost all of its frivolity, her face darkened with fear, not at what she had done, but at what they would think of her.

• • •

Each young man sat slumped in his chair, one with hands fisted in his lap, the other hanging on to the edge of the table as if it were the only thing keeping him from falling off the edge of the world. For Viviana, it was a moment seeming to last a lifetime, until she could bear it no longer.

"One of you say something, please." It was a whispered plea, but it brought results.

Marcello stood slowly, chair legs squelching against stone as his legs pushed it backward. He took two steps and stood over her; never would she have thought her own son could appear so foreboding. Bending in half, Marcello wrapped his long arms about her neck and rested his head on her shoulder, much as he did as a small child.

"Justice finds the strangest of paths," he whispered, his breath sending wisps of her chestnut hair floating in the air, "but it always finds its way."

Viviana closed her eyes and leaned her head against his, a sob of relief caught in her throat. She reached across the table toward Rudolfo.

The young man stared at the outstretched hand, at her blue eyes, violet with the redness of tears about them.

He stood, and walked away.

"Rudolfo!" Viviana found her voice through her tears, through her fears, but it was for naught. Her son's long strides helped him escape the room, and her, with swiftness.

Even as his heavy footfalls struck the steps down to the street, Viviana turned to Marcello, but in this son's eyes, she saw only her own perplexity.

• • •

For two days, Marcello doted on her, and it brought her a modicum of peace. But Viviana saw his gaze fall to the road below.

"You should take to your bed, mama," Marcello said late on the second night. "You have still not fully recovered from your ordeal. I see it on your skin and in your eyes."

"I cannot sleep."

Marcello stood and shook his head; anger made an appearance on the dear features. He kissed her forehead and retreated to his own room.

Viviana watched as the streets emptied, until only the heavy boots of the Night Watch stepped upon it.

"Mama, mama, I am here."

She heard Rudolfo's voice. With eyes closed, she dozed, dreamed. Until she felt his head in her lap.

Viviana's eyes fluttered open. There he was.

"Oh my boy, my boy," Viviana sobbed, leaning over to envelope him in her embrace. "You have come back to me, my dear son."

"I never left you, not really," Rudolfo's voice cracked with emotion. "I needed to talk. To understand."

Viviana pulled up on his shoulders. "To understand what, *cara?*"

"To understand my—" Rudolfo swallowed, his throat bobbed with the effort, "—to understand my joy at what you had done."

"Your joy?"

Rudolfo nodded fiercely, with the slightest bit of shame. "I had never loved my father as I love you, had never felt anything remotely resembling affection for him." He leaned closer. "There were many times I wished him gone, by whatever means."

Viviana's sigh trembled from her lungs. "He was a cruel and heartless man."

Rudolfo nodded. "I know. I do know. But when I saw him die, when I saw him take his last breath...the *relief.* I thought it sinful to feel this way. And then, when you told us it was you, I was filled with—"

Viviana shook him by his broad shoulders. "With what?"

"Yes, with what?" Marcello stood in the doorway.

Rudolfo lifted his chin and confessed, "Glee. I thought, how perfect for the woman whose life he made such a Hell, to help send him there. And I felt ever more ashamed. But I was wrong. I did nothing wrong. My father chose to be who he was. It was not my doing. He made me see the truth of it."

"Who did, Rudolfo?" Viviana asked, uncertain whether to feel grateful or fearful. "With whom did you speak?"

For the first time since his return, her son smiled. "Father Raffaello."

Viviana barked a laugh. Her son had confessed to one who was a party to the entire affair. Life was but one circle within another.

• • •

"I do not have very much time, but I so longed to see you."

Isabetta sat at Viviana's bedside. Viviana and her sons had talked so late into the night, yet another in which she had found little sleep, she felt little compunction in receiving her friend from the comfort of her bed.

"I was very worried when you failed to join us yesterday." Isabetta continued from the embroidered chair Marcello had placed by the bed.

"I recover still, I fear," Viviana replied.

"Did they injure you?"

Viviana turned her head, displaying the bruise on the side of her mouth, touching it delicately. "It is far less than I have received in the past."

"Why did you never tell us? Why did you never tell one of us?"

Viviana dropped her head back on her shoulders. "At first I thought I could change him. Such nonsense."

Isabetta nodded in silent agreement.

"And then I thought, foolishly, if I told no one, then it wasn't real, it couldn't be true." Viviana took Isabetta's hands in both of hers. "The mind plays tricks to allow the soul to continue. But the darkness had reached my soul and I could allow it no longer."

"What a pair we make. Your husband is dead, and mine is dying."

"And you have kept it a secret as well," Viviana said, a reproach of the tender sort.

Isabetta shrugged a single shoulder. "I stopped loving him long before he became ill, but when he did, the lack of love turned to guilt, a guilt eating away at me like the leeches the physicians use."

They simply squeezed the hands they held, these two women who knew so much of guilt as well as its senselessness.

"It is all the more despicable because of my needs."

Viviana raised her gaze at these words, but the direct look did nothing to hold Isabetta's tongue, a captive at last released.

"They say sexual need is the purview of men, but it is so strong in me, and the lack exacerbates my loneliness."

"It makes it so much harder to bear, does it not?" Viviana replied.

"You too?"

"Oh yes," Viviana nodded vigorously. "Me too. But I thought I was an aberration. I have such fantasies," Viviana continued, "I wonder what it would be like not only to love a man, in a physical way, but to be loved."

"Truly loved," Isabetta said, wistfully.

"Yes, truly loved. I want to know what it feels like to be adored and revered by a man." Viviana proclaimed it as if she wished upon Venus. "My sons love me, I know, but it is not the same. I want a man to love me, not for my family's fortune, my face, or my figure—just for me."

Viviana held her tongue, though she was mightily tempted, aching to put thoughts to words as she was to put fantasies to actions. How Viviana longed to tell Isabetta the rest of it, of the man who haunted her dreams, the burnished gold of his hair, the changing eyes, the touch of his hand still burned her skin. But she couldn't, not yet. Someday, someday for it all—the telling *and* the doing—perhaps.

"They paint us with such perfection," Isabetta mused, "yet their regard rarely comes off the canvas."

Their talked turned then, as it always seemed to, to specific works of particularly beautiful women and the men who painted them, which brought them to a fine and heated discussion of technique and craft. And, suddenly, the sadness turned to pure joy.

Chapter Thirty-Three

"Cracks and fissures appear in the hardest of stones."

The door to the secret studio smashed open as if kicked, thrust open with such force, it hit the interior wall with the boom of God's condemning thunder, the latch bent against the stone it chipped, the hinges screaming as they were pushed beyond their limits.

Fiammetta stood in the threshold, heaving like a rabid animal.

"Damn you, Viviana del Marrone."

Viviana cringed. How happy she had been, but a moment ago, to be back in the studio, to be feeling well and returned to her work. She lowered her silverpoint from the barely marked canvas in a stupor.

"Why? Why do you damn me?"

Fiammetta crossed the room like a marauding army, heedless to a knocked over stool, the clatter and crack of overturned bottles upon a jostled table. She stood inches from her friend, dark eyes black in red-rimmed, swollen skin.

"My husband spent the night in the tower," Fiammetta barked, ignoring the gasps throughout the room. "The same tower you once graced. And it is entirely your fault."

The silverpoint dropped from Viviana's hand. "My fault? Why was it my fault? I said nothing of—"

"It is not what you said," Fiammetta spewed, "but what you did, what you made us all do."

"What I—"

"Orfeo! We condemned Orfeo, now all his acquaintances are in question."

Viviana took a step back, not out of fear but with thought. Orfeo had few men of close ties, few friends, and she had heard of none who had been arrested and questioned. Any time Patrizio spent time with Orfeo was due to the relationship of their wives. Patrizio had, however, spent more than a little time with…

"The Pazzis," the tail end of her thoughts she said aloud. "Patrizio had a far closer relationship with the Pazzis then he ever did with Orfeo. Surely it is this which accounts for the government's action, and nothing else."

"Do not—" Fiammetta began, but it was Isabetta's words putting a stop to them.

"Is he well?" she asked, the only one, including his wife, to speak of Patrizio's welfare. "Is he still in custody?"

Fiammetta rubbed her eyes with fisted knuckles "He was soon released, but feels he is still watched closely."

"Everyone is watched closely," Mattea stated the obvious.

"Especially those with a long time connection to the Pazzi," Viviana would not allow the blame to rest on her shoulders.

The other women rolled their eyes. It was not over.

Fiammetta jammed her chubby arms on her thick hips. "The Pazzi are one of the greatest families of Florence. Their knighthood dates back to the Crusades."

"As do thousands of others." Viviana shook her head with a smile that could be called many things, but never pleasant. "The Crusades, when men killed other men in the name of their God."

"You cannot say the same for the obscure, upstart Medici." Fiammetta's thin upper lip curled unbecomingly.

"True," Viviana sniffed righteously, "they worked for their power and their fortune."

"By using unsavory—"

"They played the game, Fiammetta, they did not invent it." Viviana tossed back her head in frustration. "They played the game as the Pazzis did, with the Pope and the taxes and their banks. You know it, and if you do not, do not suddenly be so eager to show your stupidity or your narrow-mindedness."

Fiammetta's mouth dropped open. Never had anyone dared argue with her with such impudence. It seemed to have stifled her. But no. "The Medici have strong armed this city for the last two hundred years. Marriages. Businesses. They control it all. Is it any wonder they made so many enemies?"

"Civilized people do not kill in response. Rise up, yes. Use the same system to try to gain control, yes. Cold-blooded, brutal murder under the eyes of God?" Viviana shook her head, her skin taking on a green pallor of one pestered with illness. "Only evil itself would perpetuate such a thing."

"Come, Fiammetta, come sit. Have some wine." Natasia led the still irate woman away to her worktable, sat her upon a stool, and fetched a full goblet. Viviana caught Isabetta's eye, seeing the same question as the one bouncing about in her mind as they watched Natasia pacify and soothe.

Fiammetta drank, in silence. It seemed as if the group came to a rest.

"Did you attend d'Este's fête, Fiammetta?" Mattea asked as if to change the subject, or was it to see if this woman who held others so accountable was as prodigious with her own responsibilities. "Were you able to find out anything about Lapaccia?"

"Yes, to both," Fiammetta replied matter-of-factly. "The government no longer believes Lapaccia stole the painting but they do believe she may have taken something or she is somehow involved. They search for her still. As they see it, only the guilty run."

"Surely Andreano's—" Mattea swallowed and started again, "surely her son's help protecting the Medici should prove something of their loyalties?"

Fiammetta nodded. "Yes, of course it does, but the widow of a knight, of a chivalric knight, does not just disappear without reason."

It was the truth that had started them on this fraught-filled course.

"I fear I must tell you all something." Natasia glanced at the entrance, the battered door still open a crack. "We must be quicker. We must look faster. I shouldn't tell you; my brother should not have told me," Natasia lowered her voice to a whisper should the priest be within hearing, "but Lapaccia spoke to him just before she disappeared. She spoke of her ill health, of it growing worse. She spoke of her final requests."

They all knew of Lapaccia's condition; the attacks of the lungs had plagued her all her life, what some called *anemos* or *asma*. More than one had mixed the concoction of herbs and heated them upon the hot bricks for her.

"What if she cannot get her herbal treatments where she is?" Mattea spoke aloud their shared fear.

Isabetta reached out and took Mattea's hand. "We will find out as much as we can tonight," she said, explaining to the other women about the salon and the man who may have information of worth to them.

"Natasia and I will go to her home once more," Fiammetta volunteered for them both. "We will demand entry and do a search. Perhaps there is something in her home which will give us a clue to her whereabouts."

The women began to talk at once, strength of purpose infusing them, and for a time they chatted and worked, and chatted of their work, and that of Botticelli and his giant mural, conversations layered upon others, overlapping, mingled with amusements, much in the way it had been before, yet tinged with something, something off-color, something it had never been.

As the bells of *None* rang out, they departed as they always had, though not a one felt the same as when they had arrived.

Chapter Thirty-Four

"True capability is only learned when tested."

"I look the fool," Mattea fiddled with the layers and layers of fabric heaped upon her body. The blue and gold brocade gown brought out the highlights in her fair hair and the sparkle of her azure eyes. The same seed pearls trimming every edge of her overgown hung from her ears, and took strategic spots upon her grand coiffure of twisted and piled braids.

All of this the girl could accept, grateful to Isabetta for finding such an ensemble for her and helping her into it, though she felt weighed down by a net full of stones. In the reflective glass's gaze, however, the face looking back at her, one adorned by cosmetics for the first time in its life, gave her pause. How surprised she was by the glow upon her cheeks, how they made her blue eyes look so much bluer. How perplexing it was to see her lips reddened; how much fuller they appeared.

"I cannot be seen in public like this." Mattea shivered at the thought.

Isabetta chuckled, even more resplendently attired than her friend, wearing the one gown she had saved from better days, the one that reminded her most of those happier times. "And *you* shall not, for no one would recognize you. You are an amazing beauty, Mattea. You truly are."

Mattea dipped her chin, color rising with a peach blush.

"Speaking of which," Isabetta chirped, "What shall I call you tonight? Whom do you wish to be?"

It was an interesting question. Would Mattea ever wish to be someone else? There were many reasons why she would, many things—and people—that could be hers if she were. She also knew that she could create with her hands what few others were able to. Would the benefits be worthy enough to deny her talent?

She shook her head. All this fuss brought her thoughts in directions she need not go.

"I shall be Adelina. Adelina della Compagni."

Isabetta tossed back her head and laughed. "For one so quiet, you have the most interesting sense of humor."

"I do, don't I?" Mattea smiled, enjoying Isabetta's amusement, for the name she had chosen meant nothing if not "the little noblewomen of the company."

"And who are you this evening?" Mattea asked.

But Isabetta only waggled her pale brows at her fellow adventurer, and lowered the deep maroon veil further over her face, covering it completely, "Never mind about that now, you shall see."

Mattea squinted one eye at her. "What have you plan—"

"Put your linen in your hidden pocket, there," Isabetta said, tossing off her prodding and showing Mattea the hidden pouch of her gown where ladies tucked a perfume scented strip of cloth. Far too often, in homes both grand and not, odors abounded and overwhelmed and such scented cloths could keep a lady from swooning.

Mattea knew all about such linens and such hidden pockets. What Isabetta did not know of were the other hidden items she carried on her person. If all went well tonight, she would never have the need to.

• • •

They could barely make their way through the crowd bunched at the door. The *maggiore domo*, overdressed and over impressed with himself, took each name as they entered and took his time in perusing each guest as they entered.

"He will not know us," Mattea hissed nervously as they drew nearer and nearer to the stout, balding man. "He will not allow us entry."

Isabetta patted her arm and smiled oh-so-pompously. "Have no care, I will make it right."

"How?"

"And remember," Isabetta evaded Mattea's question, "you are Adelina della Compagni, you are allowed entrance everywhere."

The couple before them moved on, and they stepped before the self-important manservant.

"Names?" He asked, or was it a rude demand?

Isabetta raised her chin and looked down her pert nose at him, the details of which were greatly cloaked by the heavy dark veil upon her face.

"I am Natasia Soderini and this is my cousin, Adelina della Compagni, daughter of the duke of Albenga."

"Erk!" Mattea squawked, then coughed.

"Do you need some wine, cousin?" 'Natasia' asked with insouciant concern, already moving off and away. "We are done here, are we not?" This to the *maggiore domo*, who simply nodded his head, having no chance for a real reply as Isabetta turned her back to him, as nobles were wont to do.

"Come, *cara mia*, I see a wonderful table." Isabetta feigned the rolled speech of a noblewoman so well, producing a nervous twitter from Mattea.

"You are a daring woman, aren't you?" Mattea asked, composing herself, especially now that they had made it past the discerning eye of the doorman and were lost in the horde of people filling the small *apartemente*.

Mattea's information proved quite correct; this was a salon of great popularity, regardless of the condition of their city. The two women had barely made their way past the threshold, let alone to and through the receiving line. When they did, they were not the least disappointed in their host.

He was a very tall man, and fair, a physique speaking strongly of his northern roots. This was no born and bred Florentine. He resembled more the stories Mattea had read of the Goths and Visigoths who had long ago, and so very often, invaded the peninsula.

The Marchese Ranieri del Monte Pesaro wore his fair hair shorter than did Florentines, its soft blond curls winding themselves around his ears and his chin and down his forehead, almost into his startling blue eyes. The thick and upward curling mustache and pointed chin beard did little to disguise his full-lipped mouth.

They finally made their way before him, curtsying deeply, but it was Isabetta who was made speechless by his beauty.

"We are so very grateful for your kind invitation, Marchese." Mattea dipped once more as she made their introductions, almost tripping on her new name.

"It is I who am grateful to have such beautiful women call upon me." The Marchese took her hand and leaned over it, brushing his lips softly across her skin.

"You have the eyes of a northerner, Signorina della Compagni." Her hand still in his, he took a step closer. "May I call you Adelina? It is such a beautiful name."

Mattea smiled, her eyes slanted with amused censure. Though she may not wear such finery or live in such elegance, she had met more than her fair share of rogues. She could identify one as quickly and as sharply as the name of the pigments she used in her work. If this cad found her attractive, if he would ply her with his charms, she would do the same, to her own end.

"It is even more lovely when spoken by your lips," "Adelina" said, for Mattea threw herself headlong into the role, picturing her lover as she did so, the very thought of him bringing a bloom to her innate sensuality. "And may I be so bold as to call you Ranieri?"

"I would be heartbroken did you not."

"Ranieri!" The call came from the very center of the room, where there sat another dashing man, dark and not as tall, most likely a Florentine, but one neither woman knew. "Come, all is ready for our game."

Ranieri made a tick with tongue and teeth. "Oh dear, I had forgotten I promised Nestore a game of *tricche-trach*." He stood in silent contemplation. "You must sit beside me, both of you. You will be my good luck."

With long strides, the man stomped to the middle of the room, the striped board on the small table set between two chairs, Nestore already seated upon one. Instead of taking his seat, Ranieri took the chair and moved it out of the way. Shooing three young fellows, clearly already in their cups, off their perch on the settee to one side of the table, he pulled the small sofa into place where the chair had been.

"Come," he proclaimed, taking the women by the arm, he sat one on each side, and shimmied his wide, muscular form between them.

Comfortably settled, ever pleased and smiling at his beauties, Ranieri turned to his opponent. "Very well then, Nestore, try your best."

The game began, the movement of the two colored chips across the board of patterned squares, each player doing their best to get their pieces off first while blocking the other from doing so.

It was time for Mattea to begin her game as well. Like *tricche-trach*, one needed to be subtle and not reveal one's plan.

"You have chosen a difficult time to see the sights of Florence, I fear," Mattea said with sympathetic innocence as she sipped the wine, then sipped again, having never tasted one finer.

"I am not here for pleasure," Ranieri turned a look of longing upon her, "more's the pity."

Mattea batted her eyes, ignoring the rolling of Isabetta's. "You are not?"

"No, indeed. I have been invited, my dear, by both the Duke of Urbino and your *Il Magnifico*." He made a move as he spoke, of one piece only, but of such skill it blocked most equally skillful responses. "It would seem both look for my military advice."

Mattea allowed the arm he had moved to the back of the settee behind her to remain. "Are we coming to that?"

The Marchese's studied gaze lifted from the board in favor of her face, the salacious stare now a thoughtful gaze. "I believe it will, yes."

Mattea had been tutored about this man. A renowned Venetian *condottiere*, Ranieri del Monte Pesaro, his military acumen had won him his title as well as the respect of government leaders far and wide. His two books on the subject were forever in demand, as was he, by men for his expertise on the battlefield, by women for his equal proficiency in the bedchamber. Ranieri filled both roles happily and often. Such a serious declaration as the one just made could not be taken lightly or forgotten.

But something in his words did not make sense to Mattea, and presented her with the perfect opportunity, one taken with all honesty.

"I am surprised to hear *Il Magnifico* wishes to go to war," she said with as much nonchalance as she could muster. "I had thought he feasted on the traitors in our own midst to the exclusion of everything else."

Ranieri nodded, rolling the tip of his pointed beard in his long fingers as he studied the board. "This is true. And for that, he has brought me here to advise him as well."

Mattea cheered along with those around them as the marchese made a skillful move in reply. "I am sure you do so with great astuteness."

"Indeed I have. They search high and low for the miscreants yet they have not searched the convents and monasteries."

He shook his head pitifully as he made his next move on the board.

Mattea could barely breathe.

"It is as plain as can be. This was an attack made on sacred ground, by clerics," he leaned toward her, lowering his voice. "Clearly there are entanglements with ecclesiastics at all levels. The religious houses should have been the first place to look."

Mattea nodded, stunned, astounded by the sagacity. "Yes, they should have searched there first, of course." Her "they" meant the guild.

As Ranieri leaned over to make another move, Mattea caught sight of Isabetta's face. Her eyes bulged, and she flashed them, repeatedly, toward the door, mouthing, "go," silently to Mattea.

It would make their very presence questionable were they to rush away. Mattea turned the conversation with the marchese to his journey to their city, to niggle him with more questions of the same nature, may appear dubious. It mattered not, she believed he had told her all he knew that was helpful.

The high-pitched note of the *Vespruccio* in the church of San Felice gave out one toll, a warning that Vespers, and therefore the new curfew, was but a short time away.

Isabetta jumped up as if poked. "We must take our leave, Adelina. We would not wish to be caught out past curfew."

Ranieri jumped up, leering down with pure lewd intent. "You are not going, my dear?" Leaning closer, he tickled her ear with his soft facial hair. "I thought perhaps we could deny curfew its power together."

She knew what he meant. For one second, as every part of her body tingled with the thought of it, Mattea almost complied, almost.

Mattea reached up and touched this handsome man's cheek; she would not hurt him with her denial. Standing on tiptoes, she gave whisper to her truth, "Would that I could, dear man." She lowered herself with a half-smile. "I fear, Marchese, my betrothed would look poorly on such behavior."

Ranieri's own smile ran from his lips, as if Mattea had poured water upon one of her freshly painted works, their vibrant colors running and turning to brown. His hands dropped from her arms to his sides.

Scoundrel he may be, but an honorable one, she was pleased to see.

"Your man is a lucky one," he said with a graceful bow.

Mattea allowed her lips a wide smile. "Yes. Yes, he is. And you have been a most delightful host. I will never forget our time together."

Ranieri kissed her hand even as others wrangled to bid him farewell, all those who cared about the curfew. "Nor will I."

At the door "Adelina" turned back, a quick look over her shoulder.

Ranieri watched her still. Though surrounded by pandering courtiers, he offered her a sly wink in parting. She laughed as she followed Isabetta out the door and into the street.

"What was that?"

They were barely a foot from the house on the Borgo Tegolaio when Isabetta began to poke at her.

"That, my dear friend," Mattea replied with more than a fair share of superiority and satisfaction, "was the best information we have received so far on our dear Lapaccia's whereabouts. We—"

"I know *that*," Isabetta snipped with impatience. "I meant, well, what I mean is—" she stopped in the middle of the street. It grew dusky with a sun falling near the horizon, one playing hide and seek through the many structures built one on top of the other throughout the city, a sun obfuscated by thick, dark storm clouds. "When… where…how did you learn to be such…to be so womanly?"

Mattea tossed back her head. "That is a story for another time. The only thing that matters in the here and now is this." She took Isabetta's hand almost skipping along. "We know where to look, where to truly look, for the first time."

"Yes, yes," Isabetta agreed, equally as enthusiastic, though she shook her head. "I cannot believe we did not think of it ourselves. Lapaccia has devoted her life to her religion, especially since her husband's passing. *Dio mio*, she spends more time helping at the convents than she does with us."

They turned off San Remigio, onto one of the small alleyways which would lead them back to Isabetta's home and proper clothing. It was a narrow and dark passage, but one that would allow them more anonymity as they made their way to the modest home.

It was the greatest mistake they made this night.

"But the problem is," began Mattea, "which one?"

"Which one what, dearies?"

The women jumped and squealed at a male voice coming from close behind. Whirling round, the pair found themselves confronted.

"It matters not to you," Mattea told the man, or was he a boy. In the dim light in an alleyway thick with dusk and not a single lit lamp on door or post, his features held little age or wisdom, but still threatening, tall and sturdily built as he was.

"What about me," from the opposite direction came another, thin hips swaying. This man too was just beyond boyhood, near to the same age as Mattea.

The women turned round, and round again. Mattea holding Isabetta's trembling hand, pulling her with her, keeping both young men in their sights.

"Our business is none of yours, sirs. We only make for our home, just two doors from here." It was a lie, but one Mattea hoped would dissuade these *giovani* from whatever mischief they had in mind.

"Did you hear, Giuseppe? She calls us 'sir,'" the second man called out to the first.

"Then she must be very accommodating, Ignazio."

It was the worst thing to hear. These men did not want their jewels or any money the women may have on their person, they wanted them.

Now Mattea and Isabetta stood back to back, hands held still. Isabetta pulled back in disgust as Ignazio drew closer, reaching out, and yanking the emerald head chain roughly from her.

"It would seem they have much to offer," he said, pocketing the bauble and reaching out again.

Seconds. All she had was seconds, Mattea knew it. She moved.

"Oh, please, I am dizzy...I...I am fainting."

She crumbled in a ball.

The men moved toward her.

Isabetta cried out, feeling Mattea's body falling to the ground.

Mattea reached beneath her skirts for the accessories to her attire, those she had worn since gifted to her, those she hoped never to use.

"What are—"

Giuseppe was but two steps away.

Mattea shot back up, the dagger sticking out the back of her hand thrust above her head.

"*Figlio di puttana!*" Giuseppe yelled, whether he called her a son of bitch in fact or just swore with surprise, Mattea cared not at all.

"Get back!" she yelled, but to Isabetta she ordered, "Here, take it."

Without turning, she thrust the second dagger into Isabetta's hand. With a look over her shoulder, Mattea saw her friend balk for a moment at the weapon she now held, she also saw Ignazio take a step closer.

"Jab at him. Jab!" Mattea screamed. It was another order and Isabetta followed it, with great relish.

Isabetta held the dagger with both hands, as one would a fishing pole. Any movement Ignazio made, Isabetta answered with her own, the tip of her knife she stuck out, threatening, with each move. It was an awkward defense, but the malevolent growl from deep in her throat, accompanying each shove of the blade, gave it bite and kept him at bay. Giuseppe was not so lucky.

Mattea dropped into her crouch. She held her free hand out to the side for balance, while her armed hand swayed back and forth, watching his eyes follow it, knowing he had no idea what she might do, what she was capable of doing.

"We want no more of you," she snarled low, even her voice accepted no challenge. "We want no trouble. Take yourselves away and we shall do the same, forgetting your faces and your names."

But Giuseppe was a fool.

As her dagger hand swayed to the right, he lunged left. If not for her lessons, she would have been lost.

Mattea moved left and forward, her dagger up and then down, slashing his face on the way up, grazing his chest on the way down.

"*Cazzo!*" he screamed, bringing a hand to his torn face, blood dripping through his fingers and soaking his doublet as he stumbled back a step, then two.

"Giuseppe? What is it?" Ignazio yelled from behind.

It was Mattea's turn to lunge, to taunt this callow boy who would prey on young women, slashing her knife through the air just inches from his neck.

"GO!" she screamed.

He did.

Seeing his friend running from them, Ignazio followed, keeping the armed women in his sights until he was out of range of their weapons, then he turned tail and dashed away.

"Are you all right, Isabetta?" Mattea spun round.

"Yes, but—"

"Run!" Mattea yelled.

They did. Lifting their skirts, they ran like the men on the *calcio* field, hard and fast. Only once did Mattea turn around and make certain no one followed them.

Panting, Isabetta turned fraught-filled eyes to her friend and savior.

"Who are you, Mattea Zamperini?"

Mattea snickered, mirth quivering with tears, wiping her face harshly, removing the man's blood splattered on her face, burning her skin. "I hardly know."

Chapter Thirty-Five

"Closer and farther,
Together and apart."

Mattea stopped just inside the door. She had expected to be the first to arrive at the studio and to find it empty. It was not.

Isabetta jumped up at the sight of her friend in the doorway, though the man standing beside her showed no signs of perturbance.

Leonardo da Vinci stood at Isabetta's table, where she had been perched upon her stool. Spread about on the wood plank before them were the many sketches Isabetta had made of Botticelli's mural. In some there was but a single gibbeted man, in others there were the three already in place on the wall and in eternity.

But Mattea saw all Isabetta longed to hide in how closely she had positioned her stool to Leonardo's body, the fineness of the woman's dark green silk gown—one inappropriate to work, uncovered by her smock—the great care Isabetta had taken in configuring the braids of her flaxen locks. Telling most of all, she saw the look upon her friend's face, forced wide-eyed innocence over a deepening flush, a child caught in the worst sort of mischief.

Mattea knew with one glance what Isabetta was about. How well she knew the pangs of unrequited desire. All she felt for Isabetta was sadness. Mattea would make no verdict on what Isabetta needed to feel better.

"Ah, I thought I was the only one coming," Isabetta said, coming round the table as if to greet Mattea.

"It took me longer to get word to everyone," Mattea rushed her reply. "I'm sure they'll all be here soon enough."

"You have learned something of your friend?" Leonardo asked.

"Indeed I have. We have—"

Before she could say more, the door opened once again. Even as Fiammetta, now barging in, prattled on with almost motherly strife at Natasia walking in beside her, it mattered not. As soon as she saw Mattea, gaze twitching to Isabetta, looking much the same, she knew.

"You know something, Mattea. And you, Isabetta," Fiammetta accused, as if their knowledge was a crime.

Mattea nodded. "I do, but perhaps we should—"

For the third time the door opened; Viviana passed over the threshold.

"We are all present," Isabetta stepped beside Mattea, "I believe it is time to tell."

Talking with one another, talking over one another, blushing at the gasps, at the exclamations upon their bravery, at the denunciations at their foolish daring, Mattea and Isabetta eventually revealed their actions, all of them, and the motherly chiding grew to a fever pitch.

"It is pure logic. How silly of us not to think of it," Viviana muttered.

"Lapaccia would not leave Florence. She would not leave her son," Mattea was emphatic on this point. "Though we do not know assuredly, we are all fairly convinced Lapaccia did take the painting."

"Yet we do not know why," Viviana said, not with pure conviction. All shared the belief, all had hinted they held the same thought—Lapaccia protected someone, but who no one could say with certainty for the painting had not revealed her secret. How much easier it would have made this ordeal if it had.

"It does not matter, not to me. We must start searching the convents," Mattea continued, "today, this very minute."

"But we may not be the only ones looking there."

All eyes turned to Isabetta.

"Think of the man's words," she explained. "He told *us* what he told *Il Magnifico*. It may be the government has already begun their search of the religious houses."

"Then we haven't a moment to lose."

"But where to start?" Viviana mumbled.

"Let us begin with those in our own parishes," Mattea said quickly, a notion already thought of. "It will be seen as the least out of the ordinary."

"We cannot go traipsing about the city alone," Fiammetta huffed. "It is no longer the same city."

"Of course not," Mattea assured her. "We will go in groups or in pairs."

"And what do we say, *'Buongiorno, are you hiding any criminals here?'*"

More than one pair of eyes fell upon Fiammetta with growing impatience.

"Let us ask if they have any new novitiates. Tell them a group of ladies wishes to make fresh linens for all those newly arrived and initiated." Viviana had done this very thing as a young wife married to a thriving merchant.

"Perfect!" Mattea exclaimed.

"Very well," Fiammetta agreed, though none too enthusiastically. "As I am here, I will accompany Natasia to convents in this area. My carriage will await me at your home, Natasia. Come."

Taking the young woman by the arm, a mother demanding her child's attendance, Natasia could do no more than comply, turning to the group with a raised hand and a silent, apologetic shrug.

"There is freedom in being a widow," Viviana said, still drenched in her widow's weeds though they were an ill fit. "I may walk about on my own without a care for any stinging tongues." She affected a smile, yet those remaining were little convinced by it. Her olive skin still looked more alabaster than usual, save for the dark smudges about her eyes. "Though I do not think I will look at any convents, not just yet."

Isabetta pouted at Viviana. "But we must make haste. If the Eight or the Podestà, or both, search already, we are far behind."

"But do they search wisely?"

Silence answered Viviana's question.

"How many convents must there be, within the city walls alone, let alone in the hillside?" Viviana paced a circle. "Our Lapaccia would not go to just any convent. There would be purpose and reason to which one she would choose."

Viviana dropped her hands by her sides, her veil upon her face. "I will take myself to the Palazzo della Signoria. There is a listing there, I am sure. There are lists for the lists. I am willing to wager there would be one with all the convents upon it. Perhaps it would give us some direction."

"I will gladly accompany you." Leonardo stepped up. "It will go well for you to gain entry upon my arm. Especially now."

"Now? Why now?" Isabetta seemed almost to demand the explanation.

Leonardo's chin dipped as his head shook. "I fear our *Il Magnifico* is quite angry. Not only has Bandini eluded capture once more, but the pope has sent a Bull of Excommunication."

"On who?" Isabetta huffed.

"On everyone." Leonardo shrugged. "Lorenzo, the Gonfaloniere, the Priors, and more. Even the priests if they dare serve Mass, at least until his nephew, the Cardinal, is returned to him."

"*Il Magnifico* will never do it," Isabetta spat.

"No, he will not, which is why he is so angry." Leonardo turned once more to Viviana. "Have no fear, madonna, I will keep you out of the eye of his wrath."

Mattea caught the look of disappointment upon Isabetta's face; it was naked for all to see. "It is you and I then, my friend," she said to Isabetta, "which makes perfect sense, as we live so very near one another."

"Of course. Yes, of course."

Locking the sacristy door behind them, the two groups broke off in two different directions, one north, one west.

"*Buona fortuna*," Mattea said in parting to Viviana and Leonardo.

"*Sì*, good luck," Viviana repeated, taking the artist's arm. "Good luck to us all."

Chapter Thirty-Six

"Blooms are often hidden among the thorns."

"How dare you!" Lorenzo de' Medici's scream shook the walls, the thunder of it threatening to bring down the formidable tower of the palazzo itself.

Viviana and Leonardo had just entered the first courtyard of the government palace when the cry rang out. They had taken but a few steps upon the grand staircase soaring through the entire structure, on their way to the chancellery on the second floor.

Leonardo pulled on her arm with one hand, while with the other he held a finger to his lips.

Like children roaming the house past their bedtime, they slinked up the stairs to the second floor. By his lead, Viviana found herself in a part of the palazzo she had never been privy to, those which held *il private de sala de Medici*. She had heard the great Cosimo's study remained untouched, though he had been dead for fourteen years now. Lorenzo had chosen to take over his own father's salon, for Piero had occupied it for no more than five years, and even then rarely.

The staircase spat Leonardo and Viviana out in the middle of a monstrous room, a piazza with walls.

Brilliant light from the two stories of windows on the north side shimmered upon the bronze marble floor of the *Sala dell' Udienza*. Viviana flinched, the life-sized statues lining both long side walls taking her aback. Beneath the windows, the four slim stairs led to the platform stretching the width of the room. Here Cosimo the First would sit. Here, those who desired it, could have their say, in the Audience Hall.

Viviana had never been in this room, and though he led her through it with the same stealth as he had brought her to it, Leonardo pointed up in silence. Viviana's gaze followed, and stopped dead in her tracks.

Over her head, covering every inch of the ceiling, were magnificent coffers of gold. Alternating octagons and diamonds, the gold was offset by the deep blue of the Medici, of the Florentine Republic itself.

"Pure gold," Leonardo leaned down and whispered, "every inch."

"How dare you tell me he has eluded us again!"

Once more, the voice of *Il Magnifico* occupied the building, echoing eerily in this vast hall.

Leonardo and Viviana could spare no more time to admire the room. He pulled her to a small opening in the southwest corner. Leonardo stepped into the hallway, pulled her with him, and shoved both their forms into the small corner cubby created by the odd construction of the hall and the small rooms in this section of the palazzo.

"My brother is dead and yet Bandini is still free." Though he did not scream, Lorenzo growled. Viviana realized they were but steps from whichever one of these rooms he called his own. She closed her eyes for a moment, in prayer to all the gods she called hers, for to be caught like this, after one arrest, could mean her end. And yet she wanted to hear as much as Leonardo. "And that devil that inhabits God's greatest house still plagues me."

Lorenzo lowered his voice, they could no longer hear words distinctly. "Hah!" Lorenzo barked again, and the two hidden yet reluctant eavesdroppers could once more make out his words as well as his thunderous passions. "I will release no one. In fact, I will arrest more. Gagliardi!" he shouted the name of the leader of the Eight, a silent, unseen member of this off-stage enactment. "Do as del Monte Pesaro said, search all the convents and the monasteries."

Viviana squealed like a mouse, clamping a hand on her mouth.

"Right away, Ser Lorenzo," came the soldier's response, deep and clipped.

"No. No, not right away," Lorenzo objected thoughtfully. His next words came after silent seconds of rumination. "Wait until morning, a quieter time. There may be those, such as the Cavalcanti woman, among those found. To bring such a paragon through the streets in ropes may only upset the people. We need no more to turn against us."

"As you say, Ser Lorenzo," replied Gagliardi, heavy footfalls and jangling armor accompanying his words. He headed out of the room and toward the eavesdroppers.

Back through the magnificent hall, the pair ran as fast and as silently as they could. Viviana felt certain the statues would scream of her presence, so guilt-ridden did she feel for invading *Il Magnifico's* privacy.

Leonardo led her once more to the stairs, the last set leading to the third floor and the chancellery upon it.

"*Ohé?*" Leonardo called out after knocking softly upon the door, finding it opened a crack. Sticking his long head in, he glanced about. Their timing was perfect; every clerk was at his mid-afternoon rest. The chancellery was deserted.

"Come," Leonardo held the door open for Viviana, who rushed in behind him.

"Close the door, quickly," she hissed.

"We cannot," Leonardo muttered as he searched about the floor.

"What do you mean we c—"

"Ah hah!" Leonardo crowed, finding the small bronze statuette of Hercules just beyond the threshold between piles of ledgers, and placing it between the jamb and the door. Slowly the door began to close by itself, only the statue prevented it from latching.

"It locks by itself," Leonardo explained, taking no time to elucidate.

They had come to find a particular set of records and yet found themselves in a large room where the shelves were as tall as the walls, and upon them sat bound ledger after ledger.

"At least their spine identifies them," Viviana said, but with little enthusiasm.

Leonardo snuffled sarcastically. "You take that side, I shall take this."

The hunt began.

Chapter Thirty-Seven

"Collisions occur to all around."

Viviana stepped to the table and rolled the parchment out. As the fellowship crowded around her—gathered in the studio with the first bloom of the next day's dawn—they saw a list writ upon the paper with a neat and tidy hand.

"It occurred to me yesterday that there are so many convents in this city it could take us days—"

"Weeks," Fiammetta sniffed.

"—to search them all. But I know Lapaccia well. Though she has spent much time at many an abbey, there would be a reason she would choose one in particular in which to hide. So, with Leonardo's help, I acquired a list of all the convents within the city walls."

"And how many are there?" Mattea asked.

Viviana's features crinkled into an unbecoming expression; it was the one question she didn't care to answer. "Nearly sixty." Expected groans met her announcement. "But there are some we can easily cross off as well as those you visited yesterday."

A review of the list began in earnest.

"Take those three off," Fiammetta pointed to those she and Natasia had called upon yesterday.

"And these two," Isabetta took her own silverpoint to two of the convents on the list.

Fiammetta piped up, "There are still far too many for a small group of women to—"

"Let us not look at them as a whole, but at them individually, their locations, their names." Viviana grew flush. "Look here, Santa Maria Maddalena dei Pazzi. We may cross that one off with certainty."

"And this one," Mattea pointed to yet another convent established by the Pazzi family.

So it went. With heads together, thinking as one as they had so often done in the past, the women soon began to narrow the list, ridding it of those Lapaccia had never gone to or would never, whether it be for their familial connection, or the neighborhood in which it stood.

They barely noticed as Father Raffaello brought in some simple victuals of bread and cheese and grapes, though all partook of his humble bounty.

"We have narrowed the possibilities greatly," Isabetta pronounced about a bite of cheese, "but still there are nearly twenty remaining."

"Now we must not look at where she would *not* go," Viviana cried, "but with an eye to where she would."

The scrutiny began again. Looking through these eyes, those with a positive slant, four names leapt off the page.

"Seeing the names, it is hard to believe we did not think of them sooner," Mattea said, subdued. She took another piece of parchment and wrote the four names upon it:

Santa Giuliano
Santa Apollonia
Santa Caterina de Siena
Santa Caterina della Abbandonate

Viviana shook her head at the obvious distinction of the four convents: one with the name of the murdered man, one named the same as the daughter Lapaccia had lost to the plague, and not one, but two, bearing the name of their patron, the sisterhood's very genesis of existence, Caterina.

"I did not even know these three existed," Isabetta pointed to the last three on the list.

"They are very much in the north of the city," Mattea said. "Very close to the Porta a San Gallo. There is little else in the area, little reason for you to have visited it."

"How do you come to know them?"

It was genially asked, yet Viviana thought Mattea had suddenly become ill, but the pallor passed quickly as the young girl explained.

"I like to walk," she said with a lift of one slim shoulder. "I find the quiet of the north peaceful."

No one questioned her, aloud at any rate. Viviana picked up the small paper with the four names upon it and tore it in half. One half she handed to Fiammetta.

"You and Natasia will take these. We three," she flicked her head at Isabetta and Mattea, "will take the others."

Viviana saw Fiammetta's pleasure at having the one convent she did know on her list.

"However you may be able to get to one of ours quicker, as you will be in your carriage and we will be on foot."

"No you will not," Natasia proclaimed. "You will take my carriage. Now is not the time for walking."

"And I will do what I can."

All eyes turned to Leonardo.

"What can you do?" Viviana asked with more than a twinge of guilt and reluctance. What had they dragged him into?

He shrugged, yet again, simply, though there was nothing simple about their work this day. "What do you plan to do if… when…you find the dear lady?"

No one spoke. Though they all had thought of it, though they all had a vague notion, none felt sure enough of it to speak aloud.

"Exactly," the artist nodded decidedly. "It is what I must do."

With a tip of his *beretto*, he extricated himself from the room with purpose and diligence.

It was Viviana who broke the silence he left behind.

"He makes for the Palazzo. For *Il Magnifico*."

"No!" Isabetta barked. "He would not."

Remembering her night in the tower, her day in the prison

cell, and what Leonardo had done, Viviana felt certain. "Oh, he would. He is."

With the strength of purpose ignited by the brave artist's actions, the five women made for their carriages with no further delay, save to give each other an embrace. Should the worst possibilities become realities, they would part with a tender moment between them.

Viviana took her seat in Natasia's carriage. Across from her Mattea sat snugly beside Isabetta, and upon that woman's face she found the strangest of expressions.

She reached out and took Isabetta's hand in hers; she found it cold on this hot day.

"What is it? Something vexes you?"

Isabetta shook her head, as if she understood no better than Viviana did. "We will find Lapaccia today, I know it. But we will find more than we bargain for."

Chapter Thirty-Eight

"Patience may indeed be a virtue, but it does not make it easier to come by."

"What a lovely offering," Suor Michela, the abbess of Santa Giuliano, said to Fiammetta. "But I fear we have no new novitiates. We have not for some time."

"I am sure there will be some pious girls come to fill your rooms soon enough," Natasia said, though the cold dankness of the ancient convent may have much to do with its lack of popularity. "And when you do, you shall tell us and we shall help you make them welcome."

"How truly kind of you," the elderly woman's many chins warbled as she took Natasia's hand. She walked her guests out into the narrow vaulted corridor and out onto the Via Faenza.

They stood under the small canopy above the portal, for it offered the only shade to be found, and made their parting.

"The Lord will surely bless you for your kindness, as he will the soldiers," the sister said benevolently.

Natasia yelped. Fiammetta asked coolly, "What soldiers, Sister?"

"Oh, those who came last evening," the woman prattled, eager to share gossip. "They too wanted to greet any new members to our group, to assure them the terrors of late would not continue. I thought it quite chivalrous of them."

"Yes, chivalrous," Fiammetta snipped. "Thank you again, Sister. Come, Natasia, we must away. We have many other convents to visit today."

She pushed Natasia by the small of the back, not allowing a moment for Suor Michela to attempt more conversation.

Once in the carriage, Fiammetta directed the driver to the next location. "And if you value your life, you will hurry."

• • •

"It would have been too easy, would it not?" Mattea said as the three women left the cool courtyard of the convent of Santa Caterina of Siena. "How wonderful if Lapaccia were here, in the first convent we visited this day."

Though there had been many a new woman to join the order in the last few days, brought in by fear, by the bacchanalia of the last few weeks, by the splendor of this fine abbey, none were Lapaccia. Yet the three seekers had to greet each one, had to make polite—if quick—conversation, promising them all new bed linens within a fortnight.

"Nothing about this has been easy," Viviana said, feeling, even with all the uplifting changes these months had brought to her life, as if she were drowning. She could not rid herself of the gloom Isabetta's words had wrought, nor the urgency they incited.

"On to the next. To the convent of Santa Caterina della Abbandonate," she told the driver.

Chapter Thirty-Nine

"Seek and ye shall find, but be certain of that which you search."

It was a short journey up the Via San Gallo, no more than a block of fine palazzos, before the driver turned left onto the Via S. Caterina. The convent was no more than a few doors up on the right. Viviana knew they would reach it in no more than a few minutes and readied herself, but not enough.

From within the shadows of the slim alley that was the Via Mozza, the man jumped out and with one wide leap, jumped up onto the side of the wagon, hanging precariously onto the driver's bench. The women yelped and tumbled about the carriage, the horses screeched as the carriage jerked to a stop, as the man pushed aside the driver and pulled hard on the reins.

"We are undone," Mattea said, her calm acceptance of their seeming demise surprising Viviana.

"We aren't done until they hang us." Viviana regained her seat, pushed aside the curtain, and stuck her head out the window, pushing against the pull of a grasping hand that attempted to haul her back in. The hand released her quickly when she gave a chuckle.

"What the devil are you laughing at?" Isabetta fumed.

But before Viviana could answer, the unwelcomed rider stuck his head in the now uncovered aperture.

"Ladies," he tipped his head as if he bid them *buongiorno* in the finest *salata*. Turning to Viviana, there was but a flicker of a grin on his well-formed lips.

"You were followed and I think they have figured out your destination. They are no more than minutes behind you. Unless something is done to throw them off, they will get to her first."

Viviana lost any joy she had found in his presence. "She is here?"

Sansone nodded his head. "If I do anything..." his deep voice trailed off.

Viviana placed her hand on his. She felt the stares boring into her from her companions.

"Have not a care. You have done so much already. I will figure it out." She squeezed the hand in hers. "Now go!"

With a reluctant nod, he leaned down, brushed his lips across her hand, and as quickly as he had come he was gone.

"Viviana," Isabetta growled, "if we live to see——"

"Driver," Viviana ignored her completely as she banged on the wall of the carriage. She yelled once more, "Pull close to the convent's door but do not stop, only slow to a crawl."

Looking across at her friends, the small smile remained on her face, though it was not one devoid of nervous fear. "We are going to jump. I will go first, Isabetta you will follow and we will both help Mattea."

"I need no help, old woman," Mattea replied and her lips spread into a slow grin.

In seconds, they did exactly that and though Mattea stumbled, though she grunted a bit as her light body fell forward faster than she thought, the task was done without injury. The carriage began to move past.

"Go!" Viviana yelled to the driver, slapping the horse closest to her on the rump, jolting it to a speedy cantor. "Return to the Santa Caterina de Siena convent, and quickly."

Turning to her now wholly dumbfounded companions, she ordered them as well. "Inside, both of you, quickly."

Viviana tore the laces that held her right sleeve to her gown, pulled strands of her hair out of her head. "Go to Lapaccia. Hurry!"

Her friends barely got inside the tall, rounded, wrought iron gate before a small group of men on horseback rounded the corner of the Via San Gallo.

Viviana tossed herself against the wall at her back, dropped her head in her hands, and shook her shoulders, sobs raking her body. "They've gone," she muttered and moaned. "They would not listen to me, they would not listen to reason."

"You speak of Mona Cavalcanti?" The most decorated soldier, he who led the small charge looked down at her with a squint.

"I do." Viviana lifted herself off the wall, threw herself onto the side of the man's horse, and grabbed at the soldier's leg. "I begged her to turn herself in, but she wouldn't. They wouldn't."

"Where have they gone, madonna?"

"I do not know, only that they planned to leave the city, by the Porta a San Gallo."

With a clipped nod, the man gave his commands. "Return to your home, madonna. Men, forward."

And with a snap of reins, a dig of spurs, the horses and men bounded away.

Viviana watched their retreat, allowing herself a moment, a half second of time, as an audience member who had just watched an inspired performance, and silently applauded herself, before spinning round and entering the convent.

Just inside the gate, hidden in the shadows of the entrance alcove, her conspirators waited for her, having watched and heard all through the crack of the large door.

"You grow more brazen all the time," Isabetta plied a respectful rebuke.

Before she could say another word, the convent door opened.

Of all the greetings one might expect when walking into a convent, the one hailing Viviana, Isabetta, and Mattea was the last any of them anticipated.

In the crack of the open portal, a short, stout, wimpled nun studied their faces, and pulled it open, stepping aside for them to enter.

"She knew you would come."

It was as if the world stopped, time ceased.

In the void, the three women held their breath in pure disbelief. "Come." The good sister walked away, a plump hand waving, urging them to follow. "It is well you are here. She needs you."

"Thank you, dear God. Thank you," Mattea offered up the resounding gratitude as they grabbed hands, as they hurried to catch up with the quickly moving legs of the short abbess.

"Caterina," Viviana said. How magnificent it was for her to bring them to the end of their search, to one of the deceased artist's own disciples.

They stepped into the cell. One glimpse at their friend prostrate upon her cot, pale white and ghostly thin, and they thought their arrival too late. They thought her dead.

Lapaccia's hair, now more white than black, was a long tangle upon the pillow; it barely moved as she lifted her head a few inches upward, as her eyelids fluttered open.

Her weak gaze touched each woman standing above her, and a tender glimmer sparkled in her sunken eyes. With a weak shake of her head, Lapaccia closed her eyes, and put her head back upon its perch with a smile.

"You should not be here," her voice was a croak. "I prayed you would not come even as I knew you would."

Viviana dropped to her knees by the bed, gathering the frail woman in her arms. For a moment, she could do nothing but savor the relief of finding her friend, and finding her alive, if just. For the time being, it was enough.

But the questions hounded her; these months of uncertainty pushed at her back and her tongue.

"What have you done, *cara?*"

Lapaccia opened her eyes, pushing against the cot, and sat up. Fully awake; though ill, fully present.

"I did what I had to do."

Isabetta leaned over and kissed the woman on the forehead, withdrawing with a sigh, one of relief and impatience. "Your answer is no answer, Lapaccia. The city has been in the grip of utter madness and you disappeared. Did you expect us not to take note, not to fret?"

"I am sorry. I knew you would, and I do regret it so."

"The world is topsy-turvy. If you only knew." Mattea struggled to say more.

"I do know," Lapaccia replied. "I was in the piazza that day."

Fiammetta and Natasia rushed in, vexed and breathing hard. The small cell became smaller, a bowl filled to overflowing. The women shuffled about to make room for all, their feet rustling on the dusty stone floor.

"We saw my carriage upon the street. The driver told us…" Natasia hurried to explain their presence, "Oh, Lapaccia—"

But there was no time for reunions, no matter how heartfelt.

Isabetta turned quickly to the small nun now squished into the corner of the room at the foot of Lapaccia's bed.

"I take it no soldiers have been here yet?"

"Soldiers?" the prioress balked, shaking her head. "No, no soldiers."

"They are upon our heels," Viviana said with authority.

"Do they truly look for me?" Lapaccia rasped, but it was a question decidedly rhetorical, astonishment tinged with expectancy.

"You were seen, Lapaccia," Viviana said gruffly. There was no more time for a polite inquisition, no matter how ill this woman may be. They had come to save her. She must let them. "You were seen leaving the palazzo and carrying something, carrying the painting."

"Seen?" Lapaccia's pale gray eyes grew wide and she began to cough.

"Do you have your medicine?" Mattea asked, looking helpless when Lapaccia shook her head.

"We have been giving her water, boiled with mint, then cooled," the abbess informed them.

"It has helped," Lapaccia croaked. The coughing fit passed. "I destroyed it, you know, the painting."

"Wh—" Mattea began.

"Destroyed?" Isabetta croaked.

Viviana wanted answers as badly as the others, "Now is not the time," she said. "We have to get you out of here, out of Florence."

"Yes," the voice came from the doorway. "We must get you out now, mother."

Every woman within whirled about to see the young, handsome man standing in the doorway.

"Andreano!" Lapaccia yelled out; Mattea echoed the cry.

Upon her son's handsome face was pure relief, clearly his mother's whereabouts had been as secret to him as it had been to her clandestine assemblage. He held his arms out to her, but something in his mother's face, something only he recognized, held him in place.

Lapaccia stood falteringly, silently, with the help of Mattea's quick hand. Slowly, with great deliberation, her eyes never leaving his face, each step a thoughtful move, Lapaccia came to stand before her son. For one moment, she stared up at him, unbounded love glowing from her gaze.

In the next, the flat of her right palm cracked him across his face, a pummel of such power, his head whipped back on his neck, the imprint of her palm appearing instantly in a red welt on his ruddy skin.

"Lapaccia!"

"Stop!" Mattea screamed.

Amidst more gasps and cries of outrage, Andreano chuckled, silencing them once more. The truth at last came to Viviana. It was Andreano all along—Andreano whom Lapaccia protected. It made no sense; he was a member of the militia. He had, since the assassination of Giuliano, been part of the forces protecting *Il Magnifico*, apprehending conspirators, and carrying out their death sentences. Why would he need his mother's protection?

Rubbing his hand upon the offended skin, Andreano stepped into the room. "You have every right, mother. Every right in the world." His other hand he held out, held aloft with a quiver in the air before his mother. Would she take it? "But then I thought I did too. I thought I had the right to punish him. Lorenzo de' Medici killed my father."

Lapaccia's anger cracked. She took her son's hand, threw herself into his arms. "It is the notion of a child, Andreano," Lapaccia sobbed against his chest, wheezing even as she berated him. "Yes, it was a war instigated by Lorenzo de' Medici, but he did not do it alone. Lorenzo was a young man and your father was a soldier. He would have gone to war, died in it, no matter who made the decision to use force on Volterra. It was his duty."

The strong, handsome young man crumpled. Bending low, he dropped his forehead upon his mother's shoulder. "All the terrible things I have seen. I have learned the truth of the world. I understand now," Andreano moaned. "But when the Pazzis came to me, they were so strong, so convincing." He lifted his hand, dashing the tears from his face with a hard fist. "I was weak and I listened. I know you can never forgive me. All I can do is save you."

Andreano held his mother from him, straightening his spine, raising his chin where it should be as a man, a soldier, and the son of a great nobleman and knight. "Now that I know you are alive and well, you must leave Florence and I will give myself into the hands of the Medici."

"No!"

Two women cried out: Lapaccia, his mother, and Mattea, his lover.

Andreano turned to the young woman, so bereft she could no longer hide her truth in dispassionate behavior. One hand still upon his mother, Andreano reached his other out to her.

"My love, forgive me." Andreano raised Mattea's hand to his lips and kissed it deeply.

All lives hold secrets, Viviana thought yet again, as she had so often in the last few days.

"I could not risk telling you," Andreano shook his head with shame, wavy golden brown hair falling in his face. "I could not risk involving you any more than I already had. I involved all of you. I was stupid and vengeful. I am so very sorry."

Mattea held him like the anchor to the ship of her life; her shoulders and head dropped with relief, ragged breath came and went as she closed her eyes and simply held him.

"Mattea?"

It was Isabetta who dared to speak, hesitantly, a whisper of pure disbelief.

Mattea opened her eyes. Above her lover's head, every gaze was upon her.

"You were right, Isabetta, I know not who I am. I love someone whom life has decided I cannot love." She spoke pointedly. "But love him I do, with every fiber of my being."

Andreano rose and kissed her forehead. Mattea stepped out of his embrace, spoke to Lapaccia. "I can only ask forgiveness for loving your son. I would not allow him to make it known. I feared your disapproval would force him to choose between us, and this I would never allow."

Lapaccia's gaze flitted between them in silence. "All I have ever wanted for my son is love. We cannot control where our hearts takes us, try though we might." Lapaccia reached out her hands, one for each. "Neither of you need question my forgiveness, for anything."

"Oh, for the love of God. And now we are to protect a murderer?" Fiammetta cried.

Andreano whirled at her. "I committed no such sin," he spat.

"Then what did you do?" Fiammetta retorted. "You were in the painting. Your mother would not have taken it were you not."

And there it was, Viviana thought, chiding herself for her own stupidity.

Fiammetta turned to Lapaccia, seated once more on the cot. She said not a word, but gave a single nod of her head.

"What *did* you do then?" Fiammetta demanded of the young man.

Andreano's eyes, wide and forlorn, looked more like those of the child he once was. "I opened the gate. I ensured the gate opened for the Perugini mercenaries who attacked the Palazzo della Signoria."

It was the most unforeseen of answers. It seemed such an innocuous collusion. However, collusion with the dreadful Pazzis it was. Viviana's mind volleyed back and forth, between wanting to the slap Andreano as his mother had—the visions haunting her, the viciousness in the church that day wanting, demanding her to do so—and yet, she knew the desire for justice, a consuming flame which left little room for twigs of logic. How could she fault him for the same sin she had committed?

"It will come out, Andreano," Viviana stated the vicious truth with quiet sadness. "*Il Magnifico* will not stop until everyone connected, no matter how tenuously, to his brother's death is dead. I know for certain."

The hissing slash of a whisper came from the door cracked only inches open; another nun's long thin face peaked through it.

"There are guards at the gate. They know you are here, they know your son is here. They followed him. We can only hold them off for so long."

As quickly as she came, she retreated, her appearance like a shy specter.

Lapaccia jumped up with a vitality it would not seem she possessed.

"You must leave, Andreano," she grabbed him by the shoulders and spun him toward the door.

"I will come back—"

"NO!" his mother spat. "You must leave Florence."

"He cannot!" Mattea cried.

"He must," Lapaccia insisted, even as Andreano fought against her push toward the door.

Her son took her hands. Insistent though gentle, he took them from her. "I will not allow my mother to suffer for my actions anymore."

"And I will not allow my son to die. If you are killed, I would have no reason to live," Lapaccia hissed. "Will you live with that? Will you allow us both to die?"

Andreano shook his head with the vehemence of a spasm. "You would not. You could not."

"She will, Andreano," Isabetta stood behind Lapaccia. "She has the strength of ten men. Look at what she has already done for your safety! She lives for you; all she talks about is you. What is she without you?"

"You, they will kill, me they may only banish."

"You may not be banished at all, Lapaccia," Viviana chimed in. "I have been freed from my husband's sins without recourse. *Magnifico* has let it be known, you have only to tell your truth. But Andreano must go." This last she said to Mattea, though it tore her heart to do so.

Her simple words said more than Andreano could ever truly know, but it seemed to tip the scales in his mind.

Lapaccia cocked her head, face puckered in confusion, eyes narrowed upon Viviana. "Your husband's sins? What sins?"

But Viviana had not a moment to answer.

Men's voices reached them, deep and insistent, through the small crack in the door.

"Go!" Lapaccia snapped. "Go to my family in the north. One day this will pass and all may return to normal. I know it."

Andreano grabbed his mother and held her as if he may never do so again. As he held his mother with his left arm, he reached for Mattea with his right, pressing her against his side, their passion a portrait—the very definition of love and desire—waiting to be painted.

He kissed her, hard and deep, without a care for the stares upon them or the open-mouthed gap of the abbess.

"I will see you again, of that never, ever, be unsure." Andreano's voice broke on his emotion. "You are mine, heart and soul, as I am yours."

Tears streamed down Mattea's pale face. "As I am yours," she repeated his pledge.

Closing her eyes, able to bear it no more, Lapaccia pushed him from her and out the door.

"Wait!" The nun in the room stepped from her corner and into the fray. "Do not go left from here. Go to the right and then left at the end. It will take you through a very small, private chapel with a door leading out the back way and to the north."

Andreano bowed in gratitude. With a last look for his mother and his lover, he was gone.

Viviana longed for solace in which to cry, sob as she had not done through all her trials. As a mother, she felt the tearing away of a child. As one never truly loved, she felt the emptiness of Mattea's loss.

Such sentimental thoughts vanished like smoke at the clanging of armor, as armed men marched their way.

"What are we to do? Do we offer you up to the wolves after all we have done to save you from them?" Fiammetta hissed at them, standing in the center of the room, and whirling round to beseech them all. "Or do we tell what Andreano has done, send them after him? They followed him here. They must know he was involved. How much more must we do?"

"Just one more thing," Lapaccia coughed her answer, not waiting for the spasms to subside to continue her plea. She took Fiammetta's hands and squeezed them with all the strength she had left. "Give him time. I ask no more. If we misdirect them, he may have time yet for escape. It is all I will ask, no more, I swear it."

Fiammetta's face wrinkled at this woman's abject beseeching.

"Signora Lapaccia Cavalcanti! Andreano Cavalcanti!"

The door opened, pushed by a gauntlet-covered hand, as the soldier called their names. But as the women within stepped aside, allowing the portal to fully open, the mass of soldiers in the hall could see there was only Lapaccia. There was not a single man within the small cell nor any space in which to hide one. There was barely room to breathe.

Lapaccia stepped forward. "I am Lapaccia Cavalcanti," she wheezed.

The soldier had the good grace to bow, if in a clipped manner, before the highly ranked noblewoman, suspect though she may be. "Where is your son, madonna? We know he entered this holy place. We saw him ourselves."

"He is gone."

The dark and ruddy soldier nodded his boulder like head on a neck of a tree trunk. "I can see that. But where, where has he gone?"

Lapaccia shook her head, suddenly coughing too much to speak.

Viviana knew not if it was truth or diversion, but her friend paled more, white skin turning a sickly shade of blue as Lapaccia could not get the air into her lungs.

"You see how ill she is," Viviana said, stepping in, unable not to. "Please allow us to get her to a physician."

"No one leaves this room until we know where Andreano Cavalcanti has gone."

Mattea sobbed, leaning on Isabetta's shoulder.

Fiammetta stepped forward.

"I will tell you where he is," she said, her voice harsh and angry, impatient and defiant. "Do you know who I am, soldier?" Fiammetta stepped up with fisted hands upon her hips.

The man began to shake his head, until a soldier at his back whispered in his ear. The lead soldier quickly dropped a bow.

"Contessa," was all he said; it was enough.

"Good. You understand who I am, now listen." Fiammetta dropped her hands from her hips and crossed them on her chest. The women in the room, her sisters in the great sorority they had formed, held their breath as if it were their last. Would she honor their bond or would her ire, so quick to the fore, rule the day?

"Andreano Cavalcanti has run to Rome. He seeks sanctuary with the Pope."

It was the perfect answer; its logic its greatest asset. The women knew not to release their relief, knew they could not, no matter how it burst in their hearts.

"Thank you, Contessa," the soldier said, and with a nod over his soldier, sent the majority of the others on their way out the front door, the opposite way Andreano had gone. "Your assistance will be duly noted."

"As it should," Fiammetta huffed, fully in her role now.

"But I fear," the soldier continued, "Mona Cavalcanti must come with me. I must take her to the Gonfaloniere."

The women had no defense against his claim.

"But I promise you, she will be seen by a physician."

"Oh, I can promise you the same," Isabetta stepped up with a sneer, "for I shall be accompanying you to the palazzo."

Viviana stepped up beside Isabetta. "As will I."

"And I!" the rest of the women chirped.

The soldier, seasoned and scarred though he may be, tottered. Closing his eyes, his large hand rubbed hard across his forehead, as if it pained him, sending the black curls falling upon it into impatient disarray.

He opened his eyes, shrugged his broad shoulders, and bowed again, one hand gracefully arching toward the door.

"Then let us away, my ladies," he surrendered, irony thick in his deep voice.

Like a religious procession, the women of the artist sisterhood filed from the room, Lapaccia in the lead, held on one side by Mattea, on the other by Isabetta.

Chapter Forty

"The final layer of varnish glitters with brilliance;
The brush looks to the next blank canvas."

"Forgive me, forgive me!" Fiammetta barged into the studio, the last one to arrive. Her cheeks flushed, her smile bright. "I am so sorry to be late for this gathering, of all our gatherings."

It was, perhaps, the most poignant meeting of the group since its inception. For the first time in too much of it, every member was present.

"Patrizio took me on a small trip, only to Ferrara for the day, to hear a new friar speak," she babbled even as she held tightly to Lapaccia. "He was quite stirring, like no preacher I have ever heard. Savonarola is his name, a very intense young man."

"Have no fear, *amica mia*. I have only just arrived myself," Lapaccia appeased.

Isabetta stepped to her and held her colleague out at arm's length. "You look wonderful," she declared, inspired by what she didn't see.

No longer did dark circles rim the noblewoman's eyes, nor did pallor or cough plague Lapaccia as they had for so long. Though it had been many a day, she still recovered from her ordeal, from the months in the convent without the proper medicines, from the two days in the Palazzo della Signoria tower, two days of non-stop questioning.

In the end, she had kept the secret of her son's whereabouts, confusing the Gonfaloniere by telling him her son's truth, the small part Andreano had played in the cataclysm and his motivations for doing so. Lapaccia had even told Cesare Petrucci she had instructed Andreano to seek refuge among family, but realized she herself did not know to which he would turn if the Pope turned him away. As Viviana had thought, in the words there had been enough truth for the Gonfaloniere, and after consulting with *Il Magnifico*, he had granted Lapaccia her freedom, proving the success, no doubt, of dear Leonardo's mission. The woman, still gaining her strength back, agreed with Viviana; they would both be watched.

"We are lucky to have you back," Isabetta declared.

Without announcement or fanfare, the group returned to their ways, working and talking, talking of working, gossiping while working as crepuscular rays of afternoon sun found them, lit them as if from within. The pungent, sharp scent of freshly mixed paints, of flowers and herbs and oils and stone dust filled the air, and they breathed it in like a panacea.

"I feel very lucky, very blessed to be here," Lapaccia replied. "I cannot believe so many are dead, so many banished."

They rattled off names of the deceased then, some knowing those others did not.

"Can it really be as many as they say?" Viviana mused as she arranged her brushes on the table before her by size, and the pigments she would use by brightness. The next painting lived in her mind already and therein would lay no more darkness. "I have heard it said over eighty have been hung."

"I think 'tis more near to one hundred," Isabetta murmured between gentle taps of *la mazza* upon the pointed and petite *la subbia*. Creation gave her cheer never more needed, wondering how soon her husband would join the departed. "*Il Magnifico* and the Gonfaloniere believe they have them all, save Andreano, whom they may consider too lowly to hunt, and Bernardo Bandini, one of the worst. I wonder if they will ever find him."

Mattea wondered too, aloud, putting down the mortar and pestle in which she mixed some gesso. "And will I ever see my

Andreano again?"

In silence, Viviana deliberated as well, on seeing someone again, a man with green eyes who would not leave her dreams, a soldier who in the impending days of war may not be glimpsed.

"You will, my dear. True love always finds a way. As for Bandini, I have no cl—" Isabetta began, stopped by the grating of the door latch.

It was with a flash of fear—they all felt it—that they held their breaths as the door pushed open. Once it did, the sun shone yet again.

Before the man had fully crossed the threshold, Lapaccia was on her feet, making her way to him with outstretched arms.

Reaching Leonardo, she rose up on the tips of her toes and wrapped her arms about his neck. With an expression of pure delighted surprise, the tall artist lowered himself to return the embrace.

"You put your life to the hazard for me," Lapaccia said, pulling back to speak to this stranger. "How can I ever repay you?"

"We are all each other's keeper, madonna," he replied. "And those who do not do so, will not be saved when their time comes." Leonardo scanned the room and the women in it. "I was as much saved as you, I swear it."

Lapaccia rose up once more, kissing him loudly upon his bristly cheek. Leonardo's pink blush turned scarlet and the women laughed aloud as Lapaccia pulled him into the room and to the preliminary sketches upon her table.

"Will you give me some advice on my newest endeavor, *maestro*?" she asked. "For I am, as are we all, one of your disciples, da Vinci's disciples."

"That *is* who we are," Isabetta crowed with great delight, "we are da Vinci's Disciples."

Though the artist shook his head, trying to shake off the accolade, the women would not be dissuaded.

"I am your servant, madonna," Leonardo said and the two put heads together, two artistic minds at work on composition and color.

Lapaccia observed. "It is indeed sorry I am to have missed your lessons. You have taught me so much in these few minutes." Lapaccia regarded him with admiration. "What will you teach us next?"

Leonardo eyed each woman. "I think you are ready." It was a calmly strident pronouncement.

"Ready for what?" Isabetta stepped round her bench.

Leonardo made yet another slow turn, scanning the room and all its astounding works.

"Frescoes." The word spoken, he smiled wide, wider still at the women's gasps.

"Truly?" Viviana fairly squealed. The technique of *buon fresco* had eluded the group for so long. If they did apply the wet plaster to the wall correctly—that which must be the base for the painting— they seemed to create the pigments wrong, for frescoes must be done with pigments suspended in water so that the plaster absorbed the color and the painting can truly form part of the wall. Or if the pigments were perfect the plaster failed utterly.

"We *are* ready," Isabetta crowed, whether for the delight of the craft or its teacher, Viviana could not discern, and in that moment, she did not care. And yet a weed of concern blossomed in her mind.

"Will your involvement with us take away from your own work?" Viviana asked, unable to squelch the note of guilt in her voice.

Leonardo shook his head gently, "*Cara mia le donne,* it is your devotion, even though denied to the world, that has helped me see how grateful I am to have such freedom as a man can have. I need to be grateful and to show that gratitude by pursuing my work. We will grow together in creation."

A silence fell upon them then, a contented one full of relief and promise. Suddenly the very air they breathed together changed, it crackled as if from lightning.

"Men believe they are the power," Isabetta said, raising more than one eyebrow with surprise. "And perhaps, on the surface, they are. But what we have done proves it. Together, there is not a greater power than the strength of women bound to each other."

"If more women realized it," Lapaccia whispered, "I wonder

what might happen?"

Viviana smiled; she felt the joy of it in the very blood pumping through her body.

"I wonder indeed."

La fine è solo l'inizio
(The End, for now)

What is Historically Factual
and What is Not

The truth depicts, the story insists

The murder of Giuliano de' Medici as depicted is as it happened. Incidental occurrences such as the mix up of where the Medicis would meet the cardinal and Bandini's covert search of Giuliano's person are portrayed accurately to prevailing history. It was indeed two priests who ignited the primary attack on Lorenzo; Francesco de' Pazzi's mania was truly so incensed, he stabbed his own thigh as he murdered Giuliano.

Nine-year-old Niccolò Machiavelli was a witness to the murders. What the child saw would be reflected in all his writings and his political career.

The hangings as depicted and of those particular historical characters follow the truth of history. Though all accounts of the incident make mention of Archbishop Salviati's final bite upon Francesco de' Pazzi, all these same accounts invalidate their stating it as true by calling it a myth or legend. By the time the scourge of Medici revenge found its end, it is estimated that eighty to one hundred men were executed.

Caterina dei Vigri, or Catherine of Bologna, is considered one of the first notable female artists. She was an author as well, one who kept a journal throughout her lifetime as well as writing many a religious treatise. However, the "quotes" at the beginning of each chapter are of this author's creation. Many of her manuscripts and art works survive today. Caterina of Bologna died in 1463 at the age of 49. For the eighteen days following her burial, there were many graveside miracles reported. Her body was moved then, found in an incorrupt state, and placed in the chapel of Poor Clares in Bologna where she remains on display, resplendent in her habit, seated upright behind glass. Caterina was canonized in 1712. Her relationship with Viviana is purely fictitious; her impact on women and female artists of the era is not.

The summation of the political wounds inflicted between the Medicis and the Pazzis, those which led up to this heinous murder, is simply stated, but truthfully rendered. For greater details of each offense and counter offense, please see the following bibliography.

The consequences endured by Jacopo de' Pazzi, including his capture, his arrest, his death, and his multiple interments are all, remarkably and horribly, true. Fact as well, was the fate of all Pazzis; those surviving were banished and any resemblance of the family, whether by name, escutcheon, or building...was erased in all of Florence.

The letter from the Duke of Urbino, with its veiled threats, and the anonymous poem hinting at the greater forces involved in the conspiracy are also of historical record.

It was custom for traitors and debtors to be rendered on the walls of the courthouse and prison walls of Florence, forever condemned upon giant frescoes. Sandro Botticelli did in fact create the fresco of those deemed as the main conspirators on the wall of the Palazzo della Signoria, but it was later removed.

The Compagnia e' Neri—the Company of the Black Ones— was a religious confraternity found in all Italian cities. In the tradition of Christ's Cavalry, they held their mission as sacred, to accompany and give comfort to those on their way to their death. The verse they chanted along the path was one written by a Bolognese lawyer who belonged to that city's confraternity. Gregorio Roverbella (c. 1410–88) intended the prayer, "For those who are on their way to justice."

The Bull of Excommunication indicted upon Lorenzo de'

Medici and the many members of the Florentine government was indeed enforced by Pope Sixtus IV.

It is true that many of those involved in the assassination of Giuliano de' Medici and the attempt to assassinate Lorenzo found sanctuary, for a time, in the multitude of convents and monasteries replete within the city of Florence. Lapaccia, a fictitious character, was not one of them. Nor was there a painting, a rendition of the *Feast of Herod*, created with the conspirators rendered upon it.

There was no Society such as the one depicted here; at least, not any known in the time period covered in this book.

And, lastly, it would be a dishonor not to acknowledge those words of Leonardo da Vinci taken from his own journals, notebooks, and letters. The direct quotes are:

> "There are three sorts of people in our world, signorina, those who see, those who see when they are shown, and those who shall never see."

> "Time stays long enough for anyone who will use it."

> "The greatest deception men suffer is from their own opinions."

> "All our knowledge has its origins in our perceptions."

> "As you begin your work, you must study the others, and you must make your decision and learn cohesively from there. You should look at certain walls stained with dampness, or at stones of uneven color. If you have to invent some backgrounds you will be able to see in these the likeness of divine landscapes, adorned with mountains, ruins, rocks, woods, great plains, hills and valleys in great variety; and expressions of faces and clothes and an infinity of things which you will be able to reduce to their complete and proper forms. In such walls the same thing happens as in the sound of bells, in whose stroke you may find every named word which you can imagine."

> "Where the spirit does not work with the hand, there is no art."

Acknowledgments

We are never alone

A great part of this work was inspired by the power of my female friendships, those that enabled me to survive years of great personal difficulty. It is to such kinship—one seemingly particular to women—that I hope to pay homage with this series. My survival, and this work, would not have been possible without those friends, most specifically Jennifer Way (1973–2012), Hannah Arbuthnot, and Stephanie Estes Saccoccio. To them I send all my love and gratitude.

I send thanks as well to the talented and generous C.W. Gortner, my Leonardo.

I am indebted to Christy English and again to Hannah Arbuthnot for their time and advice.

I am beholden to my agent, Shannon Hassan; her belief in me and this work reignited my passion for my true purpose and gave me back my own belief in myself.

My gratitude extends and expands to my editor, Randall Klein, for his devotion to this book, for helping me turn a good story into a great story. And to the wonderful team at Diversion, Sarah Masterson Hally, Trent Hart, Laura Duane, Beth Brown, and all those whose names I do not know, but whose support and encouragement on my behalf has been so vital to this book, I say, *mille grazie*.

Writing is a very solitary profession, but it is also a passion, one that needs a particular form of empathy that only other writers can offer. I am forever indebted to those writers who have helped me in my journey, especially Kate Quinn, Stephanie Dray, Heather Webb, Marci Jefferson, Nancy Bilyeau, Anne Easter Smith, Diana Haeger, and all the wonderful members of the Historical Fiction Co-op.

In the bibliography, there is noted the "Online Gazetteer of Sixteenth Century Florence." This is an amazingly detailed map of early sixteenth-century Florence developed, at that time, by one "Stefano Buonsignori (or Bonsignori) who designed the large axonometric ("birds-eye view") map of Florence displayed in the Gazetteer. He was an Olivetian monk (a local Tuscan order of Benedictines) skilled in map making, and near his monastery (which is shown in the lower left hand corner of the map) was a panoramic view of Florence that may have helped to inspire his creation."

I can never thank Caroline Castiglione, Ph.D., enough. Dr. Castiglione is an Associate Professor, Italian Studies and History, at Brown University, and availed me of this map. And though my years of research have made Renaissance Florence a very real place for me, this map brought it ever more alive and I am extremely grateful for her assistance and that of R. Burr Litchfield, Professor of History (Emeritus) at Brown University and his students, who digitized the map, making it, and Renaissance Florence, available to all.

Lastly, there are no words in the English language that can express my gratitude to my partner, Carl James-Cordean…who brought me back to life.

Bibliography

Knowledge is the key to all life

BOOKS

Alberti, Leon Battista. 1435. *On Painting*. Trans. Cecil Grayson. 1991. London, England: Penguin Books.

da Vinci, Leonardo. 15th Century. *Philosophical Diary*. Trans. Wade Baskins. 2004. New York, NY: Barnes & Noble Books.

Dersin, Denise. Editor. 1999. *What Life Was Like at the Rebirth of Genius*. Richmond, VA: Time Life Inc.

Earls, Irene. 1987. *Renaissance Art: A Topical Dictionary*. Westport, CT: Greenwood Press.

Field, D. M. 2002. *Leonardo da Vinci*. New York, NY: Barnes & Noble Inc. By arrangement with Regency House Publishing Ltd.

Fine, Elsa Honig. 1978. *Women and Art: A History of Women Painters and Sculptors from the Renaissance to the 20th Century*. Montclair, NJ: Allanheld, Osmun & Co. Publishers Inc.

Machiavelli, Niccolò. *History of Florence and of the Affairs of Italy from the Earliest Times to the Death of Lorenzo de' Medici*; with an introduction by Hugo Albert Rennert, Ph.D., from a Universal Classics Library edition, published in 1901. No translator was given. Presented in eight books comprising 55 chapters and an introduction.

Martines, Lauro. 2003. *April Blood*. Great Britain: Random House.

Mee, Jr., Charles L. 1975. *Daily Life in Renaissance Italy*. New York, NY: American Heritage Publishing Co.

Rogers, Mary and Tinagli, Paola. 2005. *Women in Italy, 1350–1650: Ideals and Realities.* Manchester, UK: Manchester University Press.

Simonetta, Marcello. 2008. *The Montefeltro Conspiracy.* New York, NY: Doubleday.

Toman, Rolf. Editor. 2011. *The Art of the Italian Renaissance.* Postdam, Germany: h.f.ullmann.

Vasari, Giorgio. 1550. *The Lives of the Artists.* Trans. Julia Conaway Bondanella and Peter Bondanella. 1991. New York, NY: Oxford University Press.

INTERNET

R. Burr Litchfield, Online Gazetteer of Sixteenth Century Florence. Florentine Renaissance Resources/STG: Brown University, Providence, R.I., 2006.

"Lorenzo de' Medici." *Encyclopedia of World Biography.* 2004. *Encyclopedia.com.* (September 12, 2012). www.encyclopedia.com/doc/1G2-3404704367.html

Reading Group Guide

In discussion, other truths may be found

1. In the very first chapter, much is revealed about the four women and what they are about in a few short words. Discuss the first impressions derived about each woman; how do they differ and how are they similar? What do their actions expose about them? What expectations were developed and were they met or not?

2. As Viviana, Fiammetta, and Patrizio are walking to the Duomo, as they see the Medici contingent returning as well, Viviana believes she sees something: "Her pale eyes narrowed against a bright flash of light, a reflection..." What did Viviana see and why was it so shocking for her to see it?

3. As Giuliano de' Medici is being murdered and the attack is launched on Lorenzo de' Medici, the vast majority of the congregants run from the cathedral. Viviana does not. Why doesn't she? What is it about her that is revealed in her actions? What happens to her by staying and watching the entire massacre take place?

4. Is Viviana's expectation of comfort from her husband, as she returns from witnessing the assassination, a reasonable one? Why does she expect it? Did she receive the reaction she should have expected? What does Orfeo's behavior reveal about him?

5. What is meant by the line, "She was a woman passionate of her craft, and all the more tortured for it?" Do the same conditions still exist today? How are they the same as and different from

the current status of women?

6. As Viviana reminisces about her cousin Caterina and the genesis of the Secret Society of Saint Caterina, she wonders, "if she would have embraced her newfound purpose with such rigor if her marriage to Orfeo were different. Blessings are so very often disguised as curses." To what notion does this refer? Discuss the incidents, the existence or nonexistence of it in the context of the story and in general. Discuss agreement or disagreement with the last sentence of this quote.

7. In Chapter Seven, Viviana puts out the signal for the Society to meet: "With shaking hands, Viviana removed the dead flowers from the vase at the saint's feet, replacing them with eight fresh, brilliantly white lilies, pilfered on their way past a resplendent palazzo garden. Around the saint's feet she arranged eight small stones from the pile always kept at the base of the niche, all on the eastern side, where the morning light would shine upon them." Discuss each part of the indicator and what they mean. What would a meeting set for two o'clock in the afternoon look like?

8. Viviana's divergent religious philosophies are sparsely revealed. What are they? In what ways do they differ? In what ways do they reflect the philosophies of many of the era? What does such disparity of thought set the stage for in the coming years?

9. Discuss the meaning of the statement, "A hatred once born can grow and prosper." Who does it relate to in this story? Does it relate to more than one person? If so, to whom can the words be applied and why?

10. Having learned the basic motivation for the assassination of Giuliano and the attempted assassination of Lorenzo de' Medici, is there any justification for such action? Why or why not? What does this action, and the entire conspiracy say about the Pazzi family in general?

11. How is imagery and metaphor used in the passage where da Vinci discusses time (the final line is a direct quote): "Time comes and goes in fits and starts. Slow times are marked by

mundane passages where little changes, little dust rises from the streets of progress. Oh, but when time comes at you, it becomes a rushing battalion armed with catapults of change, fair boulders of it. Time stays long enough for anyone who will use it." Are there examples of history that correlate to these images and metaphors?

12. In Chapter Twenty-One, Leonardo da Vinci states that, "All our knowledge has its origins in our perceptions." What does he mean by the statement, both in terms of art as well as in life itself?

13. It is often stated that rank—the nobility or lack thereof—has no place in the Society. Is this true? If not, what role does rank play? How does it affect the interpersonal relationships among the group?

14. In Chapter Twenty-Seven, Viviana taunts and insults her abusive husband. Could there have been a subconscious motivation for her to do so? How do the acts relate to those that happen later on in the story?

15. Did Viviana's decision to put Orfeo in the painting, knowing what would happen to him, come as a shock? Was she justified in the act? Why or why not? How did the act change her, not only in her daily life but in her as a person?

16. When Viviana is arrested and the Gonfaloniere interrogates her, it is stated, "but he never asked her the proper question." What was the right question the Gonfaloniere should have asked Viviana? Would she have told the truth?

17. Was Andreano's part in the conspiracy justified? Why or why not? Was it understandable? Why or why not?

18. Discuss the six members of the Secret Society of Saint Caterina. How are they different and how are they similar? How do these similarities and contrasts manifest themselves in their work and in their lives? The future of these characters is left unresolved. Discuss directions their lives may take in the next book.